LITTLE MAN

KENT SIEVERS

ISBN:
978-0-9976189-1-4

For the little man in the doghouse.

1

The house loomed dark but for a single bulb over a kitchen table holding a paper with the glaring print *"Notice of Eviction"*. Hot water urged suds over dirty dishes. From a portable radio in the window over the sink, Janis Joplin sang of freedom and having nothing to lose. The lyrics rang hollow as Alex stood alone at the sink staring out into a night as dark as his mood. The sheriff could arrive any time now. Twenty years paid on a thirty-year mortgage meant nothing now that his savings and unemployment benefits had run out.

Shoulders slumped under the weight of an uncertain future, Alex bowed his head and wept at the thought of his little girl not having a house to come home to. *She's probably a full-grown woman by now.* He just couldn't shake the image of her waving goodbye from her car seat. His tear-blurred sight focused on the refrigerator and the faded, red, construction paper heart she'd given him that awful day. *Love you Daddy* had been scrawled on the heart in his daughter's innocent hand.

A radio DJ cut Janis' mournful song short.

"We interrupt our regular programming to bring you a scheduled Presidential address."

"There is no doubt that times are still tough," began the President. "But from where we stand, for the very first time, we are beginning to see glimmers of hope."

"Glimmers of hope my ass," Alex growled, shutting off the water then snatching up his dishrag. He plunged his hands into the scalding dishwater only to yank them back, hissing in pain as he heard the first thunderous knocks at the door.

"Sheriff's Department! Mr. Capstain, we have a court order!"

Alex glanced to the kitchen table and the official notice that would change his life. Panic consumed him. *Not now. Not yet. I'm not ready.* He darted to the refrigerator and plucked his daughter's gift from under a magnet. Clutching the paper treasure to his chest, he ran through the empty house, whimpering as he took it all in one last time. He'd planned for this moment, yet, when faced with walking away, all he could do was put his fists to his temples and howl.

"Mr. Capstain!" the deputy shouted again. "It's time, Mr. Capstain. The bank is taking possession. Don't make this harder than it needs to be."

"You should be proud, son," Alex said, after collecting himself and opening the door, "I paid on her for twenty years. Did most of the finish carpentry work myself."

"I'm sorry, sir. I'm just doing my job," said the deputy. "Are you Mr. Capstain, the homeowner?"

"Yessir," said Alex. "I'm Mr. Capstain, but apparently I'm no longer a homeowner." As he said it, he fought back the urge to cry, staring through, rather than at the deputy.

"Do you have a place to go? Relatives or friends?"

"I'll figure it out. I've got my truck packed. I'll just back it out of the garage."

The deputy stepped aside. When Alex's feet wouldn't move, the deputy cleared his throat.

"I-I'm going," Alex said, raising a shaking hand to the doorframe for support. "It's just that everything is going to change."

The deputy rested his hand—more caring than forceful—on Alex's shoulder. "I understand."

Alex accepted the gesture gracefully. "The garage is unlocked and—" He paused to fish a small ring of keys from his pocket, handing them off, "—and I don't need these anymore. I marked them—" He fought back a sob.

"Thank you," interrupted the deputy, saving Alex the embarrassment of breaking down. "I appreciate your cooperation," he said, gently.

Eyes brimming, Alex took a long, hitching breath and stepped into the night.

* * *

The doghouse sat amid the trees on a snow-covered vacant lot. Inside, wrapped in a secondhand parka and two army surplus blankets, Alex Capstain lurched to consciousness. His breath came out in great puffs, their vapor illuminated by stabs of light streaking past his makeshift front door.

Exhausted with eyes matted and cloudy, he managed the first word of the day, "F-fuck." A bone-deep shiver made his jaw chatter. Disappointment and relief washed over him in equal measures. Part of him had hoped he'd never wake, yet, faced with a new day, hope overtook the fear and depression that always consumed his nights.

Frozen snot caked his yellow-gray mustache, he plucked at it, then probed the pockets of his parka for a cigarette gleaned from a public ashtray days before. "Butt sniping," he called it. Lipstick left by the cigarette's previous owner went unnoticed as he struck a cardboard match and filled his lungs with the street version of second-hand smoke.

Much as he detested the thought of bedding down with hundreds of other castoffs forced indoors by the cold, he knew he wouldn't survive another night in the doghouse. Tonight he'd have to make the move to the St. Vincent homeless shelter.

Menthol exhalations swirled from his nose and mouth as he looked up at his gray plywood ceiling and smiled, "Good morning, ladies," he said to the busty pin-up girls tacked overhead. They smiled back from their weather-warped magazine clippings as he let loose a phlegmy, staccato cough.

Through the doghouse walls and the drawstring hood of his parka came the whine of weekday commuter traffic. A frigid day of dumpster diving beckoned. Unlike weekends when the bar trash and street gutters sparkled with cans, weekdays were far less rewarding. Trash picker was a far cry from cabinetmaker, but that job was long gone, another victim of the new normal.

Hunger and the need to pee hurried the last drags on his cigarette. He twisted free of his covers, slid his plywood door aside and peered out at the morning. New snow had covered everything in a clean blanket of white.

"Beautiful," he said aloud, though no one was there to hear.

Crawling out into the snow and the blue morning light, he raised his fifty-one-year-old body to its full height of four-feet-eleven inches and stretched with a growl. He brushed snow from his pants, then reached back inside the doorway to fish his lawnmower blade from under the covers. If stopped by the cops, the blade was rusty junk to be recycled. If confronted by predators, it was a mighty sword to hold the jackals at bay.

He had kept the weapon close at hand these last few weeks. North downtown regulars were disappearing in greater numbers than a want of warmer climates could explain. Even his neighbors, four men who'd built makeshift shanties in the lot next to his, had vanished without warning or goodbye.

Shuffling through the ankle-deep snow to the back of his house, he brushed clean his trash picking stroller and tucked the lawnmower blade safely inside its seat before pulling the zipper of his threadbare blue jeans to relieve his near-bursting bladder.

With the exception of the heavy parka, the stroller was his most prized possession. He'd used wire and string to cobble the conveyance together from an abandoned Winnie the Pooh baby stroller and a busted-up plastic cooler. It was a light, smooth-rolling Cadillac compared to the heavy shopping carts used by his competition.

A cartoon donkey stared forlornly from the stroller's seat. "Good morning, Eeyore," Alex said, tucking away his pecker and zipping his pants. "Cheer up a little. It's a beautiful day."

His daughter had adored Eeyore. A favorite at bedtime, he could still envision her pale blue eyes moving between the book and his face, her head tucked cozily into his shoulder as he read.

"Daddy! There's no crazy monkeys in the hundred acre woods!" Amanda would declare, accusing him of inserting his own words—which he sometimes did, to see if she was paying attention.

Amanda wandered into his mind all the time now. Alex had begun to think he might see her again someday. He'd been homeless for nearly two years, but his hard work and help from friends was about to payoff. He had almost enough saved for a one-month reprieve from the street. With a little luck, real employment would follow and he could make homelessness a memory and a reunion with his daughter a reality.

* * *

Five blocks east, in front of the Harvest House soup kitchen, hungry, half-frozen men and women shifted from foot to foot, their faces blank as the day's volunteers, a snooty group from the West Omaha Church of Christ arrived in vans from their church's Angel's Wings program. The "churchees," as the street people called the do-gooders, emerged with armloads of donated food, then mingled awkwardly, working their way to the locked door to wait admission into the building.

The Harvest House was a favorite free dining destination of the street people. Though a church-based organization, unlike the other churchee soup kitchens and shelters, most of the regular staff didn't shove God down anyone's throat before serving up the food. They offered a meager breakfast every morning but Sunday. On Mondays, Wednesdays and Fridays, they served a hot soup lunch as long as their pantry held out. It wasn't much, but it meant the world to the homeless, especially in winter. It simply meant survival.

Warm light spilled into the morning's icy blue as Paul Finnegan, the kitchen manager, opened the door for the volunteers. The huddled and persevering street people watched them move into the glorious warmth of the indoors. The more animated churchees stomped snow from their shoes at the entryway, voicing brief and cheerful introductions as they moved by Paul. After presenting the donated food and listening to his instructions, they moved to their assigned tasks. Urns of hot coffee, plastic bins of bulk cereal

4

and gallons of reconstituted powdered milk were set on countertops so worn from scrubbing, their Formica patterns were barely visible.

After pulling a one-pound tube of frozen hamburger from the pile of new food, Paul directed Seth, his kitchen assistant, to put the rest in the pantry and walk-in freezer.

"Your demand is my command," said Seth, a thin, happy man, fond of rhymes, bad puns and tabloid rumors. In the homeless community, where violence and death were a constant threat, wild tales of monsters and government conspiracies were common. Seth believed every tale ever told with all of his heart. The latest was of a monster named Michael who fed on human flesh in an underground lair. It was a break from the usual man-eating alligators in Carter Lake or secret government medical tests, which meant it had to be true.

Paul placed an oversized frying pan atop a lit burner and peeled the wrapper from the frozen meat. In good times he would have browned two pounds to add to his stockpot, but the failing economy and brutal winter had stretched the pantry's shelves thin and swelled the ranks of the homeless to record numbers.

Through the serving window, Paul glanced out at the happy volunteers, a blatant contrast to the humanity waiting outside. Saddest of all the homeless souls were the severely mentally ill. When the Kilpatrick Center, a long-term care facility for the mentally ill had been forced to close, only a few of the most helpless found new placements. The rest were cast to the street. Every night, those who had survived the day, stumbled into the shelters. He had seen many who were near catatonic, silent and uncaring. Most barely made it indoors before simply settling on the dirty, wet floor until shelter staffers rolled them onto a mat and covered them with a blanket.

Seth returned from the pantry with an apron full of canned vegetables for the soup. Steam from the simmering hamburger wafted up and around Paul's face, adding a welcoming aroma to the room's warmth and humidity. He barely caught Seth's joke that the smell was "heaven scent."

"Get it?" he said, poking Paul. "S-c-e-n-t? The meat came from a church and smells good?"

Paul offered a brief smile and continued to chop and turn the browning meat.

* * *

Five blocks west, powdery snow swirled around Alex as he eyed his doghouse from the sidewalk. Hidden well off the street, his home was all but invisible. The little slant-roofed, plywood structure had been a gift from a neighboring business owner. Almost two years before, after a night of torrential rain, Alex had crawled from the limp remains of his cardboard shanty and saw a man waving at him from the loading dock of a plumbing supply business across the street. Alex returned the greeting in spite of being cold and soaked to the bone. They had exchanged niceties at a distance before, but this time the man took it a step further. His well-past-middle-age paunch jiggled as he stepped down from the dock, hopped over a puddle and quick-stepped across the street to Alex.

"I've been watching you work the hell out of those cans. My name's Arnold Perset," said the man. He was a few inches taller than Alex and much heavier. His thin, gray comb-over hair started just north of his left ear and arched across his balding pate to the far side of his head. The hop over the puddle had jostled a few strands loose to drape awkwardly down the man's neck to his shoulder. Alex looked down at the hand extended toward him. He shook it noticing the man wore both a belt and suspenders.

"Alex Capstain. Nice to meet you." He remembered trying to sound confident instead of pathetic while thinking, "This man doesn't trust his own pants. Why would he come anywhere near me?"

"I talked with a police detective friend the other day," Arnold continued. "He says you're a good man."

"If you mean William Olson, yes, I know him. Nice guy. Not like most of the cops around here. He stops by for a street update now and then. Usually trades me a good cigar for my time."

"Ah, I've been known to enjoy a good stogie myself now and again."

Alex smiled. "Well, in my case, good cigar means I didn't rescue it from an ashtray."

"I see." His round face had contorted sourly at the thought, then turned speculative, eyes twinkling. "Tell you what. Since I like having an extra set of eyes on my place, I've got an old doghouse I'll give you. Of course, you have to help me haul it across the street. It'd be a mansion compared to that cardboard."

"The cardboard would work better if I could find some plastic," Alex said, looking at the limp pile of brown. "I guess that would be a moot point if I had that doghouse."

Arnold returned his smile and offered his hand again. Alex grasped it and shook vigorously. It was nice to have someone notice his attempt at making a living, meager as it was.

Together they had hauled the doghouse across the street and into the lot, setting it back in the trees. Alex crawled in, turned around and poked his head back out, looking up at the nodding Arnold. He remembered the wave of guilt when he realized he might be taking on more than he could realistically handle. "You know I can't do much if somebody's messing around your place. It's not like I have access to a phone or anything."

"No, no, no." Arnold had waved a hand in the air. "Please, don't do anything risky. That's what my alarm system is for. It'll just be a comfort knowing there's a good man over here that's willing to talk to the police and report what he saw."

The rumble of a snowplow pulled Alex from the daydream. The cloud of ice crystals thrown by the plow's huge blade stung the craggy skin of his face. He turned away, tightening his hood in preparation for the trek to breakfast and his day's rounds.

The wheels of Alex's stroller left squiggly ruts in the snow on the sidewalk as he trudged down the line to his neighbor's shanties. They looked lifeless. Still, he had to check. Leaving his stroller, he high-stepped through untouched snow and confirmed his suspicions. Billy, Henry, Tom and, worst of all, DeAndre, were gone. Without a good-bye, everything left behind and still untouched. Something sinister had to be going on and he wished William, his detective friend, would stop by.

It was mostly the late-night discussions with DeAndre that he missed. On the night they'd met, DeAndre had strolled up to Alex's doghouse, offering to share his bottle of beer.

"Goddamn kids over at my camp is fightin' again," he'd said, shaking his head as he approached. "Don't know why I hang with that bunch. Mind if I sit?"

"Naw. Pull up a milk crate," Alex said. He did his best not to show he was scared to near panic by the six-foot-four stranger in his camp. Not wanting to offend, Alex took the offered bottle and sipped. The beer smelled and tasted sweet.

"That's a little different from the Bud I used to drink," Alex said, hiccuping as he felt the beer warm his stomach.

DeAndre chuckled, "You a newbie, ain't ya? This here's malt liquor." He held up the bottle. "It's cheap and it'll kick yo' ass in no time. Mo' bang for your buck. Do a damn fine job a' keepin' you warm in winter, too." He took a long drink before handing the bottle back.

The malt liquor and his new acquaintance's willing ear lowered Alex's defenses. It felt good to finally talk to someone about the loss of his family, his job and his house. It eased the sting of what he considered to be a crushing failure.

"Well, enough about me," Alex said after half an hour of blabbering to his new friend, "What's your story?"

DeAndre gazed at the ground for a moment, took a hit off the bottle and handed it off. His too-small t-shirt accentuated bulging, tattooed arms. Half of one eyebrow had been replaced by a ragged scar.

"I drove a Tasty Cream truck," he said. "Kids on my route used to call me the Ding-Ding Man."

Alex swallowed hard and looked up at DeAndre. The big man's wry smile revealed one gold tooth twinkling in the firelight.

"You don't strike me as an ice-cream-and-kids kind of guy," Alex cautiously commented. "Not to offend, but you're really kinda scary looking."

"No offense taken, Little Man," said DeAndre, grinning. "I was a pretty scary guy at one time. Drugs and guns . . . you name it, I did it. I thought the only way to win was to be the baddest mutha in north O. I hurt people and people hurt me."

He showed Alex his left bicep, pointing out the small round scar that looked like a cigarette burn. When he rolled his arm over, Alex could see the puckered mess left by the exit of a hollow-point bullet.

"All that bad mutha shit got me was locked up," said DeAndre. "Did two years in Tecumseh prison on some jacked up charge."

Alex managed a whispered, "Damn."

"Guess I grew up while I was inside. My parole officer got me hooked up with Tasty Cream. Had me chasin' the American dream. Trouble was, I gots two kids of my own from when I was, like, fifteen. When my baby mamas heard I had a job, they got some fuckin' lawyer to come afta' me for more child support. I was already given 'em most a my damn paychecks, but that wasn't enough for them fuckin' lawyers. Fuckers got too greedy and got the govmint to take my driver's license. Can't drive for Tasty Cream without a license, so now they get fuckin' nothin'."

"They can take your license for falling behind on child support?"

"Yessa, they can and they did."

"What's the sense in that?"

"It ain't about common sense or right or wrong," DeAndre said. "It's about power and everybody screwin' everybody else outta what they can. Ain't nobody getting rich but the politricksters and fuckin' lawyers these days. Look around, Little Man. They's a lot of us American dreamers out here and they's mo' comin' in every day."

An icy wind gust brought Alex back to the present. Little Man. He liked the nickname when DeAndre said it. God, I hope he shows up for breakfast.

After parking his stroller with the odd collection of shopping carts and wagons in the Harvest House's delivery yard, Alex stepped into the line along the yard's chain link fence. He grumbled at seeing the Angel's Wings vans. The presence of these West Omaha churchees usually meant a hefty helping of God would be served with breakfast.

"Is Pastor Asshole in there yet?" Alex asked the man ahead of him in line.

"Yeah, drove up in his fancy SUV a few minutes ago."

Sunshine added a touch of warmth to the morning's icy hue. The sidewalk looked slick where the snow had been trampled hard. Alex shifted from foot to foot hoping the churchees inside would hurry up.

Finally, Paul Finnegan flung open the kitchen door, bellowing a warm welcome.

As the line shuffled in, Seth issued his usual singsongy announcement, "Good mornin', people. I'm Seth the soup kitchen sou chef. Eat it and beat it, folks. Make room for those still waiting outside."

Having arrived later than usual, Alex was in the second group allowed in. He headed straight for Paul Finnegan.

"Morning," Alex greeted him to make eye contact. "Seen any sign of my neighbors?"

Paul frowned. "So you haven't found them yet?"

"No, sir, not a sign."

The frown deepened. "Is it possible they picked up some work and didn't tell you?"

"Anything's possible, I suppose." Alex shrugged, knowing his comment was meaningless. "But it's not like DeAndre. He has always clued me in when there's work."

Seth nosed in, "I heard there's a monster out there that's cutting people up and eating them."

"Dang it, Seth," Paul interrupted. "You'll believe anything. Last week it was alligators in Carter Lake—in the middle of winter, no less—and now it's monsters. Can't you see the man's concerned?"

Seth flinched as if he'd been slapped. "Yeah, but it could be true," he said defensively. "I heard his name is Michael and he's like, ten feet tall."

Paul put a comforting arm around him, "Seth, I'm sorry if I was rude. But you know how people like to tell stories. Some guy sees a big alley cat and before you know it, everybody's saying there's a mountain lion."

"There is a mountain lion," Seth said with conviction. "He's in the woods up by the airport."

Paul started to answer, then scrunched his tired face in defeat and turned his attention back to Alex who did not try to hide his amusement over the exchange.

Paul cleared his throat. "You know how it works, Alex. Some guy pulls up in a truck offering cash for labor and off they go."

He shrugged, still not satisfied. "I suppose."

Stepping into the line for the bathroom, Alex unzipped his parka. A glove he'd carelessly stuffed into a pocket, fell to the floor. The man in line ahead, deftly covered it with a dirty, wet shoe.

Alex gave him a small nudge. "Excuse me," he said quietly, bending to retrieve the glove.

"Oh, sorry," said the man, as if it were an accident.

That was the end of it. Any sign of confrontation meant swift expulsion and neither wanted that.

The small, two-toilet bathroom offered little privacy. Alex spent a few quality moments cleansing his privates with toilet water, then moved to the sink where he wedged his parka between his waist and the counter. He washed with liquid soap from the dispenser over the sink, careful not to soak anything that wouldn't dry before heading back into the cold.

Feeling fresher, he moved into the breakfast line.

"What'll it be today, my friend?" asked a neatly dressed, elderly volunteer with an artificial smile.

"Froot Loops and a hot chocolate. That's my daughter's favorite cereal. I'll take one of those bananas, as well, if I'm allowed."

"I pray your daughter is staying someplace warm," probed the judgmental woman.

"Florida, I think. She's probably a grown woman now, but I like to think she still likes Froot Loops."

"Too bad you can't be with her. Florida sounds good this time of year."

Breakfast in hand, Alex settled into his usual spot on the floor under the heavy wooden table that held the coffee urns. He kept his back to the wall, staying out of the way and out of trouble.

Scanning the room while munching his cereal, he watched a volunteer offer day-old sack lunches. There was no sign of DeAndre or the others, but there were familiar faces, some friendly, some predators. The new faces kept to themselves, but Alex knew it wouldn't be long before they moved on or joined a clique for protection.

Snow melting off the shoes in the coffee line formed a puddle in front of Alex. Soon a huge, rag mop swished by, followed by the smiling, upside down face of a Harvest House staffer.

"How's it going, Alex?" said the mop man.

"I'm still kicking."

"Excuse the mop. This floor is a constant battle this time of year." The face disappeared and the mop went back to work.

The morning's quiet shuffle for breakfast was shattered by the bellow of Pastor John Ahough, the televangelist leader of that morning's volunteers. "Praise the Lord Jesus. In his name we pray for guidance for these lost souls in their time of need!"

Just what we need; a little floor show with breakfast.

Pastor Ahough's hand pulled a greasy-haired kid from the breakfast line.

The boy stared blandly back as the impeccably dressed pastor's pink, manicured fingers squeezed his shoulder. The phony holy man wore freshly creased designer jeans, rectangular, brushed-metal framed glasses and, beneath his lower lip, bobbed an annoying little soul patch. When the preacher bowed his head low, working his overly-fervent prayer, the boy squinted in distaste at the man's display of inflamed hair plugs. Even from his position against the wall Alex thought the pastor's scalp looked like a miniature cornfield.

"Lord! This young man has the look of a lost soooul!" crowed the pastor, shaking the boy's left shoulder while thrusting his free hand into the air as if reaching to the heavens to give God a big high five. He raised his head, pushing his face closer to the kid's. "What's your name, son?"

"Jake," replied the boy.

Alex knew Jake was sixteen, but passed for older. He'd escaped his incestuous, drug-addicted father only to run straight into the grip of a new hell named Larry Parmenter. Each of Larry's four-member street family had specific skills and weaknesses that he exploited to the fullest in exchange for his protection. Greg was a shoplifter and Cat, Greg's toothless, meth-addicted wife, gave $5 blowjobs to anything with a dick. Jake's talent for servicing of the drivers at the truck stops across the Missouri River in Iowa, made him the best earner by far. He was Larry's masterpiece, a diamond in the rough he'd reeled in with small acts of kindness, only to beat and rape him into submission.

The prissy holy man's touching of the boy threw the territorial Larry into a rage. He shoved Jake aside to come nose to nose with the pastor.

"Shut. The fuck. Up. The boy is mine," Larry growled.

The fastidious holy man appeared dizzy with fear. He jerked a glance at his audience then squeaked, "The Lord is my shepherd. I shall not want—"

Larry grabbed Ahough's shirt, yanked him forward then shoved him back, placing a foot behind the pastor's leg to send him and his designer jeans to the muddy floor. The room fell silent.

Paul and Seth moved quickly toward the trouble, leaving behind anything that could be seen as a weapon. Out of Larry's view, the mop man discreetly unscrewed his mop's hardwood handle.

Seth slipped behind the wallowing, terrified Pastor to grab his collar then pull him out of Larry's reach. Holding up both hands as if calling for peace, Paul circled warily, keeping a safe distance. Only one hand shown from Larry's filthy coat sleeves. The other, Alex—and, of course, Paul—knew, likely held a box cutter.

"Larry, cool it," Paul placated, watching the old predator's face for a hint of intent. "You don't want the cops and you don't want to miss out on breakfast. Why don't you and your people get what you need and head on outside."

Larry smiled, nodded and relaxed. The mop man breathed a sigh of relief.

Cat, Jake and Greg grabbed all the remaining sack lunches and headed for the exit. Larry followed, but paused in the doorway, holding the room's attention. He glared back at the pastor, whose mud-stained pants now looked like he'd shit himself. Larry pointed at the pastor and summoned his best, growling, pirate-like voice, yelling, "Look! It's Pa-a-astor A-a-a-a-hole!"

Everyone in the room, including some of the churchees, burst out laughing. They all knew the pastor's rude nickname. They considered the holy man a joke, but a joke worth tolerating because he came bearing gifts.

2

A bare light bulb dangling from an ancient porcelain fixture held back the darkness, but nothing could hold back the small, dank room's crypt-like smell. It was frigid in the cellar this morning, but Michael liked it that way. Cold slowed the work, allowing him to enjoy his service to God that much longer.

Eartha Kitt's purring rendition of "Santa Baby," his mother's holiday favorite, played in his mind. The imagined music urged his naked body to sway at the hips as he selected the tools for the day's work. His current project hung in the center of the room, snoring quietly. Meat hooks hammered between the bones of the man's forearms were set wide, suspending him in a crucifix-like position.

Saving the man's soul, bringing him to true repentance had been a long journey. *Soon, very soon, it will be time.* He donned a black rubber apron to hide his swelling excitement. *Soon this fornicator will awaken and I'll release his soul.* He reached under the apron and touched himself at the thought of basking in another orgasmic conversation with the Lord.

* * *

Alex donned his coat and gloves as the soup kitchen staff hollered prayers and goodbyes. His coat zipped and hood tightened, he retrieved his stroller while considering his route for the day. Working the south edge of the neighborhood was the smart thing to do. The trash trucks were still a day away and bins would be full. He'd work west through the alleys till he hit the North Expressway, then cut south to the university campus where the smoke-break ashtrays offered excellent butt sniping.

If the morning's pickings proved slim, he could skip lunch at the Harvest House and pick up a sack lunch from a church group that frequented the park across the street from the downtown library. From there he'd hunt dropped parking meter change, working his way back toward the St. Vincent campus. He'd arrive too late to catch Nurse Liz, but sleeping over meant he'd see her in the morning. With a little luck, she'd have news of DeAndre and the neighbors.

Pastor Ahough burst from the Harvest House kitchen with a less-than-holy look on his face. "Like I need this crap," the pastor muttered, not seeing Alex standing nearby. Pastor fished muddied pockets for car keys then thumbed a key fob remote, drawing a chirp from a white BMW X3 parked across the street.

"Have a good day, sir," Alex said, "and sorry about Larry. You're lucky he didn't hurt you. He can be a real monster."

Startled, Pastor Ahough donned his holy smile and turned to Alex without missing a beat. In less than a second, the pastor's face flashed feigned concern, confusion and, finally, disgust when he realize the voice came from someone he obviously regarded as less than human.

"God only knows what diseases you filthy animals tracked in," Pastor said, looking down at the muck on his pants. "This world will be much better off without this cesspool of a neighborhood."

Alex decided to poke him with cheerfulness. "It's just dirt. Been living in it for over a year now. Hasn't killed me yet."

Seth popped his head out of the kitchen door. "Pastor Ahough, sir, I think this is your scarf."

"Oh, thank you, son," said the pastor, resuming his holy puffery. "This was a gift from one of our Sunday school classes," he said draping the gray scarf like a priceless necklace. "I'd have been crushed to lose it. Thank you so much."

Seth glanced at Alex and back to Pastor, waved goodbye and shut the door.

"Many of these filthy people," Alex continued with his own fake smile, "are not here by choice. I, for instance, managed a cabinetmaking shop not far from that new ballpark." He pointed to the stadium looming a few blocks away. "I had a nice house, too."

"I see," said the pastor. "And what personal vice was it that so unfairly took it all? Drink? Drugs?"

Alex took a long moment, his thoughts assembling like storm clouds. Just as the pastor turned away, Alex spat, "I suppose my vice was believing in the American dream."

"Well, aren't you the little street philosopher," said the pastor, turning back to Alex.

Giving in to the thoughts coming hot and fast, Alex took one step forward. "People like you are the problem." The pastor's widening eyes egged him on. "You live off of other people's good will and offer nothing but bullshit in return."

The man huffed a moment then sneered, "I'll have you know I provide the money and volunteers to keep your little shit-hole existence afloat."

"No, sir." Alex shook his head. "The members of your church provide those dollars and time. You're just like a damn politician, raising yourself up on the good deeds of others. I didn't see you lift a finger to help in there."

The pastor's cell phone rang. Still glaring at Alex, he answered at his sanctimonious best, "Praise the Lord, how may I help?" Moving in a wide arc around Alex, he headed to his SUV. The crunch of Alex's steps in the snow behind him had him looking over his shoulder. "Just a minute Phil," he said into the phone, "I've got a *little* problem to deal with."

Holding his cell against his coat, he smiled and scanned the street to be sure they were alone. "Listen, you little piece of shit, I've had enough of your kind today. It's been interesting, but if you don't get the hell away from me, I'm calling the police." He jabbed an index finger at his phone for emphasis, his eyes needling from behind those trendy designer glasses.

Alex glared back, silently wishing Larry had gutted the pompous leech rather than making a joke of him. There was more he wanted to say, but understood that men like Ahough held all the cards. Arguing further would only land him in jail. Alex shrugged, lowered his head and moved on.

The sun warmed his back and soothed an aching leg that had never completely healed after the car accident that eventually put him on the street. Vehicle exhaust overwhelmed the morning's crisp, fresh air. The few university students not headed home for the Christmas break, hiked to and from campus.

One block south and west of the Harvest House, Alex trundled onto Cuming Street. Looking east, he saw the futuristic lines of the new indoor sports arena and the towering steel of the new ballpark jutting skyward like the spires of ancient cathedrals.

Alex watched silhouetted steelworkers navigate the ballpark's metal skeleton, marveling at their bravery, then turned back west, passing the Fitzgerald Hotel. Alex planned to live at the Fitzgerald someday soon. After nearly two years of dumpster diving and odd jobs, he had almost enough saved. Sleeping rooms at the Fitzgerald were $60 a week, but they came with heat, a mailing address for job applications and communal bathroom facilities.

Nurse Liz, a nursing student and paid part-timer at the St. Vincent Shelter held his savings for him. DeAndre had introduced them after Alex had been beaten and robbed by a swarm of housing project kids out for an evening of mayhem. He shivered at the memory.

"That shit's gonna get infected," DeAndre had said, as Alex sat in the doorway of his doghouse, blood coagulating in his hair, his cracked ribs complaining with every breath. "It'll go gang greeny or somethin'."

"Do you mean gangrene?" Alex croaked. "That would be very bad. They'd have to amputate." The painful half laugh had doubled him over. "Of course, that might be better than living like this." His pained smile faded. "They took all my savings, DeAndre. Forty goddamn dollars. Made me drop my pants and took it out of my underwear. It took months to save that much."

"Don't get all twisted up about it," DeAndre had said, "I used to be one them kids. They ain't got nothin either. When I was little, seemed like beaten the hell outta folk was the only time we was in control . . . Anyways, use that dumb-ass head of yours while you still got it and come see Nurse Liz with me. She's good folk. You can trust her."

After introductions, Liz had cleaned and closed the gash on Alex's head with a few stitches.

"Damn kids got me for over forty bucks," Alex complained to her, as well. "Figured my money would be safe in my underwear. But those little bastards—excuse my French—the little monsters made me drop my drawers."

"Tell you what," Liz had said, "It's against the rules, but if you promise to keep it between us, I'll keep an envelope with your name on it locked in my desk. If you stop by for a visit now and then and some money happens to find its way into that envelope . . . Well, we'll be the only ones who know about it."

"God, that'd be a load off my mind," Alex had said as they shook on the deal.

In an alley at 18th Street, Alex spotted a radiator in a car repair shop dumpster. After checking that no one watched, he hoisted himself up over the metal edge to tilt in deep. Top heavy with the radiator in hand, he kicked and rocked to pull it out. It was worth the effort, the soft brass and aluminum in the radiator's core would go a long way toward getting his room at the Fitzgerald.

Crossing to the next block, Alex heard, "Hey you! Over here!"

Thinking it might be a shop owner wanting to bitch, Alex pretended not to hear.

"Stroller dude!" hollered the voice again.

Alex spotted an older, pony-tailed man on the corner, his hands resting on the handle of a snow shovel.

"Got an offer. Come on over," the man said.

Warily, Alex approached.

"My help didn't show today and I've got an extra shovel with no one to use it. The other shopkeepers told me the little stroller dude is cool. I assume that's you." He pulled off a glove and held out a hand for Alex to shake.

"Yes, sir," Alex said, removing his own glove to shake the offered hand. "Sometimes I do odd jobs, sweep up and such. If you've got tools, I'm a heck of a woodworker, too."

"Maybe down the line, my man," the shopkeeper said. "For now, I've got a dollar and a spare shovel, if you've got a few minutes."

"Always willing to earn a buck."

He parked his stroller, grabbed the extra shovel and went to work.

"I've seen you around," said the shopkeeper, steadily shoveling and tossing. "Do you stay at one of the shelters?"

Already puffing hard after hoisting the first half-dozen shovels full of snow, Alex said, "I will tonight because it's so darn cold. Mostly I stay at a little place over by 20th and Paul. It's not much, but it's home."

Twenty minutes of hard work had cleared the storefront and chopped several walkways through the waist-high bank between the street and sidewalk.

"Since the other guys along here say you're okay," said the shopkeeper as he pulled a dollar from his pocket, "why don't you stop by now and then. There's always something that needs doing and the damn college kids I've been hiring act like manual labor's beneath them."

"Gosh, that'd be great and thanks a million." Alex gratefully pocketed the dollar.

"Two rules, though. Don't come around if you've been drinking and no panhandling customers on this block. No exceptions. One violation and the deal is off."

"Fair enough and thank you," said Alex, knowing it was futile to tell the man he wasn't much of a drinker. He shook the man's hand again, savoring pride in a job well done.

The fresh ice melt rattled his stroller and crunched under foot as he continued on his way. He let his mind wander back to the last job he'd held before hitting the street . . . .

Desperate to fend off foreclosure, he'd taken a third part-time job at Liberty Pizza. Rather than bussing tables or working kitchen prep as he'd expected, Alex had been handed a gauzy, blue-green dress with a matching, foam crown and a torch. The dress was much too big for his small frame. His insides twisted at the embarrassing memory. He cringed as he saw himself dancing from foot-to-foot, the crown slipping down his face as he held up the dress in the torch hand and hoisted a sign reading *Get a Slice of Liberty, Only a Buck!* with the other. Some passersby waved, their smiles not masking their pity. Most of them averted their gaze. He assumed they needed to turn a blind eye to the desperation that could be a layoff away.

At 20th Street, Alex froze, faced with a dilemma. Before him stretched a rock-hard wall of dirty, white snow nearly 100 yards long. "Son of a bitch, I forgot about the Alps," he said aloud. The plowed snow strained the chain link fence surrounding the city's sprawling transit facility, making passage without walking in the street impossible.

Inbound traffic streamed endlessly, but outbound—Alex's direction of travel—was only a trickle. Crossing to the cleared sidewalk on the far side of the street meant wading into the stream of unforgiving commuter traffic. Going around the transit facility meant walking blocks out of his way. He peered back over his shoulder to gauge the risk of a 100-yard run in the gutter. No cars came in his direction. Ahead, gray metal parking meter heads jutted from the frozen barricade at regular intervals. At the far end, traffic lights were obscured by steam from a sewer grate roiling upward in a green, then yellow, then red cloud of doom.

One more peek back over his shoulder showed it was clear. Maintaining a death grip on the stroller handle, Alex dropped the wheels into the gutter, glanced back one more time, then took off with the hurried limp of a wounded speed walker. Halfway into his run, a diesel engine's rumble caught his ear. *Where the hell did he come from?* His quick pace shifted into an awkward sprint.

The engine roared in downshift.

Behind him, someone yelled, "Run, wino, run!"

Alex lurched into an all-out gallop for his life. His chest heaved, the cold air torturing his lungs. He smelled the diesel and imagined his reflection as the truck's chrome bumper swallowed him whole before his tiny body popped under the truck's huge dually tires. At the height of panic, Alex's junior high phys-ed coach flashed before his eyes screaming, "Come on Crapstain! Breathe through your nose, not your mouth!"

Then disaster struck. Just a few yards from the finish line. A stroller wheel caught in a sewer grate, ramming the stroller's handle into his groin and lifting him off the ground. A hot pain exploded in his kidneys as the stroller's contents flew into the street. Shuddering tires squealed. Alex braced for an impact that never came. The fire in his groin coaxed a sickly, low-pitched croak from his throat. Feet suddenly frozen with fear, he looked back and hunched over in agony, his hands covering his abused crotch, his mouth open and eyes wide.

The truck's massive chrome grill loomed hot, just feet from his face. The diesel engine rattled at idle, then roared as the driver repeatedly tapped the accelerator, threatening, like a bull about to charge. A blasting chrome chorus from the truck's air horn sounded just as the truck lurched forward then stopped.

The threat propelled Alex in a leap for the safety of the snowbank. He glimpsed the fast approaching EXPIRED flag inside the head of a parking meter just before pain exploded in his head. Barely aware of his blood smearing the dirty snow, he slid toward the gutter. Gears grinding, the truck rolled by, then, just before unconsciousness took him, Alex heard the driver shout "Gaawdaaamn! Wished I'da taped that for TV, Wino!"

Blackness. The sound of traffic funneled into Alex's ears. His eyelids fluttered open. Noise and light swirled into a jackhammer of pain. Slowly, the world came into focus. A chubby college girl in a wool pea coat hovered above him. She wore a ridiculous looking stocking cap with a topknot that made her look like a plump, Silkie Bantam chicken. The brightly colored topknot bobbed and flopped as she spoke into her phone.

"Yes, he is breathing, but his face is bleeding pretty bad," she said, her voice high pitched and panicked.

Alex saw his stroller nearby, its handle bent from the collision with his crotch. Someone, probably the girl, had dragged both his body and his stroller out of harm's way. The precious radiator had disappeared. He removed a glove to put a bare hand to his face. It felt odd . . . thick. With a little more probing, he discerned that a wad of napkins was stuck to a gash on his cheek. Gently pulling them away, he saw a Starbucks Coffee logo mixed with the dirt and blood.

The frustrated girl griped into her phone, angrily trying to convince a dispatcher that a paramedic was needed.

"I've never had a Starbucks," Alex said, loud enough to get her attention. "I usually get the small senior coffee at the TastyQuick down the street." His hands shook as he pressed the bloody napkins back in place.

"What? Just sit still," the girl ordered, kneeling down to him, dropping her phone into a coat pocket. "The paramedics are coming." She looked down the street then back at him. "That trucker was a real asshole. He saw you were hurt and just took off."

The girl gently removed the bloody makeshift compress. Coagulation had started, but fresh blood still seeped. She replaced the soaked wad with a fresh one. Alex smelled the coffee on her breath.

"My head hurts but I think I'll be all right," Alex said, pulling the new napkin away to eye the slower accumulation of blood before gingerly pressing it back in place. "Don't think I'll be collecting cans today, though. There goes a day's wages." Alex regretted his obvious attempt to gain a handout the second the words passed his lips.

Now embarrassed and wanting to escape, he tried to stand. The world did a half-spin that came to a halt when he sat back down.

"No, sir. You stay right where you are," the girl ordered. "You should get looked at." She took a deep, calming breath and put a gentle hand on his shoulder, "You hit your head really hard, sir. You could have a concussion."

I could have concussed balls. Thankfully his brain was in control enough to not mention the crushing pain throbbing from his crotch up into his kidneys.

Sirens sounded to the south, growing louder on approach.

Fearing contact with police or a trip to the hospital could cost him his stroller and possibly his freedom, Alex strengthened his voice. "No, I'll be all right."

"Listen, if you stay, I'll give you ten bucks." The anxious girl pulled a small wad of bills mixed with receipts, napkins and lint from her coat pocket. "My name is Amanda. What's yours?"

Her intensity and generosity stunned his embarrassment and worry into silence. "Alex Capstain," he whispered and gently accepted the ten from her dainty, soft hand. Glancing around for any other spectators, he quickly slipped it into a coat pocket.

Barely into my day and I've already made eleven dollars. Might have to reward myself with a warm afternoon at Mick's.

The sirens fell silent, but lights still flashed as Engine and Squad One arrived. Passersby, mostly students, now paused to check out the commotion. Alex watched them grimace, some even shrugging before hurrying on. Firemen and paramedics dismounted, their bunker gear loosely buckled for what they obviously assumed would be a brief event.

"Hello, my friend," said a fireman with the name "P. Collings," stenciled on the front of his heavy canvas coat. "Looks like you've had a bumpy morning. Can you tell me what happened?"

"A parking meter attacked me," Alex said, nervous and trying for humor. Collings didn't even smile. "I jumped out of the way of a truck and I punched the meter with my face," Alex admitted.

The paramedics set to work. They flushed and dabbed at the gash on his face, applied disinfectant and checked his vitals. One paramedic flashed a penlight into his eyes. He announced to his partner that the pupils were equal. P. Collings interviewed Amanda and wrote on a form atop a metal clipboard-box.

"He was unconscious for several minutes. You called him friend. Do you know him?" Amanda asked.

"These old bums are all the same," P. Collings said, speaking over the fire truck's idling engine. "We see them every day, usually after they've had a run-in with someone over cigarettes or booze."

One of the paramedics approached and spoke discreetly into P. Colling's ear. P. Collings shrugged, then keyed his radio. "Patient refuses transport, Engine One, Squad One available, returning to station."

"Shouldn't a doctor make sure he's okay?" Amanda asked, looking from Alex sitting on the ground to the medics stowing their bright orange medical boxes back into their squad.

"Well, ma'am, that would be the prudent thing to do," said P. Collings, "but these street guys?" He shrugged. "Believe me, I've seen them much worse than this. Mainly, guys like him are out here by choice. They don't like being confined and they don't want to be away from their habits, if you know what I mean. Tell me, did he ask you for money?"

"No, he didn't ask . . . but I gave him ten dollars," she admitted sheepishly.

P. Collings flashed an all-knowing smile. "He'll be fine, ma'am, I'm not supposed to share patient information, but I will tell you there was no sign of concussion. He'll have a headache. But I'm sure it's not his first."

Amanda thanked the men in general and gingerly crouched next to Alex on the curb where the firemen had moved him. From her strained expression, Alex knew she had never been this close to a homeless man. Now that the emergency had passed, her pursed lips and wrinkled nose showed acute awareness of his rank odor, a tangy-sweet mix of garbage, cigarettes and unwashed clothes. She focused on the square of white gauze held by translucent tape that had replaced her napkins. He passed shaking fingers over his face remembering the blackheads that populated the wrinkled skin of his forehead and around his eyes. When her attention shifted to his yellowed and dirt-cracked fingernails, he hurried to re-button the layers of clothing the paramedics had disturbed. She looked away from his boney, pale chest. *I must remind her of a sad little stray dog.*

"Thank you for the help," Alex said, still nervous. "I've had much worse than this little bump. Years ago, I boxed in the Golden Gloves." Regretting the lie, he turned his thoughts to the anonymity of a dark, warm corner at Mick's Tavern.

"Are you sure you don't want to go to the hospital?" the girl tried one more time.

"I'll probably have a good shiner, but I'll be okay," Alex said, slowly getting up from the curb, steadier now. "I'm staying at the St. Vincent shelter tonight," he said. "They have a nurse there who's a friend of mine. She can look me over."

"Well, all right then, I guess I'll get to my work-study on campus. Don't want to be late for my shift." She extended her hand awkwardly.

Alex gently shook the beautiful hand, so soft, tiny and delicate in his ugly fingers. "What was your name again? My name is Alex."

"I remember your name. I'm Amanda."

"Really? I have a daughter by that name," Alex said. "She lives in Florida with her mom."

"Florida sounds wonderful this time of year," she said. "It was nice to meet you, Alex. I hope you feel better."

He turned toward his stroller, still embarrassed over the whole disturbing scene he had caused this girl but turned back. "Amanda, I didn't box in the Golden Gloves, I just made that up." She smiled and nodded.

They both raised a hand in parting.

3

"The Friendliest Place In Town" proclaimed the blow-molded plastic sign hanging from the front of Mick's Tavern. Friendly was not what the fading and broken sign or the building conveyed.

Crumbling under years of misery, Mick's appeared to be held together by thick coats of cheap, white latex paint streaked with rust weeping from metal security bars. A clever tagger—more acrobat than academic—had added a finishing touch by scaling the front gate to scrawl "FUCK" above the entrance.

Steering around patches of ice that had been melting snow the previous afternoon, Alex noticed a white van belonging to the West Omaha Church of Christ's Angel's Wings program idling in front of Mick's. The driver struggled to load an unconscious man through the van's open side door.

Angel's Wings was one of the few things Alex thought Pastor Ahough had gotten right. Last winter, when the temperature had dropped below freezing, their vans appeared nightly to patrol the north downtown in search of those in need of a ride to shelter. All assumed it was a publicity stunt. No one expected the free rides to continue much past their media debut. But to everyone's surprise, a wealthy congregant had stepped up to donate the money needed to keep the Angel's Wings aloft well into their second year.

Slowing his pace, Alex saw the van driver squat to haul his soon-to-be passenger to a sitting position. Bear-hugging him from behind, the driver lifted, muttering words seldom heard in church.

"Need some help?" asked Alex.

"Sure, grab his feet will ya?"

"Man, he looks near dead," Alex commented as they hoisted the unconscious man in, his head thunking hard on the van's metal floor. Alex winced. The guy didn't even grunt.

"Don't think so," said the driver, "I felt a pulse. I wouldn't be surprised if he has some bad frostbite though. I just called the St. Vincent and Nurse Liz told me to take him straight to the hospital. Do you know who he is?" asked the driver.

Alex recognized the man's puffy, blue winter boots. "I think his name is Moon Boots. I see him pass by my table over at the Harvest House some mornings." He leaned in to touch Moon Boot's neck, the volunteer joined him in the doorway, pressing his hand into Alex's back.

"Want to ride along?" the driver asked, pressing harder. "I could drop you at the shelter after."

Alex pushed back hard, the hair on his neck stiff as he placed a hand on the lawnmower blade in his stroller. "I'm gonna go warm my bones in there," Alex said, tilting his head toward Mick's.

"I really don't think you should do that," said driver, stepping closer. "I could put that contraption of yours in the back."

When he put a hand on the stroller, Alex yanked it away, partially drawing his blade.

"All right, all right. I got it." The driver put up his hands and stepped back. "But I'll be watching for you on my rounds. Alcohol will likely get you into my van one of these days."

"Doubt it," said Alex. "I'm not much of a drinker."

The driver nodded, offering a condescending smile before swinging the door shut on Moon Boots. A moment later the van roared off.

Mick's front door sat behind a rusty security gate mangled by the bumper of an angry patron's Buick years before. This time of day customers had to request admittance via intercom. Only after the barman had looked them over through a security camera could they be buzzed in through the off-kilter gate.

"Deliveries go to the back," said a gruff, electronic voice.

"Hey, it's me, Capstain," Alex said, positioning his face in the bars so it could be seen clearly by the camera. A buzz and a click sounded. Alex pulled open the gate to roll in his stroller. He parked it to the side as the gate slammed closed behind him, then pulled open the front door.

Like landfill rats in the headlights, the bartender and mop man looked up as daylight briefly scoured the cavernous barroom. No words of welcome could be heard, only the musical clink of beer bottles as the square-jawed man behind the bar hustled beer from box to cooler. Beneath the stunted ears of a boxer—the left one barely holding a cigarette—the barman's thick neck disappeared into the open collar of a white dress shirt, its sleeves rolled up to the elbow.

Alex wove his way through the tables and chairs, his eyes adjusting to the dark, his nose adjusting to the familiar Lysol and cigarette smell.

"Morning, Jerry. Want me to break down those boxes?" Alex asked. He had applied for work at Mick's on several occasions and always tried to look eager.

"Nah, Julio will get 'em. Jesus, Alex, what the hell happened this time?"

He touched his bandaged cheek. "My face got up close and personal with a parking meter."

"Was it an accident or did someone help the two of you meet?"

"Just trying to get out of the way of some jerk in a semi."

His gaze drifted to the upright, lighted cooler and the package liquor within. Mick's carried everything from the cheapest malt liquors and fortified wines all the way up to some fairly good single malt Scotch and Irish whiskeys. The package liquor cooler that Alex admired contained strictly the cheap shit, catering to the man or woman who wanted a quick drunk at the least cost.

"Goin' with the cheap shit as usual?" asked the barman.

"Jerry, I'm in the mood to celebrate," Alex replied, rubbing the bills in his pocket. A forty-ounce bottle of beer would last him most of the day, but a real can of Budweiser would taste much better. After an inner debate, he compromised. "I'll take a bottle of Colt, and the cheapest decent cigar in your humidor."

"We've got a buck-fifty machine-rolled that's really pretty good."

"Deal," said Alex.

It pained him to watch his ten-dollar bill reduced to a five and some change.

Jerry made a big production out of unwrapping the cigar, cutting the cap and formally presenting it to Alex. Grinning, he tossed in a handful of matchbooks onto the bar top in front of Alex. "Don't use them all up at once." The bottle of Colt followed.

Alex saluted him with the cigar and scooped the matches into a coat pocket. Beer in hand, he headed to a heavy wooden chair in a dark corner. It was his usual spot, directly under a vent that blew warm air in the winter and cool in the summer. The bottle hissed as he broke the seal. The hair on his arms stood in anticipation. His body's involuntary reaction surprised him. *I'm not turning in to an old street drunk am I?*

The beer tasted sharp and a little sweet. It stoked his internal furnace, warming his bones from the inside out while the warm air on his shoulders and neck warmed his body from the outside in. One packet of matches and a glass ashtray sat next to the bottle, now dewy with condensation. He struck a match and roasted the end of the cigar then lit a second, taking several long draws to bring the tip to an even red glow.

Julio had mopped his way over to the beer boxes and was breaking them down. The phone rang and the bartender answered. The predictable rhythm of the place, the rich taste of the cigar combined with the lightness of the alcohol sliding down his throat brought on a pleasured sigh. Alex took another sip of beer. *I've been on the street a lot longer than I thought I'd be. Is this how alcoholism starts?* That thought brought on a wave of depression that grew until it felt like a rip tide pulling him out to sea.

A chair screeched across from him startling Alex from his dark thoughts. Jerry sat down, a tall wooden box under one arm and three shot glasses gripped between the tips of his fingers. The glasses clinked as he set them on the table.

"Julio!" the bartender bellowed. *"Aqui, por favor, I have a surprise, a sopresa,"* he said in butchered Spanish.

Julio abandoned his mop and box breaking duties. He sauntered over to lean on the back of a chair, smiling and curious.

"Sit. Ah, *sentarse*," said Jerry.

The two cigars protruding from the barman's shirt pocket looked to be better than the one Alex had purchased.

"That phone call was my daughter in Denver," he said. "It seems I'm a grandfather for the third time."

"Well, I'll be," said Alex, smiling. "Congratulations."

Seeing Julio was smiling only to go along, Jerry pounded his chest with, "*Bebe*, Julio."

Julio's eyebrows shot up. "*Usted es un nuevo padre?*"

"New father?" Jerry laughed. "No, Julio. I'm a grandfather. Ah, *abuelo*." He held up three fingers. "*Tres*."

"*Si, tres*," said Julio, now shaking the bartender's hand and smiling sincerely.

From the tall wooden box marked Middelton's Very Rare Irish Whiskey, the barman pulled a half-empty bottle. "I brought this in because I had a feeling today would be the day." He uncorked the bottle. "My wife bought this for me when our first grandchild came into the world. Funny her buying me, a bartender, a bottle of booze, but she knew I'd never spend 150 bucks on a bottle of whiskey for myself."

Alex's jaw dropped when the man poured a finger of whiskey into each shot glass. *$150 a bottle. Son of a bitch.*

"I take a taste only on very special occasions and I feel like sharing this one with you two right now."

"I have a daughter too," said Alex, brightening. "I think she's in Florida. Haven't heard from her for a while."

"Well, then I suggest we make a toast to the children." He held his shot glass high, offering a toast. "To the children! That's *niños* to you, Julio."

Julio's smile widened.

The first sip took Alex's breath, but rewarded him with a thousand earthy flavors as it went down warm and smooth.

"Now, because I'm in a generous, grandpa kinda mood and it's Christmas Eve, here's a cigar for each of you. You don't have to smoke them here. Put'em away for later. Julio, you and I should get back to work." He waved a hand at the abandoned beer boxes.

Julio downed his drink and returned to work straightaway. Alex finished his whiskey more slowly as did the bartender. Alex felt Jerry's pleasure in watching him treasure the rare treat. "Man, this is amazing, Jerry. Thanks a million."

"My pleasure, Alex . . . " He hesitated. "Personal question. How long you been on the street?"

"Oh, over a year now. Almost two, I guess." He carefully rolled the shot glass between his hands. "I kinda lose track of time. I can tell you it's been a lot longer than I thought it would be." He took another tiny sip followed by a long draw on the dollar-fifty cigar.

"Ever want to get a place, get off the street? It's got to be miserable out there this time of year."

"I'm working on it. Almost have enough saved to pay for a month at the Fitzgerald. It's nowhere near the house I had back before my layoff." His sighed then pushed his shoulders back. "Once I get a real address, I should be able to get a job. That's probably about as good as it'll ever get for the likes of me. This new normal everybody talks about has me setting my sights a lot lower."

A loud buzzer startled them both. Jerry returned to the bar, his voice regaining its gruff edge as he answered the intercom.

Alex finished his whiskey, part of his beer and most of his cigar before his sleepless nights caught up with him. Between the vent's warmth, the alcohol and his safe surroundings, he didn't have a chance. In his slumber, his dreams wove a mixture of old and new, flashes of happier times at the cabinet shop interrupted by the violence on the street. Choking on an occasional snore, his mind barely registered the comings and goings of the bar's meager lunch crowd.

On the verge of waking, Alex's unconscious mind vividly took him back to the sidewalk in front of Mick's and the chill he felt on Moon Boots' flesh. He awoke with a start. A new bartender stood over him and for a second, Alex thought it was the van driver about to do him harm. He raised an arm in defense, emitting a tiny whimper of fear.

"Sorry, Alex," said the afternoon barman. "Didn't mean to scare you. Jerry told me to let you sleep, but the owner's coming in soon and he wouldn't be too happy to see you sleeping back here with your stroller parked out front."

The bar had more customers now, a table full of construction workers from the high steel of the new stadium and a few regulars from the St. Vincent. Alex looked out through the bar's cigarette-tarred windows to see the ruddy glow of streetlight. "Gosh, Jimmy, what time is it?"

"A little after six. Why? Got an important business meeting to get to?"

Alex ignored the slight. "Thanks for letting me catch some shut-eye, Jimmy. I must have been more tired than I realized." He stretched and rubbed his eyes. "You take my bottle of beer?" he asked, staring at the empty table.

"Nah, I looked over one minute and it was here, the next it was gone. Sorry, man."

"That's okay, I think I'm laying off that stuff for a while. I've been getting a little too comfortable with it, if you know what I mean." The bartender said nothing, just ran a wet bar towel over the table, a message to get moving.

Alex stood and panicked at the thought of losing the cigar Jerry had given him. A pat of his shirt pocket reminded him that he'd packed it away for safe keeping.

His stroller and his trusty blade were where he'd left them. The weather was worse than ever as he stepped from the cover of Mick's entryway into a bitter wind. Low clouds sailed past the downtown high-rises, their upper floors seemingly lost in the sky.

It was a short, torturous walk to the St. Vincent. Icy wind pierced the seams of his coat, sneaking through his multiple layers of second-hand sweaters underneath. As he turned the corner onto Nicholas, he hugged the side of an empty building, cutting the wind by half. The sprawling St. Vincent campus spread out before him. With the exception of the usual street corner whores and dealers, the area looked quiet. Still, as long as he was out of the wind, Alex took an extra moment to scan the landscape one more time. Someone might have seen his stroller at Mick's and assume he had money.

The St. Vincent campus filled both sides of the street. Women and children were housed in a brick building while the larger, men's building sat opposite. The place bristled with locks and security cameras.

Satisfied that the coast was clear, Alex pulled his gloved hands up into his coat sleeves to better protect his fingers. He curved an awkward grip around the bent handles of the stroller and stepped back into the relentless wind. A powerful gust took his breath. *Good God, I'm glad I'll be inside tonight.*

For many, the price of admission to the St. Vincent was the risk of losing what had to be left outside. Streetlight streaming into the cars parked near the shelter revealed backseats filled with clothing, utility bills, kid's drawings and photographs, all mashed together with the fast food wrappers and the plastic bag trappings of homelessness.

After parking his stroller in the shadow of a seldom-used doorway of the women's shelter, he wished it well and prayed it would still be there in the morning.

The glare of floodlights lining the shelter roof obscured the crowd gathered outside. Alex swallowed his fear and headed into the shuffling mass of silhouettes clouded in cigarette smoke and frozen breath. A hand shot from the crowd to grab his arm. Alex yanked his arm free, stepping back and raising it to fend off an assault.

"Sorry, Little Man. Didn't mean to scare you."

Much to Alex's delight, he realized his neighbors had returned. DeAndre, Billy, Henry and Tom were huddled together to fend off the cold. DeAndre's handshake and broad, smile nearly brought tears to Alex's eyes.

"My god, I thought you guys were gone. Hurt or something by whatever's been making folks disappear."

"Not hardly," said Tom, the group's de facto leader. Tom was about Alex's age, a little taller and lean with thinning blonde hair. He'd owned a lumberyard until alcohol got the better of him. "Looks like you should have been with us," he said, eying Alex's bruised and bandaged face.

"It's nothing." Alex shrugged. "Ran into a parking meter trying to get out of the way of a truck."

"We been livin' the high life," said DeAndre, tilting his head back and smiling broadly.

"What do you mean 'the high life'? Where have you been?"

"It was Billy. He did it for us," said Tom. "Go ahead, Billy, and tell him about it."

"I s-s-scammed a Gold Star card for the casino across the r-river," Billy stuttered, his chest puffing with pride. He was the youngest, a ferret-faced, eighteen-year-old with acne-scarred cheeks. "Had us a s-suite on the top floor for t-two days. Man, we had room service, cable TV and warm beds just like we was high rollers."

"No shit?" Alex noticed the boy's stutter diminished as he fell into a rhythm.

"The management caught on last night and it was just like a fuckin' Chinese f-fire drill with us all piling outta there."

"Nobody got pinched?" asked Alex.

"Nah, we all m-made it out alive," said Billy. He produced a shiny card from his shirt pocket and held it out with a pinky finger extended. "I'm a m-member of the Gold Star Club," he said, with a nasal lilt that complimented his upturned nose. The act drew a round of laughter and self-congratulation for their successful misadventure.

"You guys eat yet?" asked Alex.

"Yup," said Henry, a sullen, middle-aged man who seldom spoke.

"It's green wieners and green beans tonight," said Tom. "Us Gold Star Club members are out for our after-dinner smoke. You better hurry, though. The line's gonna close soon."

Cigarette butts littered the tiny courtyard outside the entrance to the men's building. Alex shoved his way to the grimy glass doors. The instant he entered, the noise and smell made him question his decision to come in from the cold.

"Nice to see you, Alex. Hope you're stay'n the night," hollered the night manager from behind the front desk. "Better get in line. It's gonna close soon."

Alex waved at him and followed his advice. Those who had already eaten milled around the front desk or propped themselves against a wall, waiting for the line for sleeping mats and blankets to form. Beds and cots were a premium here. Every inch of the shelter floor would be needed for tonight's overflow sleepers. As the long, cafeteria-style tables emptied, the shelter staff would fold them up and roll them aside.

Unlike the sleepy-eyed breakfasts at the Harvest House, meals at the St. Vincent were fast-paced, watch-for-trouble affairs. Alex took a seat alone at the end of a table, eyes scanning the room.

Alex felt a presence approach from behind. An orange jump-suited offender-to-work trustee slammed a heavy ceramic cup to the table hard enough to make Alex flinch.

"Coffee?" he asked, thrusting a plastic thermos forward.

"Yes, thank you, sir," said Alex, ignoring the man's overt aggression. The man splashed coffee in the cup and moved on.

Alex sipped his hot beverage, forked in a few green beans and took a bite of his hotdog as the heat and humidity of over-crowded room closed in. His coat remained on for fear of theft. Sweat beaded on his forehead, his eyes narrowed on the hotdog. Tom was right. An angled look at the wiener showed the skin's green shimmer. What little taste the food held was lost in the stench of humanity and industrial cleanser. *Beggars can't be choosers.* He bent over the tray and shoveled in the rest of the food like everyone else around him.

The din shifted from loud conversation and scraping plates to the metallic clink of tossed flatware and crash of stacking china and plastic food trays. Shelter staffers armed with mops and yellow, rolling buckets formed a line at one end of the cafeteria floor and began their backwards, swaying march toward the remaining diners.

Alex gulped the last of his coffee, hoping a new gurgling, heavy feeling in his gut would pass. A trip to the St. Vincent bathroom was something he hoped to avoid until the room quieted. If there was a drug deal to be made or sexual act to be sold or forced, the bathroom was the place and screams for help would be lost in the cacophony of the evening meal.

A new, more ominous gurgle started at the top of Alex's stomach, rattled through his belly and roared down into his bowels. He leaped from the table and ran for the bathroom in a hobbling clench.

The bathroom door crashed off the ceramic tile as Alex burst in, pants already dropping. Landing safely on a cold toilet seat, his ass exploded with a force that he was sure rivaled the eruption of Mount St. Helens. *Fucking green wieners.* His arms wrapped around his belly. Cold sweat followed. He fought the threatening shivers, pressing his head in his hands, elbows on his knees in slow recovery. Quiet echoed in the cold porcelain room. From distant stall, a powerful, James Earl Jones voice rose up, "God bless you, my man," said the owner of the voice who flushed and made a quick exit.

Minutes ticked by in silence. The rumbling in Alex's guts subsided. Although his insides were still tentative at best, he felt remarkably better as he stepped from the bathroom back into the crush of humanity.

"If you want a sleeping mat," a shelter worker's voice bellowed over the loud speaker, "get in line now! First come, first served. We don't have enough for everybody but we do have plenty of blankets."

The noise throughout the big open room lessened to a mere rumble as the men moved to comply and the last of the tables were folded away.

Quickly taking his place in the line, Alex studied the profile of a tall, thick-chested man in front of him. The man's intelligent eyes scanned the room from behind black, thick-framed glasses. Judging by the condition of his clothes, he hadn't been on the street for long. He wore dark blue jeans, new leather work boots and a heavy corduroy-and-sheepskin coat.

"This your first night?" asked Alex.

The man didn't respond.

Alex tried again, a little louder. "This your first night? You're not alone. Most people don't realize they're only a paycheck or two away from all this."

"You talking to me?" The man looked down at him in surprise. Sharp curiosity gave way to watchfulness in his eyes.

"Yeah. Don't want to be too nosey, but I haven't seen you here before. This your first night?"

"No," The admission sounded forced. "But I'm still a bit . . . new to all of this."

"Well, just make sure you watch your stuff. If you go to the bathroom be careful and take everything with you or it won't be around when you come back."

The man glanced around then looked Alex up and down, his eyes losing their wary edge. "Thanks. I've been here for a couple a weeks. I had a friend named Antonio. We watched out for each other until he disappeared."

A shiver rippled down Alex's back. "Did you know him long?"

"No, I met him here. Nice fellow. He showed me around. Said he had a fight with his wife and she kicked him out for drinking. Said he stayed here a few nights a month."

"So what did you do before landing here? I used to manage a cabinet shop myself, but I got laid off and one thing led to another."

"I was a university professor before I got sick," the man said. "Eventually insurance ran out and . . . well . . . ." He shrugged.

Their conversation faded as they approached the front desk. Both accepted sleeping mats and a thin blanket. Alex looked through the crowd for DeAndre. Unable to spot his old friend, he decided to settle down with his new one.

"Your friend probably went home to his wife," Alex assured the professor when he saw him searching the room.

"Oh, I don't know," said the professor. "Last I saw Antonio, he was drunk and hitting on a big Indian girl at the Blue Diamond bar. He said he'd catch up with me here later but he never did."

The professor took off his coat and balled it up for a pillow. He untied and pulled off his boots and socks to look at his toes.

"Make sure you tuck those socks into your boots," Alex said, as he settled his mat. "Then tie the laces together, wrap them around your arm and keep them under the blanket. Shoes get stolen in here all the time. Some of these guys would kill for a pair of boots like yours."

The man's intelligent demeanor faded as he fiddled with his toes, oblivious to Alex's suggestions.

"It's smart to be checking your toes," Alex continued. "If they start feeling numb or turning bright red or purple make sure—"

"I'll cut your fucking head off!" screamed the suddenly wide-eyed professor. "Get back or I'll cut your fucking head off!"

Alex recoiled. "Hey, no problems here, friend," he said, collecting his mat and slowly moving away. "I'll just go over here and leave you be."

Head jerking as he looked around, the professor's rant continued. Alex retreated, his gaze searching the room. *Did you really think you could find an intelligent new friend at the St. Vincent?*

"They's room up by the front desk with us, Little Man."

Alex spun around and saw DeAndre's towering frame.

"There you are. I looked for you guys. You say you're up by the front desk?"

"Yessir," drawled DeAndre. "Around the corner from the front desk. It's kinda bright, but it ain't so crowded."

Alex hoisted his bedding up over his head then followed DeAndre through the parting crowd.

"Sounds like you made a new friend," said Tom, smiling as Alex approached.

"Christ, I almost shit myself," Alex laughed. "Seemed like a nice enough guy 'til he went off on me."

Billy chimed in, "I t-talked to that guy a w-week or so ago. He asked about s-s-some guy n-named Ant-tonio or s-something. C-course I didn't know he was from the l-loooooony b-bin." The boy twirled his fingers at the sides of his head to emphasize his point.

"Speaking of loony, any of you guys ever get a ride in one of Pastor Asshole's vans?" asked Alex, shifting the conversation.

Henry, the quiet man of the group, spoke up, "I did once. It was kinda nice. They preached a lot of bible stuff at me, but that was all right. Saved me a long walk on a cold night."

Alex arranged his blanket atop his mat. "Well, I had a run-in with one of their drivers this morning, The guy was pushy. Not bible pushy like most of the churchees. This one was scary. I saw him in front of Mick's. He was putting Moon Boots into his van and I offered to help. Poor Moon Boots was really out of it."

"Moon Boots was unconscious?" asked Tom.

"Yeah, out cold. Looked like he drank himself half to death—"

"Moon Boots don't drink," Tom interrupted. "Can't because of his medication."

Alex sat quiet for a moment, rethinking what he'd seen. "If he wasn't drunk, he must have been awful sick."

"That driver should have called an ambulance," said Tom.

"He said he called Nurse Liz and she pointed him to a hospital, so I figured it was cool," said Alex, tying his shoelaces together wrapping them around his arm. "But then it got weird." He stopped and looked around at the listening men. "I was leaning in the van to check Moon Boot's pulse and I swear the driver put his hand on my back and tried to push me in with him."

"Might have been a misunderstanding," reasoned Henry. "If he was helping Moon Boots, it'd be a shame to accuse him of something bad."

"I suppose," said Alex, "but with all the regulars that have gone missing . . . ."

"I've been asking around about that," Tom said. "A lot of guys think it's the cops. You know, back in the depression days, the cops used to load vagrants into trucks and dump'em in the next town down the road. It wouldn't surprise me if they were doing it again. It is getting crowded around here." He craned his neck to look back across the open room packed with humanity.

Alex waved a hand in the air. "Think about this. Could it be something more sinister?" When his friends frowned back, he shrugged. "Okay, Tom, your idea's as good as any. Especially after my the conversation I had with Pastor Asshole outside the Harvest House this morning."

"You actually talked to that clown?" said Tom.

"Yeah." He couldn't contain his grin. "By the way, you all missed a hell of a floorshow at breakfast. Pastor Asshole had a run-in with Larry. Long story short, Asshole ended up in the muck on the floor looking like he'd crapped his pants."

The image brought a round of laughter and a farting noise, courtesy of Billy.

"Anyway, I was outside as Asshole was leaving," said Alex. "I said hello and he went off on me. Actually said the world will be a much better place without the likes of us."

"Did he say will be, like it's a done deal, or did he say would be, like it is a possibility?" asked Tom.

Alex considered for a moment. "No, he definitely said will. To my mind, it would fit to use the church vans to make us somebody else's problem."

"And it would explain the money to keep the vans rolling," said Tom. "Hell, it'd be easy 'cause everybody trusts 'em."

"Lights out!" a staffer called out over the loud speaker, putting an end to conversation. Seconds later, the flip of a breaker switch darkened all but the few safety lights over the front desk and exit signs. The room quieted but for the occasional cough.

Someone on the far side of the room yelled, "Good night, John Boy." Someone else yelled, "Good night, Mary Ellen." And so the nightly ritual continued until all the Waltons and more than a few non-Waltons had been named.

Behind the front desk, Alex saw the night man settle into his word-find puzzle. Rolling over to minimize the overhead light, Alex noticed a small, shabby Christmas tree standing near the television on the far side of the room. Its tiny lights still glowed softly. Around the little tree's base where presents should have been, homeless men drifted toward sleep.

Damn, that's right, it's Christmas. Heard that at Mick's.

The usual nighttime depression flowed through his blood, dimming the warmth he had felt. He forced himself to envision happier Christmases, the ones with little Amanda decorating their own Christmas tree.

In the illumination of the twinkling colored lights, she held the first ornament to bless the tree. It was always the delicate, red, blown-glass heart, he and his Elaine had purchased on their first date. Amanda held it with two hands. Alex lifted her high and she hung it on a branch with care.

"Love you, beautiful girl," he said, setting her down to kiss the top of her head.

The ornament was the only personal item he'd left behind in the eviction. He'd hidden it under the basement stairs, hoping someday to return.

He let himself be enveloped in his memories of his little girl. Amanda on Santa's knee holding a carefully crafted letter. She couldn't hide her fear of the jolly fat man in red. Elaine had stepped back to snap a picture. Amanda's chin had trembled just before her arms sprang out and Alex swooped to the rescue. How he had hugged her tight then placed her letter safely in Santa's hands as she tearily waved goodbye to the magical man.

Why didn't she answer my letters? Alex wondered. *She was always a daddy's girl. What did I do to make her never want to see me again?*

4

Michael stumbled upon God's plan and his own magnificent purpose while taking out the trash. It was a brisk fall morning. The leaves on the trees lining the sidewalk outside his building had turned, but not yet fallen. Their color seemed bright enough to taste.

Pre-school children, costumed for Halloween, filed by on the sidewalk across the street. Dressed as tiny super heroes and cute animals, they marched holding hands, escorted by attentive teachers who brought them to a halt to wait for a signal to cross the street.

The last child in line, a red devil in a black plastic mask, stared at Michael malevolently. Michael shook it off as an oddity of the moment in spite of the chill running up his spine. When Michael dared to look back, the devil child smiled and jabbed his little pitchfork at him, adding a snake-like flick of his tongue. *Kids being kids*, Michael told himself. He turned away to step into the alley where the trash bins were kept.

A shopping cart heaped with junk sat next to the dumpsters. A jumble of noise between the dumpsters caught Michael's ear. His brow furrowed. Backing to the far side of the alley, he sidestepped slowly, then peered between the bins, fearing a feral cat or raccoon.

"Oh Christ!" said Michael, seeing a sickly bum masturbating. The old man's back was against the wall and pants around his ankles. An open wine bottle cradled in his underwear. "There's kids across the street, man," Michael whined. "Knock that crap off and get out of here."

"Eat me." the old bum hollered back. Without missing a stroke, the wino hocked and spit a wad of phlegm that mercifully hit only the Hefty bag in Michael's hand.

Dropping the trash, Michael stormed at the bum in a rage. The bum flung his bottle in defense. Its foul, purple liquid splattered as Michael caught it one handed. In a rage, he sent it whistling back, its base hammering the bum's temple with an odd, muffled tink.

"Fuck all y'all," groaned the bum, slumping down the wall as the bottle shattered on the alley bricks. Fists clenched in fury, Michael stomped forward then froze in horror. The fabric of reality ripped before his eyes. This was no wino. Grinning at him from between the dumpsters was a yellow-eyed demon. Michael backpedaled in horror. The demon screeched, then lunged. Hot, sulfuric breath kissed Michael's face as the demon's razor-toothed maw snapped inches from his nose, issuing strings of silvery spittle. Michael's hands reacted without hesitation. He was outside of himself, watching from above as he went on the attack, snatching the broken bottleneck and stabbing it deep into the demon's right eye. The perverted pile of flesh and teeth jerked then went rigid, squealing as Michael twisted the jagged green glass.

Reality shifted. Michael returned to his body, vision swimming. When the world came into focus, he looked down to see his hands coated in blood and gore.

"God forgive me," croaked a voice from between the dumpsters.

Michael's gaze shot from his hands to the old man. One eye lolled, the other oozed red through the green glass funnel. Michael stared in disbelief as the spark in the man's remaining eye faded. The world went gray.

Michael fell to his knees, raising his hands to the heavens. "Lord, help me," he cried.

The answer came from the dead man's gaping mouth. It was a long, mezzo-soprano note, so pure, so devoid of pretense, that Michael had no doubt of its heavenly origin. A warm, golden light shone from around the dead man's head, a halo casting the world in warmth. Michael bowed his head, feeling God's loving embrace.

Slowly, the sound of morning traffic returned. Michael stood, instinctively wiping his hands on his pants. He discovered he had an erection. His mind spun with questions, both religious and sexual. The carnal connotations confused him, but then sex had always been a tangled mess. His mother's perverted boyfriend had seen to that with his wine, dirty magazines and painful, secret sins.

Safely back in his room, a steaming hot shower washed away the blood. As water poured down through his hair and over his shoulders, he recalled the bum's repentance. His erection returned and he masturbated with a ferocity he'd never known.

For the first time in Michael's life, climax was magnificent satisfaction. During an orgasm that seemed to last for hours, God spoke to him in a clear, loving voice. The Lord expressed elation for his finding his way, instructing him to continue what he'd started in the alley. Tears of joy mixed with the shower's baptismal waters as Michael milked the last pleasured spasms. He was born again, destined for greatness as "Michael, one of seven who stand before God."

* * *

Alex woke before sunrise, his dark mood of the night before replaced by an unexplainable cheer. The twinkling Christmas tree that had been so depressing the night before now seemed a beacon of hope. *By God, this will be my last Christmas at the St. Vincent.*

At the front desk, a shelter staffer scooped coffee into a huge percolator then powered the television, muting the sound. After rubbing the sleep from his eyes, Alex saw that DeAndre, always the early riser, was up, most likely in the bathroom.

Soft light from the television mixed with the comforting aroma from the percolator to stir the lighter sleepers. Christmas morning at the St. Vincent was off to a peaceful start.

Tom, Billy and Henry slept on as Alex quietly packed up, returning his mat and blanket before tiptoeing to the front desk for a Styrofoam cup of coffee. He inhaled its invigorating aroma and scanned the room. No sign of DeAndre, but he did see the professor sitting on his mat, babbling to himself. Alex watched, as the bespectacled man formed a square with his thumbs and index fingers. He put the square to his eye as if sighting a target before stopping to smile and nod with satisfaction.

Failing to discern the ritual's logic, Alex turned his attention to the muted television, where Ralphie from "A Christmas Story" silently lobbied for a Red Rider BB Gun.

A commotion at the shelter entrance further brightened Alex's morning. Nurse Liz pushed through the front door with a cardboard box in her arms and her backpack over her shoulder. Smiling broadly, Alex jumped up to help.

Liz's eyes twinkled when she peeked around the box to see who had held the door. "Merry Christmas, Alex," she whispered. Her whole body seemed to smile when she was happy.

"Merry Christmas to you, too," Alex whispered in return. "Can I get you some coffee?"

"Yes, please. Black," she said, her eyes homing in on his damaged cheek.

Liz's office was small, sparse and bright. Her desk and a four-drawer file cabinet sat on one wall. An aging exam table, supplies locker and floor lamp filled the other. Yellowing posters described the symptoms of frostbite and the dangers of STDs. The room's only personalization came from Liz's laptop screen where every few minutes the picture would change. Currently it displayed a picture of Liz making faces with a group of girls all wearing hospital scrubs.

"So, Alex, how did you get that shiner?" Liz asked, as Alex set their coffees on her desk.

"I jumped out of the way of a truck over by the city bus yard," Alex said, perching himself on a rolling stool with squeaky wheels. "Long story short, I smacked a parking meter with my head."

Liz nodded, listening while her hands palpitated his neck. "You need to be more careful, Alex. You're no spring chicken anymore."

"Liz?" Alex said, looking at the ceiling as she examined his neck, "do you know a guy we call Moon Boots?"

"I know of him, but we've only spoken briefly."

"I saw an Angel's Wings van pick him up yesterday and he looked pretty bad. The driver said you told him to take him to a hospital."

"I never received a call like that, plus I'd have told him to call 9-1-1."

"Could you do some checking? He's not the only one to go missing lately."

She frowned down at him. "Certainly, I'll make some calls."

Without her having to ask, he unbuttoned his shirt for her stethoscope. A little Santa was clamped to one of the ear tubes.

"I really wish you'd think about getting off the street," Liz murmured as she listened to his chest. "Take a deep breath for me. Another. Good. This winter and your smoking aren't doing your lungs any favors." Finished, she flipped the stethoscope to hang around her neck. "How close are you to getting that room at the Fitzgerald?"

Alex re-buttoned his layers of shirts. "I'm working on it. Had a radiator in my stroller that might have added a good chunk to my sleeping room account, but I lost it in that run-in with the truck. I'm gonna run by the spot this morning and see if it's buried in the snow or something."

An understanding smile crossed Liz's face as she opened her supply cabinet to pull a fresh bandage from a box.

"There was one good thing to come out of it," Alex tried to sound upbeat to keep her smiling. "I met a nice young woman, college girl like yourself. She gave me ten dollars."

"So, I've got competition willing to pay for your attentions. Is that what you're telling me?"

"Never. You'll always be my number one girl, Liz." Alex rolled his eyes at her as she applied the bandage. "But, I have been thinking about her a lot. Said her name's Amanda just like my daughter and I think she's about the same age, too." An awkward silence followed as Liz jotted notes in a ledger. "Made me wonder about my little girl, this being Christmas and all, you know."

"As I recall you said you never heard from her after your wife took her to . . . Florida was it?"

"Yup, Florida." He stared at the floor.

"If it would make you feel better, I'd be happy to help you contact her. You write the letter and I'll mail it," Liz offered, closing the ledger and placing it in a file drawer.

"Gosh, that'd be great."

She reached under the desk for her bag and pulled out a notebook and a pen from a pharmaceutical company. She held them out to him.

Alex took it, savoring the warmth of her kindness. "I'm already feeling a lot better." He pressed the notebook and pen to his chest, nodding. "Just seeing you on Christmas morning is the best gift ever."

"Aren't you a charmer." She even giggled.

"Speaking of Christmas," asked Alex, "why the heck are you here? Don't you have family?"

Liz sighed and pursed her lips. "Mom's a drinker and we always fight when I call. She's up in South Dakota. I live here with my aunt on my mother's side while I'm going to school. I'll probably call Mom this afternoon, but I don't have high hopes of cheerful conversation."

"I'm sorry. That's a real shame. How about your dad?"

"All I've seen is pictures." Her gaze shifted to the desk. "Mom told me he died in a motorcycle accident when I was four."

"Oh, gosh, I-I . . . " fumbled Alex.

She waved a hand to reassure him. "Not a big deal. Anyway, I figured I'd work a little this morning, have dinner with my shelter family then my aunt and I will go see a movie late this afternoon. It's kind of become our holiday tradition."

"Movie theaters are open on Christmas?"

"Sure. A lot of people are doing it now. Speaking of Christmas traditions, I've got a little something for you." She perked up again as she reached into the box she'd carried in with her. "Now this is between you and me. I don't want the whole shelter thinking I've got gifts for everyone."

"No, no, no. Liz, you didn't have to . . . "

"I know, but it's my pleasure, Alex," she said, placing a palm-sized package in his hand. "Stop your yammering and open it up." Her eyes twinkled with anticipation.

Alex tore off the Looney Tunes wrapping paper to reveal a small cardboard box. At first he thought it was a small trinket, but the heft of the box indicated something more substantial. He opened the container and was stunned to see a tiny travel alarm clock. "Well, I'll be. Liz, this is too much. You really shouldn't have."

"Hush up. You'll need it once you get your own place." Joy lit her expression.

Alex took a moment to figure out how it worked then set the time and an alarm. It beeped cheerfully. "Holy cow. Won't be late for work with this baby around."

"It's small enough to carry with you. I have more batteries in my desk drawer when you need them. It takes one AA. Now, ah, it looks like you've missed something."

Removing the velvety plastic piece that had held the clock, Alex looked again.

"The lid, Alex. Look in the lid," Liz said, wiggling with excitement.

He flipped the lid over to see a tiny envelope taped inside. He gingerly removed it and took out a small, handwritten card that read, *This entitles Alex Capstain to one month at the Fitzgerald Hotel.*

His mouth opened but all he could manage was a squeaked, "I-I don't . . . ." He looked up at Liz, his eyes wide and moist.

"You earned it, Alex. You had most of the money in your envelope." She threw up her hands in mock surprise. "Amazingly, when I checked that envelope just yesterday, I saw that Santa had made an early delivery. He left just enough to make one month's rent."

"But Liz—"

She held up a finger to stop him. "Don't question Santa, Alex. He knows who's been naughty and nice and apparently you've been very good this year."

Still stunned that his nightmare of homelessness might be coming to an end, Alex leaned over, wrapped his arms around Liz and hugged her small frame as she patted his back.

"Oh, I brought something else," Liz said as she reached into her box and pulled out a newspaper. "These are the help wanted ads from today's newspaper. May I suggest you do some homework so that once you get your room, you can hit the ground running?"

One hand wiped at his eyes as the other took the newspaper. "It'll be nice to use one of these for something besides a blanket or kindling." Seeing her eyes a tad moist, he managed a crooked smile then focused on putting the clock back in its box. "Can you hold onto this till I'm moved in? I'm afraid it'll get messed up in my pocket. I doubt the Fitzgerald's manager is around to take in new renters on Christmas."

"Of course, Alex," she said, putting the clock in a drawer. "But I expect to hand this back to you tomorrow. If you have questions or need help, let me know."

"Looks like I've got everything I need right here." He waved the want ads as he backed out of her office, grinning like he'd just hit the lottery.

In the glow of the TV, he took a long time deciphering the ads then used the pharmaceutical pen to make some tiny notes in the newspaper's margin. *Bus line - Close to shelter - Roommate?* He thought about how nice it would be, working a steady job with a real roof over his head, maybe even a house again someday. Of course that set him to thinking about his daughter, wondering if she would remember her childhood home. He opened the notebook and started to write.

> *I hope all is well for you in Florida. Sorry I have not written for so long. By now you are probably a grown woman and I'm sorry I wasn't around to see you grow up. I wrote many times when you were little, but I'm guessing your mother never let you see them because I never heard back. Things are looking up for me. I'll be moving to a new place soon. If you do get this letter, please write back. I'd just like to know that you are okay and know that I love you.*
> *Love, Dad.*

He tore out the letter, folded it and placed it in his pocket. It had been so long, he couldn't remember the address, but he figured with the help of Liz and her fancy computer, she could find it for him.

Those not awakened by the percolating coffee and light of the television, were stirred to life as the clerk flipped on the television's sound. The scary-looking department store Santa scolded Ralphie before rudely shoving him down the slide.

"Overnighters need to be out by nine!" said the deskman over the shelter's loudspeaker. "Those who volunteered to help with the holiday dinner meet at the kitchen serving window. Everyone else, return your bedding and be back by 4:30 for the turkey."

Alex pocketed his new pen and stuffed the notebook into his layers of clothing over his chest. Before leaving, he tried to catch Liz's eye for one last thank you, but a line had formed at her door. He made his exit, thinking that he had his own Santa Claus duties to attend to.

5

Alex stepped from the shelter into a morning flocked in a fuzzy, white hoarfrost. He breathed deep. *What a beautiful day to be alive.*

With a little money in his pocket and the St. Vincent Christmas dinner being the day's only free meal, Alex decided that if they were open, he'd spring for breakfast at the neighborhood TastyQuick. Afterward, in his quest for a gift for Liz, he'd risk a run to the heavily guarded trash-picking holy land of the Alpine Ridge apartments. What the rich university kids residing there considered trash was legendary.

Other than a coating of frost, Alex's stroller sat untouched. His hand automatically checked that the blade was accessible as he backed it out of the women's shelter doorway and began the mile-long stroll to breakfast.

At the bus barn where the Alps had been such a hazard the day before, Alex took advantage of the deserted streets, skirting the ice mountain at a leisurely pace. He imagined himself in an episode of the Twilight Zone where a man discovered he was the only living being left on earth.

At the scene of his unfortunate collision with a parking meter, he looked for his lost radiator but found only a bloody Starbucks napkin frozen into the snow.

He pulled the napkin free and placed it in his pants pocket. *She has the same name and is the right age . . . .*

Memories came flooding back. The friendly-scented Play-Doh and a tea party with his daughter. They sat at a tiny plastic table with tiny plastic chairs. Amanda prepared Play-Doh cupcakes with all the seriousness of a master chef. She had tasked Alex to make chocolate star toppers for the brown balls of doh she'd iced in pink. From a plastic, Fun Factory press, Alex extruded a brown, star-shaped log, which he planned to cut into stars. When he held it up for Chef Amanda's approval, she put delicate little hands to her cherubic face and giggled, "Daddy, it looks like star poop."

On the deserted north downtown street, Alex smiled. Eyes still closed, he treasured the image of those little girl hands, comparing them to those of the college-age Amanda. *What are the chances?*

"Control your expectations," he mumbled and opened his eyes on reality. Down the block, the TastyQuick's red neon *OPEN* sign glowed.

Alex parked his stroller by a window near the front door and braced himself. He had little hope that the holiday would soften the TastyQuick management's abrasive attitude toward the homeless. He entered, stomping snow from his shoes. The assistant manager kept his pimpled face buried in his paperwork.

"You can't use the bathroom unless you buy something," said a female working behind the counter.

"I'll take a number one with a small senior coffee," Alex said and slapped the needed money on the counter to show his irritation.

His mantra, *You're all just a paycheck or two away from joining me,* echoed through his mind. He shut it down when he saw the wariness—*or was it real worry?*—in the woman's eyes as she punched in his order.

He remembered his own panic when multiple jobs could not keep pace with the bills. By the time the bank took the house, he had been so confused and depressed, he remembered believing his misery was deserved.

"Egg, ham and cheese sandwich and a senior coffee!" hollered the cashier.

Alex settled at a table and peeled the breakfast delicacy from its paper wrapper. Slowly he savored each bite. When the last bits of cheese were nibbled from the greasy wrapper and the last crumbs picked from the table, he pulled the newspaper from inside his sweaters and went to work with Liz's pen.

The words *apply online* eliminated many possibilities. Distance eliminated still more. The most promising ad by far was one for the Hilte Linens and Uniform Company. Not only was the job within walking distance, the ad said they provided uniforms for their employees. Alex imagined the looks of respect from passersby as he walked to and from work in a crisp shirt with his name sewn above the chest pocket.

His research finished and plan in place, Alex borrowed the key to the restaurant bathroom, took care of business and offered a cheery "Merry Christmas," to the TastyQuick staff as he exited. The lone counter clerk waved back half-heartedly. The assistant manager, who had moved his paperwork from the counter to a table, offered Alex an extended middle finger.

A brightening sky bolstered his good mood as he pushed his stroller toward the Alpine Ridge complex. The exertion and slowly rising temp had him unzipping his parka to let in some air. The cigar gifted to him the day before peeked from his shirt pocket. *Now's as good a time as any.* He paused to bite off the cap before firing a match to bring the cigar's tip to a fiery-red glow then walked and puffed like a steam engine, relishing the cigar and what he giddily thought might be his final day on the street. He envisioned his cozy room at the Fitzgerald with a bookshelf, books from the second hand store and maybe even a radio.

At the apartments, Alex studied the scene from a distance, scouting the enemy lines for weakness. A u-shaped driveway framed the buildings on three sides. At one end of the drive a compact car sat next to a small and very empty guard shack with its swing arm barrier. An automatic, rolling metal gate blocked the other end of the drive. No Trespassing signs were posted prominently.

Moving closer, he saw heavy condensation coating the windows of what he surmised was the security guard's car. He had caught the enemy sleeping. Alex crossed the street, watching the Ford Escort for signs of life, then slalomed around the swing arm gate, his stroller's big rubber wheels rolling quiet as a ninja's tread as he headed for the cover of a walled trash enclosure in the back of the complex. The rich kid dumpsters were newer and cleaner, with much quieter plastic lids than the grungy dumpsters he was used to.

Alex gasped as he cracked open the first lid on a goldmine of goodies. "I'll be damned," he whispered. "Moving trash."

Not only had he successfully crossed into the trash-picking holy land, he'd stumbled onto the trash picker's holy grail. Moving trash was what people in a hurry threw out in lieu of packing.

Into his stroller he tucked a clock radio, a hair dryer, kitchenware and some contraption he'd seen on television called a "George Foreman Grill". The best find of all was a shoebox filled with cheap costume jewelry. Most of it was tarnished junk, but gleaming from the bottom of the box was a silver, heart-shaped locket.

Finding the locket set Alex's heart pounding in anticipation. He hurriedly untangled the chain and tucked it into a shirt pocket. Were he captured on his way back through enemy lines, his gift for Liz would likely go unnoticed.

His stroller filled to capacity, he began his escape. Approaching the turn that led to the exit, Alex paused and peered around the corner.

"Shit," he muttered, leaning on his stroller full of loot.

White exhaust puffed from the tailpipe of the guard's car and defroster lines formed on the back window. Alex waited, fearing a resident might appear to sound the alarm. Five excruciating minutes later, the exhaust ceased and the car rocked as the guard settled. *Aha. Ran it long enough to heat up the inside.*

As fog reclaimed the car windows, Alex took off as swiftly as his bad leg would allow, his full stroller still running silent. He imagined himself as the pilot of a stealth fighter jet swooping around the car and the swing-arm gate. Back on the public sidewalk, he considered a victory dance, but decided not to push his luck.

His nerves calmed the further away he got, but his heart quickened each time he the thought of presenting the gift to Liz. He considered what to put in the locket. A picture was the norm for this sort of jewelry, but that was impossible and he couldn't imagine anyone wanting to look at his ugly mug anyway. He decided to keep it simple and heartfelt.

He rolled his stroller into an alley behind a convenience store. Plastic milk crates provided a seat beside a dark green dumpster that magnified the warmth of the sun now high overhead. His eyes twinkled and the corners of his mouth formed a smile once his ugly fingers figured out the locket's latch mechanism. Once it was open, he pulled out his pen and notebook and traced the heart's outline. After much thought and several attempts at a sentiment, he had the words just right. Inside the heart outline he printed in small letters *"Thank you. Love Alex."*

He carefully tore the words from the notebook paper, folded the ragged paper heart to fit, smoothed it in place then snapped the little silver charm shut. For a long moment he imagined the look on Liz's face. Giddy with anticipation, he dropped the present back in his shirt pocket and secured the notebook and pen back inside his sweaters. Just a mile away, the shelter and Liz waited. It wouldn't be long now.

Standing, he stretched and turned to collect his stroller. Its heft reminded him that he still had loot to deal with. A stop by his doghouse to hide the goodies was in order.

The mid-day sun cast a shortened version of his already small shadow on the convenience store wall. Alex failed to notice that more shadows joined his. A powerful shove sent him face-first into the concrete block. Pain and stars filled his vision as he slid down the wall, his hand inside his stroller, dragging it to the ground.

"That's my shit now!" growled Larry. Alex found himself surrounded. Cat and Greg to his left, the dumpster and Jake to his right.

Larry produced his box cutter, smiling as he slid the razor blade into view. Only Alex's hand moved to grip his lawnmower blade. Larry kicked the loaded stroller away. The sadistic delight in the predator's eyes vanished as the lawnmower blade slid out and arced to cut with a sickening thud deep into Larry's shin. He howled with pain and stumbled back. Quick as a tomcat, Alex was up and on his feet, his blade already arcing toward Larry's head. The swing went wide as Cat's heavy girth knocked Alex off balance.

The jackals paused to consider their not-so-easy prey.

"I was just going take your shit and knock you around a little, but now I'm gonna open you up for Christmas." Larry sneered, sliding the box cutter's blade in and out, in and out. He charged with blinding speed, burying his shoulder into Alex's chest, knocking the wind out of him in a body-slam against the wall.

The swing of Alex's blade came far too late. The steel bounced feebly from Larry shoulder as it flew from Alex's grip to clatter on the alley bricks. Pinned against the wall, Larry sawed at his midsection, Alex felt the razor slice through layer after layer of clothing until his attacker issued a pleasured grunt as the little blade scraped over something hard. *My ribs?* His body a confusion of pain, Alex turned his gaze to Jake's dark, sullen eyes. *Why are you letting him do this?*

Larry yelped with sadistic delight. He let Alex drop to his knees then looked down, triumphant evil dancing on his face. Eyes wide, he raised the box cutter as he considered his next cut, but before he could strike, Jake stepped in and delivered a powerful right hand to Alex's jaw. Alex fell back, his head connecting with the convenience store wall as he struggled to overcome the shattering pain and stay in the moment.

"What the fuck ya doin'? He's mine, asshole," Larry roared and turned his attack on Jake, grabbing the boy's hair and repeatedly punching him in the stomach so as not to damage his moneymaking face.

"Wait ... Stop," Jake croaked. He pointed up to a security camera focused on the alley. Gasping for air, swallowing back the acid forced into his throat, he managed, "If somebody ... calls ... the cops ...."

Through rapidly blinking eyes, Alex saw Larry cuff Jake's ear. The next moment Cat and Greg pawed through the stroller before standing it upright. Larry unzipped his pants. With a guttural laugh he pulled out his cock to loose a stream of urine. The steaming piss made a rat-a-tat-tat sound on Alex's coat and face. He kept his eyes closed and stayed as still as death.

"Jake, go through his pockets," ordered Larry.

"But you just pissed on him."

Through slitted eyelids, Alex watched Larry knock Jake to the ground with a powerful open-handed slap. Silent, Jake obediently crawled forward and began to probe, frowning with disgust.

With Larry's attention drawn to the salable items in the stroller, Jake performed only a cursory search. From Alex's coat pockets he pulled string, bits of wire, a matchbook and plastic bags. When the money came out of Alex's front pants pocket, Jake met his eyes, peeled off two dollars, enough to satisfy Larry, then tucked the rest back with a flicker of a smile, mouthing, "Sorry, Alex, Merry Christmas."

Hearing the predators' feet shuffle off down the alley, Alex let unconsciousness take him.

* * *

"Si-ilent night, ho-oly night ... " Bing Crosby's smooth voice contrasted sharply with the electronic ding-ding-ding of car keys left in an ignition switch. At first, Alex thought the church van was part of a dream, but feeling himself being lifted from the alley floor, he reconsidered and fought to surface to full awareness. Crosby crooned on that everything was calm and bright. *The fuck it is.* His head bounced off the van's corrugated metal floor.

The van's side door slid to close, the noise and the van's warmth helping to clear Alex's fog. With clarity came pain. Frozen fingers throbbed. An ache started low on the back of his neck, crescendoing to a pinpoint of agony behind his eyeballs. Brain synapses began to fire more reliably and the memory of Larry's blade returned.

His throbbing, stupid fingers probed the gash in his coat where Larry's blade had passed. Something tangled on a finger. *Tendons? But there's no blood.* In the dim illumination of the van's dome light, a corkscrew wire glinted. He realized it was the wire binder of his notebook. Larry's blade had cut deep into the paper, catching in the wire at the end of the stroke.

The van swayed as the driver crawled in. A door creaked then slammed in closing. The dome light went out. Warmth and fumes from the van's exhaust system drifted up through the metal floor as the van thunked into gear. It quickly picked up speed, bouncing on the pot-holed streets. Abruptly the floor fell away then shot upward, punishing Alex as a rear tire encountered a small crater. Light from passing streetlamps pulsed across the driver's face.

Alex cleared his throat then made an attempt at humor. "Are you my consecrated driver?"

Familiar eyes flashed in the mirror. Alex's skin pebbled with gooseflesh.

"I see you're still among the living," said the driver. "Had me worried there for a while. Hate to say I told you so, but I did say I'd get you into my van someday."

"You taking the scenic route to the shelter?" His mind frantic, Alex struggled to sit up.

"Have to finish my route, then I'll drop you," he said. "Don't want anyone else dying piss-drunk in an alley on Christmas."

"I wasn't drunk. I got beat up."

The pulses of streetlights ceased as they rolled under a tangle of freeway ramps, silhouetting the driver against the windshield. A reflective green sign read "480 EAST COUNCIL BLUFFS." The van climbed upward, traveling east. More signs, directions to Kansas and Sioux Cities.

Why take me over the river? Alex fought the sudden terrifying vision of being tossed into the icy Missouri.

On the radio, Bing Crosby sang of coming home for Christmas. Alex rolled to the side door. His fingers searched and finally found the latch. He yanked frantically, feeling his chances of survival growing thinner by the second. Cold air blasted as the latch released, but Alex was too weak to lever it much past a crack.

"Hey! What the hell!" yelled the driver, stepping on the brakes.

The shift in inertia threw open the door. Alex pitched himself out, tumbling with fabric and flesh ripping on the incline's grooved surface. He rolled to a stop against the concrete divider. The van stopped thirty yards ahead. White back-up lights flashed on as the van rolled back through its own cloud of exhaust. Alex hauled himself up. Ignoring his wounds, he gripped the ice-cold guardrail for support as he willed his bloodied, half-frozen limbs to function. His legs pumping, his feet slipping and sliding on the mix of ice, snow and gravel at the base of the divider.

"Stupid son-of-a-bitch!" yelled the driver.

Halfway down the ramp, Alex dared to glance back. Only the van's red taillights shone, as they grew smaller, heading over the river bridge into Iowa.

Alex made it to the cover of a dumpster-lined alley before his adrenaline gave out. Rancid cooking grease caught in his nose. Glistening legions of cockroaches and moldy food flashed through his mind. Trundling forward, he tapped the dumpsters as if hunting for a ripe watermelon. Hollow tones meant the receptacle was empty, no insulation. Deep tones and the smell of grease meant rats, roaches and rotten food. The third dumpster he tapped sounded promising. He lifted the lid. The bright smell of shredded paper and foam packing peanuts beckoned. He leaned on the bin's front edge, but was unable to summon the strength to pull himself up. Laying down right where he was seemed less crazy by the second. He decided he'd earned a quick nap. *I'll just lie down and sleep this all away.*

He lost his balance, falling backwards. The bin's metal lid crashed close, waking Alex as he stumbled. Plastic milk crates painfully greeted his backside. Summoning his last drop of strength, he stacked the crates into a stairway to salvation before stepping up then up again, lifting the lid. As he rolled in, swaddled by paper and plastic peanuts, the heavy lid slammed down making the container's sides and his eardrums vibrate. *Is it still Christmas? Oh, God, I can't remember.*

After unconsciousness took him, images flashed through his mind like the windows of a passenger train rolling through a crossing. Each window was an out-of-order glimpse of the past. Steaming hot chocolate after shoveling snow with Amanda ... Standing in church wearing an uncomfortable suit as he eulogized at his father's funeral ... The fevered argument when Elaine announced she was leaving for someone who could provide what she believed she deserved.

Then an all too familiar nightmare returned.

Hot water rose in the sink and the sheriff's deputy pounded at his door. His cozy little house spun like Dorothy's in the Wizard of Oz. The hiss of airbrakes and the slam and rattle of metal on metal greeted his eardrums. Alex's eyes flashed open to a sliver of light and an overhead rumble.

Trash truck!

He felt the bin rise. Scrambling in the paper surrounding him, Alex's feet found the dumpster's bottom. He pistoned himself upward, bursting from the bin to come eye-to-eye with the driver. For the briefest moment, both froze in disbelief. Then the driver screamed. Alex's scream back sent the startled driver into motion, his hands grabbing at controls. The bin landed hard, its lid punishing the top of Alex's head and driving his jaw down on the bin's metal edge.

"Jesus, dude," shouted the traumatized driver, crawling from his truck. He stared at Alex who struggled to hold the lid off his head. "You look bad, man,"

"I don't give a shit what I look like, just help me climb out," said Alex in a shaky voice. "Why are you collecting trash today?"

"The holiday screwed up the schedule. Jesus, you know better than to sleep in these things. Don't you know you could end up crushed and in the landfill?"

Without much effort, the driver helped Alex climb up and out. He held onto one arm as Alex worked to gain his balance. "You look like death warmed over, man. I'm calling the paramedics."

"No! Screw the paramedics!" Alex almost shouted. "I just need to get to the St. Vincent. A nurse there, Liz, can take care of me."

"Dude! Come here!" the driver commanded, easily pulling him toward the truck cab. "You're not going anywhere. You're half dead and don't even know it."

The driver tilted down the truck's side mirror then forced him to look at himself.

Alex saw the face of a monster. Blood matted his hair. His battered face looked like a patchwork quilt of scabbed-over wounds, his skin underneath a pasty white. He did indeed look like death warmed over. He dropped to his butt on the ground and leaned against the truck tire as the driver called 9-1-1.

For the second time in two days, paramedics from Station One rolled up to help him. They went straight to work with a quiet proficiency that frightened Alex even more than the reflection of his face.

"Do you know what month it is?"

"December."

"Do you know where you are?"

"In an ambulance."

"Do you know why you are here?"

"Larry Jenkins gave me a beating, then some weirdo tried to kidnap me and I bailed out of his van on the 480 bridge . . . Hey, you guys need to tell the cops about the church vans. There's a serial killer driving one."

The two paramedics exchanged glances.

"Sure, okay," murmured one paramedic, flashing a penlight at his eyes. "Had much to drink today?"

"Nothing today, sir. I had part of a beer yesterday at Mick's."

With the exception of the siren, engine noise and click of the red and blue strobe lights, the ride to the emergency room transpired in silence.

An embarrassing hospital gown replaced Alex's filthy clothes. A male assistant in scrubs cleaned his facial wounds and applied antibiotic cream. A cute nurse patiently listened to Alex's wild tales, tucking a second blanket around him just as the police officer arrived.

"Thank God you're here," said Alex. "You have to get word out about the church vans."

The young officer held up one finger. "First things first. My name is Jason Grant and you are?"

"Alex Capstain."

"Nice to meet you, Alex," he said as he wrote on his clipboard. "Now, what's all this about church vans?"

"It's the Angel's Wings vans from that televangelist's church. There's a weirdo driving one of the vans. I saw him take Moon Boots and last night he tried to get me but I got the side door open and jumped out on the 480 bridge."

"I see. Ah, someone tried to steal your . . . moon boots was it? Do you mean those puffy snow boots like Napoleon Dynamite wears?"

"Napoleon who?"

Officer Grant let a tiny smile escape. "So, you're saying one of the van drivers tried to steal your boots?"

"Nooo," Alex elongated the word for emphasis. "Moon Boots is a nickname. For a man. I'm talking about a man. I don't know his real name. Us street people just called him Moon Boots because he always wears those funny astronaut boots."

"Okay, I get it. Pardon me for being slow." He tapped his pen on his paperwork, obviously puzzling over what to write. "Could it be that the van gave your friend—Moon Boots—a ride to a different shelter or even the hospital?"

"I suppose that's possible, but lots of regulars are gone, guys that have been around for years. You guys don't see it, but I live out there."

Silence fell. Alex watched the young man's expression change as he struggled with how to proceed. The cop sized him up from head to toe, obviously cataloging his many wounds. Alex remembered the guy who had cleaned him up mentioned his face looked like someone had taken a belt sander to him. He fisted his hands in frustration. *How can I get the cops to believe me?*

Chart in hand, the cute nurse reappeared to wrap an automatic blood pressure cuff around his left arm. "Still feeling okay?" she asked, watching the numbers on the machine.

"Been better. This officer thinks I'm crazy."

Not commenting, she smiled, her eyes moving from Alex to the grimacing young police officer.

"Will you excuse us, Mr. Capstain?" asked Officer Grant. He motioned to the nurse to follow him outside the curtain. Alex didn't bother telling them that nothing was wrong with his hearing.

"Is this guy a regular?"

"If you're asking whether he's previously been admitted, the answer is no, as far as we can tell. But, he is a vagrant, so he could have come in under another name." Paper rustled. "The paramedics were familiar with him. Apparently they treated him for, ah—Here it is—a head wound early yesterday morning but didn't transport."

"Was he acting weird or anything when they brought him in?"

"He was very excited, talking about kidnapping and church vans and getting the word out. He calmed down when we told him you were coming." When the curtain moved, Alex slitted his eyes as if asleep.

"As street people go, he's not like most of the drunks and addicts we get in here. He says he has daughter in Florida and that he used to work at a cabinet shop. Seems like a sweet old guy who's had a run of bad luck."

"What can you tell me about his medical condition?"

"Mild concussion. No surprise there. He's suffered multiple blows to the head by the looks of it. He's got multiple abrasions on his face and extremities. The sort of injuries usually associated with a motorcycle accident."

"Any alcohol or drugs show up in the blood tests?"

"We only did an alcohol level and that was negative. A drug screen would take a couple of days."

"Thank you, ah, Cathy is it? I think I will at least take his statement if that's all right."

The curtains parted. Alex blinked as if waking up as the officer pulled up a chair. He positioned his clipboard with pen in hand before looking directly into Alex's eyes.

"Okay, Mr. Capstain. Where do you want to start?"

6

One of Detective William Olson's earliest memories was of his mother. She had been mad as a hell and stuffing clothes into plastic trash bags. He was six or seven maybe, sitting attentive and out of the way on a cracked vinyl couch with his younger sister Danielle. In silence they watched as she hauled the bags, two at a time, out of the house to their new, but rusty Ford Galaxy.

He recalled the feel of his thin, undernourished arms hugging a cardboard box stuffed with a G. I. Joe action figure and the soldier's tiny clothes, helmets, boots, guns and knives. Joe was the one "big toy" he always chose to take with him when it was time to leave.

Obscenities flew between his mother and the hare-lipped fry cook who'd taken them in. They fought over how she'd attained the new car, with words like "sex" and "whore." Each time she exited, the wooden screen door slammed open against the shabby hardboard siding and peeling paint flew. When the screen banged shut, William and his sister flinched.

His memory of the yelled words clarified.

"While you and your kids live in my house. I'm the only one you fuck!" screamed the fry cook.

"I fuck whoever I want," his mother screeched back. "Nobody owns me and I don't owe you shit, not any more!"

William had seen his mother's signal to follow just before she rammed the screen door one last time and marched into the night. Danielle ran to hug the legs of the fry cook, he knelt to hug her in return. Tears streamed down their faces as William approached to pull his sister free. The boyfriend looked them both in the eyes and told them to take care of each other.

"We will," William had blubbered, knowing he would really miss this boyfriend. Most of them weren't so nice.

"Where you gonna go?" the fry cook shouted to his mother from the front step.

William listened close, knowing this was his mother's favorite part of a break-up fight. It made the boyfriend feel like crap and usually revealed whether they'd be sleeping in a shelter or on the street.

"We'll live in the car 'til I find someplace."

And they had.

Now, past fifty with some graying at the temples, William earned his way as a detective with the Omaha Police Department. He felt eons away from waking up in homeless shelters or falling asleep to the sound of his mother "paying the rent" with a new boyfriend.

Life hadn't turned out too bad. Despite those harsh times, he and his sister had survived. They grew up to be strong and self-assured out of stubborn determination. Danielle had married a construction worker who eventually landed a cushy job with the City of La Vista. With their two kids, they lived a secure and comfortable life. He married a much younger woman and had two boys of his own. Though the teenager made William's hair grayer by the day, he held onto the memories of how bad his own childhood had been and took satisfaction in providing a good home for his kid to resent.

Until recently, he couldn't imagine not wanting to go to work. Times changed. His aging body had become a challenge and friends he'd worked with for years were retiring. The majority of new recruits replacing the good guys came off as bullying, self-interested jocks who saw everyone outside their clique as a threat.

Just this morning as William dressed after his workout in the station's weight room, he'd watched a cadre of young officers gang up on a fellow rookie named Jason Grant. William thought Grant showed promise. He was a bit of a loner, but only because he wasn't a bully. He took the time to listen. It was his listening skills that made him a target this morning.

"If I had a dollar for every fairytale a bum told me," crowed one of the rookies, "I'd be able to retire before I get as old as Detective Olson over there." The rookie glanced to William who responded with the obligatory middle finger.

"Listen, newbie," said another with Jersey Shore abs. "When Sarge finds out you spent two hours writing a report on an old drunk, you'll be eating shit sandwiches for a week."

The "Sarge" they referred to was Sgt. Harry Gurdlich, an aging, muscle-bound knot of ignorance whose reputation as an "outdoor dawg" was legend. The police union made sure Gurdlich kept his job, but they couldn't prevent his being penned in the north downtown rather than moving on to easier duty in the suburbs out west.

"The old guy wasn't a drunk," insisted Officer Grant as he changed from his uniform into blue jeans and a sweatshirt. "In fact, he seemed very intelligent."

Jersey Shore abs laughed. "You believe this guy? Officer Grunt's first cry-me-a-river story from a street shit and he wants to take the fucker home and tuck him in bed. Jesus, dude, get a clue. They're all fucking losers or they wouldn't be on the street."

Olson admired Grant's lack of intimidation.

The kid merely shook his head and continued. "He's had a run of bad luck and somebody beat the hell out of him yesterday. I thought he deserved to be heard. Besides, he knows a lot more about how things work on the street than we do."

"You should listen to him, boys," William raised his voice to add. "There's a lot to be learned by listening to experienced folk, even if they are on the street."

The jocks leered at William suspiciously. Beneath their gelled and fauwhawked hair, he could almost hear their tiny brains conjuring slurs like, old school, has been, antique.

He glared back, rising to leave as two of the youngsters mindlessly scratched the "junk" they kept cradled in tight briefs that were the male equivalent of a push-up bra.

Grant caught William at the elevators outside the weight room.

"Detective Olson, sir, I thought you might want to see this," he said, holding out a copy of a report.

"Is this what you were working on last night?" asked William.

"Yes, sir. I think you might know the man involved. At least he says he knows you. His name is Alex—"

"Capstain?" interrupted William.

"Yes, sir. He's in the hospital—"

"Is he okay?"

"Just in overnight. He got roughed up. Said he also jumped from a van on the 480 bridge to escape a kidnapper. It's all a fairly wild story, but . . . since you know him, I thought you'd want a heads up."

William's cell phone rang. The name *Liz Caldwell* showed on the miniature screen. Putting the phone to his ear, William offered an apologizing look at Grant who raised a hand in parting.

"Hi, Liz. I just heard about Alex. I'm holding the report one of our officers took from him last night."

After a bit of small talk, William reluctantly agreed to meet Liz at a trendy downtown coffee shop.

* * *

Sunshine had coaxed the city from hibernation. The post-Christmas, pre-New Year's crowd conversed loudly over a caffeine chorus of steam wands and grinding beans. The coffee shop's blue beadboard and tobacco-colored walls had been plastered with European coffee posters and burlap coffee bags. Liz sat at a table under a vintage poster proclaiming *"Absynthe, La fe Verte."*

Standing in line, William searched the shop's blackboard menu for the word coffee, but saw only jumbles like Latte and Machiato. The customer ahead further aggravated William's coffee insecurity by ordering a "skinny, sugar-free half something-or-other with an extra shot of god-knows-what."

When his turn finally came, he blurted, "Can I just get a decaf coffee?" He glanced at the room, expecting a hush as though they'd just seen him shit on the floor.

The spike-haired barista looked down his—or her—pierced nose and spoke in condescending exaggeration, "Will a decaf Americano do?"

"Sure, whatever," said William. *And that will probably set me back six bucks.* He smiled when the total only came to a little over three dollars.

Waiting for his drink, he considered what he knew of Liz Caldwell. They hadn't communicated all that often, but she had proven to be a reliable contact at the St. Vincent. Better than her predecessor who had been arrested for selling narcotics to shelter guests. Sgt. Harry Gurdlich had made that bust, further fueling rumors of his protecting the territory of the dealers who worked the nearby street corners.

William glanced around and spotted Liz. Like many of the coffee shop's customers, she gazed into a laptop, the screen casting cold, blue light in the ruddy, yellow-green glow of the shop's eco-friendly compact florescent bulbs.

"Decaf Americano," shouted the barista.

Sure, tell the whole place I'm an old guy who can't handle caffeine. William gave the genderless kid his "cop stare" as he scooped the cup from the counter. First, he blew across the steaming hot concoction then took a sip. *Surprisingly good.* He nodded at the snooty server before dropping a tip in the marked jar. He got a roll of the eyes in return.

Liz pulled herself from her studies as William approached.

"Good morning, Miss Caldwell," he greeted her formally.

She smiled back at him. "And good morning to you, Detective Olson."

He sat, holding up the cup. "Pricey, but good stuff. Glad you nursing students can afford a place like this."

"They have free Wi-Fi." When he frowned, she explained, "Internet connection so I can do research."

"So, did you get to check on Alex at the hospital this morning?"

"Only talked to him on the phone, He told me a little. He sounded good, but some of what he had to say . . . " her voice trailed off as she shook her head. "Something is not right. I'm worried."

"I talked to the officer who interviewed him early this morning. He said Alex was in rough shape but he'll be okay."

"It's not his physical condition," she emphasized. "He claims someone is preying on the homeless population and even has a mental list of regulars who have gone missing."

"He didn't list them for Grant. Is it possible our little friend is falling off the deep end? Some of the things in the report were sort of . . . out there, if you know what I mean."

She nodded. "That's something I need your help to straighten out. I saw him Christmas morning at St. Vincent's. He claimed then to have witnessed an Angel's Wing van pick up a man named Moon Boots. He said that Moon didn't look very good."

"That was in the report. Nothing unusual about that sort of thing, though. That church always ups their presence in the north downtown around the holidays to catch the free publicity."

"I know, but Alex seemed very agitated. He said the driver of the van claimed he had talked to me and I told him to take Moon to a hospital." She paused for a sip of her latté. "I've thought more on it since calling you. First, I wasn't there that morning and, second, I would have told the driver to call the paramedics, not transport him."

"So, maybe the mystery driver was mistaken and talked to somebody else at the shelter."

"I asked that. No one could remember a phone call from anyone out cruising for Angel's Wings. I also called every hospital in the area. No one fitting Moon's description was seen in either emergency room that morning. I also contacted Open Door Mission and Stephen Center. Moon hadn't been to either of those shelters."

William grunted. "I've never heard of a guy named Moon Boots. Are you sure he even exists?"

Liz cocked her head and raised her eyebrows at the challenge. "He does, I've met him, Detective. Right now, however, I'm more concerned about Alex." She stared at her laptop screen a long moment then looked up with a pinched expression. "If it was mental illness that made Alex jump out of a moving vehicle, I need to know."

He considered the genuine sadness and worry she showed. *She's gonna burnout young.* Almost in defiance of his assessment, her eyes hardened like a boxer raising his gloves in defense. *Abusive father in her history?* He opted to tread lightly. "I'll have to admit I was concerned for his mental state after reading the report. I'm going to see him in a bit if you'd like to come along. Maybe I can drill down a little deeper into the details and figure out what's going on."

"Wish I could join you, but I've got check-ups scheduled at the women's shelter. I won't be able to visit him until this afternoon." She paused for another sip of her drink. "It would be a real shame if he were starting to lose it," she continued. "He's saved enough money to get off the street for a month and he's hoping to turn that into employment."

"Really?" William brightened. "He's getting a room? I've been after him to do that for forever. He wouldn't take any money from me. Hm, you know, maybe this beating and mix-up over the van are like just bumps in the road for him. He is one tough little man."

"Who has had more than his share of bumps. Can you call me after you talk to him?" asked Liz.

"Will do. So, beyond Alex's problems is there anything else of note going on at the shelter?"

"It's winter." She shrugged. "Newcomers have us packed to bursting every night. We even have them sleeping in folding chairs. This break in the weather will help, but it seems there's more new faces every day."

"The camps along the river are growing too," said William. "Most people don't see it when they drive by, but if you look into the wooded areas south of the airport they're full of little shanties."

Both fell silent and almost simultaneously turned their gazes to the street. The world was changing, and not for the better.

To break the melancholy, William held up his cup. "So, this is called an Americano. If it didn't cost so much, I might even come here again. What is it that you're drinking?"

Liz lifted her cup, "This is a skinny vanilla latté with an extra shot."

William's eyebrows knitted and Liz smiled.

"Skinny refers to non-fat milk. The milk has been steamed and frothed then mixed with vanilla syrup and two shots of espresso instead of one, hence the extra shot."

"Espresso I've heard of. It's just really strong coffee that's served in tiny little teacups, right?"

"Pretty much. Tell you what," Liz said, handing William her napkin, "write down your email address and I'll send you a link with all sorts of great information on coffee drinks."

William wrote carefully. Liz actually giggled at his capitalizing the first letter and his squiggled attempt at the @ symbol followed by "aol.com."

"AOL, huh? Not a Dot-Gov, so you use a computer at home."

"What's that supposed to mean?" he asked defensively.

She grinned and tapped his empty cup. "It means you may act like the 21st century is passing you by, but you are still as sharp as they come."

"Age has nothing to do with smarts, Liz."

She sobered. "And Alex Capstain is another example of that."

William nodded as he stood. "I will call you and, if you hear anything, you will call me."

Outside, he stopped in surprise. Officer Grant sat alone at an outdoor table, sipping coffee and eating a danish.

"Kinda cold out here, rookie. Are you following me? Want to see how an old guy does it?" William asked, smiling.

"Yes, as a matter of fact I do." Grant said without hesitation.

Curious, William pulled out a metal chair and sat down.

"What's on your mind, Officer Grant?"

"First, the name's Jason," said the young officer. He carefully applied a napkin to his sticky fingers before looking directly into William's eyes. "I was wondering how you did it all these years."

"Did what?"

The kid sighed hard. "Endured the job. It—well, it isn't anything like I thought it would be."

"Did you think it would be saving kittens from trees and hugs from old ladies? If you did—"

"No," he interrupted. "No, not the interaction with the public. I enjoy that for the most part. I'm talking about dealing with the macho dicks in the department. They're like a pack of dogs all vying for dominance. I swear I spend more time fending off the leg-humpers than I do serving the public."

William leaned back in the chair, smiling at the apt "leg-humper" description. "I won't tell you it was better back in the day. In some ways it was worse. A lot of shit was swept under the rug then. The biggest difference now is something you just said."

"Excuse me?"

"Jason, you just said you were in it to serve the public. That's a foreign concept for most of those dicks you were talking to this morning."

Officer Grant studied him a long moment, "Does it get better? I like a little back and forth, but the crap Gurdlich's disciples dish out is getting old."

"It'll get better with time. I had a couple of good partners over the years. There's more than a few of us that get into this business to serve. Just keep your head low. It won't hurt to laugh at their jokes. You don't have to contribute. Just go along enough that they don't see you as a threat."

"Threat, huh? So I should ignore what I can't do anything about? Gurdlich was getting a face fuck from a hooker in the alley a few weeks ago and I—"

William abruptly sat forward. "He was what?"

"He was getting a blow job from a prostitute. He calls it face fucking, but from what I hear it's more of a torture session than sex. All the guys say it's one of the perks of being the big dawg."

"Christ Almighty." William ground his teeth. "That sort of crap would not have been tolerated in my day. He'd get one warning. If the brass didn't take care of it, then his fellow officers would."

"Well, that's not how it works now. I was the one who got a warning after I asked if we should tell somebody about it."

"What do you mean?"

"I mentioned reporting Sgt. Gurdlich and the next day somebody wrote, 'RAT' in the dirt on my car. I found it written on my locker, too."

William's gaze swept their surroundings.

"Nobody followed me, if that's what you're looking for," said Grant. "It's been weeks since it happened. I think they forgot about it."

"I wouldn't be too sure about that. Not many know this, but Gurdlich's going to retire soon."

Officer Grant smiled. "That would solve a lot of problems."

"In the long run, maybe. But, in the short term, watch your back. Even good cops get hinky when a fellow officer's pension is on the line."

"So, he just gets away with it?"

William flinched at Grant's disappointed tone. "Yup. Wish I could say different. Even if I raised a stink the brass would shut me down. These days doing the right thing takes a back seat to politics."

The young officer slumped in his chair, his jaw hard as his hands tightly wadded the soiled napkin. He threw it at a trashcan. The napkin bounced off the rim, landing on the sidewalk.

"If it's any consolation," William said, rising to pick up the errant napkin, "I've been doing this a very long time and discovered one important truth. What goes around comes around. You just have to be patient."

7

On his way to see Alex in the hospital, William picked up a gift in the clearance bin of a mega sports store not far from downtown. The coat was an odd color and a little big for Alex's small frame, but had a fur-edged hood and thick polyester fill. Before bundling it into a paper grocery bag, he pulled the tags and dirtied it up on the floorboard of his car.

He took a circuitous route to the hospital through north downtown, thinking through Alex's claims in Grant's report. The area seemed more crowded than ever. An anonymous anthill of despair as people and cars moved to and from the St. Vincent. *Perfect hunting ground for a serial killer.*

Just past the north expressway, the hospital facility came into view. It was an incongruous collection of architectural trends. The structure still showed some of its original stately red brick, while additions displayed the computer-punch card blandness of 1960's concrete and the ugly, smoked-plastic bubble windows of the following decade.

At the front desk, William flashed his badge and inquired about Alex.

"Looks like he'll be going home later today," the plump woman behind the reception desk said. She directed him to a short-term care area adjacent to the emergency department.

William stopped at the open curtain divider. Alex occupied a chair next to his bed, his pants already on under his hospital gown. He grimaced as he leaned forward struggling to pull on socks.

"If I were you I'd wait for a pretty nurse to help with that," William said.

Alex straightened, his dry lips offering a smile. The yellow-green healing around the gash on his cheek and fresh scrapes on his forehead and nose made him look like he'd slid into home plate face first.

Careful to hide his reaction to Alex's condition, he went for a casual greeting. "Looks like you're determined to leave. Not enough slap and tickle with the nurses to keep you entertained?"

"The nurses are cute and very nice, but no one gave me a choice," Alex said, shaking William's hand. "They need the bed for paying customers."

William caught a whiff of piss and garbage, wafting from the open trash bag containing the rest of Alex's street clothes. "I found you a little something." He handed Alex the paper bag.

Alex just stared at the bag. "You really shouldn't."

"Just open it," William urged. "I dug it out of the lost and found at the station. Looks a little big for you but with all your layers it should be okay."

Alex slowly withdrew the coat and sat back in the chair, his battered hand slowly smoothing the fur around the hood. "Goddamn, somebody just left this and never came back to claim it?"

"Yup, probably some absent minded kid, but . . . it's yours now."

"I should give you a little something for it, maybe a couple a bucks for a police charity or something."

"Save your money, Alex. Liz tells me you'll be getting a room." He knelt down to Alex's level, helping him with his socks while looking him in the eyes. "You can repay me by not getting pissed by the questions I have to ask you."

Alex's gaze held his. "I'm not crazy if that's where you're headed."

With the filthy socks on, William reached for Alex's shoes, "Funny thing about crazy. It never seems crazy at the time. Back when I was working the south precinct, we had this guy that would come into the station every now and then and take off all his clothes. We called him Elephant Man because of the size of his trunk." William paused for effect and was rewarded with a flicker of a smile.

"Anyway, I saw him on the street one day—fully clothed, of course— and he told me all he had to do was miss a pill or mix up the order, and all of a sudden, taking off his clothes at the station seemed like a damn good idea. After hearing it explained, it's always seemed to me that there's a fine line between sane and crazy."

"Trust me, William, I've still got both oars in the water," said Alex. He took a deep breath and ran shaky, frostbitten fingers through his hair. "I ask myself if I'm crazy every morning I wake up in a goddamn doghouse. Some days I think I am for not laying down for the big sleep, but then there's this voice inside that tells me it'll all work out."

William loosened the laces on Alex's shabby canvas shoes and slipped them on his feet.

"I know I wasn't imagining the bad intentions that van driver had for me. And I saw how he handled Moon Boots. It just didn't feel right," Alex continued. "I can't say for sure that he's hurting people, but he sure prickled the hair on the back of my neck. And what other explanation could there be for his heading to Iowa with me?"

William finished cinching the shoelaces. As his mind lined up the facts, his gaze settled on the bandages on Alex's knees through the torn holes in his pants. "Tell me about this Moon Boots character." He settled back on his heels. "I know most of the street regulars. How come I've never heard of this guy?"

Alex scooted forward on the chair seat, perking up at William's interest. "I don't think he lives on the street. He must have a subsidized apartment or lives with a relative or something. He comes to breakfast at the Harvest House a lot of mornings, but I only see him once-in-a-while at the St. Vincent."

"Why the name Moon Boots?"

"He wears those big puffy boots with the plastic soles, just like Napoleon Dy-No-Mite."

"Napoleon who?"

"Never mind, I didn't get the reference either. I mean puffy boots like the astronauts wear. Anyway, I saw those boots walk by my usual spot on the floor at the Harvest House most mornings. Maybe the guys over there know his real name."

William groaned as he stood. "Goddamn knees aren't what they used to be."

"Tell me about it," said Alex, looking from his own battered legs to William's face. "So, are you really going to look into this?"

"I'll do some snooping around but no guarantees. Are you going to be all right? Need a ride?" He waved a hand to emphasize nonchalance so as not to pressure the poor guy. "Where you staying tonight? Not back at your doghouse, I hope."

"Liz said she'd have someone come get me in a little bit. I was hoping I could stretch this into an overnighter because the food's good and these beds aren't half bad."

"Why not check into the Fitzgerald and hole-up until you're healed a bit."

He looked up with disgust. "Can't waste the Fitzgerald on healing time. When I get that room, I'll have thirty days to find a job. I'll need its bathroom and clean smell. My doghouse just ain't good enough. I don't get a job I'll end up back there. No, I have to make good use of the Fitzgerald."

"So, where will you stay?"

"Liz pulled some strings. She got me a bunk in the living quarters at the shelter. They usually save those for young guys with families who stand a better chance at finding a job. She thinks I can stretch it out for a week, maybe more if I work in the kitchen. That'll give my face time to heal."

William watched him take his soiled clothes from the hospital bag before pulling out Grant's copied report and a pen. "You're sure it was an Angel's Wings van that you tangled with?"

"Honestly, I was pretty out of it when he picked me up in that alley. But, it was the same guy that took Moon Boots and he was driving a church van then. Those details I remember clearly."

"Speaking of the alley, what do you want to do about Larry? The guy needs to be locked up."

Alex's fingers hesitated in buttoning his layers of shirts and sweaters. "Nah, don't do anything. He'd just get out and hurt me worse. It's my word against his and nobody believes an old homeless man."

Their eyes met again. "I do and so does Liz. And there are others. I think you underestimate how many people are rooting for you Alex."

"Well, I thank you for that. But you coming here to get the facts . . . well, you taking me seriously on the church vans is plenty. Something really bad is going on, I just know it. If you're gonna check on Moon Boots, I've got a few other names to add to the list of the missing."

After taking down the names, William made Alex tell his story all over again, sifting for nuances unseen in Officer Grant's report.

Ending on the scare he gave the garbage truck driver, Alex slumped and blew out a long breath. "If we're done, I think I'll take a nap in this chair until I get picked up."

"Take care, Alex." He handed his card to Alex who carefully slid it into his new coat's pocket. "Call if you need anything. I've got a lunch date at the Harvest House."

"Say hello for me. If they've got the green chili soup today, you gotta have a big bowl. It's the best in town."

* * *

By the time William parked and entered, the lunch crowd at the Harvest House had thinned out. The cleaner, more up-scale dressed church volunteers helped with cleanup under the watchful eye and sweaty brow of the man he figured to be the supervisor of the center, Paul Finnegan. As he approached the man, he unzipped his coat revealing the badge and gun clipped to his belt.

"If you're looking for a free lunch, the soup's running low," Paul said with a warm smile. "What brings the police to our humble kitchen today?"

William glanced around as nearby people deliberately moved away, trying to be casual about distancing themselves.

"Can I assume you are Paul Finnegan?"

"Yes, sir."

"Alex Capstain spoke highly of you."

Paul's expression tightened with concern. "He wasn't in for breakfast this morning and now there's a cop in my kitchen. Please don't tell me—"

William interrupted him with a raised hand. "He's okay. In the hospital briefly after a pretty rough night, but okay."

Kitchen work had stopped and everyone, including the church volunteers watched and listened. Nodding at the audience, William leaned a little closer to Paul. "Got someplace more private to talk?"

"Get the man some of the good stuff," Paul called out to another man pointing at an aging Mr. Coffee machine on the rear counter of the kitchen.

William followed Paul back toward his office. A worker the supervisor greeted as Seth met them halfway, handing each a heavy ceramic mug of coffee then hurrying away. The office was little more than a closet. The bulletin board over the cluttered desk hung heavy with yellowed notes. William settled onto a creaky, wooden library chair crammed beside the desk as Paul took a 1960's era metal desk chair. The office, like the center, reeked of overuse and no amenities or money.

"Excuse my office. I gave my secretary the year off," Paul said with a cautious smile. He leaned back, his hand clasped behind his head to critically eye his visitor.

"Sorry if I'm getting in the way of your kitchen work. My name's William Olson, I'm a detective with the Omaha PD." Paul leaned forward long enough to shake William's hand, then settled back, again in evaluation mode.

"Alex is being discharged today from the hospital. He'll be fine, but a fellow named Larry Parmenter knocked him around pretty good."

Paul's eyes narrowed. "You want to do the world a favor?"

"If I can."

"Get that son-of-a-bitch Larry off the street. We had our own run-in with him the other day. Darn near cost us our biggest benefactor."

William set down his mug and took out his notebook and pen. "What happened?"

"He roughed up John Ahough, pastor of the West Omaha Church of Christ."

"The guy with the television ads and Sunday morning TV church service, right?"

"That's him. And you don't have to say it. I know Ahough's a little over the top, but if it weren't for his church, our pantry would have lot of empty shelves." Paul took a slurp of hot coffee, swallowing hard.

"This is probably nothing," William offered cautiously, "but in addition to his fight with Larry, Alex had a run in with one of the church's van drivers."

Paul frowned. "I heard he and the Pastor had words that morning, too."

William sipped his brew and considered the new information. "When you say Larry roughed up the pastor, what do you mean?"

"It was Larry being his asshole self. Pastor Ahough was doing his televangelist bit on a kid that hangs with Larry and the mean old bastard took offense. Got in his face then tripped the pastor onto the muddy floor. No one was really hurt. Well, the pastor's pride took a beating."

"And that was the end of it?"

"Unfortunately not." Paul sighed. "Larry yelled out the pastor's nickname—Pastor A-Hole—and everybody laughed. I think that did the most damage."

"That would have been entertaining." A smile touched William's lips then vanished.

"Pastor's people cleaned him up as best they could. The floor was a real mess that morning. He made me promise not to let Larry in the building when he or his people are here. Larry's pretty hit or miss on coming in for breakfast and the Church of Christ only comes in once a month, so I figured I'd deal with it when and if it happened again."

"And the pastor left right away?"

"He stayed to clean up then kinda stormed out in a huff. That's when he and Alex exchanged words. My kitchen helper said he saw him arguing with Alex outside." He stiffened. "Don't tell me you're here because the Pastor is making trouble. Did Alex do something to tick him off?"

"No, Mr. Finnegan, relax. I dropped by to tell you about Alex and check on his report of suspicious activity involving the church vans. Alex thinks there's something sinister going on. He says regulars are disappearing. What can you tell me about a fellow named Moon Boots?"

"That would be Terrance. He comes in for breakfast a few mornings a week. He lives in Section Eight housing near Davenport and 24th."

"Got a last name to go with the first?"

Paul looked up at the ceiling in thought. "Sanford. Yeah, Terrance Sanford. But he hasn't been in for a few days. He's kinda memorable."

"Have you heard of any problems between the street people and the church vans?"

"No. Some of the guys whine that they get preached at during the rides the church provides. But most don't look a gift horse in the mouth."

William flipped to the list of names Alex had provided and showed them to Paul. "How about these guys? Seen any of them lately?"

"Now that you mention it, I haven't." Paul studied the list thoughtfully then pointed to a name. "Oh, I heard this fellow's in jail. But these others," he shook his head, "I don't know about them."

William thanked Paul for his time. When he stepped back into the kitchen, Seth stood in his path, holding a tray with two servings of soup, bread, shiny apples and napkin-wrapped utensils.

"It's not every day we get a visit from one of Omaha's finest," he said, smiling nervously. "Would you care to join us for lunch?"

"No, I should . . . ." William hesitated at the look of a child's dashed hopes in Seth's eyes.

"It's green chili, Alex's favorite," Seth coaxed. "He says it's the chilies that keep him from getting sick."

"And I do need to eat, I guess. Thank you."

Seth smiled and led the way to a table that glistened, still damp from cleaning.

"You boys want something to drink?" asked a large woman, her washcloth in hand.

"I've got coffee." William held up the mug he'd carried from Paul's office. When the enthusiastic woman looked disappointed, he added, "Could use a glass of water, though."

"Same," Seth called over his shoulder.

After setting out the food, Seth watched William take the first spoonful of soup then eagerly asked, "Is Alex all right? I heard what you said to Paul and I was just wondering 'cause he wasn't in for breakfast."

"Yes, he's going to be okay. They patched him up at University. Should get out later today. I'm sorry, I didn't introduce myself. I'm William and you are . . . ?"

"Seth, the soup kitchen sou chef," he proudly announced.

Paul sauntered out of his office. William glimpsed his quick inspection of the kitchen. Refilled mug in hand, he joined Seth and William.

Out of the blue, Seth blurted, "Some of the guys say there's a government conspiracy to get rid of the homeless and they're kidnapping people to do drug testing."

"Let the detective eat in peace, Seth," Paul patiently ordered. "That's just the conspiracy theory du jour. I thought we talked about this."

"Sorry." Seth whispered and slumped over his soup.

"I'm pretty high up the ladder in the police department, Seth. I haven't heard of any such plans. But, it wouldn't hurt to keep a close eye on all the regulars. If you see something suspicious tell Paul and he'll call me." When Seth perked up, William looked to Paul who flashed him a "don't encourage him" glance.

"So, Paul, who are today's volunteers?" asked William between spoonfuls of the soup. "I assume it's not Pastor Ahough's church."

Obviously wanting to share his appreciation of them, Paul raised his voice enough to be heard beyond the table, "No, these good people are Baptists from North O. They're a lot more fun than those West Omaha folks."

"You know that's right, honey," called back the big woman with the washrag.

After a wink at Paul, William focused on his meal. Alex hadn't exaggerated. The soup was delicious. Buttery with an added zip from the green chilies. When he finished, Seth jumped up to get him a second helping.

Using all the communication skills the years had taught him, William spent the next half hour gently probing and gathering information, sharing just enough of his own dysfunctional childhood to gain Paul and Seth's trust.

8

In the alley behind the Blue Diamond Bar, the glow of a wire-caged floodlight seemed swallowed by the night. Beyond the bulb's reach, Michael watched as a huge American Indian woman wearing a lightweight jacket and heavy black skirt stumbled from the bar's back door, trailed by a gaunt little drunk with the prance of a poodle eager to mount a bitch in heat. Michael's nostrils contracted on the pungent scent of lust tainting the cold night air.

The woman allowed herself to be pinned against the building while the man stood on tiptoe to kiss her neck. He groped her crotch through her skirt. She tilted her head back, moaning and cooing her desire. She bent her knees so her big hands could unbuckle, unzip and rubbed him in awkward and brief foreplay. Abruptly, she pushed him back, lifted her skirt and tugged her underwear's crotch to the side.

Lust defied the cold as the gaunt man's pants fell to his knees. He waddled a half step forward to mount her against the wall. She reached down to guide him. Michael's eyes widened as she squeezed and twisted. The john wrenched backward yelling in agony as the woman bore down, her lips drawn back from her teeth in a snarl. Her free hand formed a rock-hard fist that slammed the side of the man's head, dropping him in a heap to the alley floor.

Looking far less drunk than she had moments before, she cursed, delivering a kick to the man's head before kneeling to strip him of valuables. After she disappeared around the corner, Michael moved in. The fornicator sprawled on his back, pants down, pockets inside-out, blood streaming from his nose and ears.

He rolled the man to his back then knelt and found a pulse. One tug had the pants again covering his white nakedness. He lifted and draped the limp form across his shoulders effortlessly. Keeping to the shadows, Michael headed to his workshop and the satisfying work ahead.

Not many minutes later, the naked, cold man hung from the huge metal hooks piercing his forearms. The fornicator once again lurched to consciousness, the whites of his eyes gleaming in his terror. Of course, the adrenalin-fed impulse to survive made him struggle to stand on feet bound together at the ankles. However, the agony of the movement created a scream and trembling stillness. His gaze wildly searched the shadows beyond the lone light bulb's circle. Finally Michael stepped into the light. He wore only a black rubber apron. A long, thin boning knife skillfully balanced in his right hand.

A keening wail rose from the man's throat.

"Hush," Michael crooned, stepping close to study the man's bruised and swelling face. It sagged on one side, allowing slobber to trickle down his chin.

"What the f-f-fuck?" the man muttered.

"Will you repent?" Michael asked.

"Is . . . this . . . Hell?"

"Yes. This is a hell of your own making," Michael answered in singsong fashion. "Will you repent?"

"Yes. I repent. I f-f-fucking, goddamn repent." Tears mixed with slobber and mucous fell to the floor in long stringy glops.

Michael fisted his free hand and punched the man hard in the stomach, shouting into his distorted face, "Blasphemer!"

The man wretched, then gasped for air, coughing, gagging, groaning as his body swayed on the hooks.

"What's your name?" Michael demanded, wrenching the scrawny chin to look into his unfocused eyes.

"My name's Dave," he rasped through chattering teeth. "Who-who the fuck are you?"

"I am Michael, one of the seven who stand before God." He paused to revel in the echo of his powerful voice. "I am here to expunge the sickness and offer your soul to the Lord." He paused again then put the knife to work.

Screeching, primal noises of agonized humanity punctuated the gibberish of imagined ancient tongues echoing off the dank, brick walls as Michael delivered the purifying cuts.

"Hear me, Devil," Michael bellowed, shaking one of the man's amputated ears. "You possess this man no longer!"

As he sliced and sawed, pinched and probed, the rant of madness grew evermore exquisite, pulsing in joy through his body. Michael's sex throbbed for release. Discreetly, one hand reached behind the apron to ease his aching loins.

In one moment of excruciating clarity, the fornicator shrieked, "Fuck me and get it over with faggot!"

With blinding speed, both of Michael's hands clamped around the man's throat. The close-up view of the man's bulging eyes staring back at him in blankness released a childhood memory . . . .

Ten-year-old Michael hovered on a mattress in his bedroom.

His mother's boyfriend gazed out the nearby bedroom window. "Look at them fly'n rats," the man murmured as he put his cock back in his basketball shorts.

Michael knew the flying rats were a flock of pigeons roosting on the roof outside that window. He hadn't told anyone he'd encouraged the birds to gather by feeding them cereal spirited from the breakfast table.

When the boyfriend left, Michael painfully sat up to look out at his flock. He slid open the window, anger and frustration rising. Claws scratched the shingles as the birds teetered to him, expecting food. Quick as a snake, Michael snatched a bird by the neck. He yanked it inside, ignoring the flapping and feathers that whipped into the air. He had been this terrified and now relished terrifying the bird.

After he pinned the flapping wings between his legs, the bird struggled only briefly. In its helplessness, its fight gave way to submission. Michael well understood how it felt. In that rush of understanding, a strange arousal swept over him. He'd never been in control of anything, let alone something so precious, so helpless.

The bird's tongue, a tiny sliver of pink, darted in and out as Michael squeezed. Soon its silvery-gray breast convulsed involuntarily. Michael stared as the bird's bulging, yellow eyes looked through rather than at him. When the light in the bird's eyes dimmed, Michael eased his grip then gently blew on the pigeon's face, breathing life back into a dying fire. The living light flickered back. He squeezed again. The cycle of terror, submission and rebirth continued until the light would return no more.

In the dank cellar, Michael stared at his hands as he squeezed. His fingers were much larger and stronger now. The light faded from the fornicator's bulging eyes. Michael loosened his grip, blowing gently on the man's sagging face. The light returned.

"God forgive me," the man whispered.

True repentance ushered angels from above. It was time. Michael placed his blade to the dying man's neck and sliced the big artery. Warm blood showered Michael's face and apron as God's loving glow encircled the man's head, growing in brightness and warmth. The voice of the angels sprang from the man's slackening mouth. Michael pleasured himself under his apron, speaking to the voice in his head as he reveled in God's glory.

* * *

"I'm heading to bed to do a little reading, dear. Want me to leave the television on for you?"

"No, Aunt Deb. I have a report to finish for school and a few emails to deal with for the shelter," said Liz. She sighed over the array of work that was sprawled across the table in her aunt's dining room.

In her favored green flannel nightgown and ratty, pink slippers, Aunt Deb leaned against the doorway, cradling a Sue Grafton Alphabet Murder mystery. "All right, dear. When you come up would you turn down the heat a degree?"

"Yes, ma'am." Liz didn't bother hiding her fatigue in the acknowledgement.

The older woman hesitated, her expression turning concerned. "How did your phone call to Elaine go?"

Liz shrugged. "You know your sister. Angry at the world. Apparently everyone's out to make her miserable, me included."

Aunt Deb clicked her tongue in disgust. "Did she sound like she'd been drinking?"

"Of course. I only managed a 'Merry Christmas' before she lit into me about not being there to take care of her."

"I'm sorry, dear, but you know you are where you are supposed to be. She made a mess of things in her younger years and now she wants to blame everyone but herself."

The ding of an email arriving on Liz's laptop perked her up. She tapped the keys.

"Is that something from the shelter? Some word on Alex?" Aunt Deb asked.

She shook her head. "Just spam. The crew at the shelter isn't big on email, but I was hoping to hear something from a police detective."

"A police detective? How exciting. A handsome, young detective per chance?"

Liz threw her a warning glance. "He's married and old. So, no, I don't plan to run off with him anytime soon."

"Just trying to live vicariously through you, dear." In reality the woman was far from apologetic, as she hugged her Grafton book. "Don't tell me what he looks like. I'd like to imagine that for myself. Does he wear a gun and badge?"

"Of course, Aunty, on his belt. You can see it when he unzips his coat."

"Ah, yes." She squinted, her expression turning dreamy as she looked up at the ceiling. "I can see him now. Hm, I can even hear that zipper." As she looked back at Liz her eyebrows offered a naughty wriggle, drawing a "you are so bad" smile from her niece. "If you do hear from the detective, I'll be up for a while." She held up her book. "You know how I love a good mystery, make-believe and real."

Exasperated, Liz huffed, "I'll be sure to keep you posted."

* * *

From inside his idling car, William watched a pair of Angel's Wings volunteers coax a coatless drunk from the sidewalk to their van. He tailed them to the St. Vincent where they helped the man inside. He had seen nothing of a van with a single driver as Alex had described and no sign of anything but kind-hearted and patient volunteers helping people in need.

Tomorrow he'd gather information from both Moon Boot's apartment and the West Omaha Church of Christ. Tonight's activity was as much a trip down memory lane as it was time to think and observe.

Even now, thoughts of living in a car outside the St. Vincent hovered just below the surface of his life, like a threatening toothache that never quite matured but wouldn't go away. Luckily, he'd never had to endure a winter in the car. His mother's mood swings—which he now understood to be a bi-polar disorder—had created a wild ride between boyfriends and shelters in winter and boyfriends and the car in summer.

The chirp of his cell phone brought him back to the present. His wife's text read, *"Would you call Mike and tell him he has to be in by midnight? Not listening to me."* William blew out a sigh of frustration. *Damn kids don't know how good they've got it.*

When his son answered, they lapsed into their usual argument.

"Why, dad? I'm old enough to drive. Why can't I do what I want?"

"Because I'm your father and you still live under our roof . . . ."

It ended with his son half-heartedly agreeing to be home soon. William dropped the car into gear and headed home to see that he arrived safe and sound.

* * *

Alex spent a restless night trying to sleep in the trustee's quarters. His injuries and over-active mind made it difficult to appreciate slumber in the luxury of indoor living. Liz had gone out on a limb for him with the Rich Skelton, the shelter director. Men with families were always first in line for trustee status. Liz asked the director for an exception and Alex promptly answered Skelton's summons to make his case. Tall and unassuming with white hair and glasses, the man offered a sturdy hand shake as Liz made the introductions. Alex knew Skelton's eyes read him cover to cover.

Careful not to reveal that Liz had helped him save the money, Alex laid out his plan. All he needed was time to heal so that he could start looking for work the minute he moved to the Fitzgerald.

Skelton let a long moment pass before pronouncing, "Liz is vouching for you, Mr. Capstain. Please, don't let her down."

In the dark of the trustee's quarters, Alex rolled over, his skin itching, body aching and mind repeatedly playing the words "please don't let her down".

Shortly before sunrise, bathroom needs called. Stiff and aching, Alex sat then stood, the pain masked by a touch of vertigo that dissipated with some deep breaths. On his walk back to his precious bunk, he saw DeAndre

71

wrapped in a blanket, sleeping upright in a folding chair. The big man had come in too late to get a mat. Alex passed by in silence so as not to disturb, but caught a whispered, "Hey, Little Man."

Alex awkwardly settled into an open chair next to his friend. "Sorry we haven't had much time to talk," Alex whispered, "I was training in the kitchen last night."

"Ain't nothing to worry about. I got in late anyways. How you feelin'?"

"I've been better. Having trouble sleeping. My skin's itchy from the frostbite and my head, neck and ribs hurt."

"I hear it was Larry that gave you the beatin'. I catch that mutha fucka alone, I'll beat his ass sorry."

"Nah, he's not worth the trouble. You don't want to go to jail over a piece of shit like Larry."

DeAndre reluctantly nodded agreement.

"I've been wanting to talk to you about something," said Alex, "but if you'd rather get some more shut eye . . . ."

"Ain't much shut eye to be had in this damn chair. It's diggin' into my back like a bitch." He shifted in emphasis. "So, what's up?"

Alex took a deep breath. He hadn't been this nervous since asking a teenage Elaine to prom. "I've got enough saved for a month at the Fitzgerald. Once I'm healed up, I'm moving there. I, ah, I was wondering if you wanted to be my roommate."

DeAndre turned to better see Alex, the chair creaking in protest. "I gots a little money, Alex, but not near enough for that. They bound to charge more for two in a room."

"Yeah, I thought about that. How about you just use my mailing address for job applications? Once you're employed, you could move in with me."

As Alex waited expectantly, DeAndre's heavy sigh punctuated his silence. "Alex, youse a good man, but ain't nobody hiring a thug like me. Don't you remember I got a record and ain't got no drivers license?"

"I'll leave it up to you." Alex pulled the want ads from inside his sweaters. He tapped a finger on an ad he had circled. "There's a linens and uniform company south of here that's looking for help. That's where I'm applying. You know where it is?"

DeAndre took the paper, squinting at the circled ad in the dim light. "I'll give it some thought. Mean times, sun's comin' up. How 'bout we walk on over to Harvest House and get in line? They might be about open by the time we get there."

"I'll buy the coffee," Alex joked, seeing DeAndre's willingness to consider the roommate offer as a good sign. "Can't wait to show you the new coat my detective friend found me."

Minutes later, the brisk morning shown in their clouded breath as the new sunlight peeked through the stadium construction to the east. Despite the early hour, ironworker silhouettes moved like ants on the steel beams and both men marveled in their fearlessness.

"That's a damn nice coat, Little Man," said DeAndre. "That fur around the hood is stylin'." He frowned. "But don't it mess up you see'n somebody sneakin' up on you?"

"A little. When I'm walking by myself, I usually pull it back like this." He pulled back the hood so the fur still covered his ears but greatly improved his peripheral vision. "After I get a job and save up my next month's rent, the first thing I'm gonna buy is a decent coat for you. That sweatshirt and windbreaker getup you're wearing can't be very warm."

"I gots a couple a t-shirts under. I'll be all right, Little Man. Winter ain't gonna last forever. Afore you know it we be sweatin' and swearin' at the damn mosquitos. Can't never find my size anyways. Speakin' of that, I'm too damn big to crowd beside your eatin' spot at the St. Vincent. What we gonna do 'bout that?" he said, gold tooth twinkling.

"Well, if you insist, I suppose I could join you topside, at a real table, I mean," Alex said, his frozen breath puffing around his fur-lined hood. "Say, Tom and the other guys aren't going to be mad that we went to breakfast without them, will they?"

"Nah, they's not gettin' along anyway. Billy and Henry are fightin' worse than ever. Tom's talkin' about movin' someplace warmer. Plus, Henry's goin' all Bible-thumper. He keeps preachin' God to everybody."

"They're not using the church vans are they? I'd stay the hell out of them 'til Detective Olson figures out what's going on."

"Henry might climb into one. Like I say, he likes the church crap they's preachin'. The others? I don't think they ridin' the Angel's Wings."

Breakfast was a quick affair with Alex sharing a table with DeAndre. A heavy crowd forced them to gulp food and move on to make room for others. They barely had time to warm up.

"What's your plan for the day?" Alex asked as they stepped back into the frigid air.

"Hell if I know. I gots me a hidey-hole in an old warehouse, but in the daytime I gots to crawl in through the old steam tunnels so nobody sees me. I'm thinkin' 'bout walkin' over to the labor pool. Maybe pickin' up one a' them off-the-books jobs. I hear the renderin' plant might be lookin' again. I'll need to start savin' if we gonna be roomies."

Alex's scabbed face wrinkled in a smile. "Really? Think you might want to?"

"Ain't makin' no promises but I'm thinkin' about it."

* * *

At his breakfast table, William savored his Wheaties accompanied by half a peanut butter sandwich. Per his usual breakfast ritual, he alternated between a spoonful of cereal and a nibble from his coffee-dipped sandwich.

He wrinkled his nose after a gulp of Folgers. *Disappointing. Maybe I'll grab an Americano on the way to work.*

His wife, Susan, descended the stairs, interrupting his caffeine daydream. She wore one of her tight-fitting business suits. He admired her still-trim figure. *Good genes there, Suz.* He knew better than to say that aloud, though. Meaning and compliments got crazily swirled these days.

"Meeting today?" William asked.

When he exaggerated an inhale of the intoxicating scent of her soft skin, shampoo and make-up and smiled, she smiled back in appreciation. He congratulated himself. *Actions speak louder than words.*

"Just the usual monthly manager's meeting," Susan said.

William stood and walked to the sink to rinse his breakfast dishes before setting them in the dishwasher. Susan dropped two slices of raisin bread into the toaster. The comforting smell of the warming bread mixed with her scent as William sidled up to her, nuzzling her neck, wrapping his arms around her waist.

She relaxed in his arms just until the toast popped up. Before pulling away she murmured, "Tonight, dear. Come straight home tonight. We'll skip the news and go to bed early."

After a pat of her firm bottom, William sighed and let her go. "It's a date."

He headed for the mudroom and his winter coat.

* * *

Terrance Sanford a.k.a Moon Boots lived in a once stately house converted to multiple sleeping rooms. A red and white sign out front read *"Quiet sleeping rooms- Reasonably priced - Inquire within."* Shifts in the building's foundation had opened cracks in the brick walls and set the front steps off-kilter.

William buzzed room 203. A mumbled, indiscernible response sounded through the aging intercom, followed by a buzz and a click from the interior door. The door opened easily. Its scarring showed it had been kicked open so many times, the electronic latch was useless. Urine and rancid cooking oil scented the entryway. He climbed the narrow, creaking stairs, not wanting to touch either the dulled wooden banister or the soiled wallpaper. An old man wearing boxers and a stained, wife beater undershirt greeted him at the second-floor landing. The man led him to the open door of a cluttered and filthy living area then dropped into a ratty, wingback chair, rocking to and fro, his gnarled hands gripping his white cane tipped in red.

William hung back at the doorway.

"Howdy," the man said, his gray, clouded eyes looking toward, but not at William.

"Good morning, sir. Is this 203?"

The man tilted his head to the left.

William stepped back and eyed the next door down the hallway. "Thank you."

"Yer welcome, Officer."

"Excuse me?"

"You smell like a cop."

"Ah, okay. Well, like I said, thank you."

The door to Moon Boots' room stood cracked open. When William knocked gently, it swung inward.

An ancient, gray-haired man in a fraying, over-sized suit coat stood by a table, in the middle of a phone call. Without looking at him, he motioned for William to enter.

"How the hell did he get all the way over there? I see. Well, I got no way to get there. I'll have to make some calls. How do you spell that? Okay, thank you. Goodbye now. I'll be in touch."

He dropped the phone to its cradle and turned his attention to William. His faded eyes looked him up and down. "You must be the detective that called the building manager."

"Yes, sir," William said, opening his coat so his badge was visible.

"Can't thank you enough for calling." The man extended a wizened hand. William dialed back his grasp at the weakness of his handshake. "My name's Jerry. Terry's my brother. I check on him once a week or so. I live up north and don't have a car. It takes me hours to get here on the bus."

William started to speak.

The old man held up a hand then carefully lowered himself into a kitchen chair. "Hang on. I gotta write this down or I'm gonna forget." He turned over an envelope atop the stack of mail that littered the kitchen table. William handed him a pen. Twisted, arthritic hands scribbled *Arlington Campus* then some words William couldn't make out. He folded the envelope, his hand patting it on the table.

"I didn't know he was missing until the manager called me. Now, these Arlington folks say they have him." One arthritic finger tapped the note.

"I'm sorry, sir. I'm playing catch up here," said William. "You say your brother was missing but now you know where he is?"

"Yessir. The manager hadn't seen him for days. He thought Terry was staying with me until you called him this morning. On the phone just now, these Arlington people say he's at their campus."

"And where is that?" William gently retrieved his pen and pulled his notebook.

"Supposed to be some new shelter over in the Bluffs."

"And he's there now?"

"Yes, they said it's on the east end of town." He opened his note. "MacPherson and Kainsefield. I don't know how I'll get him. He needs his meds. Had a seizure at Arlington. That's why they looked in his wallet and got this number. If he don't get his meds he's gonna have more."

"I've got some questions I'd like to get answered. How'd about I give you a ride over there right now?"

"Works for me, young man."

In the confines of his car, William appreciated that his passenger smelled of nothing more than bacon and mildew. The old man squinted as the winter sun reflected off vehicles, bridgework and sparkling ice flow of the slow moving Missouri River beyond. Two hazardous-looking hulks of metal and rust loomed over the Interstate shortly after crossing into Iowa.

"What the hell is that? Was there some kinda accident?" Jerry asked, gazing up through the windshield.

"Apparently that is somebody's idea of art," William explained.

"Well, that somebody's got more money than brains," Jerry quipped. "I'll be goddamned if that don't say 'Welcome to Council Bluffs and here's a sharp poke in the eye.'"

William laughed in agreement. Across the I-80 bridge and into Iowa, the landscape changed to fast food, truck stops and casinos. The old man's sour expression didn't change.

The northeastern corner of the city appeared far more inviting than the western entrance. Brightly painted Victorian style homes had been built on steep hillsides by the wealthier inhabitants of long ago. Snow-frosted trees surrounded them creating a sedate and picturesque atmosphere.

Arlington Campus came into view as the residential neighborhoods gave way to another area of commercial property at the far edge of the city. It was a multi-story, tan brick building, new enough that landscaping waited for spring.

William liked that the parking lot and sidewalks had been cleared and ice melt sprinkled. He didn't think the old man would have appreciated a steadying hand on his elbow.

After introductions at the front desk, a smiling, middle-aged attendant in tidy sweater and jeans escorted them to the dining hall where Terrance Sanford and his puffy, blue plastic boots, sat by himself. Around him, apron-uniformed staff cleared remnants of breakfast while sounds of lunch preparation drifted from the kitchen.

The woman didn't touch him, but bent until the lone man looked at her. "Terry, this is Detective Olson from the Omaha Police. Will you talk to him?"

Jerry took the chair beside him. Terrance turned, his face lighting up in slow recognition. A couple of tears tracked down his weather-chapped face. When Jerry pointed at William taking a chair across the table, Terry blinked and squinted.

"He drove me over, Terry. Wasn't that nice of him? He understands about your medicine," Jerry spoke as if addressing a small child. "Is it okay if he asks you some things?"

Continuing to stare at William as if trying to figure him out, Terry nodded.

"Terrance, can you tell me how you got here?"

Terry cleared his throat. "I-I woke up in the park. That's right. The park." He glanced at Jerry who patted his arm in encouragement.

"Can you tell me which park?"

"Had a lot of trees and black squirrels. I woke up and started walking. Then a car took me here."

William leaned forward. "Terry, did anyone try to hurt you?"

"No. No." Instead of shaking his head, he nodded and shivered and nodded again. His voice continued in a flat tone, "I just woke up in the park and a car took me here. They have black squirrels in the park."

Jerry shook his head. "I'm sorry, detective. He's not going to be much good until we get him back on his meds. He's not quite right after a seizure, if you know what I mean. His seizures really mess him up."

The older brother looked at William's pen tapping in frustration on the open notebook then squeezed his sibling's arm. "Terry, can you try real hard to remember what happened before you woke up in the park?"

"There were squirrels and I woke up."

"It will take a good day or so before he gets back on course. I'll get a dose of his medicine into him now, but he still may not be able to remember. Sometimes he does and sometimes he doesn't." Jerry leaned into another long hug with his brother, then looked back at William. "He's really pretty good when he's on his meds."

"How about I get the two of you home and I check on you tomorrow afternoon?"

"I'd be grateful, detective. C'mon Terry, let's get you back home."

Jerry stood, using gnarled hands to help his little brother up. They wobbled a moment then steadied. William followed slowly behind ready to catch the first who stumbled.

The facility's director waited for them by the front door reception desk. A pleasant woman with gray hair, white blouse and khaki pants, she came out from behind the desk, her attention focused on Terry. She squeezed his hand and looked him in the eyes. "I'm glad you've found your way home, Terrance. You had us worried."

William introduced himself. "Thanks for taking care of him and making that call," he said. "Can you tell me how he got here? He's quite a ways from home."

"I was told a car dropped him off. We're a fairly new facility and all of the faces are new. It wasn't until he had his seizure that we paid him much attention. As far as who dropped him off, I'm afraid I can't be of much help."

9

It's like walking on a cloud. William stepped carefully on the ultra-thick, red carpet in the lobby of the West Omaha Church of Christ. Top notch and very expensive fit and finish stretched everywhere, with deep, rich hardwood trim and hand-carved doors. He tilted his head back and almost gaped at the crystal chandelier hanging from the vaulted interior of the huge spire adorning the church's front facade.

Not knowing where the church offices were, William followed the sound of orchestral music wafting from beyond the multiple sets of wooden doors directly in front of him. He worried about interrupting something important or drawing undo attention. His hand gradually pulled one double door open just a crack. The sanctuary looked more like an opulent Broadway theater than a church.

"Heels, people! I'm still hearing heels clomping like a stampede of farm animals," shouted a late 60-ish, athletic-looking man in black pants and a black turtleneck. Throwing his arms in frustration, he viciously yelled, "Run it again!"

The stage crew—also dressed in black—scurried to make ready, frantically communicating through headset microphones and bobbing about like basketball players in a full court press.

As William slipped in, the stage lights blinked out. He stood still, straining to hear then felt more than heard muffled movement. The lights came up on angelic young girls in white robes who swept in from both sides of the stage to converge then part like a human curtain. A spotlight shone into the void to illuminate a casually dressed, slightly overweight man with spiky, blond-brown hair highlighted at the tips. A thin wireless mic curved around one cheek. He tilted his face up into the glare of the spotlight, his expression loving as though God were in the catwalks and singling him out. After the appropriate half second of silence, the man burst into song.

Hell of a voice. The crudely phrased thought had William glancing around as if someone nearby might have sensed it. He slowly raised his hand to the handle of the door and eased it open just enough to slip back into the lobby. He almost knocked down an approaching elderly woman.

His hands reflexively caught her arms. "Oh, I'm terribly sorry," William sputtered. "Please excuse me."

As his hands dropped away, she regained her composure and tugged at a flawless and expensive suit jacket. "Yes, well . . . Can I help you?"

William went for his most charming smile to enhance his flattery. "That's quite the production in there. This certainly isn't like the church my mom took us to when we were kids."

His greeter relaxed enough to return the smile. "Pastor Ahough believes church should be a fun as well as uplifting experience. I had actually stopped going to church altogether until a friend invited me to services here. Are you interested in joining our congregation?"

"Possibly," William said, elongating the word. "In the future I might give it a try. At the moment, my primary interest is in the Angel's Wings program. I work downtown and see the misery of the homeless almost daily. It wears on a person, you know?" She nodded as he expected. "I've seen the news reports on the good work this church is doing. Maybe it's the time of year, but something told me to come by."

The woman patted his arm. "Well, I've never worked on Angel's Wings myself, but those who do say it's very rewarding. We have a packet of program information in the office. If you'd care to wait, I'd be happy to get it for you."

"Perfect. I'll just stand here and soak up the, ah, grandeur."

As she scurried off, he actually examined the postings on a series of bulletin boards in a hall just off the main lobby. He found separate calendars for numerous groups, items for sale, and a great deal of Sunday school artwork reminding William of those delightful years before his boys had out-grown refrigerator art.

Two men engrossed in a conversation stepped from the church's main hall. William recognized Pastor Ahough from the late night TV commercials. The other man had the demeanor of haughty self-assurance. He didn't know him. Once they'd cleared the lobby's glass front doors, William moved forward to watch from the edge of the lobby's opulent holiday decorations. In the parking lot, the two men stopped at the door of an aging Pontiac Firebird. The driver rolled down his window to talk with them.

"Here you are, sir," the helpful woman spoke from behind William.

He turned as if startled. "Oh, I'm sorry. I was lost in thought. We have to quit meeting like this."

"Goodness, that's quite all right," she said, laughing. "Here's everything you need to know about Angel's Wings. I included information about what the church has to offer. For you to think about," she added.

"Thank you so much, Ms . . . ."

"Johnson. Mary Johnson. I'm one of the church secretaries. And you are?"

"William Olson. It's very nice to meet you, ma'am." He gently shook her liver-spotted hand. "Trust me, I'll look this over with careful consideration. Thanks again."

She beamed at his feigned sincerity. *At least you can still charm the ladies, the old ones that is.*

As William leaned on the latch-bar of the church's front door, he ducked as if reluctant to reenter the cold. Through his lashes he watched the two men climb into a white BMW X-3 and depart. The Firebird backed out to follow. As its brake lights flashed, he stared at the driver's profile. It was Sgt. Harry Gurdlich.

* * *

"Sleeping at the shelter tonight?" Alex asked as he and DeAndre shuffled slowly from the Harvest House.

"Maybe, maybe not," his friend waffled. "First I gots to see what's doin' at the labor pool. May hafta sleep in my hidey-hole if I work too late. Can't sleep in no foldin' chair again tonight."

"I hear ya." Alex gently rubbed his itchy face, careful to avoid his wounds. "I didn't sleep much last night, either. I hurt in places I didn't know I had. Kinda wish I could take a nap when I get back to the shelter, but I'm sure there's kitchen work waiting."

"That's whatcha get fo' bein' a workin' man," DeAndre teased as he settled a broad hand on Alex's small shoulder. "You watch yo' self headin' back now. I gots to get to the labor pool."

An awkward moment followed. Alex wanted to say something about the roommate deal but held his tongue. DeAndre didn't respond well to pressure. The big black man jerked his head in a nod and moved away in a longer stride than Alex's aching knees could manage.

Headed in the opposite direction, Alex caught a distant glimpse of Larry's old station wagon cruising the neighborhood like a shark in search of food. He glanced back at DeAndre who was already a long city block away. On the alert, Alex pressed on, pulling back his fur-lined hood to aid his peripheral vision.

Making it safely to a block from the St. Vincent, he relaxed a little. His thoughts turned to Liz. His gloved hand found the silver locket heart ferreted away in his pocket. Since he'd missed Christmas and his move to the Fitzgerald had been delayed, he decided to wait until he was totally back on his feet before giving it to her. The locket nestled next to his letter to

Amanda that had also survived the attack. He still needed Liz's help in looking up her address. *Hope my girl still lives in Florida.*

The screech of tires sent Alex leaping back from the street. He stumbled over a curb but regained his balance. Over his shoulder the big green station wagon idled roughly. Behind the wheel, Larry grinned at him. He couldn't force his feet to move as the four doors creaked open. Larry and his family crawled out.

"We've got unfinished business, you little fuck," Larry spit out.

Alex felt his defiance melt as he frantically glanced around for an escape route. He couldn't help whining, "You already cost me my stroller and everything in it. Why-Why can't you just leave me the hell alone?"

"I never got to open my Christmas present," said Larry, sliding open his box cutter.

"The cops know what you did to me." Alex stared at the almost hypnotic weaving of the box cutter. "But, I-I told them I wouldn't press charges. You hurt me again and they'll come looking for you."

"Maybe they will," Larry said then thrust his face out with, "maybe they won't. I'm thinking nobody gives two shits about a little runt like you."

Alex edged to one end of the car planning to break and run for help. Laughing nervously, exposing his meth-rotted teeth, Greg blocked him. Jake watched from behind the car, his crossed arms and pained expression indicating he didn't want to take part but knew he was powerless to prevent it. Alex faked a move toward Greg then turned to dart in the opposite direction. He ran face-first into Cat's huge, sagging breasts. Three bodies hit him like ravenous wolves taking down a kill.

Larry fisted Alex's hair, easily dragging him backwards toward an alley despite his kicking and screaming. One of his flailing feet caught Larry hard in the kidney producing a grunt of pain. The enraged man reacted with a boney fist to Alex's ear, followed by a boot to the groin.

As Alex fought not to vomit, Larry growled "He's all mine." The hulking outlines of Cat and Greg loomed. "You heard me!" Larry yelled near Alex's ear. "Go keep watch at the car."

Desperately, Alex shot out one shaking hand to claw for a hold on the corner bricks at the alley's mouth. The forward motion of the struggle swung against the wall. Larry tugged violently, pulling free a fistful of gray hair. Instantly, he grabbed again and yanked harder. Alex's fingers gave way.

Glimpsing the flash of the box cutter, Alex closed his eyes and sent his mind back to his tea party with Amanda. He could hear her giggle and smelled the cozy little house . . .

From far away came a heavy, melon-like thud then nothing. No cleaving of flesh, no pain, no warm gush of blood. Alex slipped back to the present, straining to hear and feel, his eyes still pinched shut, too terrified to look. *It would be just like the sick bastard to bait me with hope then slash it away.*

Fingers stroked the side of Alex's face. A panicked nausea rose as he opened his eyes. DeAndre towered over him, his broad, black face scrunched in concern.

"You okay, Little Man?" DeAndre asked gently.

The nausea subsided and Alex nodded.

"Damn labor pool was closed. Told you I'd beat his ass sorry."

Strong arms and hands helped him away from the wall. Alex made it to his knees, but the movement aggravated the nausea. He barely turned away from his helper before his breakfast spewed onto the alley's cement. When his stomach was finally empty, he balled up his fists, balanced against the brick wall and let loose a squeal of pain and frustration.

"It's all good, Little Man," DeAndre said, his hand patting his shoulder.

"Why me?" Alex wailed, his forehead propped against the cold bricks. "I'm a good man. I did everything I was supposed to do."

"Life ain't fair for nobody no mo'. You know that," DeAndre reasoned. "We need to get outta here. Larry don't look too good and his people will be comin' to check on him."

Alex glanced at the old predator. His nose had been pushed back into his face. Blood seeped from his ears and eyes. He sprawled awkwardly on his back.

De Andre raised his head, listening. "We gotta go." He scooped Alex into his arms and ran for the far end of the alley. They were half a block down and headed for the St. Vincent when shouts from Jake, Cat and Greg rose from the alley.

* * *

In his car in the parking lot of the West Omaha Church of Christ, William opened the packet of Angel's Wings information. A pocketed folder bore a picture of Pastor Ahough, arms in the air, looking up to Heaven. *Your Invitation To Celebrate God's Glory!* read the banner above his likeness. *Intended for framing, I bet.*

A full-color, elaborate church magazine occupied one folder pocket. The cover picture was the pompous-looking man William had seen leaving the church minutes before. The cover story had been titled *"Meet Our Own Angels"*. In smaller type, below the photo label of *"Lead Angel"* he read the man's name.

"Hello, Mr. Barry Jennings," William muttered. "Something tells me you are not putting the angel in the Angel's Wings program."

William pored over the brochures and paperwork listing requirements for the volunteers, how to dress, what to expect and more. The church lady, Mary Johnson, had added a recent schedule, listing sixteen volunteers. They worked in pairs, rotating into the night and weekend shifts.

Lead Angel Barry was not on the schedule. *That makes for an odd number of volunteers. Prefer to work alone, Mr. Jennings?*

He pulled his cell phone from its holster and dialed his reporter friend at the newspaper. When he got switched to her voice mail, he clicked off. This wasn't something he wanted on a recording. His mind kicked into overdrive. *Was it possible that the city could be involved in this?* He replaced his phone and pointed his car toward downtown.

Relieved be out of the snooty western suburbs and back in familiar territory, William turned north at 16th Street. He rolled past a little strip of hell known to the hookers and addicts as Glass Alley. Next to the alley rose the dilapidated shell of the former Fairbury Cannery. The landscape improved as he continued north, passing junkyards and grain elevators before the crumbling industrial neighborhood turned into run-down family homes made softer by the snow covering debris-littered yards surrounded by the semi-security of chain link fences.

Just past the ball fields at the west end of Carter Lake Park stood Nite Hawkes Cafe, a favorite of his back when he was in uniform. The lunch crowd wasn't a crowd at all. William slid into his favorite booth beneath a Norman Rockwell print of a runaway boy and tough-looking yet softhearted cop.

"William! What brings you to our neck of the woods?" called out Tracy Hawkes, the restaurant's co-owner.

"Howdy, my lovely. Just had a hankering for your world famous hot beef sandwich. Say hello to your husband for me when he comes up for air." He craned his neck to catch a glimpse of Dan Hawkes snagging an order from the ticket wheel.

"Hell, he's not that busy. Dan!" Tracy yelled over her shoulder. "Look who's here!"

Her mustachioed husband smiled through the cutout and waved a spatula.

Tracy poised her pen over her order pad. "So, hot beef sandwich?"

"Yes, ma'am. And, ah, could I use your phone?"

"Let me top off some coffees and get your order turned in. I'll bring our cordless back." She bent down to whisper, "Gotta keep it in the kitchen instead of under the counter, though. It's grown legs a time or two, if you know what I mean."

"I certainly do. I'll wait."

She frowned at him. "Something happen to your cell phone?"

84

"Ya know, sometimes it is a good thing to not have your own number flagged on caller I.D."

"Ah, gotcha. Love your cop shit." With that, Tracy scooped up a coffee pot and took a circuitous route back to the kitchen, filling cups and joking with the regulars along the way. After ringing up a group of rough-looking men in brown coveralls at the cash register, she returned with the phone.

"How's the homeless traffic up here these days?" he casually asked.

"Good God, there's more every day." She shook her head. "And it's not just your usual bums anymore, either. There's whole families living in their cars. It's a regular 'Grapes of Wrath' up here. We get half-a-dozen in every day looking for work, sometimes begging."

"Any of the regulars talk about strange goings on in the north downtown?"

"Nah, no more than the usual tin foil hat stuff. Have you heard there's a mountain lion in the woods out by the airport?"

William chuckled, shaking his head. "That one comes around at least once a year."

"Order up!" hollered Dan from the kitchen.

As Tracy returned to her duties, he dialed the phone. "Manuela Garcia, please."

"Newsroom. This is Manuela."

"How's my favorite Latina reporter today?"

"That depends on who's calling."

"Your favorite policeman."

"Well, that's taking a lot for granted. I know plenty of policemen."

"And me better than most. It's William. Have you ever heard of a guy named Barry Jennings?"

"Jennings is a pretty common name, but there is a Barry Jennings who owns a big chunk of the north downtown and Jennings Meats. The guy's a socialite, one of those most eligible bachelor types. Are you looking to set us up?" The keys of her keyboard rattled in the background as she talked.

"No, but I'll see what I can do when I talk to him. I'm just following up on something for a friend."

"Looking at our clips, he appears to be generous to his church and a number of local charities. Hm, we did a feature on his remodel of an Old Market loft few years back." Keys sounded. "Most of what we have on him is in the society stuff. He certainly is a looker when he puts on a tux."

"Thanks, Manuela. If he gives me good vibes, I'll give him your number. Say, you don't show an address for him in your computer, do you? I hate Googling on my phone."

"So I'm just a Google to you, is that it?"

"Oh, *mi amor*," crooned William, "Google is so bland. You, sweetheart, are at the very least a Yahoo!"

"Your Spanish *es muy malo*," chided Manuela, before reading off Jennings' address. "William, you wouldn't call if this weren't something bigger than a hunch. What's going on?"

"It's probably nothing, but it might not hurt to put Mr. Jennings' real estate dealings on your radar. *Adios, la mujer del corazon mio*."

10

"Got some aspirin?" Alex asked the trustee manning the front desk. After telling the kitchen manager that kids had attacked him not far from the shelter, he'd been excused from kitchen duty and had managed a few hours of restless sleep. It hadn't helped his head to stop hurting. He wondered how much more his battered body could take.

"Sure, Alex," said the trustee. "You don't look much better than when you came in."

Alex massaged his temples. "Yeah, well, hope I'm not in trouble with the shelter director for missing the morning." His fingers worked into his scalp. He hesitated then tilted his head down. "Is there a bald patch on my head?"

"Kinda thin and looks sore in one place, but it don't look too bad." He handed over a tiny paper packet containing two pills. "And don't worry about Mr. Skelton, DeAndre and I told him what happened. He wants you to see Nurse Liz when she comes in."

Sounds from the kitchen indicated preparation for the evening meal were underway. Deciding to pitch in rather than sit around in worry for DeAndre, Alex headed for the bathroom to wash up. His mind still wrestled with guilt. The ultimate injustice would be if his friend got pinched for dealing with Larry.

The bathroom mirror showed the slow progress of healing. In spite of the missing hair and a few new knuckle marks on his ear, he no longer looked like death warmed over. *Thank God. A few more days and I'll be ready.* A weak cough reminded him of his damaged ribs. Any laboring job would involve lifting. *Maybe another week before I go to the Fitzgerald and get that job.*

The kitchen had yet to hit the steamy rush that accompanied the prep and the cleanup involved in feeding hundreds of men.

"Gotta earn my keep," Alex said to the kitchen manager as he stepped into the steamy room gleaming with stainless steel. "What can I do to help?"

The man patted his shoulder in comfort and directed him to a metal stool to keep him off his feet as he peeled and chopped vegetables, a basically mindless task. He attacked a large bin of potatoes, peeling long thin, strips skin from the spuds. The monotony let his thoughts drift to worry.

What if they find my hair in Larry's hand? Hell, throw me in jail, instead of DeAndre. Let the government take care of me.

He tossed a peeled potato into a bin full of water, then took his frustrations out on the next unfortunate tuber until an errant stroke caught the ridge of a knuckle. Glancing around the hive of kitchen activity, he sucked on the scrape. *Fuck being a victim and fuck this! I'm getting a room and a job and prove to everyone that I'm not a loser. I'm going to mean something in this world.*

Bright laughter and a bustle of activity interrupted his brooding. A group of well-meaning university kids were taking a turn in the kitchen. They nudged one another and laughed as they performed tasks just as menial as peeling potatoes. Their playful attitude improved Alex's mood. *Liz will be in soon, too. I can ask her about that address for Amanda when she checks me over.*

A happy and somewhat familiar voice rose above the kitchen's din. It took Alex a moment to spot its source. The peeler in his hand froze as he spotted the girl. It was Amanda, the plump college girl who'd rescued him from the truck. One of the students noticed Alex's stare and nudged Amanda to look back at him.

Embarrassed to be caught staring, Alex returned to his potatoes. One tear then another trickled down his cheek. *Jesus, what the hell is wrong with me?* He grabbed for an onion, peeling away its papery outer layers to cover his abrupt weepiness.

A hand touched his elbow. He looked up into Amanda's eyes, his sight now blurred with tears.

"You probably don't remember me," she said. "I called 9-1-1 after that truck almost ran you over."

Throat tight, unable to speak, Alex dipped his head.

"Well, I just wanted to say 'Hi.' And I hope you're feeling better."

He merely nodded and the girl started an awkward retreat.

He cleared his throat and sputtered, "That ten dollars was a real lifesaver." Rapid blinking cleared his sight just as the girl looked back at him. "Your name is Amanda, right? I remember because I have a daughter by that name. You, ah, look a lot like her, I think."

"Yep, that's my name. I just wanted to say it's nice to see you again," she said, her fingers fidgeting with her apron. For a moment she frowned. "I don't mean to pry, but, ah, why are you crying?"

He held up the peeled onion. "It's this, I guess."

"Must be a strong one since you haven't cut it yet."

He lowered the onion to stare at it as he repeatedly swallowed and fought for control of his tears.

"Hey," her voice turned perky again, "if it makes you feel any better, you're the reason me and my friends are volunteering. I thought it was high time some of us lived up to the college's motto. It's 'Education in the spirit of service.'" When he looked up, she smiled warmly and rested a dainty hand over his. "I just wanted to say hello. I'll let you get back to work."

She pulled her hand away and started to turn.

Looking at that hand so like his daughter's, he blurted, "I think I might be your father."

She froze. "Excuse me?"

He wiped at his eyes with his free hand. "I'm sorry. I don't know what I'm saying." He heard her nearby friends snickering. "I'm just a stupid old man."

Amanda glared at the kids and they resumed their chores. She lowered her voice so only Alex could hear. "You must miss your daughter very much."

The trickle of tears flowed more freely. "I'm sorry," Alex repeated. "These darn onions . . . ."

She eased a cautious arm around him and he let her. Her head ducked so their gazes again met. "Didn't you tell me she lived in Florida?"

He nodded. "Her mother took her." The words rapidly spilled out. "She ran off with a rich lawyer and left me with all the bills. I-I tried to keep the house for my Amanda, but I lost my job. Then the bank took it. I have nothing for her to-to come home to," he blubbered.

Her eyes shiny with her own tears, Amanda squeezed him tight. "I wouldn't care about the house, if I were your daughter. I would be proud to be her, but, well, I already have a dad in Chicago. I grew up there with both my parents."

Alex took a deep steadying breath and nodded. He glanced around to find the entire kitchen staff silent and watchful. *Fucking pathetic.* He sat straighter and she stepped away. "I do miss her and our home."

Amanda cocked her head as if coming to a decision. "Tell you what, Alex, I'm a little lonely living so far from home. Would you consider being my Omaha dad?"

Alex sniffed, shrugged and loosened a hint of a smile. "Thank you for not making fun or getting scared. I'm just a silly old man who's hit a rough patch."

"Rough patches I understand. So, Dad, is it okay if I get back to work?"

"Ah, you have my permission," he said, playing along. Though he felt crushingly foolish, hearing her call him 'dad' had warmed his heart.

* * *

By the time he finished his kitchen duties, Liz was in her office. A wave of her hand and a smile welcomed him through her open door. She studied his face after he settled in the chair by her desk. "How are you? I heard you had another problem."

"I'm a little sore here and there, but I don't think anything's broken. Darn kids." Her flinch told him he hadn't deceived her. He hurried on. "I sort of embarrassed myself with those college kids in the kitchen. Thought you should know . . . in case it comes up."

"What happened?"

He stared at the peeler-scraped knuckle. "The girl that rescued me from the truck the other day? Her name's Amanda, just like my daughter. She volunteered here . . . you know, to help out in the kitchen . . . with some friends."

"And?"

He shifted in the chair. "And I don't know why, but I told her she might be my daughter."

"Oh, Alex."

Her watery words snapped his head up. Tears indeed welled in her eyes. He gulped. "It's okay. Really. She handled it well. In fact, she gave everyone in that kitchen a lesson in class and grace, me included."

When Liz reached for a tissue, Alex pulled out the letter he'd written to his real daughter. He had to stuff the chain of the heart locket back in place. *Another time*. He set the letter on the desk. "I wrote this a while back. Do you think you could help me look up my daughter's address? She's in Florida but I can't remember my ex's address."

Liz stared at the envelope a long moment. "Your daughter could be out on her own by now. You said she was college age. When parents remarry, some kids keep their last name. Do you know if she did?"

"No. And I can't remember my wife's new last name either . . . Jesus," he reached for the envelope, "what was I—"

"I tell you what," Liz interrupted, "I'll do a little poking around the internet, maybe dig around Facebook and the other social networks. It's a long shot, but if I come up with something, I'll let you know. She might even be looking for you, too. Wouldn't that be a wonderful surprise?"

Alex brightened. "I never thought of that. I guess she would have trouble finding me here. Ah, could you hold onto the letter?"

"Certainly. I'll put it with your savings," she said, dropping it into the top desk drawer. She looked up at him until he met her eyes. "And I want you to know I don't think your little slip up means you're foolish. It just shows how much you miss your little girl." When he reluctantly nodded, she folded her hands on the desk in a business-like manner. "Where do you stand on your moving plans?"

"I asked DeAndre if he wanted to room with me."

"Really? Roommates can be trouble. Are you sure?"

"It'll work," he affirmed. "He's been a better friend than I deserve. I owe him a shot at getting off the street just like me. Another week and I'll be healed up enough. Do you think Mr. Skelton will let me stay that long? I could be out sooner if need be."

"A week should be fine, Alex. Mr. Skelton and everybody else I've talked to is rooting for you."

"So, what are the two of you cooking up in here?" asked a voice from the doorway.

"Hello there, William," said Alex, meeting the man's smile with his own. He let pride color his voice with, "We were just talking about when I might move to the Fitzgerald."

"Soon I hope."

"A week, maybe less," Alex said. "My face should be healed up enough by then."

"Speaking of that," William said, narrowing his eyes, "do you remember the unwanted ride you took the other night?"

"Hard to forget."

He stepped into the small office, closing the door then leaning against it. He held up his hands to keep Alex and Liz in their seats. His eyes focused on Alex. "I have a theory, but I need your help." He pulled a magazine from inside his coat. Handing it to Alex, he tapped on the cover photo. "This fellow look familiar?"

Alex's heart rate increased. "Yeah, yeah. That's him. That's the van guy right there."

With a Cheshire cat smile, the detective took back his magazine. "By the way, I found your friend Moon Boots."

"He's all right?" Liz asked before Alex could.

"He's fine. We found him at a new shelter over in Council Bluffs. His brother took him home with him. Apparently the man has some sort of seizure disorder."

"Did the church van take him over there?" asked Alex.

"Moon Boot's couldn't remember how he got across the river. From what I gathered, he woke up in a park not far from the shelter and someone in a car helped him inside."

"How'd he end up all the way over there?" asked Liz.

William held up a hand. "Like I said, I have a theory. I need to do a bit more digging to change it to accusations."

Alex sagely nodded his head. "Whoever it is, they are trying to make us someone else's problem."

William chuckled. "Good guess, but . . . we don't know that for sure."

"Sure we do." Alex couldn't contain his rising excitement. "That jerk Ahough told me as much outside Harvest House. He said the neighborhood would be better off without us. Said we tracked in disease."

"Okay," said William. "Let's say I agree with you. I still have to prove wrong doing. Prove, as in facts, not suspicions." Alex felt disappointment smother his enthusiasm as William continued, "For example, the church could claim they thought they were trying to help the overcrowding on this side of the river. I doubt they'd get in much trouble for that."

"He's right, Alex," Liz added. "We need to stay quiet about this. Right, detective?"

"Absolutely, please do. They don't know I'm watching. It's possible there are other forces at work here and I need to tread lightly."

"Other forces?" Alex asked.

William shrugged. "Nothing in life is simple."

All shared a laugh over that statement.

* * *

Alex, DeAndre and the rest of the gold star club neighbors stood outside the shelter with the other smokers. For once no wind pierced their clothes. Low clouds threatened snow, keeping the temperature from dropping to single digits. They shuffled from foot to foot as a police cruiser rolled by slowly.

"P-probably looking for a s-scape goat to p-pin something on." Billy quipped. Their little huddle cursed agreements.

"Hey, Alex," called a voice from the cruiser.

His back to the vehicle, Alex froze in fear.

"You and that big nigger, get over here. Don't make me get out in the cold."

Exchanging wary glances, Alex and DeAndre silently agreed to play it cool. Still, they approached the cruiser with caution.

Streetlight glanced off Sgt. Gurdlich's scalp as he and his rookie driver peered from the cruiser. Both had lower lips bulging with chewing tobacco.

"What happened to Larry Parmenter?" Gurldich demanded.

Remaining calm, Alex didn't miss a beat. "Don't have a clue. Why? Did someone finally give him what he deserves?"

"He's in a coma at the hospital. Somebody smashed his face. He looks like a fucking pug dog." Gurdlich's eyes fixed on DeAndre then glared in menace at Alex. "Our report says you were the last one seen with him."

"Don't know what you're talking about," Alex said, squelching the rise of fear.

"Really? I have witnesses that put you two together."

"Who?"

"His woman, Cat for starters."

Beside him, DeAndre chuckled and he humphed.

"Cat'll wrap her lips around anything, including a dirty lie," said Alex. "Look at me. Do I look like I'd stand a chance against Larry, let alone hurt him?"

"You might not be much—" He pointed a finger at DeAndre. "—but your big buck nigger could do some major damage." Gurdlich punctuated the accusation with a stream of brown goo, forcing Alex to sidestep. "What do you see in this little guy, blackie?" he probed. "Is it a gay thing? You warm for his form?" The sergeant's tongue poked at the inside of his cheek, bulging it outward as he feigned stroking a cock. "Why, little Alex here probly don't even need to kneel to suck that jungle snake of yours."

DeAndre crossed his arms. "You a sick mutha."

Gurdlich responded with another stream of tobacco juice that spattered DeAndre's pants. He then laughed. "Hey, look. Ol' blackie's dick's leakin' just thinkin' about it."

In an instant DeAndre's hands closed on Gurdlich's throat. The sergeant spit his chew into his face. The rookie cop threw himself over Gurdlich's back to viciously jab DeAndre between the eyes with the steel ball in the hilt of his nightstick. Cross-eyed, the big man stumbled back and dropped to his knees. Alex caught him, his ribs screaming against the weight.

Gurdlich coughed then sputtered, "Bottom line . . . if you and your nigger boyfriend . . . don't want to end up in jail . . . you'll keep your traps shut . . . about Angel's Wings."

"What the hell are you talking about?" Alex shouted back.

"We know you've been . . . bad-mouthing the Angel's Wings. It stops . . . fucking right now or both of you . . . both go to jail for attempted murder."

DeAndre groaned, shaking his head to clear his vision.

"Look, Officer Pembroke," Gurdlich said to his young driver who still leaned forward, his eyes wide with agitation. "We had it all wrong. It's the nigger that's sucking the midget. He's already on his knees ready to receive."

"Michael will bring God's vengeance," DeAndre mumbled.

"Hear that? Jesus, now he's fucking delirious with desire." Gurdlich laughed then his driver joined in. "Let's get out of here, kid, and leave these two love bunnies alone."

As the cruiser sped off, the gold star club members rushed forward to help DeAndre to his feet.

"What the hell was that about?" asked Tom.

"Nothing," Alex said. "Just Turd Lick bitching about my police report on the church vans He's just trash talking."

Henry patted a comforting hand on DeAndre's broad chest and broke his usual quiet to ask, "Who the heck is Michael?"

"What?" slurred DeAndre.

"I heard you say something about Michael and God. What did you mean, man?"

DeAndre rubbed his fingers across his forehead. "Hell, I don't know what you're talkin' 'bout, Henry. Damn, my head hurts."

* * *

A plastic bag of ice on his forehead, DeAndre sat beside Alex in an isolated vigil in front of the shelter's big-screen television.

"What do we do?" Alex whispered. "Gurdlich said Larry is in a coma."

"Hope the mutha fucka never wakes up."

"Not that simple. Didn't you hear him say he has a witness?"

"Cat ain't no witness. Nobody'll listen to that old ho'."

"He pulled out my hair, DeAndre, I've seen it on those CSI shows. If they find my hair in his hand . . ."

"You in a DNA file somewhere?"

Alex frowned. "Not that I know of."

"Then don't be worryin' 'bout it. That science bullshit you see on TV ain't nothin' like real. B'sides, if he had proof, we'd already be locked up."

11

Whiskers surrendered to the shining scissors in Alex's hand. The gray clumps of hair tumbled into a towel draped across a sink in the trustee's shower room. Three weeks of indoor living had done a lot for Alex's looks. The bruising was all but gone. The road rash had faded. This morning a face emerged he hadn't seen for what felt like a lifetime, as he pruned his coarse, gray mask of homelessness.

Deciding his beard had been tamed to the point that a razor could take over, he balled up the towel, set it aside and lathered up. The razor's twin blades prickled long-hidden flesh, shearing whiskers made soft by hot water and foamy, sweet-smelling Barbasol cream. The razor clogged quickly. Alex tap-tap-tapped it on the sink's edge, the sound conjuring a memory . . .

He occupied a hospital bed, immobilized by broken bones and plaster casts. A male nurse bent over him to shear his stubble with a disposable razor that he tap-tap-tapped on a thick plastic basin of water.

"Heck of a way to end a workday, eh, Mr. Capstain?" said a police officer standing at the foot of Alex's bed.

Alex stared back through a thin fog of pain medication.

"The doctors tell me you're lucky to be here," the officer continued. He held a clipboard with Alex's driver's license, registration and insurance card attached. "Good thing you were wearing your seatbelt."

"I suppose," Alex murmured. "My truck totaled?"

"Most likely," said the cop. "The driver's door was crushed into the middle of the steering wheel. Pretty sure the frame's bent. The camper shell was ripped off. Like I said, you're one lucky guy."

"How about the stuff inside the camper? Had just about everything I own in there."

"We picked a ton of personal stuff off the street and threw it back in the truck. You'll have to check it when you're released. It looked like you were in the middle of a move or something."

"Or something. You know, all of this is the last thing I need."

The nurse finished and gently wiped his face clean with a warm washcloth.

Alex sucked in a deep, painful breath. He looked to the ceiling to blink away the embarrassment of tears. "I'm sorry, officer. A lot of things are weighing on me right now."

The uniformed man exchanged looks with the nurse then continued, "No worries, sir. I truly understand you've just been through something very traumatic. Your insurance should help."

"Nah, no job, so no health insurance. That truck was a beater. I only carried liability." He pinched his eyes closed to capture a thought. "But, ah, didn't the other guy hit me? His insurance should cover it."

"That's correct, sir, but we can't locate him. Witnesses said he walked away from the accident. The car's VIN comes back to a to a Ricardo Velasquez, but the plates were stolen. Even if we do find him, it's likely he has no insurance. He's probably on his way back to Mexico, if you know what I mean."

A burst of anger cleared the fog in his mind. "So you're telling me my truck is totaled, I can't work and the guy responsible gets a walk?"

The officer ran a hand over his own face. "If we find him . . . he'll probably be deported or go to jail."

"Tell you what, take me to jail instead." Alex squirmed as his anger pumped adrenalin and frustration into his battered body. "That truck was all I had left. I was living in it, goddamn it. Saving money for an apartment." His balled fists thumped the bed. "God damn it all to hell! Can't I get a fucking break? Take me to jail, officer. Three meals and cable TV would be a helluva lot better than where I'm headed."

Finished tidying up the hospital room, the male nurse stopped long enough to pat Alex's arm and glare at the officer.

"No, no, no. I'm sure you don't want that," the officer tried to placate him. "Don't you have family or someone that could take you in?"

The pain ricocheted around inside his chest. "No."

The nurse spread his feet and folded his arms across his chest to stare down the officer. As a flush rose above his dark blue collar, the cop awkwardly pulled Alex's papers and one sheet from his clipboard. "I'll leave this with you." He started to put the paperwork on the foot of the bed, but the nurse scooped them up and carried them to the bedside table. "Ah, there's a copy of the report for your insurance, if they ask for it. Your truck is at the city impound. There's a receipt there with a map on the back. Sorry to tell you, but there is a towing and handling fee to get your vehicle out . . . Or you can let the city take it for scrap and they'll wave the fees." When Alex didn't respond, he nervously glanced from him to the nurse and back. "Ah, he did a good job with the shave . . . And, I'm sorry . . . about all this. None of it's fair."

Coming back from the memory, Alex stared hard at the much older face reflected in the mirror. He toweled off the last bits of Barbasol. Butterflies fluttered in his gut as he thought of the job interview scheduled that afternoon.

He emerged from the trustee's quarters savoring his cleanliness and progress. He grinned in spite of his underlying nervous tension. DeAndre waited for him in front of the big-screen TV.

"'Scuse me," DeAndre said with a gold-toothed smile. "Have you seen a Mister Capstain? I'm lookin' for him and he's no where to be found."

Alex playfully punched his arm. "You're a big dork. I feel kind of naked without my beard. One of the trustees trimmed up my hair last night. How does it look?"

DeAndre feigned a hypercritical assessment. "Lookin' good, my man. More than lookin' good. You are lookin' fine. Now, you got what you need for the big day?"

Alex patted his right front pants pocket that bulged with his envelope of rent money.

"Let's go do it, Little Man. I'll walk you there."

As they stepped from the shelter into the cold, Alex's hands went straight to his face. "Damn, this feels weird."

DeAndre smiled.

After a few steps, Alex offered, "About that job interview I have today . . . Well, I have an extra application form if you're interested."

Momentarily surprised, DeAndre smiled crookedly. "Sure, if you got a pen, I'll do it at breakfast."

Alex promptly unzipped his coat, showing off the two pens in his shirt pocket. "You know, I haven't thought about pens and pocket stuff for a long time. It feels pretty good."

At the Harvest House, they listened to Seth's usual eat-it-then-beat-it speech to the line of waiting people. Everyone then shuffled forward without any pushing and shoving. All were equally grateful to be given what awaited.

In the warmth and humidity of the busy kitchen, Alex felt eyes on him. He longed for the anonymity of his usual hiding spot on the floor under the big wooden table.

"Hey, Alex, you get a vasectomy or something?" Seth hollered, anxious to deliver the punch line.

Alex's eyebrows knitted in confusion.

"'Cause you look pretty dang impotent." Seth laughed at his own joke.

"Ha, very punny," Alex shot back while DeAndre glared at Seth.

Froot Loops and hot chocolate added to the perfection of Alex's day. DeAndre munched on cornflakes and milk. Both were sipping dregs of cereal from their Styrofoam bowls when Paul Finnegan took a seat beside them.

"You're making us mighty proud," Paul said, extending his hand to Alex. He then clapped a hand on his shoulder. "I have to say you're about the hardest working guy I've seen. And you look damn good with that shave and haircut, too."

Alex sat up a little straighter. "Thank you, Paul. I'm not out of the woods yet, you know. Still have to get a room and then a job. Do you know anybody over at the Fitzgerald?"

"Gerard's the main man over there," said Paul. "Good fella, kinda strict, but he has to be to keep things on an even keel."

Alex pulled Liz's small notebook from his pocket, clicked a pen and made a note of the name.

"I could make a call to let him know a good man's coming over," Paul offered.

Another smile lit Alex's face. "That'd be great." Then he sobered. "I probably wouldn't have made it so far without this place."

"No need to get all sentimental, Alex." The supervisor's head wagged. "We've all been there . . . This place and what it provides is our way of paying back. These people need us and, in turn, we need all of you. Think about that. We'd be nothing without you needing us." He looked at the two amazed expressions. "You never thought of like that, did you?" He shook their hands, " So, I'm thanking you for giving me purpose."

"I'll be damned," whispered DeAndre.

* * *

On the short walk to the Fitzgerald, DeAndre glanced frequently at the quiet man at his side. As the red brick of the hotel-turned-long term residence came into view, Alex sensed his friend's concern. He knew DeAndre caught the show of nerves in his flexing jaw.

"Feels like everybody's watchin'. Everybody's expectin', don't it?" said the big man, looking down as if concentrating to make his long-legged stride match Alex's shorter one.

"Man, you've got that right. I don't know if I'm up to this," Alex said, deep-breathing to combat his internal butterflies. "I'd hate to disappoint everybody."

DeAndre laid a hand on his shoulder then squeezed gently. "People's watchin', Alex, but we ain't expectin'. Everybody just wants to make sure you be safe and gettin' what you need." He nodded his big head in all seriousness. "It's nice to see some good fo' a change."

"I noticed you didn't ask for that job application at breakfast." Alex decided to broach the awkward subject that had been nagging him. "You don't really want to room with me, do you?"

They slowed at the corner of the Fitzgerald.

DeAndre's lips pursed, his expression troubled. "Wouldn't put it that way. Look, it ain't about you. What I gots now . . . well—" He wiped a hand over his lips. "—that's as good as it gets for me. Anything else is just trouble. Thought I'd be dead a long time ago but here I am. I'm free and I gots me a hidey-hole. It's kinda cold but that's okay 'cause it's free, too. I'd like someplace warm, but . . . well, that leads to responsibilities, taxes and govmint shit—you know, answerin' to people—I ain't no perfect roomie, either," he added for emphasis, crossing his arms and leaning his back against the building. "They's lots you don't know about me."

They stood quiet for a long moment, just watching the morning commuter traffic roll by. Behind them steel grates covered the Fitzgerald's first floor windows. A red neon vacancy sign flickered above their heads.

Alex's stomach tightened over his frustration with his friend's sense of hopelessness. He couldn't let it go. "But you deserve better, DeAndre. You're a good man. A lot of people would be a lot worse off if you weren't around. Hell," he said slapping his own chest, "I'd be dead a couple times over if it weren't for you."

"Watchin' over folk out here, helpin' 'em get better is what I do, Little Man. At least, I think it's what I'm s'posed to do. If I had regular responsibilities, I wouldn't have no time for that."

Considering his words, Alex leaned his back to the building, arms crossed to match DeAndre. "I tell you what, once I get back on my feet, I'll make sure you get a few comforts. A real winter coat would be a good place to start. What do you think?"

"Deal!" DeAndre stood straight and stuck out a hand that Alex shook. The big guy then looked around as if to see if anyone watched. "Think I'll head back over to the shelter to see what the other gold star club members is up to. You gonna be all right in there?"

"I'll be fine. Got my money in my pocket and I made it here safely, thanks to you. Now if you're expecting a goodbye kiss after taking me to breakfast and seeing me to my building . . . well—"

"Hey now!" DeAndre interrupted, quickly jamming his hand in his pocket. "Not on the first date, I don't. I ain't that easy," he added with a grin. "Thanks for understand'n."

Outside the Fitzgerald's front door, three steps led up from street level. Just beyond the entrance, the office sat on one side of a long hallway opposite a wooden stairway. Decades of dust clung to the electrical fixtures. The carpet had been worn through to reveal the hardwood floor beneath.

Take-out menus and gypsy cab phone numbers graced a bulletin board next to a line of little brass mailboxes. Alex stared hard at them, a smile lighting his face. *A real mailbox. I'll get catalogs again.*

He found the office behind thick, bullet-resistant glass, bolstered by a metal cage.

"Hello?" Alex called through a shiny metal tray below the window.

A chair creaked and a tall, thin man appeared. "Can I help you?"

"I'd like to inquire about a room, please." The sound of the words finally coming out of his mouth sent his heart soaring.

"Just for the night?"

"No, sir. I'd like a room for thirty days, if that's possible."

"You must be the fella Paul called about."

"Yes, sir, that's me. My name's Alex Capstain and you must be Gerard."

"That would be me," the man said offering a bony hand under the window for Alex to shake. "Normally, a thirty day stay requires a deposit . . ." Alex tensed, seeing his job hunting time cut dramatically. " . . . but, since you come with references, I'll wave it."

Alex puffed a relieved breath. "Darn near gave me a heart attack."

"Of course, one month will be $240 in advance. Can you handle that?"

"Yes, sir," Alex said, retrieving the envelope with his savings. His hands shook as he reverently laid it in the window's metal tray.

Counting the money, Gerard didn't look up. "You want an upstairs room or down?"

"What's the difference?"

"Heat rises. In the winter, upstairs is warmer. In the summer it gets hot up there and we've got no air conditioning."

"I'll take an upstairs room," said Alex. "If I'm lucky enough to be here 'til summer, I'll be so happy, the heat won't matter."

Gerard slid the rental agreement under the window and Alex proudly produced a pen to fill it out. A pair of shiny, brass keys and a smaller, steel key put the finishing touch on the deal. Picking them from the tray along with his receipt, Alex realized he had no keychain or wallet. *Have to remedy that soon.*

"Your room is up the stairs, halfway down the hall on the right," said Gerard. "One key works the street door. It's locked after 10 p.m. The other is for your room. The smaller key is for your mailbox. Bathrooms are a communal affair and you can trade in your bed linens for fresh ones every two weeks. Any questions?"

Alex took out his notepad, "So, what's my mailing address gonna be?"

"Address is right there on the receipt. Your room number is 206. Any other questions?"

"No, sir. Can I go up and look at my room now?"

"It's yours, my man. You paid for it."

The wooden stairway creaked and sagged and the handrail jiggled in his grip. The air indeed grew warmer as he climbed. At the top of the stairs a pair of tarnished light fixtures dimly revealed flaking paint and cracking plaster. Closed doors lined both sides of the shadowy hall illuminated by the faint glow of bare bulbs at either end. Searching for 206, he heard televisions and muffled conversations from behind a few of the doors.

He sighed at the beauty of his room number, the number two in thin brass nailed in place followed by a zero and six in white paint. His key slid in and turned easily.

"Home sweet home," he murmured, opening the door to a cracked linoleum floor, neatly made-up twin bed and a folding table and chair. He palmed the wall and found an antique, push-button light switch. Depressing the top button fired a sixty-watt bulb in the middle of his cracked and water-stained ceiling. On the table, a towel and washcloth sat next to a laminated list of house rules.

Just beyond the sooty glass of his room's single window a pair of pigeons roosted. They shifted but remained in place as he stepped closer to take in the view from his window. To the west stretched the university's old gymnasium, parking lots, streets with traffic and the tip of the TastyQuick sign. To the east loomed the stark, high steel of the baseball stadium.

After removing his coat, Alex sighed over the warmth surrounding him. He gently lowered his backside onto the creaking innerspring mattress, bounced twice just for the hell of it then laid back. For a long moment he savored being alone and warm at the same time.

He rose to hang his coat from a hook screwed to the back of his door. His smile broadened. *What a relief not to worry about the coat every second of every day.* From its front pocket he pulled the precious little travel alarm and meticulously spun the little red alarm hand to six o'clock, the time he'd gotten up every morning before his layoff. After making sure the alarm switch was in the off position until bedtime, he put it in a place of honor in the center of the folding table. As he read the Fitzgerald's rules, the clock's little quartz movement ticked beside him. He let his mind wander to how his new morning routine would unfold.

He then realized he had yet to reconnoiter the communal bathroom. Still amazed that he had a door to lock, he secured his room and found the bathrooms at the far end of the hall, the door illuminated by the dim light fixtures. Breathing in the aroma of strong cleanser and underlying mildew, he surveyed five toilets with dividers and doors, five porcelain sinks and three metal shower stalls, each with a single shower head and short plastic curtain. It reminded him of his high school locker room, except for the rust and peeling paint.

Alex returned to his room, aware of feeling a mix of elation and relief, tainted with nagging uncertainty. He blinked back tears. *Welcome home. Welcome to the new normal.*

By noon, he had read and reread the ad and the notes he'd made for the job application on his horizon. He closed the notebook Liz had given him to replace the one destroyed by Larry, stood, stretched and took a deep breath to calm his nerves. He looked at the travel clock. *Time to go.*

To be safe, he'd given himself three hours for the two-mile walk to the Hilte Linens and Uniform Company. He preferred to be early and prepared. He was to meet a man named Harold, fill out some forms and take what he was told was a low-key physical abilities test.

After hustling down the stairs, he hesitated at the office window. "Wish me luck," he called out to Gerard.

Barely glancing up, the man waved back automatically.

Hilte Linens and Uniforms was south and a little east of the Fitzgerald. On his trek through the business district, he encountered office workers on lunch break spilling onto the sidewalks before their high-rises. The occasional head nod or "how's it going" surprised him. Considering it was far better than the wide berth they'd given him weeks before, his tentative smile turned into a genuine one. He drew himself up and walked just as purposefully as those around him.

At a bus shelter filled with waiting passengers, he stopped to inquire about the bus system. A congenial, ancient black woman pulled a schedule from her purse and insisted he take it with him.

"Buses run along here every fifteen minutes," she said with authority. "But you can't count on 'em in the winter. I'd plan an extra half hour to forty-five minute cushion, just in case." Everyone in the shelter nodded agreement.

The cushion he'd given himself for this morning's walk left him standing outside his destination with a whole two hours to spare. When traffic allowed, he crossed the street to a Holiday convenience store and stepped inside. Behind the counter a heavyset, well-past-middle-aged woman greeted him with a nod and a "howdy."

"I've got a job interview across the street at three o'clock," Alex said. "Is it all right if I wait in here out of the cold?"

"Sure, grab a seat over by the window," she said.

"I don't have a lot of money to buy anything. Is it still okay?" He cringed that the question hinted his confidence had slipped a notch. *Habits are hard to break.*

She looked him up and down. "Where's the interview?"

"That Hilte uniform place over there," he said, pointing. "I can wait outside if it's a problem."

"Nah, that's okay. Grab a seat and take a load off."

Relieved that she found him acceptable to be in her store, he settled at a narrow booth and pulled out his notebook, the job posting and the bus schedule. A steady stream of laborers entered to buy cigarettes and beer. The computer for the gas pumps beeped incessantly as the counter woman played the pump buttons like a concert pianist.

When the afternoon clerk arrived, the woman hung her apron and pulled her cash drawer, taking it to the back to count. Minutes later, she reappeared, carrying her winter coat and a box of pastries.

"So, what's your story?" she asked, sliding into the bench seat across from Alex. She opened the pastry box then turned it to him. "These were gonna be tossed as day-olds. I don't need 'em all. Help yourself."

Alex plucked out a chocolate-coated donut with a grateful nod. "First job interview in a long time. Been digging out for a while after a layoff."

"Jail?"

His head snapped up in pride. "No, ma'am. Did spend some time at a shelter and on the street, though." Seeing her expression as nonjudgmental, he added, "A time or two I wondered if jail wouldn't be a little nicer."

The woman's eyebrows lifted at his honesty. "You a drinker or a druggie?"

"No, ma'am. But I understand those who were tempted and fell victim. It's tough out there."

"You got that right," she said, studying the fruit filling of her pastry. "I figured I'd be retired by now. But, thanks to the stock market, a couple of mergers and a bunch of greedy, dumb-assed CEOs, I'm working a convenience store register. You want some coffee?"

"I can't . . . I mean, I need to save—"

"On the house," she interrupted. "It's about time to dump the pots and make fresh, anyway." She slid from the booth and Alex stood with her. "Nah, sit," she said. "I'll get it."

When she returned, Alex was still standing and only sat after she did.

"You ever worked at a commercial laundry?"

"No, ma'am."

"Quit with the ma'am business. Call me Betty." She pointed to her nametag.

"Okay. No, I never worked at a laundry before. Don't know what to expect."

She touched the wedding ring on her left hand. "My husband worked the Hilte laundry line for fifteen years. It's hard work, hot with lots of lifting."

"I'm not real big, but I'm a hard worker. My last job was managing a cabinet shop. I worked my way up to that." He held out his hands and turned them over. "I can make just about anything with these hands."

"The only thing you'll be making at Hilte is a sore back and minimum wage to start. Where you living?" she asked before washing down a bite of her danish with stale coffee.

"I have a room at a hotel about two miles from here. Don't have a car so I have to stay close. How about you, how long have you been—"

A thunderous bang rattled the window. Arms covering their heads, they ducked sideways in fear of the window shattering. When it didn't, they sat up. On the other side of the glass, a crazed, bespectacled face smeared a greasy trail across the store window.

"Barb! Call the cops," screamed Betty. "He's back. I think he's gonna break it this time."

Alex leaped from the booth to race for the front doors. Outside, the crazy man stepped back to form the weird finger sign Alex had seen him make at the shelter.

"Professor!" Alex yelled, pushing open the doors.

The man turned his wild gaze to Alex. "I'll cut your fucking head off !"

"It's me, Alex!" he shouted back. "Alex, from the shelter. You know me. Are you still searching for Antonio?"

"Get back," the professor warned. He cocked his head as if to get a better look at Alex. His tone changed to a little less menacing, "I can do it. I can cut your fucking head off."

"I think I know where they took Antonio. If you calm down, I'll tell you," Alex said slowly and distinctly.

The professor sighted him with his fingers, "If you're full of shit, God will punish you."

"I talked to the police, Professor. I think I know where Antonio is."

The madness dimmed and shifted into a bland stare. He lowered his hands.

Alex moved a little closer, speaking quietly, "It's all right. I think the church vans took him to a new shelter."

He shook his head. "Is he in Hell? I told him he'd go to Hell for fucking the whores."

"No, he's not in Hell. I think he's in Council Bluffs."

Alex waved to a stack of ice melt bags then sat down. The man cautiously joined him.

"Do you think you could rest here?" Alex asked. "I could run inside and be right back with some coffee. You like coffee don't you?"

"Yes, coffee would be lovely," the Professor offered, looking straight at him with an intelligent gleam emerging behind the glasses.

The minute Alex cleared the door Betty demanded, "What the hell is up with that guy?"

"He's off his medicine. I've never seen him hurt anybody. He's just scared and confused. Are the cops coming?"

"Any second."

"I'll talk to him until they get here. Is it okay if I give him my coffee?"

"Hell, give him a danish too, if it'll keep him happy."

Just after the man had sampled a bit of coffee and danish, a cruiser rolled up. As the officers met at the front of their vehicle, Alex recognized Jason Grant, the young man who'd taken his report at the hospital.

He held up a hand, holding them off momentarily. "Professor, these gentlemen are going to take you someplace warm. If you promise not to give anybody a hard time, I'll ask them about Antonio."

"You did say you knew where Antonio is, right?"

"I think so. Now, they're going to have to put cuffs on you. If you fight they'll hurt you. You don't want that. You cooperate, I'll tell you what I know."

"Oh, I don't like being a bother."

"That's good. I'll talk to them then they'll help you in the car," Alex said glancing at the two officers who nodded.

"Very well," he said, politely.

"Officer Grant, I don't know if you remember me—"

"Alex, right? I hardly recognized you without the beard. What's up with this guy?" he said, eyeing the professor, finishing his coffee and roll.

"He's one of the mental cases from that Kilpatrick place that closed down. He's off his meds. If he goes wacko on you, tell him you know where Antonio is. It seems to calm him down."

"You want to ride with us? We could drop you at the shelter."

"No, I've got a room now and—wait, what time is it?"

The young officer looked at his watch. "Two-thirty."

"Whew, I've got a job interview at three."

"That's cool," Grant said, holding up his fisted hand.

Alex gave him an awkward fist bump.

As the cops approached him, the professor carefully set down his empty cup and dutifully turned, putting his hands behind his back. Alex entered the store and stood at the door with Betty to wave goodbye as the cruiser backed up.

He sighed with relief and turned to the friendly clerk. "Well, I'm going to get to that interview a little early. Thanks for your kindness."

"Alex is it?" she asked.

"Yes, Alex Capstain."

"When you're in that interview, tell Harold that Betty said to give you a shot."

"You know Harold?"

"He's my husband."

Alex's brow furrowed. "I thought—"

"Yeah, like you, my husband worked his way up. Now, he's in charge of human relations. He does the hiring for Hilte."

12

"Christ, walking into this place is like stepping back into the '70s," said Sgt. Gurdlich. He sat in a deep-tufted, high-backed semi-circular booth, flanked by Barry Jennings and Pastor Ahough.

"Does Warren Buffett really eat here?" asked Gurdlich.

"Yes, I'm told he prefers the T-bone steak and Cherry Coke," said Jennings.

Clad in white shirt, black vest and black slacks, a waitress wound through the tables of old-money geriatrics to deliver a basket of bread, butter and glasses of water. She stared down Gurdlich's sexually aggressive leer, took their order in a crisp, no-nonsense manner and left.

"The investors will be touring the neighborhood next Tuesday," Jennings cut right to business, "Gurdlich, you'll prod the riffraff away for the day, correct?"

He munched on butter-slathered French bread, eyeing his arrogant dinner partners. "The whores won't like it much, but I'll herd them north. I'll do a drive-by before I start my shift to make sure they stay put," he said, around a mouthful of bread.

Jennings looked across the table at the pastor. "John, you're issuing the press release for Sunday's evening prayer service, correct?"

"The release will stress the church's good work and the neighborhood's improvement."

"And if the more astute of the press want real numbers?"

"Ambiguity is our friend and they've got weekend airtime to fill," said Ahough. "If one of them does bother to ask, I'll just tell them to look around that area. The change is obvious—Sergeant, we'll need you to move the prostitutes on Sunday as well. I'd hate to hold the prayer service with that abomination on display."

Gurdlich shrugged. "The girls will do what I tell 'em. The dealers aren't as cooperative but I'll give'm a heads up on the possibility of media. They won't come within a mile of the place."

The no-expression waitress returned with their order on a circular tray and set it on a fold-out stand a bus boy opened for her. Gurdlich snickered as their plates were set before them. Jennings and Ahough had ordered sandwiches while he would enjoy a T-bone and a Cherry Coke.

His eyes followed the departing waitress's ass. "Damn, I'd like to tap that."

He picked up on the disgusted glances exchanged by Jennings and Ahough so he decided to poke them a bit. "You know, if the hookers were at your little prayer service, we'd get a shitload of press by calling it the second cumming. Get it?"

The affronted pastor dropped his head while Jennings' eyes slitted in warning. "This isn't a joke. We have a great deal at risk here . . . including *your* future."

Gurdlich's smile melted into a sneer. He cut his steak a little more forcefully than necessary. "I get it, boys. You find me distasteful. Well, that's just too damn bad because . . . " He waved his steak knife at them, " . . . you need me." His fork shoved a bloody hunk of savory meat into his mouth. Only two chews later he said, "I'm not afraid to get my hands dirty, while you two make your big bucks, right?"

"Your salary as head of security, added to your city pension should go a long way toward washing your hands," Jennings ground out, looking around to see if any one had overheard.

"And you're not the only one who's gotten their hands dirty," said the clergyman, not bothering to sugar coat his hate. "Between the vans and the shelters, I've had more than my share of contact with street vermin."

Gurdlich took a sip of his Coke. "Speaking of that, Barry, you need to lay off those runs across the river. Try some legitimate picking up and dropping off to cover your ass. That little guy that got away from you made some noise."

Jennings shot a worried look at the pastor. "How so?"

Gurdlich turned nonchalant, enjoying any discomfort he could create. "He ended up in the hospital and the hospital called us. One of my rookies took a report and filed it before I could shit-can it."

"Damnit, John!" spat Jennings.

"Nothing to worry about," Gurdlich said, then let his full mouth smack wetly. "It would be your word against his and I doubt anyone will pay attention. He lives in a doghouse, believe it or not. I heard he might get a room at the Fitzgerald, but that won't last."

Jennings ground his teeth before asking, "Any other street news we need to know about?"

He casually mopped the bloody juice from his steak with a hunk of bread, before looking up at Ahough. "Remember that guy Larry you had trouble with?"

The pastor cringed. "How could I forget? It was only by the grace of God that I was able to turn the other cheek."

Gurdlich rolled his eyes. "He's at the hospital in a coma."

"Did you . . . ?" Jennings let his question trail off as if he didn't really want to know.

"No, not any police. We never had to touch him. We think it was a big buck nigger named DeAndre. He hangs with that Alex and his bunch of loser friends."

Glancing around, Jennings raised a warning finger to him, as if the racial slur might be overheard.

Gurdlich exaggerated looking around, too, then shrugged in a feigned apology. "Sorry, didn't mean to offend your sensitive ears. We think the under-privileged, African American male slammed Larry's face into a wall. Medics aren't sure he'll recover." He belched then swiped at his mouth and tossed the soiled cloth napkin on the table. "Thank you for lunch, gentlemen. I need to get to the station."

Jennings slid to his feet. As Gurdlich stood, the businessman spoke in his ear, "Keep us posted on this doghouse fellow."

He nodded. Two steps away he turned to let the curvy waitress pass and heard Ahough's too loud whisper, "How much longer do we have to tolerate—"

"Shut up," Jennings cut him off. "It's coming together, John."

* * *

William's early sentencing hearing took most of his morning. Back at his desk, the report on Larry Parmenter snagged his attention like a rusty nail piercing the sole of his shoe. *Goddamn it, Alex, you better not be tangled up in that mess.* He picked up his desk phone to dial the medical facility.

"Nothing new to report on Mr. Parmenter," said the charge nurse. "He's in a coma. There is brain activity and he's breathing on his own."

Later, he parked his car in front of the Fitzgerald, letting the engine idle as he considered whether to broach the subject of Larry with Alex. It would be a shame to tarnish the little man's celebration of getting off the street. With a heavy sigh, he cut the engine. Inside he stopped at the window of the caged office.

"How can I help you, officer?" asked the old man who stepped to the glass.

"Really?" William sputtered, raising his hands in question. "I look that much like a cop?"

The bony shoulders shrugged. "Either a cop or a city inspector and I know most of them."

"Whatever. For the record, I'm not here on official business. I'm here to invite a friend to lunch."

The man looked at him in puzzlement then his demeanor relaxed. "Name's Gerard. I'm the manager and owner," he said, extending his hand under the security window.

"William Olson." He shook the man's thin hand noting his arthritic fingers. "My friend was supposed to move in yesterday but I don't know if he made it. His name is Alex—"

"Capstain, the little guy. Yeah, he's in 206, if you'd care to go knock on his door."

"206."

"Yes, sir, up the stairs and half-way down the hall on the right."

One hand on the loose stair rail and one foot on the first sagging stair, William looked over his shoulder at the watchful Gerard. "You know, Alex is a carpentry genius. You might think about putting him to work."

"Ah, yeah. You sure you're not a city inspector?"

William chuckled and continued his climb. Depressing as the dingy flophouse hotel was, he was pleased to see Alex making progress. The last thing the man needed was to get tangled in the mess with Larry Parmenter. He rapped his knuckles on the door marked 206.

"Who is it?"

"A friend with a free lunch if you're up to it," William called out. When the door opened on an unfamiliar face, he almost apologized. "Ah . . . hello?"

Sleepy-eyed, Alex smiled. "Don't recognize me without the facial foliage, eh?"

"I'll be damned. You clean up good, my friend. Can I buy you a lunch to celebrate your move up in the world?"

"Real nice of you. I'll get my shoes on." As he tightened the laces of the first old tennis shoe, Alex glanced up. "Any word on Larry?"

William frowned in surprise. "You know about that?"

"Yeah, Sgt. Gurdlich got on my case about it in front of the shelter night before last." He worked on the second shoe. "Asked if I was the one that put Larry in the hospital." He sat up, hands on his knees, an expectant expression on his face, as if waiting for the classic cop follow-up question.

"So, you want me to ask, so I hear it. Okay, did you do Larry any harm?"

"No, I did not hurt him in any way." He locked gazes with William. "For the record, we tangled near the shelter. He tried to hurt me, but I was able to get away. Gurdlich's trying to pin this on me, isn't he?"

William crossed his arms and leaned against the doorframe. "No, but it could be trouble, Alex. I won't lie to you."

"And I won't lie to you, either," Alex said firmly. "I did not put Larry in that condition. But I won't pretend to be bothered by him getting what he deserved, either."

Sensing there was much more than Alex was giving him now, he decided to be patient. "So, where we going for lunch? It's my treat."

Alex smiled and took his coat from the back of the open door. "How about TastyQuick?"

"Are you sure? I was thinking maybe a big, juicy burger and a shake at Burger Lust."

"Maybe when we celebrate my first paycheck and it can be my treat," said Alex, "Today, TastyQuick would be great."

"So, you're saying . . . You had an interview? You got—"

"Yup," Alex interrupted him. "I got hired. I start at the Hilte Linen and Uniform Company next Thursday. A few days of training, then I start part time. If I can handle the work, they'll take me full time."

Grinning, William extended his hand and Alex shook it vigorously. "All right, TastyQuick it is."

* * *

At the restaurant, Alex headed straight for the assistant manager who'd given him the middle-fingered farewell on his last visit.

"I'd like to introduce my good friend, Detective William Olson with the Omaha Police Department," Alex said.

The acne-riddled manager looked up, his expression flat from obvious boredom. "Nice to meet you," he said in monotone. "What can we get for you today?"

Alex decided not to let it go, especially with William beside him. "You probably don't recognize me without my beard and baby stroller."

Now wary, the manager glanced at William then looked Alex up and down. "Sure, you're the senior coffee and an egg and cheese muffin."

"That's right, my good man. But today I'll have two single burgers, a large fry and a medium Coke."

"O-o-okay." He looked at William "And for you?"

"Just a number one with a Coke, small." The detective slapped a twenty on the counter before the guy could even ask who was paying.

Alex held up a hand. "In case I can't eat all of my second burger, I'll need a to-go box to take back to my apartment." He proudly jingled his keys on a piece of copper wire twisted into a key ring.

"Of course, sir," the assistant manager said too politely and set a Styrofoam box on their tray.

Carrying the laden tray, the grinning Alex led the way to a booth. As William slid into his side, Alex didn't miss the man's crooked smile.

"Did you enjoy that?"

"The little jerk has been rude to me since the first day I walked in here," said Alex, carefully setting aside the extra box. "So, yes, I enjoyed it."

He sank his teeth into the first burger and closed his eyes to savor the greasy taste and aroma. Chewing slowly, he kept his eyes closed as his hand searched for the Coke to wash it all down. "You don't know how long I've waited for this." At William's chuckle, he opened his eyes.

"Glad I could be here to watch. I vow to never take food for granted again."

After touching drink cups as if toasting, they ate and drank in silence for a few minutes.

Alex caught William studying him before the man asked, "Do you have a fallback if the uniform place won't take you full time?"

He nodded, proud that he had considered all possibilities. "The guy that runs the used record store just north of campus says he'll give me a few hours here and there. I'll just have to save every penny, work odd jobs and keep applying for a full-time job."

Alex pulled a few french-fries from their carton. The salty flavor tasted heavenly. "God, TastyQuick's fries are the best. These sure beat the cold dumpster fries."

"Damn, Alex. You didn't—"

"The crap I've done out there . . . " Alex interrupted, tilting his head to the street beyond the storefront. He stopped eating to lean forward in sincerity. "If it wasn't for friends like you, I don't think I'd have made it. I'm not too proud to be grateful, either."

Looking a little embarrassed, William shifted and went back to eating. An awkward moment passed before he spoke again. "You know taxes are gonna take a chunk. And some companies only pay every two weeks. If your rent comes due and you don't have a paycheck yet . . . Well, you gotta keep the positives going. I want you to promise you'll ask for help."

"I don't think I'll need to, but thank you for that." He snapped his fingers. "Hey I forgot to mention that I put in an application at Mick's Tavern, too. Think I'll stop by there on my way to a shelter dinner tonight to show off my new look."

"Great idea," William encouraged him. "If I were you I'd hit every bar up here. Cleanup guys are always coming and going. Who knows? You might be able to work up to bar-back and even bartender. They make damn good money, with tips and all."

Alex realized his friend was stretching to think up alternatives to keep him off the street. He pictured himself behind the bar at Mick's. As short as he was, the image was not appealing.

Conversation lagged as they ate. On the restaurant's big-screen TV, CNN News broadcast the latest unemployment numbers. Alex shook his head as the talking heads did their best to put a positive spin on the official report.

"What world are those damn news people living in? It doesn't take a rocket scientist to see those unemployment numbers don't make any sense. Hell, the shelters are packed and new people are coming in every day."

William glanced around at other scowling customers watching the newscast. He cocked his head at Alex. "What is it that keeps you going?"

"What do you mean?"

"The world certainly hasn't done you any favors, but you keep plugging along."

Alex shrugged. "Don't have much choice in the matter. Sometimes I think about giving up, laying on a good drunk and settling into in a snow bank for the long sleep, but something always pulls me out of it. Like friends. Ya know what I mean?"

William's eyes locked with his. "Promise me you'll ask for help if you . . . well . . . I worry that if this job thing doesn't work out . . . "

"Stop with that, Will." Feeling a sense of certainty, he sat up as tall as he could. "I'm managing my expectations. It would be hard if I have to go back to the street, but—"

"Hold it. The Olson basement still has a couch with your name on it. You know that, right?"

They stared a long moment at one another before Alex slowly shook his head. "Nope, won't have it. My life is my life. I got myself into this and I'll get myself out."

William broke eye contact and set to wadding up his food wrappers. "Okay, I understand. Just know the offer's there."

"Appreciated, but my luck is turning around."

William looked back at the television and sighed heavily, "Think this economy will ever turn around?"

Alex savored his final fry before commenting. "Hilte giving me a shot is a good sign. So, maybe . . . Who knows anything for certain? I've thought a lot about the how and why I got here." A sip of Coke washed down the fry. "Just being an honorable, hard working guy used to be a ticket to the American dream." Seeing he had William's full attention, he continued, "Greed screwed it all up. There aren't enough honorable people left. Everybody, and I mean everybody, from the highest CEO to lowest welfare queen, thinks they deserve more than they've earned."

"Ain't that the truth," said William. He pulled reading glasses from a breast pocket then looked at his cell phone to clumsily thumb the keypad.

"You gotta call?" asked Alex.

"No, just looking up a definition. I had this American dream conversation with my teenage boy the other day."

"Mike, right? How old is he now?"

"Sixteen and aching for a damn car."

"His own car at sixteen? Hell, I didn't have a car 'til I was out of high school. Wait," Alex said with a slap to the tabletop and a laugh. "I'm over fifty and I don't have a car. Probably won't be buying one anytime soon, either."

"There you go," said William, still working the keypad. "He actually told me that he deserved a car. I asked him why. He said his friends have cars, so he's entitled to one. He threw out that it's part of the American dream."

Alex wagged his head in disgust. "It's that damn MTV. My wife watched that garbage. She left me for a lawyer to live like a rock star."

"Hey, it used to be MTV. Now, it's every goddamned channel. Ah, here it is on Dictionary dot com."

Alex stared from William's face to the phone. "You have a dictionary on that little thing?"

"Yeah, but I have a love-hate relationship with this thing." William showed the small screen to Alex then turned it back to read aloud, "The American dream. The ideals of freedom, equality, and opportunity traditionally held to be available to every American."

Alex quirked a half smile as he put away his glasses. "Funny, but I don't hear the words 'new car' in there anywhere."

"No, but he interpreted the word 'equality' to mean, 'my friends have one so I get one, too.'"

Alex shrugged. "Smart kid."

"Smart-assed kid is more like it. I told him to take his free car argument to the closest car dealer and see how it worked out."

"Ah, the joys of parenthood," Alex said, his smile fading as his gaze turned distant.

"What are you thinking about, my friend?"

"Oh, nothing." His hand rubbed his forehead. "Just my little Amanda, what she would have been like as a teenager."

"I'm sorry, buddy. I didn't mean to—"

"Hey, Will, I enjoy hearing about your kids. I'm a good listener."

William's eyes flashed a mischievous twinkle. "If you're done eating, I've got a little surprise for you in the trunk of my car."

Together they cleared their table and tossed the trash. Alex spotted the assistant manager as they headed for the exit and waved goodbye. The guy waved back, this time using all five fingers of his right hand.

"So, Alex, all those stories you told me about the cabinet shop. That was all true right?"

"All true, every last word."

"Follow me." William motioned him to the back of his car. "Consider this a little housewarming gift."

He opened the trunk. Next to a heavy, bulletproof vest marked with POLICE in big block letters sat an orange bucket brimming with tools. Alex's mouth dropped open.

"A lot of this came from my grandparent's farm. It's old stuff, some of it's a little rough but most are pretty serviceable tools." He handed the bucket to Alex then reached back in the trunk and pulled out a pair of old handsaws. "I put an edge on the cutting tools and I had these sharpened for you. One's a crosscut, the other's a rip. There's some hardware in the coffee can and a bottle of wood glue."

Alex searched for words. "William, I thought you were a street kid, not a farm boy—"

"My mom had a lot of issues," William interrupted. "Grandpa was a farmer in Kansas. I didn't even know I had a grandpa until Mom died. He was a tool nut, Alex. Turns out, it sorta runs in the Olson family. I kept Grandpa's really good stuff and I've got a garage full of my own tools. I think Grandpa would be pleased to see these put to good use."

"Do you have a minute to drive me by my doghouse?"

"Of course. Something over there you forgot?"

"There's an old pallet or two. I could use the wood to practice with." He palmed a block plane and pretended to stroke the edge of a board. Man, it feels good to have tools in my hands again.

Moments later William parked at the curb in front of the doghouse. Insisting William wait in the car, Alex hopped out, hammer and crowbar in hand. He attacked the pallet, then retrieved a few things from his doghouse. Over the next few minutes his small stack of boards grew at the back of the car.

William again opened his trunk. "Got something in mind already?"

Alex took a satisfying breath and nodded. "Yup, Gerard's probably going to raise the rent when I get done with the place." After the pry bar slid into the bucket, he held the hammer handle in his right hand, the fingers of his left caressing the dulled metal of the well-used and scarred head.

"How's the balance on that old hammer?" William asked.

"Not bad at all. Craftsmen built this country with tools like these. I'd put the old stuff up against the new any day."

"Gonna build a frame for the girlie pictures you took from the doghouse?" William teased.

Alex laughed, his left hand patting his chest where the magazine clippings rested under a rinsed-clean sweater. "Can't just leave the girls out in the cold. Hm, now that you mention it, I should do something nice for them."

Back in front of the Fitzgerald, William helped unload the trunk, placing the wood against the building foundation. Alex pinched moisture from the eyes he turned on the detective. Their manly handshake became a brief embrace.

William closed his trunk then hesitated. "When you get back on your feet, do you wanna come by the house on a free weekend and show me some old school cabinet-making tricks?"

Alex hefted the bucket of tools. "You think about a project and we'll build it together."

"You're on. I'll be checking back with you." With that William slid into the driver's side of his car and drove off.

It took Alex a couple of minutes of swallowing the lump in his throat before he felt ready to climb the steps to the Fitzgerald entry, the bucket in his right hand and boards tucked under his left arm. Aware of Gerard watching through his security window, Alex set down the bucket and lumber then wiggled the rickety stairway railing before setting to work. He used a chisel to cut shims from a dry edge of a board, squeezed glue into the railing's gaping joints then tapped the shims into place with his old hammer.

"Been meaning to do something about that," Gerard said, out of the office now, his hands in his pockets, peering over Alex's shoulder.

"The old wood's just dried out. Years of expanding and contracting with the weather weakened the joints."

Gerard huffed in disgust. "Drunks hanging off the rail and a couple of fights on the stairway probably didn't help, either."

Alex nodded agreement. "Let me know what else you need done and I'll put myself to good use around here."

"Plumbing?"

"Excuse me?"

"Can you do plumbing?"

"Basics like install new wax ring on a toilet, replace supply lines, valve and flapper ball. I noticed you had more than one toilet wasting water upstairs. Your sinks are easy, old-school rubber washers. Some of the old chrome p-traps look pretty corroded. You might consider replacing them with PVC. That won't cost much."

Without waiting for a go-ahead from Gerard, he jiggled the railing again and went to work on the main post.

"I'm no good if you need bigger inside-the-wall plumbing stuff," he continued as he worked. "Start messing with the pipes in an old place like this and things can get outta hand pretty fast."

Gerard waved a hand at his office. "I've got a storage room full of hardware and paint if you'd care to see it." After a few more moments of watching Alex, he shifted his feet. "Ah, things work out around here . . . Well, I might give you the key and a break on the rent."

Tapping a large shim into the base of the banister post remarkably improved in the railing's stability. Alex gripped and shook it hard but it stood solid.

"I'd like that a lot," Alex pronounced, pride swelling his chest. "I start a job next week so I'll have to work around that. A regular paying job has got to be my first priority."

Gerard stuck out his bony hand. "Well understood."

13

The quick freebie to avoid arrest went on and on. On the cop's duty belt, a ring of keys beat against the metal of his dangling flashlight. Pinned against the alley wall, the kneeling Leticia desperately concentrated on the key's rhythmic clink close to her face. She couldn't gag again. Any sign she didn't like it stirred Gurdlich's cruelty.

The big hand fisted in her hair tightened as his other hand squeezed the back of her neck. His pace quickened. She dared a glance up just as his grimace turned to a toothy, evil grin. He released her neck only to pinch her nose tight. Her struggled panic to breath resulted in happy-sounding grunts as he came. Sparkles appeared then her vision dimmed.

She dug the fingers of one hand into his rumpled uniform pants, trying to turn away for air. His pinching fingers and fist of hair twisted harder as she struggled. When she began to bite down in desperation, the thumb and forefinger pinching her nose shifted to dig a thumb into her left eye.

He crazy. He gonna kill me!

Her right hand clawed at the gravel of the alley, closing on a huge nail. With all her might, she rammed the nail into the base of his cock.

"You fucking bitch!" Gurdlich roared, releasing her.

Just as she gasped, his big hands slammed her head into the brick wall. The burst of pain and ringing in her ears made her own scream sound far away.

She stabbed again but her puny weapon sliced through empty space as she fell back on her ass in the dirty snow lining the alley.

Glancing up, certain he would kill her, she jerked her head, dodging Gurdlich's baton as it whined past her ear to send shards of brick from the alley wall to sting the back of her neck. She rolled to scramble on all fours, Gurdlich's arm wrapped his chest as he wound up for a backswing. A sickening thud dared her to look back. Wide eyed, Gurdlich dropped to his knees as his gun hand searched for his pistol. Her pimp's leather-wrapped, lead-filled sap whizzed in to deliver a second crack to the back of the sergeant's head and he crashed to the muck on the alley bricks unconscious.

The yellowish whites of her pimp's eyes shone and his nostrils flared in his agitation. He stared from the hulk of the downed cop to her.

"Get your ass outa here," he snarled, as he toed Gurdlich onto his back.

Her hand cradled the side of her aching head. She stumbled to her feet watching him yank at the man's service belt. "He was gonna kill me, Leon. I had to."

"You didn't have to do shit but take it anyway he give it to you. What you stick him for? Stupid bitch! Now, get on outta here." The swing of his arm had her scurrying backwards, almost twisting her ankle on her platforms. "And don't follow me. I got to go hide his fuckin' car. You go out the other end a' this alley."

She tried to think where she was and where she could go. *Goddamn, my head hurts.* The back of her hand swiped at the taste of him on her lips.

"I said move it!" Leon yelled, making her cringe. He stomped the cop's cell phone and portable radio to bits. "He come after you bitch, ain't nothin I can do. You hide 'til you hear different. I'm outta here. Git now."

After shoving the service weapon in his waistband and palming the car keys, Leon sprinted to the alley entrance. He hesitated, looked around the empty street then headed toward Gurdlich's nearby cruiser.

A moan from the cop startled Leticia. She looked around then scooped up her faux gold lamé purse. After a moment of dizziness, she clicked it open. Her fingers found a small, contact solution bottle filled with the bleach she used to clean the needles in her hit kit.

"See how you like it, asshole." Sneering down at the repulsive man, she placed the bottle to her crotch as though it were a penis and squeezed a stream of bleach onto Gurdlich's face. He didn't react. When the bottle was empty she returned it to her purse and scurried to the far end of the alley, her shoes clattering in the stillness.

* * *

Gurdlich slowly resurfaced to consciousness. The pain in his cracked skull barely registered beyond the agony of the liquid scalding his eyes. Rubbing at the chemical with his snow-wet coat sleeves didn't help. Each breath sucked bleach fumes into his lungs and throat. He coughed and wretched like the hooker he had been . . .

Hooker. How long ago? Shit!

His hands fumbled at his waist. No radio and no gun. Fighting panic, he focused to shut off the pain so he could problem solve. *Water and radio in my cruiser.* Carefully, he rolled to his knees. Bile rose in his throat. He swallowed it down.

Pain. Head. Eyes. Pecker. Bitch stabbed me.

His hand reached out for the building's brick wall. He tried to pull himself up.

An arm wrapped around his thick neck as a new attacker straddled him from behind. He struggled but pressure on his carotid took the fight out of him. Prayers whispered in his ear as he spun down to oblivion.

Blackness . . . .

Odors permeated his rising consciousness. Even with bleach-burned sinuses he could smell rotting flesh. Cold and naked, he hung with his arms outstretched and feet bound together. Pain overwhelmed him. His damaged lungs urged painful coughing fits. The tiniest movement of his eyeballs scraping in their scorched sockets brought agonizing awareness. Finally, working up the courage to open the blistered lids, his worst fears were realized. The world before him was a nearly blank sheet of milky white. His sorrow came out as quiet, muffled cries. Then a voice interrupted.

"I am Michael, one of the seven who stand before God."

Gurdlich turned his head to the voice. "You won't get away with this," he said hoarsely. "The whole city will be looking for me."

"Let them. God offers you a choice. Repentance for the sickness will deliver you to heaven. God's angels swarm in the ceiling above you and demons hover below. Each divine mission brings me understanding of his purpose and God grants a new vision."

A hand wiped across his face.

"Like Saul of Tarsus your sight has been taken. Will you learn as well as he?"

"Keep talking bible shit, asshole. When my boys . . . get hold of you . . . they-they'll take more than your fucking eyes."

Michael put his thumbs to the enflamed eyelids and rubbed hard. "Blasphemer!"

The pain drove freakish noises from Gurdlich's mouth.

"My loins fill with the Lord's power. Soon, yes, soon God will grant me a pleasured conversation. But now . . . oh, hear me, sinner," Michael crooned, "and repent of thy sickness so we can both bask in the glory . . . ."

Barely hearing those final words, Gurdlich mercifully welcomed the black void of unconsciousness.

* * *

Industrial washing machines loomed like giant cycloptic robots inside the steamy sprawl of the Hilte Linen and Uniform laundry facility. Sheet and towel-filled canvas carts formed a line from the machines through the tall, plastic stripped doorway of the sorting room.

Dwarfed by the machines, earplugs and eye protection in place, Alex waited for instruction. He'd passed the physical test in spite of his diminutive stature and was about to get his first hands-on experience.

"Just call me Hootus," yelled the one-armed instructor over the industrial din.

Alex made a mental note to ask the origin of his name sometime later. Today was about learning.

There was no magic to loading the upright laundry behemoths, only repeated bending and lifting in stifling heat and humidity.

"Slow down, little dude," Hootus had shouted as Alex jumped into the work with enthusiasm. "You gotta work smart to make it through the day. Eventually you'll be running three machines, so timing is everything."

Waiting for his lone machine to finish, Alex watched the sheets tumble and whirl, worried he'd be too short to retrieve the wet linens at the back of the washer. He could easily craft a wooden step stool with his new tools and pallet wood and was about to ask if he could when the machine spun down.

Hootus instructed him to open the machine's giant, porthole-like door, taking care to avoid the inevitable rush of steam. With the door open, Alex rolled the canvas bin into place and stood on his toes, reaching in to grab the tangle of wet sheets. Hootus put his arm out to stop him. His thin, whiskered face wore a huge smile.

"This is the cool part," Hootus yelled.

The trainer handed Alex the metal control box at the end of a thick cable attached to the side of the washer.

"This box not only starts the load, it empties it, too," said Hootus.

Alex studied the round, industrial buttons at the base of the box labeled "DUMP" and "ROTATE." Pointing a finger to the dump button, Alex looked at Hootus and received a nod. To his amazement, pushing the button made the rear of the machine rise, tipping the front forward as though bowing to its master. Half of the load spilled from the washer's mouth to the canvas cart like gum from a guilty student's mouth. Hootus pointed to the rotate button. Alex jabbed it. The drum spun a little, urging more of the load forward. Alex pushed the button again, this time holding it long enough to empty the drum.

"I never get tired of that," Hootus yelled, patting Alex on the back.

* * *

At the end of his second day of training, Alex stopped into the Holiday station after work. Betty still manned the counter. He proudly marched in with a smile.

"I can't thank you enough," Alex told her. "I think they like me, and I enjoy the work. My trainer's a guy named Hootus."

Betty nodded. "Hootus is a good man. He's probably trained half the people on the floor. He'll do right by you."

"Ah, Hootus is an interesting name," probed Alex.

"You're not the first to ask," said Betty, her smile contradicting the weariness on her face. "It's a nickname. He'll have to tell you the story. Let me just say it involved paint remover and his private parts. The rest you get from him."

"What are you doing here so late? Don't you usually work mornings?"

"It's Friday. I always pull a double on Friday. Payday makes the beer fly out of the cooler."

A short, pig-faced man approached the counter. "You're out of Miller Lite in the cooler. Got anymore in back?"

"Yes, sir," said Betty. "Can you give me a minute? My help went to get dinner and I've gotta watch the pumps."

When the man huffed impatiently, Alex spoke up. "Is it something I can get for you, Betty?"

She considered a moment then pulled the walk-in cooler key from under the counter and extended it to him. "I appreciate it, Alex."

Crates and boxes of beer, pop and milk filled the small cooler but for an isle to facilitate restocking of the wire shelf display from the merchandise stacked against the back wall. After taking care of the pig-face customer, Alex peered out the cooler door. "Betty, if you like, I'll restock the rest of the cooler."

From behind the counter she gave him a thumbs-up then returned her attention to the gas pumps. A few minutes later, Alex emerged with a stack of empty cardboard boxes he had broken down for the trash bin.

"You can just set those by the back door," Betty said. "Before you leave, I've got a little something for you."

Task completed, Alex waited patiently as Betty dealt with a customer cashing in a winning scratch ticket followed by a rush of customers buying gas.

"Thank you for your help, Alex." She cocked her head. "I know you're as tired as I am."

He rubbed at the weariness in his eyes. "Yeah, but it's a good tired, ya know what I mean?"

Betty handed him a white plastic sack and a five-dollar bill.

"There's no need for that. I offered. You didn't ask. Friends do that, right?" He pressed the offering back in her hands.

"I won't take no for an answer," she said, forcing him to accept. "Even better, I think we should make this a regular Friday tradition."

Looking in the sack, he saw it was filled with pastries. "Gosh, thank you."

"They're the day-olds. Would have to throw them out anyway."

He held up the money. "As long as I've got a little cash, mind if I pick up a couple things?"

"Now, you're the customer. Go get what you need." The beep of a gas pump turned her back to her work.

In the meager grocery aisle, he grabbed a jar of peanut butter and a loaf of white bread.

Betty laughed as she rang up his purchases. "You remind me of the college kids. The only thing you missed is Ramen noodles."

"Wish I'd gone to college," said Alex wistfully. "Might have been able to ride out this economy a little better if I had."

"I don't think you missed much. Student loans, maybe. Work ethic and people skills will go a lot farther than some damn piece of paper when times are tough." She squinted at him then nodded. "Yep, work ethic and people skills. Those two things you have in spades."

Though her comment sent a burst of pride through him, it also sent an embarrassed flush up his neck. Grabbing his plastic sack of food, he gave her an awkward wave and headed for home to drop off the sack then head to the St. Vincent for dinner with DeAndre and the gang.

Despite his underlying fatigue he kept to a brisk clip, barely noticing the cold en route to the shelter. His hand repeatedly reached inside his coat to pat his shirt pocket and the surprise tucked safely within. Tonight, if she was still at the shelter, he would give Nurse Liz her belated Christmas present.

Streetlights added an amber tinge to the deep blue of the winter evening. Lights shone from various windows in the high-rises and traffic poured into downtown. In the distance, parking lot attendants twirled their red-coned flashlights trying to attract customers headed to an event at the sports arena.

The security lights at the front of the St. Vincent beckoned as Alex approached. Liz's familiar computer bag-laden silhouette stepped into the street, her arm raised as she waved goodbye to someone. He picked up his pace to catch her as she crossed to the women's shelter parking lot.

"Mind if I escort a lovely young lady to her car?" Alex called, his rush and anticipation causing his breath to puff out in great clouds of white.

Liz's smile brightened the darkness. "You certainly may, young man. So how'd the training go today?"

"Quite well. My trainer seems to like me," Alex said, extending his arm toward her beat up Honda Civic. "I think it's likely they'll take me on part-time."

"That's wonderful, Alex. Does part time earn you enough to keep your room?"

"Not quite, but eating at the St. Vincent will help. I've got a few other odd jobs lined up that might be enough to make the difference. Oh, and Gerard—the manager at the Fitzgerald—says he'll discount my rent for doing maintenance work."

"I am so proud of you," Liz said, leaning against her fender.

He sighed with contentment as he joined her. "Hm, Do you remember back on Christmas when you gave me that alarm clock?"

Liz nodded.

"I had a present for you that day, but Larry messed everything up." He pulled the silver-plated locket from his pocket and let it dangle from his fingers, the St. Vincent light appropriately dancing off the metal.

"Alex, what's this? You shouldn't—"

"Didn't cost me anything," Alex interrupted. "I snagged it and a bunch of other good stuff over at the Alpine Ridge." His childlike smile dimmed. "Don't know why I waited so long to give it to you. I think I was embarrassed about the delay in my moving to the Fitzgerald."

"Stop blaming yourself for everything." She gently took the chain from his fingers to study the gift more closely. "This is incredibly thoughtful."

"It's hard to see out here, but it's a locket. I put a little something inside. You should check it out when you get—"

She pulled a penlight from her blue hospital scrubs under her coat. "I'll check it out right now, if it won't embarrass you. Here you hold the light."

As she bent forward into the narrow beam, Alex saw tears glistening in her eyes. He swallowed a lump in his throat to better focus on her fragile fingers working the clasp. The silver heart popped open. They stood a long moment as she bent to read and he held the light steady for her. He thought her fingers trembled as she carefully clicked the locked closed. His own fingers fumbled to turn off the light and hand it back to her.

Liz cleared her throat, pursed her lips then raised her gaze to meet his. "I don't know what to say. This is so beautiful."

"I know a picture is the norm for lockets, but I figured you wouldn't want to look at my old mug anyway."

Liz threw her arms around him and hugged tight. It was the first real affection he'd felt in a very long time. The warmth of it made his own eyes brim with tears. With the St. Vincent lights on his back, he hoped she wouldn't see the tears on his shadowed face.

"Liz, whenever you're having a bad day, I hope you'll look at that and know what a good thing you've done in helping me. Quite honestly, I probably would have died if you hadn't been here to help."

She reached out to grasp his hand then looked in his eyes. "You don't give yourself enough credit."

After another brief hug, she set her computer bag on the hood of her car to tuck the locket into a small zippered pocket. When she turned back to him, her expression had sobered. "Now, I have news that is a little less, ah, up-lifting. Larry Parmenter is out of the hospital. Paul, over at Harvest House called to say he saw him this morning."

Alex felt the blood drain from his head. He took a deep breath and stared into the darkness.

"Did you hear me Alex?"

"Yes-Yes, sorry. I'll be on the lookout for him." He nodded confidently and motioned her to the driver's side of her car. "Now, you should probably be on your way. Somebody might get the wrong impression. You know how these guys talk." He tilted his head to the crowd gathered outside the men's shelter.

"Let them." Liz winked at him before unlocking her door. She stood a moment studying him. "Thank you again. It means the world to me."

He stood on the sidewalk and watched her car until it turned a far corner. Reliving the past few minutes, he joined the line for dinner.

As the line inside moved forward, he found the Professor working the food delivery window. The man's eyes looked dull and disinterested behind his thick-framed glasses.

"How's it going, Professor?" Alex asked.

"As well as can be expected," the man replied in monotone.

Alex moved on, frowning down at his tray of food. At the long cafeteria tables, he joined Billy, Henry and Tom.

Settling in, he looked around. "Where's DeAndre tonight?"

"Don't know," said Tom. "Saw him at the Harvest House this morning. He said he had a line on some cash job. Didn't say what it was."

Alex looked back at the window. "So, when did the Professor come back? Did you guys see him working in the kitchen?"

"I talked to him last night," said Tom. "He came outside for a smoke before lights out. Said he'd been at some hospital. He seemed kind of out of it, but at least he's not screaming about cutting off heads."

"He told T-Tom he's a psycho," said Billy.

"That's schizoaffective, not psycho," Tom explained. "It's supposed to be something like manic depressive but worse. At least, that's what he says."

"I t-talked to some guys that said they knew him b-before went loony and got put in that hospital p-place," said Billy. "They s-said he t-taught human s-s-sexuality. I think we should c-call him D-doctor Dildo or P-professor Pussy."

Henry slapped his hand on the table. "Darn it, Billy. I told you I don't want to hear that sorta talk anymore."

"D-dildo, dildo, fuck, shit, p-pussy," Billy goaded. "Go hump a b-bible or something."

The glaring Henry stood, picking up his tray. "You won't like Hell, you know."

"P-p-pussy!" Billy taunted in a quivering falsetto.

Henry stormed off to sit by himself.

"T-Tom, I think we should kick Henry out of the gold star club," said Billy.

Tom sighed. "There is no goddamn club. How many times do I gotta tell you?"

"I hear Larry is out of the hospital," Alex offered a change of subject.

"Heard that, too," said Tom. "I also heard he's mov'n pretty slow and looks like a bulldog with his nose all smushed into his face."

"Couldn't have happened to a nicer guy," said Alex. "I think he—"

The front doors crashed open. A cluster of police rushed into the entryway. Voices fell silent throughout the dining hall. Despite the sudden arrival of cops obviously on a mission, all heads turned away and conversation automatically resumed.

"Can I have everyone's attention?" hollered an older cop with captain's bars on his collar. His voice faded into the crowd noise of men intent on ignoring the police presence.

An ear-piercing whistle over the shelter's P.A. system silenced the room. "These policemen are asking for our help," boomed the shelter's night manager's voice. "Now, shut the hell up and listen."

The captain stepped to the office window and took the mic from the manager's hand. "Earlier tonight Sgt. Harry Gurdlich went missing while on duty."

"Check with the hookers!" an anonymous voice yelled from the crowd.

Laughter and smart-assed retorts followed.

A second shrill whistle brought the room back under control. "Quiet down and let the officer speak!"

"Sgt. Gurdlich's cruiser was found abandoned in a parking lot up by Carter Lake."

"Maybe he jumped in the lake!" said a different anonymous voice, earning a round of muffled laughter.

"If anyone has information as to his whereabouts, I'm leaving contact information at the front desk."

"Some hooker probably bit his dick off," said Tom, his sarcasm and disgust obvious.

Alex leaned forward and spoke in a soft voice, "Are we sure DeAndre is working?"

"Shit," spat Tom.

14

Pastor Ahough led a prayer as Angel's Wings volunteers held hands outside the West Omaha Church of Christ. Barry Jennings was not among them.

William watched from his idling car in a distant corner of the church parking lot. When the pastor broke from the group to set off in his SUV, William tailed him. The SUV stopped in front of the City/County building adjacent to the Douglas County courthouse in downtown. William circled the block to the south. Waiting at the traffic light, he watched Ahough unload folding easels and several poster boards covered with brown craft paper.

By the time the man had carried his various items through the City/County building's revolving front doors, William had pulled into an empty meter. Minutes later he followed the pastor to the Omaha City Council chambers. People scurrying into the room indicated a meeting was about to commence. Someone held the door for the burdened Ahough who smiled his greasy smile then ambled down the sloping aisle to a front row seat. William eyed the moderately crowded room before slipping into a seat toward the back and on the side so he could observe both Ahough and the council members. After setting his phone on vibrate, he automatically pulled out pen and notepad.

The seven members of the council quickly droned through scheduled business. A bored looking television cameraman recorded the meeting for posterity. The chairman called for public input and immediately acknowledged the good pastor's raised hand. Ahough set up his easels and placed his still covered poster boards in place to the side so council, audience and cameraman could view them.

He stepped back to the microphone on the small podium that faced the council's semicircular desk. "I'm Pastor John Ahough with the West Omaha Church of Christ. I reside in the Regency Park neighborhood, 10242 Chaney Circle."

The council president welcomed him warmly. William didn't miss the exchange of confused glances among the other council members. He'd bet money the guy usually addressed them in private.

Using the practiced boom of a voice meant to project, Ahough spoke as he walked toward his easel. "I think everyone in the chambers can hear me without the microphone."

Following the appropriate chuckles, Ahough's intentions became clear as he dramatically pulled the paper from his poster boards. No longer bored, the cameraman focused on the display. Everyone in the room shifted for a better view. The pastor looked around the room with confidence as his "congregation" took in the images of dilapidated buildings, trash-heaped vacant lots and homeless men and women huddled into Angel's Wings vans. The council member stiffened as though they obviously realized they were about to endure a public shakedown.

"No one knows better than I, the hurdles faced by our homeless community," Ahough began. "For years my congregation has helped feed and counsel those who have lost their way in north downtown." His hand motioned to his evidence. "For the last two years we've offered the Angel's Wings program, providing a safe ride to shelter for those in need."

The people behind the desk displayed tight smiles as they nodded like puppets. The council president turned on his mic and assured the pastor that they were aware and appreciative.

"Much of the thanks for this good work goes to one of my most generous congregants, Barry Jennings, whom I'm sure you all know. The Jennings family has been a generous contributor to needy causes across this fine city for many years."

Ahough paused, sighed then frowned as if perplexed. He appeared to choose his words carefully. "Mr. Jennings came to me after last Sunday's service." He shook his head to emphasize his dismay. "He expressed frustration that although we've saved lives, helped thousands and done a great deal to improve the north downtown, redevelopment and jobs have not followed."

The council members leaned forward as if hanging on his every word. When the cameraman swung his lens toward them, two nodded as if to get their understanding on tape.

"In fact," Ahough continued, "Barry put it to me in a clever way. He said, 'Pastor, aren't we doing a disservice by teaching men to fish where there are no fish to catch?'" He cleared his throat for effect. "By fish, dear council members, he meant jobs. Barry believes in the north downtown with every fiber of his being. His family's business started and once thrived there."

Sweeping an arm toward his display, he quickly looked around the room as if urgency demanded everyone be as concerned as he appeared. He then faced the council members, his palms up and trembling. "Much as he'd like, he can't solve the problems in north downtown all on his own. He needs help from the city to which his family has been so generous."

William smiled, in awe of the man's dramatics. *The council didn't even see this coming.*

Ahough drew himself up as if regaining control of his emotional outburst. "Mr. Jennings and I have been moved to talk with developers. There is interest, but they sense a lack of commitment from you, the City Council. Without exception, they all say the north downtown needs tough love. Tough love, council members, as in declaring the hardest hit areas of the north downtown as blighted. This small step alone would make federal funds and favorable loan terms available to those hungry for a sign that the city cares about the less fortunate."

The cameraman moved his focus across the faces of the now openmouthed council members.

"If need be," the pastor bellowed in a carefully crafted crescendo, "you must seize the worst of the properties through eminent domain to make sure eyesores such as this—" he pointed to the bombed-out looking skeleton of the former Fairbury cannery, "—does not remain an anchor around the neck of progress."

A smattering of audience applause accompanied the council president's gavel. He called for a brief recess. As Ahough returned to his seat, the members adjourned to the anteroom off the chamber. The murmurs in the room reminded William of people at church striving to be respectful. The pastor folded his hands in his lap and stared over the council desk as if in prayer.

The wait was short. The council resumed their seats. William read the faces of polite, well-managed people. Each took their turn at countering the pastor's claims without appearing argumentative. They had an entire city to manage, after all. In the end, it was predictably agreed the worst blocks as suggested by Pastor Ahough's research should be designated as blighted but that the use of eminent domain should be used only as a last resort. The man raised his hands as if graciously acquiescing.

You sneaky sonofabitch.

William's cell phone vibrated, the screen indicating it was Chief of Detectives, Dan Armour. William exited into the hall to answer.

"Sorry to interrupt your evening, but we're calling all hands. Harry Gurdlich's patrol car was found abandoned over by Carter Lake a short time ago. The car was intact with nothing taken as far as we can tell, but no sign of Gurdlich."

"That's a little out of his district. Was that his last reported position?" asked William.

"No, his last check in was from the vicinity of 16th and Nicholas. Will, I need you to put everything on the back burner and press your contacts with the homeless community. The uniforms are getting nowhere."

"Can't imagine anyone in north downtown being too broken up about Gurdlich's disappearance. You know my thoughts on the beloved guy, Dan. It was only a matter of time before something like this happened."

"No argument there, but still, he is a fellow officer. We don't ignore our own, whether liked or not."

* * *

Working late into the night, William probed and cajoled all of his contacts. Without fail, both the homeless and those who cared for them confirmed what William already knew. Gurdlich was involved up to his eyeballs in illegal activity.

A tired-sounding Dan Armour answered his cell in the wee hours of the morning.

"You won't like what they're saying about Gurdlich," said William.

"He's a bad cop with a lot of enemies," his boss responded. "Tell me something I don't know."

"According to my guys on the street, he likes to hurt the working girls. Tortures them with rough oral sex—something he calls a 'face fuck'—in exchange for letting them operate."

"Jesus," Armour groaned.

"Come on, Dan. This isn't the first time something like this has been found. It just happens to be spotlighted on our watch. The street cops all know Gurdlich expects it as a perk of his job."

A long silence ended on Armour's heavy sigh.

"How does a guy this bad keep his job?" Will demanded, confident his boss was in his corner. "Is the force changing that much? Even if the brass turned a blind eye to that kind of behavior, back in my day we'd have dealt with a scumbag like Gurdlich privately."

"Yeah, well, those days are long gone, my friend." Despite his comparative youth, Armour's voice sounded like an old, old man's. "Lawyers wiped out that thing called common sense a long time ago. Wasn't profitable enough for them."

"And one look around you shows where that crap is taking us."

Armour perked up, as if getting his second wind. "Preaching to the choir, buddy."

"Sorry, Dan. I'll step off the soapbox for us cogs-in-the-wheel. Back to Gurdlich. I had one of my informants say he saw him hassling the hookers on 16th, north of the junkyards about an hour before he was reported missing. The guy says he didn't stick around to watch. Says Gurdlich scares the hell out of him."

"Did he know who runs that bunch of girls?"

"No, but Vice probably would."

"A lead. Good. What time is it? Shit! Will, go home, hug that beautiful family of yours, and get a few hours sleep. Is there anyone we need to hunt down overnight or in the early morning?"

William pinched his tired eyes and decided to trust his gut. "This might sound a little strange, but—in the morning, mind you—you might talk to Pastor John Ahough and Barry Jennings."

"About Gurdlich? Kind of uptown folks for him, aren't they? Will, what's going on?"

"I was checking on something for a friend and stumbled into Jennings, Gurdlich and Ahough, as in together. They met then . . . " he yawned, "had lunch together."

"You tailed 'em?"

"Yeah."

"Is this little favor for a friend something I need to know about?" Dan asked in a crisp commander's tone.

"Nah, it's minor. I can fill you in later. Still, that little meeting was damned odd. Know what I mean? My gut tells me it wouldn't hurt to poke around a little." He started his car. "For tonight, I think you just need the troops working the hooker angle. Get 'em out of their cruisers and tapping on people's shoulders. As much as most hated Gurdlich, someone's bound to dig up something."

"I'll put in the call. You go home!"

William's house was dark. The family's yellow Lab—Big Jake, named in honor of John Wayne—greeted him at the door.

"Hey there, big guy," William whispered, scratching under a floppy ear. "All quiet on the home front?"

The dog smiled and wagged. William let him out into the backyard, waited a few minutes before letting him in then listened to the somehow peaceful sound of the dog following him upstairs. After peeking in on both sleeping kids, he tiptoed into his own shadowy bedroom. Jake collapsed at the foot of bed. William stripped off his a .40 caliber Sig Sauer in its paddle holster then quietly settled it in the bedside table lockbox on his side of the bed.

As he slid between the sheets, his wife rolled over to wrap a warm arm around his chest. "You're ice cold," Susan murmured but still snuggled closer.

He maneuvered an arm under her shoulder and tilted her toward him. "Sorry, hon. Guess you'll just have to warm me up."

"Tell me you're being careful," she said sleepily against his neck.

"I'm being careful." His chuckle stopped abruptly when she tensed and pushed up to stare into his face.

129

"This isn't a joke for those of us waiting at home."

"Ah, you heard about Harry Gurdlich."

"It's all they talked about on the evening news."

He tightened his arm, settling her back onto his chest. "I'm sorry, Suz. If it helps, I'm pretty sure this isn't some random act against a cop. Regardless of what they're saying on TV, Gurdlich was no straight arrow."

"The breaking news bulletins kept blurting the same damn reports over and over, showing the officer's picture. The boys got pretty worked up. I finally had to turn it off."

William ran his fingers through her hair and savored how she softened against him. His lips trailed from her cheek to her ear. "I'm being very careful," he whispered before nipping her earlobe and moving to her lips for a long, deep taste of the woman he loved more than life itself.

Despite his fatigue and her worry, they let the moment evolve then slept deep. When morning's thin light lightened the shadows, William awoke, still partially entwined with Susan. He breathed in her scent before giving into the impulse to kiss her awake and go for round two.

As they lay together in the afterglow, a squeak and rush of water in the boys' shower brought them back to earth. William listened, imagining his sleepy-eyed son's routine. Cabinet doors thumped followed by the blare of a docked iPod playing B.B King.

"Hm, Mike must be worried about me," William murmured. "He's playing my music instead of that heavy metal crap."

"And the detective makes a brilliant observation," Susan teased as she untangled herself

He flipped the warm covers back and shivered. "Well, we both better get showers before the hot water is gone."

As William dressed, he looked at the neatness of their bed Susan had made up while he showered. He felt her watching as he slid the paddle holster into his pants. He drew the weapon to check that a round was chambered. At her flinch, he glanced up and caught the flicker of both pride and apprehension in her eyes. She stepped close to hug him one more time. Her hand stroked down the Kevlar vest under his dress shirt before she headed for her shower.

In the hall, outside the main bathroom, his youngest, eleven-year-old David, searched for socks in a laundry basket.

After reluctantly allowing his dad to hug him, the kid nodded to the bathroom door and whined, "Would you tell him to hurry up?"

William nudged open the door to the steamy enclosure and fingered down the volume on the docking station. "So you decided to go with actual music this morning," hollered William over "The Thrill is Gone".

"What?" called out his oldest from behind the shower curtain.

"Real music," said William. "Not your usual noise."

"Just playin' what was on the iPod."

William glanced at the mp3 player's screen and saw a "blues" playlist had been selected. "Save some hot water for your brother."

"Whatever."

"I love you."

After a moment's hesitation, Mike replied, "Love you, too."

Downstairs, William pocketed a duo pack of strawberry Pop Tarts and stole a swig of orange juice from the carton. Obviously hearing the fridge and the foil wrapper, Big Jake nudged his side.

"No stray morsels today, pal. Be glad you're a dog and staying home, buddy," he said, ruffling the dog's fur from head to tail. "Today is gonna suck for us cops."

The opening garage door revealed a driveway covered in three to four inches of snow. William groaned. Fluffy white flakes steadily floated straight down from a heavy, gray sky. He checked his watch then rolled the snow blower from the back of the garage.

Winter in Omaha. *Oh, well, at least I've got a house with a driveway to clear.*

He primed the two-stroke motor and pulled it to start. He had his attack plan down to a science. Cut down the middle of the driveway, then alternate sides, working his way toward the edges to avoid turning the chute.

Four rotations into his run, his eldest son appeared with the snow shovel and went to work on the front steps. *I'll be darned. I didn't even have to ask.*

Eight minutes later, William shut down and parked the snow blower back in the garage. He smiled broadly and waved goodbye to his son, who didn't return the smile, but did manage a wave.

He thumbed on the speaker to his phone and auto-dialed as he eased from the driveway.

"Morning, William," Dan Armour greeted him.

"Morning, Dan. I'm back on the street. What's the news from overnight?"

"We've been combing over Gurdlich's recent arrests, rousting parolees, talking to family and friends. We found some fairly interesting stuff in his finances but nothing to help us locate him."

"Vice got nothing from the hookers?"

"According to Vice, nobody is getting any illegal lovin' in or around north downtown." Armour's heavy sigh sounded clearly over the phone. "They say the hookers have vanished."

"Interesting. Gone to ground, huh? That tells us something right there, but I doubt the girls are on holiday. They're just working somewhere else. What about forensics on the car?"

Computer keys sounded before Armour answered. "Just sent the preliminary report to your phone. But long story short, the driver's side was the only part of the car wiped clean of prints. We figure it was dropped in the park to throw us off. No blood in or around the car and it was left in a cleared paved parking lot, so no footprints."

"The airport's across from the main park entrance. Do they have any cameras pointed that direction?"

"Their cameras aren't on the park but they are on Abbott Drive. No sign of his car from that side so whoever parked the car came in from the west. He—"

"Shit! Stupid asshole!" barked William.

"What?"

"Sorry, boss. Bastards have forgotten how to drive in the snow. Just had a pick-up do a 360 in front of me. This damn snow is going to screw up our investigation and kill me in the process."

"Sorry. Drive safe, Will. The wrecks are piling up all over town. We stopped taking accidents reports an hour ago. It will be slow going, but we're re-canvassing the neighborhood around 16th and Nicholas this morning. A lot of the businesses were closed last night."

"Hell, half the buildings are empty in that neighborhood. Probably a lot of homeless nesters hole up in them for the winter."

"Reports say, ah . . . yeah, we have already checked out a few. With the news hawks watching our every move, the chief gave us the green light to go where we need and do what's necessary. When we find an opening, we'll go in and worry about warrants after the fact."

"One thing about this snow," said William, steering around a sand-spitting snowplow. "Anyone going in or out will leave tracks."

"Good point," said Armour. "We ran our own canines through the alleys last night. They're mostly air scenters, though. Great for chasing a perp, but not so hot on tracking after the fact."

"Dan, I hate to say it, but we might want to have cadaver dogs on call."

"Already in the works. The cold will delay decomp but that won't matter to their noses."

"You know, I might have better luck than Vice if I work the hookers from a different angle. I'll head to that area. While I'm at it, I'll dig around for more known hiding places." He tapped his brakes as he approached the traffic backed up at a barely visible traffic light. "Have any luck reaching Pastor Ahough or Barry Jennings?"

"Davis and Gratz are headed to talk with Jennings right now. Your instincts regarding Gurdlich and Jennings were correct. Those interesting financial transactions involved them. What the heck did you stumble into? What were you working on?"

"I was checking out reported suspicious activity regarding the Angel's Wings vans. Went to Pastor Ahough's church to talk to him and saw the odd threesome leaving together like they were the best of friends. I decided to hang back and watch the vans and Gurdlich for a while."

Armour grunted. "Yeah, Gurdlich at church. I can see the red flags there. What was going on with the Angel's Wings?"

"At first, I figured it was just another wild tale like the mountain lion in the woods by the airport."

"Ah, yes, that one comes around a couple times a year."

"Well, this tale actually checked out. I've got two guys that were taken on unwanted rides over the river by an Angel's Wings van. There's a new shelter on the east end of the Bluffs and they're being dumped in a park nearby."

"Interesting approach to cleaning up the north downtown."

"It's also interesting that the driver in both cases was Barry Jennings."

"Hm, classy guy dirtying his hands. Another red flag."

"Dan, you know how the sports commission's been calling for a clean zone around the new ballpark?"

"Yeah."

"I was at a City Council meeting last night when you called about Gurdlich disappearing. Pastor John Ahough spoke on behalf of Jennings and persuaded the council to declare a big chunk of the north downtown as blighted. Said his church has worked hard to clean up the neighborhood and the council needed to do their part. That opens up tax incentives, eminent domain and all sorts of loopholes to benefit developers."

Cars crept through the driving snow as William waited for Dan Armour's response. He could almost hear the wheels turning in his boss' brain.

"Really," Dan drew out the word. "Think this has any bearing on Gurdlich's disappearance?"

"Nah. My gut tells me it's the hookers. Street philosophy of 'What goes around, comes around.' Jennings and Gurdlich may have been working this redevelopment scam together, but I don't see—"

"Maybe," Dan interrupted, "they had a falling out. Gurdlich threatened to expose their game, or maybe he was squeezing them for more money."

He knew his boss didn't have his street experience and was anxious to fit puzzle pieces together. He had to rely on his people skills to nudge the man to his way of thinking. "But that would be the end of Gurdlich, too. I just don't see it. My vote is still with the hookers."

"Well, either way we need to have a sit down on this, William. You may be old enough to be my father—"

"Let's say older brother," he corrected him.

"Okay, older brother, but you should have clued me in sooner on all this that may or may not fit together."

"Sorry, boss. I was waiting for the pieces to fall into place. Who knows? Maybe it is all related."

15

The 6 a.m. beep of his travel alarm coaxed Alex from sleep. His dream of the doghouse had been so vivid, he'd slept with his legs bent to accommodate the tiny space. He smiled and rolled to his back, relieved to see cracked plaster overhead rather than plywood.

On his way to the communal bathroom, he stopped at his window to check the weather. Fluffy white flakes drifted down so thick nothing could be seen over a block away. The snow stuck in narrow piles atop the telephone and power lines. From his second floor window the white and yellow dividing lines could still be seen against the darker street surface below, but not for long. Alex decided the coffee and newspaper time with Gerard would have to be cut short this morning.

He frowned at the soreness in his fingertips as he pulled on his pants. After arriving home the night before, he'd distracted himself with an hour of sanding the woodwork in the upstairs hallway. The refinishing work was slow going, but his persistent efforts were beginning to show. *Only a foot at a time, but worth it.*

He set down for his morning's necessities in the bathroom, squinting at a puddle from a leak in his toilet's water tank. *Can't let that go much longer. Got to get to it.* He closed his stall door as a huge man waddled by wearing only shit-stained briefs and dingy tube socks. A tremendous thud came from the neighboring stall as the man landed on a toilet. The porcelain throne creaked under the man's girth. Alex winced.

"Hey, you the little fucking handyman?" called the fat man between flatulent expulsions.

Hope for a quick retreat dashed, he answered, "Yes, I suppose that's me. Just trying to fix the place up a little."

"Well, knock that shit off. You make too much noise and I can't sleep."

"Sorry if my work disturbed you. I try to keep the noise to a minimum and I stop by nine o'clock."

The man's big feet shifted then the TP dispenser rattled. "I don't give a fuck. That fucking sanding last night drove me insane. I couldn't hear my TV."

"Hand sanding at the end of the hallway was louder than your television?"

"Are you calling me a liar?" The fat man shifted and the toilet seat groaned.

"No, sir, but you said you couldn't sleep. Turning off your television might help—"

"You are disturbing my peace," he shouted. "I'll file charges on you." The toilet flushed.

"Okaaay, whatever floats your boat," Alex mumbled. Hearing the man's stall door open, he planted his feet against his door. That security had him saying louder, "The owner and some of the other tenants seem happy with what I'm doing. Perhaps you should talk to Gerard about it."

"Fuck that Nazi Gerard!" The fat man slapped Alex's door making him jump and press his feet harder. "He's an asshole. You, I'll make sorry. Today I'm calling the authorities on your ass."

Alex peaked from under his stall door. Seeing no fat feet or legs, he flushed and cautiously slipped back to his room, skipping his daily shower.

After dressing, he ate a leftover pastry for breakfast, then wrapped saved aluminum foil around a peanut butter sandwich that would serve as lunch. He grabbed his coat, pocketed the sandwich and tiptoed downstairs to the office without sight or sound of the fat man.

"Any news on that missing cop?" asked Alex, through the office window.

Gerard lowered his newspaper and took a quick sip of his coffee before opening the office door for Alex to enter. "He's still missing. Paper says his car was found up by Carter Lake."

Alex poured only half a Styrofoam cup of coffee and drank it standing up. "I heard about it during dinner at the St. Vincent. It was only a matter of time before someone took the sleaze bag out."

Gerard frowned up at him. "He's a bad cop?"

Alex peered out the window to see if anyone lurked in the hallway. "Crooked as hell and mean. We all just try to stay off his radar."

Morning news blared from the little television on Gerard's desk. Gurdlich's uniformed photo hovered over the shoulders of the grim-featured talking heads. He shook his head at their fictional descriptions of the sergeant, obviously fed to them by the police public relations machine.

Alex poured a little more coffee then fidgeted beside the doorway. "Ah, Gerard, who is that really big guy in 209?"

"That's Leo, the world's largest pain in the ass. Why'd you ask?"

"I think I'm going to have to limit my upstairs work to business hours on my days off. He says my sanding disturbed him last night. He threatened to file charges."

Gerard rolled his eyes. "Jesus, that guy's a whiner. He's got a screw loose. Threatens to report everybody about everything. He caused me a lot of trouble until the city inspectors wised up."

Alex sipped his coffee. "Is he a telemarketer or something? I hear him on the phone all the time."

"He lives on that damn phone." The paper rustled as Gerard moved to an inside section. "All he does is call government agencies to report bullshit. He's running some sort of government disability scam and doesn't have to work. He plays his TV, eats and complains. The inspectors told me everyone down at city hall ignores him. Don't worry about it, Alex."

"Just the same, maybe I'll work on other projects at night and save the hallway woodwork for the daytime. Just to keep the peace, ya know."

"Sounds like a plan. Wait a minute. What do you think of this?" From under the newspaper on his desk, Gerard pulled a chunk of carpet and handed it to Alex.

"What's this?"

"You've been pestering me to re-carpet the hallways. I found a deal on this over at the Habitat for Humanity ReStore." Gerard grinned at him. "I figured it would get you off my back."

"Dang, Gerard, this will look real nice."

"It's a commercial grade and I got it for a song. You ever lay carpet before?"

"Nope. But I think Tom, a buddy of mine from the St. Vincent, has laid carpet. Those guys are always looking for cash jobs. I'll ask if you like."

"Yeah, let's do that. They're holding it for me until we're ready. We can use my truck, but we might have to enlist some more of your friends to haul it here and get it up the stairs."

"Heck, my best friend, DeAndre, is big enough to carry a whole roll by himself."

Gerard toasted that idea with his coffee cup.

"You know," Alex said with a twinkle in his eye, "maybe we could get some of the tenants in on this. They might treat this place better if they put some elbow grease into fixing the place up. Well, maybe not Leo."

"I like that. It's about time we all started taking a little more pride around here."

Alex tipped his cup to drink the last of his coffee. "I better get moving to make it to work on time. That snow's gonna slow me down."

Fat, white flakes settled into the fur around his parka's hood as Alex stopped on the Fitzgerald steps. A snowplow rumbled by on its first run, the giant front-end blade sparking on the concrete street. A block east, he crossed at the light and turned back to gaze at the Fitzgerald.

I live there. I actually live there and I'm not homeless anymore.

He canted his head, envisioning the exterior of the building after a good power washing, some new trim and paint. The bones of the building might be old, but he could have the once stately exterior of the hotel gleaming by the end of summer if all went well.

Other than a few muffled hellos and nods from fellow pedestrians, the walk to work proved uneventful. The cold crept through the soles of his shoes, though. *Living indoors is making me soft, but that's okay, too.*

Before opening the door to Hilte's employee entrance, Alex shook and swatted the snow from his coat. Due to the shift change fellow employees crowded the break area. Alex looked over the line up of break tables. He smothered the urge to hide under one of them rather than take a seat while waiting for a locker to open up.

"All yours, my man," said a small Hispanic man as he pulled his coat and lunchbox from a locker. "I hear it's snowing pretty good out there."

"Yeah, no wind though. Snow's kinda nice when it's not blowing through the seams of your coat."

"You got that right," said the man, tossing Alex the locker key.

He placed his coat and peanut butter sandwich in the locker. The brass key's safety pin allowed him to attach it to the interior of his pants pocket. That security avoided a five-dollar lost key charge. After donning safety glasses and disposable earplugs, he punched the time clock and headed for his station.

Cartloads of tablecloths waited for him. Technically he was still in training, but Hootus left him be after his first few days. The work had a meditative feel now that he had it well in hand. With the earplugs in place, he was aware of his breathing and heartbeat as he watched the fabric and soapy water tumble by the porthole windows.

A touch on his shoulder startled him from the hypnotic spin of the machines. Two uniformed police officers stood behind Hootus.

His eyes looking worried, Hootus leaned in close and shouted over the earplugs and machinery, "Alex, these officers need a minute with you."

"What about my machines?" Alex hollered back.

"They'll be all right for a minute. Follow me to the break room."

The four of them walked from the floor, every eye in the facility watching.

Away from the noise, Alex and Hootus removed their earplugs and glasses. Harold Wilson, the HR manager, entered. Seeing a few curious employees watching through the break room door's glass, Harold suggested the group of four follow him to a conference room near his office.

All remained standing, the tension palpable, expressions calculating.

"Mr. Capstain, we're looking for an acquaintance of yours," said the older officer, "a big man named DeAndre."

Alex swallowed hard as his skin prickled. "We're friends. I see him at dinner most nights but I don't know where he goes during the day."

The younger officer consulted his small notepad. "That would be at the St. Vincent Homeless Shelter, correct?"

"Yes, sir." Embarrassed, Alex glanced at Harold and Hootus before looking back at the officers. "But I'm not homeless. I've got a room—"

"We know," interrupted the older officer. "You stay at that roach-infested flop house on Cuming Street."

Alex clamped his jaw but held onto his temper. "Can I assume this is about Sgt. Gurdlich's disappearance?"

"Damn right it is," said the younger officer. "We suspect your friend is involved, maybe hurt the sergeant, possibly hurt him real bad. If you withhold information you could be charged as an accessory."

Aware that his new supervisors had taken stands beside him, Alex folded his arms across his chest. "I said I don't know where he stays other than the shelter. He had a shanty at 20th and Paul but it's too cold now. Sometimes I see him at breakfast—"

"Mr. Capstain," the older officer interrupted, "we'll haul you in right now if you don't start cooperating."

"No, you're not hearing me, officers. I don't know where he goes when he's not at breakfast or dinner. Period."

The younger officer sneered. "The shanty you mentioned? That was next to the doghouse you were living in, correct?"

An embarrassed flush crawled up his neck. He felt a gentle hand settle on his shoulder as Hootus said, "Excuse me, gentlemen, but I doubt your embarrassing Mr. Capstain will speed your investigation."

"Shut up," snapped the younger officer. "You've got ex-con written all over you. You want to be next?"

Harold smacked his hands together. "That's it, officers. Your questions were asked and answered. Your disrespect in this place of business — "

Hootus interrupted, his voice cool and low, "Paid my dues a long time ago, boys." He stepped forward a half step putting Alex slightly behind him. "Mr. Capstain, on the other hand, has never been in trouble with the law. As a private citizen that you have sworn to protect and serve, he deserves a bit more respect than I'm seeing from the two of you."

"Never in trouble? Maybe not charged, but Mr. Capstain here was suspected in the beating of one Larry Parmenter," the older officer stated flatly.

Hootus laughed but without humor. "Suspected is a long way from anything. I suspect you're a bigot who presumes anyone not in a uniform is the enemy."

Harold reached across Alex to pat a calming hand on Hootus' chest, his steely eyes on the uniformed men. "For the second and last time I will point out that Mr. Capstain has answered your questions. You will give me your badge numbers and the name of your supervisor then turn and leave through that door. Any further incursions onto this property will require a warrant."

Alex tried to plead his case between his protective supervisors. "Honestly, guys, I've told you all I know. If you really want to locate Gurdlich, ask the drug dealers and hookers on 16th Street. They had more contact with him than DeAndre did."

The older man slapped a note with their information into Harold's outstretched hand. The younger officer glared down at Alex as his partner pushed him toward the exit.

Alex dropped into a chair at the conference table and lowered his head into his hands. Hootus and Harold took the seats on either side of him.

"I can get my stuff out of my locker and be out of here as soon as you like."

"I don't think so," said Harold.

"You don't need me dragging trouble into your business." Alex looked from one to the other, his eyes burning with the rise of frustrated tears.

"Alex, half the people working here have had run-ins with the police," Harold reassured him. "I'm not prepared to pass judgment until we know more about what's going on." He nodded confidently. "According to Hootus you have been an excellent trainee. Besides, it sounded to me like those officers were on a fishing expedition."

"Alex, was what they said true?" asked Hootus, his manner several notches calmer than moments before.

"What part?"

"About the doghouse. You really lived in a doghouse and worked your way back off the street?"

"Yes, sir. I lost my house to the bank after a layoff. I'm not a drinker or a druggie, just naive."

Hootus slapped him on the shoulder and tugged until Alex looked him square in the eye. "Ready to get back to those machines?" He pointed to Alex's pocket where the safety glasses and earplugs waited.

"Yes, sir, for as long as you'll let me," Alex said, still feeling defeated and just waiting for the shoe to drop.

Hootus followed him from the conference room. Alex's shoulders sagged under the weight of the world.

"Put those assholes behind you and just get through the day," said Hootus as they walked. "Tomorrow we'll start training on the press and fold line."

Alex nodded then poked his earplugs in place.

* * *

Harold waited for Hootus to return to the conference room.

The supervisor sighed heavily as he studied the HR man. "If you let him go it'll probably kill him. He had the beginnings of the thousand-yard stare just now."

"What do you mean?"

"I saw that look in prison. On the faces of the ones who've been pushed too far. They just give up. Get this stare like they're gazing into the next world. Eventually those men just shrivel up and die."

Harold scrubbed his face. "You know that sometimes they work out and sometimes they don't. If he has a problem with violence, it wouldn't be fair to the other employees—"

"Alex?" Hootus stopped him. "That's bullshit and you know it. Those cops were just desperate. You said as much yourself. I think they were friends of that missing cop. They're just grasping at straws."

Harold shrugged. "So what do you suggest?"

"Ride it out. Alex is a good man who's been through the wringer. Chances are this will all blow over once they find the missing cop."

16

Head down and energy drained, Alex walked home after finishing the day of mind-numbing, repetitious work that meant nothing to anybody. He slid his shoes through the mushy snow, not caring how wet or cold his feet became. He didn't bother to pretend for people who greeted him along the way. *Pretend. I've been living on make-believe.* He deserved none of his recent good luck. *Yeah, because the luck has run out. The only place you truly belong is the street.*

The snow that had been bright and clean everywhere that morning now stretched before him as dirty and hopeless as he was. It only took one day for the snow and the insignificant Alex Capstain to melt back into ugliness. Waiting for a light to cross the street, he watched an Open Door Mission van pick up an anonymous collection of homeless men and women from the steps of the downtown library. The sight made him curse the part of him that refused to surrender to charity. The mission van rolled past slowly. Alex scanned the faces within and suddenly felt very alone. *They'll be warm and fed long before me.*

His brood deepened as he continued into the north downtown. The new, multi-million dollar ballpark loomed over an aging industrial landscape dotted with new businesses that had bet their futures on a stadium that would draw crowds only a few weeks a year.

At Webster Street he took a detour, trudging through the plowed snow to where his cabinet shop once stood. He envisioned the faces of the dozen or so employees that for decades had shown up for work, lunch bags in hand, happy and proud of what they produced.

Looking up at the high steel and gleaming glass, he thought back to the day his boss and friend since high school had come to him with shaking hands and worried eyes. He held a newspaper with the headline reading *North Downtown to be Transformed.*

"Hey, that's the new sports arena everybody's been gossiping about," said Alex, looking at the newspaper. "What's the problem?"

"Look at the map," said his boss.

Alex took the paper for a closer look. "That can't be right. That parking lot's right on top of this place. Has anyone talked to you about this?"

"Not a soul. This is the first I've heard."

"Well, it's gotta be a screw-up. Call the newspaper. Get them to run a correction. Everybody's gonna think we're going out of business."

There had been no correction, only a slow march to the inevitable destruction of a productive business for the sake of what the city fathers called progress. In the end, the cabinet shop owner was paid a fair price for the blighted property. Unable to find comparable space for what he could afford, the man had looked to the bank to finance the move. So began a slow downward spiral of impossible mortgage payments, higher taxes and expensive new code requirements that had been grandfathered out at their original location.

"Don't worry about me, boss. I'll find something else," Alex said the day his boss announced he was giving up, selling out and going to work for Home Depot.

That something else had never materialized. Now, years later, Alex stood in an empty, ten-dollar-a-space parking lot where the cabinet shop had once thrived. To the east the sports arena's futuristic lines already looked old next to the gleaming glass and jutting steel of the new ballpark's skyboxes, light towers and massive scoreboard.

Monuments to leisure and ego.

He turned to the west where the crumbling remnants of industry that had fueled the engines of long-ago growth sat dormant.

"This can't last," he said aloud, shaking his head.

Head and back aching, he trudged on toward the burgeoning homeless shelter that sat in the shadow of the empty splendor.

Television news vans lined 16th Street, just south of the St. Vincent, their microwave masts thrust high in the air. At the street crossing, Alex paused to watch the brightly-lit circus of cameras, stylish winter coats and hairspray. He grimaced as a blonde woman spoke into her microphone, probably repeating the same old commentary on Gurdlich-the-saint gone missing. Alex rammed his hands into his pockets in disgust.

"Ridiculous, aren't they?" said a voice behind him.

Alex spun and stepped back.

Between cars parked parallel to the curb stood a dark-haired woman with a huge, leather purse that matched a leather coat too short and form fitting for the weather.

"I'm sorry, what did you say, ma'am?"

She sighed, looking past him. "The TV circus. It's pathetic."

Uneasy, Alex glanced around. "I wouldn't know, ma'am. I'm just on my way to dinner."

Her intense dark eyes focused on him. "Are you staying at the St. Vincent?"

"No, I have a room, but I eat there sometimes." He wet his lips "Ah, are you with the police?"

"Not even close. I'm a newspaper reporter. My name is Manuela Garcia."

A ringing cell phone drew her attention. She pawed it from the bottom of her purse then silenced it.

Alex waved an awkward hand as he turned to move on. "Have a nice evening."

"I think you're right," Manuela raised her voice.

Alex paused and frowned at her. "Right about what?"

"Pastor Ahough's vans. Someone is using them to haul the drunks out of north downtown. He screwed up with you and Moon Boots."

A shiver ran down his back. He stood taller, his defenses on alert. "Moon Boots and I aren't drunks."

"See? Hence the screw up."

"How do you know me?"

"We have a common friend, Detective Olson." She too glanced around but no one stood within earshot. "He's told me about you and I've been doing a bit of nosing around."

Alex shook his head. "You know, if you're working on the missing cop, I'm afraid I can't be of much help."

"That's among the things I'm checking out. I've already heard the city's official line of bullshit. Now, I'm trying to find out the truth."

Alex gave in to his growing curiosity. "And what have you learned so far?"

"Hey, who's the reporter here?" she quipped then smiled.

He wasn't disarmed.

"Okay, I'm told Sgt. Gurdlich was no choir boy." The cell phone chirped again and she silenced it without looking. "Did you know him?"

"You got a cell phone. Do you have a tape recorder, too? Something ends up in the paper and I'm a sitting duck out here."

Her shiny dark hair swung as she shook her head. "No, I wouldn't do that without asking permission."

"Are we off the record? Is that what you reporters call it?"

"Yes, off the record, strictly for background."

Alex shifted so he could lean against the closest car looking as if the two of them merely watched the other news people. "Sgt. Gurdlich was as bad as they come."

The cell phone in her hand beeped again.

He glanced at her. "That's not some kind of recorder?"

"No, just a cheap phone." She flipped it open to show him the screen. "See? My kids are texting me to settle an argument. Stupid stuff, fighting over the TV."

That got a chuckle from him. "How many kids do you have?"

"A boy and a girl, both in junior high. Rotten age."

He folded his arms to keep his hands warm. "I have a daughter. I think she's in Florida with her mom. I wrote her a Christmas letter but I don't know where to send it."

"Really? I could help you with that. I've got all kinds of resources. Once this mess with Gurdlich is cleared up. In fact, there's a lot of things I'd like to talk to you about. You are an interesting man, Alex." She dropped the cell phone in her purse, withdrew a business card and tapped it on Alex's elbow until he took it. "You said you have a room. Olson mentioned the Fitzgerald Hotel down the street. You still there?"

"Yes, ma'am," Alex said, pocketing the card. "I'm there for the month, longer if I can hang onto my job."

She studied his face. "So, why the Fitzgerald?"

"Nothing else is close enough to the St. Vincent or the Harvest House."

"Why is that important?"

"Even full-time jobs around here barely cover rent. Eating at the shelter makes a big difference."

"I hadn't thought of it that way. William told me you once lived in a doghouse. Is that true?"

He shrugged. "Yes ma'am. Wasn't a bad place 'til this cold spell set in. Speaking of cold," he said, with a shiver, "aren't you miserable in that little coat?"

"Now that you mention it, yes, I am." She moved to the driver's door of her car. "Need a ride to the shelter?"

"No, it's not much farther, I can probably walk there just as fast."

"Can I talk to you later about homelessness and getting back on your feet?"

He scuffed his wet sneakers in the snow as he considered his returned sense of hopelessness contrasting her positive take on his recent accomplishments. He stood up and looked her straight in the eye. "Yes, ma'am, you can. But you'll learn I'm not that unusual. There's a lot of folks out here just like me. My friend DeAndre calls us American dreamers."

Alex saw something dark cross Manuela's face. *Recognition? Fear?*

"Ah, is your friend a very tall man?"

"Yeah, big as a house. Strong, too."

Her expression turned shuttered, her eyes harder. "Alex, who do you think wanted to do harm to Sgt. Gurdlich?"

He grunted. "The question is, who didn't." Another shiver coursed over him. He slapped his hands and arms against the cold. "DeAndre likes to fly under the radar, like me. He wouldn't hurt a cop. Gurdlich, on the other hand, was mixed up with the drug dealers and hookers. If I had to pick who wanted to harm him, I'd say the hookers. Rumor is he likes to hurt them."

"If you hear anything regarding Sgt. Gurdlich, would you call me?"

"Probably not." She frowned, but he cocked his head. "I didn't pay my cell phone bill this month."

"Noted," said Manuela, her dark eyes flashing in the streetlight as she brushed a strand of that long, black hair behind an ear. "Can I catch up with you in a week or two? I want to talk more about this American dreamer business."

When she smiled, Alex thought it was brighter than the television lights across the street.

She assumed a cajoling expression. "I know a cigar shop where we could talk. It would be my treat."

"You *have* been talking to William," Alex responded, returning the smile. "Forgive my flirtation, but smoking a cigar with you would be the highlight of my decade."

Her laugh tweaked a joyous spark in his chest. He was grinning broadly when she asked, "So, it's a date then?"

"Yes, ma'am."

With that, Alex waved goodbye and continued on to the St. Vincent. Her questions nagged at him. *Why the interest in the Fitzgerald? Does she know something about DeAndre?*

Dinner was already being served as Alex entered the shelter. Anticipation and a new energy made him eager for news from the street as he joined his friends who were nearly finished with their trays.

"Any word on old Turdlick?" he asked.

Tom waved a crust of bread at him. "The cops are looking for DeAndre. I heard they even put the screws to Larry and his bunch."

"They put the screws to me, too," said Alex. "Showed up at my work."

"You gonna be okay?" Tom asked with a concerned frown.

"Don't know. Even the HR guy backed me, but he didn't look too happy in the end. My trainer tried to smooth it over. I'll just have to keep my head low 'til this Gurdlich thing blows over."

"The hookers killed Gurdlich," announced Billy. "I heard one of them b-bit off his dick and ate it. I don't know why the c-cops are looking for D-DeAndre."

Henry reared back. "Bit off . . . That's a nice mental image to go with our meal!"

"Children, don't start," warned Tom.

His appetite departing, Alex sat in silence, poking at his food and worrying about DeAndre.

A heavy ceramic coffee cup slammed down on the table. The startled Alex jumped in his seat. He looked up to see a malevolent smile on the face of the orange-jump-suited work-release inmate who'd taunted him weeks before.

Alex snapped. "Fuck you and your fucking coffee!"

The sneering man glared back. "Least I ain't beggin' for food like a fuckin' dog." He glanced up as his uniformed supervisor moved in their direction. When the inmate pushed off, the man turned his attention elsewhere.

Tom lowered his voice, his eyes round. "Last thing you need, Little Man, is to get banned."

Anxiety and uncertainty swirled in Alex's confused brain. "Sorry, guys. I'm just a goddamned old fool, thinking I belonged any place but the street."

"What are you talking about?" Henry demanded. "Ask yourself that question when you're sleeping alone in a warm bed tonight. Wherever DeAndre is, I'm sure he ain't gonna be warm."

Alex's insides knotted with worry. "Shit! I know, guys. I'm sorry. Guess I didn't realize how hard all these changes would be. The street just won't let go. Does anybody know DeAndre's hidey-hole? I could take him some food on the way home."

"I've seen him come out of that busted up cannery over by glass alley," said Tom. "Can't imagine he'd spend much time there, though. It's a goddamned rat's nest of crack heads and creeps."

Alex put his inmate-delivered coffee cup on his tray then stepped out of the cafeteria table's bench seat. "You guys want any of this food? I'm heading to the Fitzgerald."

All shook their heads.

"If Nurse Liz is around tomorrow you might ask her about DeAndre . . . Hell, what am I saying? I'm probably going to lose my job tomorrow, so I'll be here and can ask her myself."

"Hey! I hear Larry's looking for you. We'd be happy to walk you home," said Tom.

Alex shrugged indifferently. "Nah, I'll be fine. He's probably pimping at the truck stops this time of night. Plus, you don't want to miss the line for sleeping mats."

Alex stepped out the front door and into a cold night clouded with worry and cigarette smoke from the after dinner crowd. An Angel's Wings driver had parked at the curb. A wizened old man exited the open side door. As the man teetered past, the driver swung the door closed then turned to face Alex.

"Fancy meeting you here," said Barry Jennings.

Alex blanched. "You leave me alone. There's lots of witnesses."

"I wouldn't dream of *bothering* you here. You caused me no end of trouble jumping out of the van and talking to the cops."

"The hospital called the cops, not me. I'm just trying to stay off the street. I've got a job now and I don't need trouble."

Looking around at those watching, Barry's smile turned to faked laughter. He moved in close as if telling a secret to a friend. "This toilet bowl area will soon be flushed," he whispered then waved Alex a goodbye and climbed into the driver's side of the van.

* * *

In the milky light and shadow of Gurdlich's vision, a glimmer of water dripped somewhere nearby. His mind perceived each drop growing heavy and round, trembling until it fell, like overripe fruit to shatter on the floor below.

He faded in and out of an endless cycle of escape into darkness before waking to gasp for breath while trying to stand to ease the shards of pain streaking down his arms suspended from the hooks. The distorted position of his heavy body squeezed his chest, constricting his lungs. Between the agony in his arms and the pressure in his chest, he could only stand for short periods without losing consciousness. He tried a deeper breath so he could stay awake and figure out what was going on. The odor of his own watery shit dribbling down his legs gagged him.

Am I dying? Dying people always shit themselves. Stand up, you lazy bastard. The cavalry will be here soon. You're a cop. Missing. They'll hunt for you . . .

He caught the squeak of a hinge and creak of wooden steps.

"Who's there?"

"If it's you, guys . . . God, get me out of here. I'm fucking blind. I think I shit myself. This sick fucker's been cutting on me."

146

The footsteps quickened, as did Gurdlich's heart.

"You shouldn't a' hurt that girl," said an oddly familiar voice.

"I-I'm a police officer. Being tortured. Help me. I'm dying. P-Please," begged Gurdlich.

"Told you Michael would bring God's wrath," said the voice. "You a sick man."

Gurdlich's mind raced to put a face with the voice. He'd heard this Michael thing . . . "DeAndre Easton, it's you isn't it?"

"Yessir. I told you not to mess with Michael. He protects people, you know. He's an avenging angel. Talks to God an' everything. He saw your boy thump me on the head an' he saw you hurt that little girl in the alley . . . What's wrong with you, Sergeant? Why you got to hurt people?"

A tremendous shiver racked his naked body. "Yeah, yeah," he whined. "I must be sick, like you said. I-I don't know why I do it. But-But if you'll let me go, I promise to get help. Whatever Michael wants, I—"

"You must repent," interrupted the much more powerful voice of his torturer.

Something metallic clicked. Straining to hear and locate the mad man, he realized the dripping had ceased. A blast of icy water punished his naked body. He howled like a lap dog left outside to freeze in the snow.

"I can't send you to heaven smelling like that," said Michael.

Gurdlich fell silent. Hanging limp again, his mind drifted. *I won't stand up next time, I'll just slip away. He won't hurt me anymore.*

* * *

Tossing in bed, Alex chafed at the squeak of his old mattress springs.

What the hell did that Jennings asshole mean by flushing the neighborhood?

The tick-tick of his travel alarm lulled him to sleep. In what seemed only minutes later, his eyes flashed open to see the clock's second hand mark the last tick before the alarm blared.

Watchful for the whiney fat man, he grabbed the world's fastest shower, scurried back to his room and dressed for work.

Maybe today will be better. You were just overtired last night.

The brisk aroma of coffee further brightened his outlook as he descended the stairs to meet Gerard in the office.

"Good morning, my man," Alex called through the office window.

Gerard looked up, his eyes tired and bloodshot. "Good morning." The man stood slowly and opened the door.

Alex plucked a Styrofoam cup from a stack next to the coffeemaker and poured from the glass pot. Craning to see the newspaper on the desk, he asked, "Any news on Gurdlich?"

"What?"

"Sgt. Gurdlich, the missing cop. Have they found him yet?"

"Oh, that. No, nothing yet," said Gerard. "They're talking about bringing in cadaver dogs . . . Alex, we need to talk. Did you see the posted notice on your way in last night?"

Feeling doom settle on his shoulders, Alex dropped into the chair beside the desk. "No. Why? What's wrong, Gerard? You look like hell. Are you feeling all right?"

"No, I'm not at all right. The city power brokers have a boot on my neck."

"What? What's going on? You're scaring me."

"Alex, after you left yesterday, I had a line of inspectors at the front door. The first was from the EPA. He said his office received a complaint about unlicensed contractors remodeling the building."

"Leo, right?"

"That's what I thought at first."

"You said the city didn't pay attention—"

"EPA is federal. Apparently there's a law called the Toxic Substances Control Act." He held the notice up for Alex to see. "I can be fined $3700 for each violation."

"And working on your own property is a violation?"

"Yes, some things can be. Unless you're licensed by the EPA. It started with the lead paint thing and asbestos, anything hazardous . . . Shit!" Gerard's face flushed red. "To become licensed, you have to take a $300, government-approved class."

"$300? What kind of shakedown is that? What's hazardous here? I wear a mask when I'm sanding. What the hell more—"

"Oh, it gets better," Gerard interrupted, wrinkling the EPA notice in his fist. "Shakedown is right. A new city inspector came in after the federal man left. He claims I have those asbestos problems and my plumbing and electrical isn't up to code. Lying bastards, all of 'em! None of this is legit, but I'll have to take them to court to prove it. That means hiring an attorney and court costs. Like I've got that kind of money!"

Just like the cabinet shop. "What are you, ah, we gonna do?"

"Nothing I can do. I have to close down or go broke paying fines."

Alex fought rising tears. "So they'd put people on the street rather than letting them live in an old building they're fixing up?"

The hotel owner wagged his head and slumped. "They don't give two shits about that. Legalized extortion is what this is. I concluded it ain't Leo. Somebody's out to steal my property. Take a listen to this interesting little coincidence."

Gerard pressed the play button on the office answering machine, zipping through the messages until he found the one he wanted.

"Hello? Mr. Gerard Roundtree? Uh, this is Mr. Strong. I represent the Jennings Development Corporation. We'd like to talk about your property on Cuming Street. As you know, the area has been designated by the City of Omaha as blighted. Please call at your earliest convenience. The window of opportunity to get top dollar for your property is a small one . . . "

Gerard mashed the stop button, knocking the answering machine to the floor.

17

"That fucking Jennings and Pastor A-Hole," Alex mumbled. "They've been planning this. I should have stayed in the damn doghouse. What the hell was I thinking?"

He yanked open the office door, slamming it into the wall. Screaming with rage he kicked at the wood railing he'd fixed in his first days at the hotel. It creaked but didn't break. Growling, he grabbed the banister, wrestling it back and forth until anger turned to frustration and he stormed out to the street.

He halted to read the yellow paper glued to the front of the building. It was a painful reminder of his first eviction. This time he had three days to evacuate the premises.

The American dream is dead. Killed by assholes like Jennings and Ahough.

Lost in depression, paying little attention on his walk to work, he slipped on a patch of ice and went down hard. Daggers shot up his spine. A back spasm took his breath. Sitting up, he tried to relax the pain away until he realized people were coming to his aid. Embarrassed, he waved them away, got to his feet and marched on.

The walk to Hilte Linens stretched his strained muscles, until only a twinge remained. The woman who'd given him the bus schedule on his first walk to work, waved hello from across the street. Alex waived back just as a police cruiser jumped the curb in front of him, barely missing his feet. Two officers emerged with guns drawn.

"On the ground, now!" one of them shouted.

Mind blank with shock, Alex dropped to his knees then laid down, salt and muddy snowmelt staining his pants and new coat. A knee landed painfully between his shoulder blades. Gloved hands yanked his arms back for the hurried slap of cold metal cuffs. The knee left his back then one officer gripped his coat collar and the other the cuffs to painfully yank him back to his feet. With his arms jacked up behind, they slammed his torso onto the cruiser's muddied hood.

"What the hell, guys?" Alex whined.

One officer's broad gloved hand pressed his head to the warm car hood while the other frisked his torso and fingered his pockets.

Close to his ear, the frisker growled, "You got any needles or drugs, knives or guns we need to know about?"

Alex inhaled the cop's Old Spice aftershave and coffee-tainted breath. "Just a small pocketknife in the right front."

The knife, his pocket change and his wallet landed on the hood.

"What the hell is this about? I'm on my way to work and can't be late."

"We had a report of a suspicious character. You match the description. Stay on that hood while we run your information."

Both officers crawled back into their cruiser. They hadn't bothered to take his I.D. Minutes ticked by. The officers did nothing but talk, smile and sip coffee. Alex turned his head toward the bus stop as the bus pulled up. He saw the woman who'd given him the bus schedule climb aboard. Her face reappeared in a nearside window. Frowning and concerned, she shook her head as the lumbering vehicle pulled away. His back cramped again due to the combination of his position, the cold and his wet clothes. He guessed twenty minutes passed before the officers emerged to remove the cuffs.

"Your information checks out."

"Can I put my pocket stuff back in my pants?"

"Yeah. Hope we didn't make you too late for work," said one officer as he adjusted his stocking cap over his ears. The Old Spice guy grunted a laugh.

As Alex slid his wallet back in place, that one moved in close, to whisper in his ear, "You don't tell us where your big nigger friend is and tomorrow your information may not check out. In fact, we may even find illegal drugs on your person."

Alex stiffened, fighting the sense of desperation clamping his chest. "DeAndre didn't do anything and I don't know where he is." He turned to look up at the two men. "Last I saw him was at the St. Vincent a couple of days ago. I don't know where he went from there."

"Very well, sir," said Old Spice, placing his hand on Alex's back as though they were buddies. "Have a nice day and be careful out there."

As the cruiser backed, Alex stumbled away to avoid a crushed foot. The officer riding shotgun gave him a one-fingered salute at they pulled into traffic. Panicked, late for work and filthy, he considered not going at all, then thought better of it. He set off at a near run. His back protested all the way to the cleaners, as his jumbled thoughts tried to make sense of the incident.

He was just ramming his time card into the machine, when Hootus found him. "What the heck happened to you?"

"I know. I'm fifteen minutes late. I slipped on the ice walking to work."

"Oh, man! You all right? I fell down last winter and cracked my butt. Cracked it all the way up the middle."

Alex forced a smile. "I'm okay. Just wet and dirty."

"Seriously though," Hootus spoke in a lowered voice and looked around, "you know trainees can't be late."

"It's been a bad morning and it won't happen again."

"Well, your time card talks, but I won't. No worries . . . for now. One more time and I won't have any choice but to let you go. Rules are rules."

As usual, carts with soiled linens lined up all the way back to the sorting room. Today they contained hotel sheets. Alex hurried to make up for lost time. His back protested as he loaded his first machine. By the third, the daggers returned, stabbing with each bend into the canvas cart. Between loads, he pressed his back against the washers, their warmth and vibration dulling the daggers. In the bathroom at lunch time, he saw how pale his face had become.

Hootus eyed him as Alex entered the break room. "You look like crap. Hey, man, are you sure you're okay? I mean, if you're sick . . . "

"I'll get through the day, come hell or high water," Alex muttered, his eyes cast to the floor.

Harold entered and motioned for Hootus to follow him.

"I'll be back, Alex. Harold's got a crabby look. Better see what's up."

Alex lowered himself to a chair and waited for the inevitable.

* * *

"Hootus, we gotta let him go," Harold said as they entered his office.

"Boss, he was only five or so minutes late. Said he fell on the ice."

"I know you like the guy, but it's not just about being late. He looks like he slept in the gutter or just got off a binge. I watched him and he's not keeping up on the floor."

Hootus sighed and ran a hand through his hair. "Yeah, a couple of people complained to me."

"His fellow employees aside, corporate got a call from the police." His raised hand stopped Hootus before he could comment. "Hootus, you know shit runs down hill. We just—"

"Wait," Hootus interrupted. "Can I at least tell him we'll take him back once he gets squared away?"

Harold considered a moment. "Okay, that's fine. But this police matter needs to be cleared up. I'll put it on your shoulders to be positive he's free of baggage and ready to work."

* * *

Alex knew the second he saw Hootus' face.

"Alex, come on back to my office."

The minute the door closed at his back, Alex blurted, "You don't have to say it, Hootus. I'll go. Sorry to let you down."

"You didn't let me down. This is coming from higher up." His supervisor's eyes got a distant look as he murmured, "I know the street can be a bitch to shake."

"I thought getting a room and a job would solve everything." Alex fought not to whine. A man has to retain some dignity, but damn this hurts. He shook his head. "It just seems to be making things worse—"

"Harold thinks you're drinking," Hootus interrupted him. "I don't. You look more like you feel real hurt, physical hurtin'. Did something happen?" His eyes narrowed. "Did the cops rough you up?"

Alex knew this man would understand. "They made me lay down in the street, cuffed me and made sure I was late for work. They asked questions I can't answer."

151

"That sucks. Harold says once you get squared away we can try again. Where should we send your paycheck?"

The Fitzgerald eviction notice flashed through his mind. "The St. Vincent, in care of Liz Caldwell would be the safest." He shifted to ease his back. "So, that's it? Do you want me to finish out the shift?"

"No, I'll handle your machines. You need to get some rest." Hootus squeezed his shoulder. "I'll walk you out."

Tears threatened as his throat tightened. Deep breaths held back the waterworks until after he awkwardly shook Hootus's good hand and hit the street. Alone in the cold, he blubbered like a baby. He glanced at the Holiday station, thinking he should say goodbye to Betty and apologize for letting her down, as well. Embarrassment made him walk on.

Heading north with no particular destination in mind, he struggled to put one foot in front of the other. He half hoped the cops would hassle him so he could take a swing and get tossed in jail. *At least there I'd have a bed and three meals a day.*

At Cuming Street he looked west to the Fitzgerald and north to Mick's Tavern. He chose north. The Fitzgerald was a tangle of worry. Mick's, on the other hand, was dark, warm and welcoming. Those thoughts lifted his spirits a fraction.

After the buzzer welcomed him inside, Alex approached the bar with a smile for the bartender. "How's that new grand baby?"

The man flipped out his cell phone and slid his finger on the screen's surface until he found a picture. "Ain't that the prettiest little Christmas present ever?" he said. After Alex's silent nod, he asked, "What'll it be today, my friend? Been a while since I've seen you. You been busy?" A frown flickered as his gaze took in Alex's appearance. "Everything all right?"

"I'll take a bottle of Night Train," Alex said, flatly. "And everything's going as well as can be expected."

The barman dutifully pulled a bottle from the upright cooler then traded it for the required amount of money. "You're more of a Colt .45 man, as I remember."

"Just a little switch-up to celebrate," Alex forced out. "Nothing to worry about."

At his usual spot and careful of his sore back, Alex removed his heavy parka and spread it over the back of his chair. Mud and salt caked in the fur around his hood. He brushed at it, disappointed that he'd soiled William's gift.

Easing down into the seat, he cracked the aluminum seal on the bottle of Night Train and tried to close the door on all his worries. *Yeah, I'll take a short vacation of forgetfulness. I've certainly earned it. Fourteen months of work, saving, dreaming, all wiped out in a matter of days.*

A gulp coaxed a hiccup. The sickly-sweet wine felt warm going down. Another sip tamed the ensuing hiccups. A healthy swig got the process of forgetting underway.

The bar's heater came on overhead like a warm summer breeze. Perfectly timed with the warm rush of the alcohol, it melted the worry from his shoulders and eased the pain in his back. *A brief vacation.*

By the time the bottle was half gone, the world turned fluid and everyone looked friendly. Too buzzed to finish the Night Train before his nap, he concentrated on screwing the lid back on the bottle before tucking it into his crotch for safekeeping. No one was stealing this one as they had the bottle of beer on his last visit.

Hours later, raucous laughter woke him. Through the bar's dingy windows Alex saw daylight still hanging in there. Unscrewing the cap from the bottle, he brought it to his lips. The now-warm wine tasted like shit, but he kept drinking, reveling in the blackness of his mood. Soon, the comforting alcoholic fog returned though tainted by a nagging sense of guilt he staunchly ignored.

Through blurred eyes, Alex looked around the room. Tired-looking construction workers had taken over, warming up after hours in the frigid steel and concrete of the new baseball stadium.

Working their asses off for what? Nothing but bullshit. Fuckers destroyed my cabinet shop job for one that one that won't last. Their work will be done in six months, then what will they have?

The bar's mop man, Julio, walked past, donning his coat to go home.

"Adios!" Julio said, waving goodbye to the bartender.

Adios my ass, you fucking wetback. I shoulda had your job. Woulda been a hell of a lot easier than washing those fucking cum-stained hotel sheets at Hilte.

Nature urgently called. Using the table for leverage, he pushed from his chair then stumbled to the bathroom. His fingers fumbled with his zipper. Unable to maintain control, some piss stained his pants before he could point himself into the urinal. A shimmer of dizziness led to the urge to vomit. Pee dribbled onto his hands and pants in his rush from the urinal to a stall. He planted his hands on the sides of the stall and spewed into the toilet below him. The smell of the foul, purplish-black liquid gushing from his guts wafted back. He vomited more. Stomach empty and head starting to throb, he managed to get his zipper up. Carefully walking to the sink, he washed his pee-smelling hands before cupping water and rinsing his mouth.

As his vision cleared fractionally, he looked over the sink. Even the faucets and soap dispenser had been scrubbed. The floor below gleamed, even in the corners and around the stall supports. *Nice work, Julio. You deserve the job more than I do.*

Turning, he caught his reflection in the mirror. His muddled mind blanked for a moment at the stranger staring back at him. He leaned forward to get eye to eye. *Being the upstanding citizen, Alex Crapstain hasn't worked out too well, has it, fella? Who gives a fuck, anyway? You can't do anything right.*

Back out in the bar room, he downed the warm syrup in the bottom of his first bottle then walked to the bar to buy more.

"What the heck. Make it two bottles. Homecoming awaits," he said, smiling bitterly as he awkwardly clawed his wallet from his pocket.

The afternoon bartender looked him up and down. "Homecoming?"

"Yessssir," he slurred. "I'm retiring from the so-ci-etal grind and heading home tonight."

"Alright then," said the bartender, handing over the bottles, each in a tall paper sack.

Alex slapped down a few dollars. "Keep the change, my good man. All the times I've come in here, it's high time I left a tip."

The bartender frowned and murmured an uncertain, "Thanks."

Alex returned to his dark corner to continue drinking himself into oblivion. He watched the bar's owner, a small man who dressed like a cowboy, slide behind the bar to collect the morning's receipts.

The guy elbowed the bartender and flicked a hand at Alex. "He been there all day?"

"Just since late morning." Alex saw the cowboy start to say something, but the bartender held up a hand. "He's been buying, not freeloading."

The scowling owner rounded the bar and headed toward him. "Hey, partner," he called out in a raised voice. "Time to mosey on home."

Alex cocked his head. "Go fuck yourself, cowboy. And the h-horse you rode in-n-n on."

Just behind the owner, the bartender spoke up, "He's harmless, boss. That's the first noise he's made all day. I'll call him a cab."

"No need for that, my good man," said Alex. "I'll m-mosey off under my own p-power." He pushed up, again using the table for leverage and balance. "Outta my way, partner."

When both owner and bartender stepped back, he yanked his coat from the chair. The room tilted so he spread his legs. One arm slipped easily into its sleeve, but the second arm couldn't find its home. The owner stepped forward to assist him with the coat, while the bartender tucked his bottles into his pockets. A man on each arm, they unceremoniously escorted him to the front door.

Once outside, the owner ordered the bartender back to work. Alone with Alex, he shoved him into a snowdrift. "Get your wino ass off my sidewalk, partner," he said. "And don't bother coming around anymore. Your kind don't loiter on my property. You are banned and barred. Got that?"

As the door closed behind the man, Alex rolled over and sat up. He reached out for the cold metal of the nearby streetlight and pulled his way to his feet. Leaning a shoulder there, he checked that the bottles were still intact and pushed off in the direction of home.

By the time he passed the St. Vincent, the cold air had cleared his head enough that he identified the drug dealers hanging around. He offered a middle finger salute. They failed to notice.

Not even worthy of their attention. Crapstain, you really have hit rock bottom. Time to celebrate some more.

He walked and drank. By the end of his second bottle, he reached his lot. He cracked the seal on his third and stared at his waiting doghouse. Leaning on a light pole for balance, he tilted his head back for a long chug. Puffy white flakes floated down from the darkening sky like angels coming to welcome him home.

A tire hidden in the snow tripped him a few feet in front of his house. He landed on all fours. His bottle tumbled from his hand. He frowned at the purple spilling into the snow but couldn't figure out what it was. Numb to the cold, he crawled to his front door and poked his head inside. *The old place picked up a musky smell while I was out.*

Something growled. He shook his head trying to listen harder. Its winter slumber disturbed, a raccoon charged him. Alex jerked backwards, the animal biting and clawing his face as he screamed against its fur. One roll in the snow convinced the coon to give up. Its fat rear end bobbing up and down, it ran into the trees at the side of the lot. Alex patted his chest as if that would slow his racing heart. Turning onto his hands and knees, he crawled back inside not bothering to slide the door shut behind him. He curled into his familiar fetal position. Slowing his churning mind, he focused on Amanda and living an unending dream with his beautiful girl.

* * *

The Fitzgerald buzzed with activity. Hotel residents filled the sidewalk, stuffing their belongings into whatever conveyance they could find. William circled the block so he could park across the street then waited for a break in traffic to cross. Several of the Fitzgerald people eyed him warily as he read the yellow eviction notice then climbed the steps. Inside he found a painfully-fat man with a pony tail and stretch pants two sizes too small arguing with Gerard through the office window.

"This is unacceptable," yelled the fat man. "I'm not moving. You're the one who will have to make other arrangements."

"Are you retarded or stupid or both?" said Gerard. "It's your beloved government agencies that are forcing you out, not me."

The man bared his teeth as his face reddened. "You can't talk to me like that. I'll sue for-for slander." His jowls jiggled as he whipped is head to William. He pointed. "This man is a witness."

William smelled ass and sour body odor. He held up his hands and backed away. "Hey, I didn't hear a thing."

"Listen, Leo," Gerard said, leaning up to the window, "I'll give you the inside scoop."

Leo leaned forward as if drawn by the hint of conspiracy.

"Don't tell anybody else, but I've got the private number for the Governor. You need to call and tell him what's going on."

The fat man nodded hungrily. Gerard ran a finger down his own empty palm. "Oh, there it is," he said with a wink to William. "It's 1-800-eat-shit."

Leo huffed and turned for the stairs in the wake of Gerard's laughter.

William replaced him in front of the window. "What the heck's going on? What's with the notice out front?"

The humor of the moment vanished as Gerard's eyes narrowed. "It's a shakedown, pure and simple," he stated flatly. "I had a string of inspectors come through yesterday. They found violations for shit that doesn't even exist. Bastards told me I had three days to get everyone out or they'd start levying fines."

William's brow furrowed. He looked at the floor then back up at Gerard. "Did you watch the news last night?"

"You mean that story about the neighborhood's being blighted? Yeah, quite a coincidence, ain't it? People contacted me before that aired."

"Let me guess. Developers wanting to do you a favor by taking this troublesome property off your hands."

"Just one, so far. I know a hustle when I see one." Gerard blew out a long, tired breath. "I'll have to comply with the city order and vacate, but sell to those sharks? No. Fucking. Way. I'll wait and see what happens." He frowned. "If you're here to see Alex, he was off to work hours ago."

"Actually, I'm here to ask a favor."

"Don't tell me. You want to buy my hotel."

"No, I've got enough headaches." He quirked a smile and glanced at a bulletin board next to the mailboxes. "Hm, I see numbers for Gypsy Cabs and take-out food."

"Yeah, need a ride to lunch?"

He continued studying the board. "No, I'm good. It's the other numbers I'm interested in. You know, the ones for personal services not usually on the menu."

"Is this a professional interest?"

He looked back at the speculating man. "Yes, but I'm not out to make a vice bust. It's about the missing sergeant. Word is he tangled with the girls on 16th, but no one can find them. I was hoping to come at it from a different angle."

"Well," Gerard said, rubbing his jaw, "you know I would never allow that sort of activity in my hotel, but if a trusted tenant were in need of company, I know of a few women who supplement their income in creative ways."

"A trusted tenant would appreciate the help," said William. He rapped his knuckles on the window shelf. "And you have my word that I won't let it come back on you."

Gerard flipped through the dog-eared Rolodex on his desk and wrote down a few numbers. He glanced up the stairs and around the empty hallway before slipping the paper under the window. "I want you to know, none of these girls are street walkers. 16th Street is pretty much a last resort for a working girl."

"I figured as much," said William. "It's a long shot. I was hoping to find somebody who knows somebody. You know what I mean?"

"Working the back door," Gerard commented with a wink.

"Yeah, so to speak. So, how is Alex taking the news of eviction?"

"Not very well. He left in a huff. I'm worried about him."

"When he comes home, could you ask him to call me?" William said, sliding his card under the window. "Tell him I have a basement couch, dinner and a good cigar with his name on it. That might cheer him up."

"Will do."

Gerard's phone rang and William waved goodbye.

18

Of the three phone numbers Gerard provided William, only one belonged to a landline with an actual address. The old craftsman-style house had fallen into disrepair. Discarded car parts and plastic toys poked through the snow on a front lawn. Three ice-packed, off-kilter steps led from the sidewalk up to the yard.

William chose to step up through the snow rather than risk the icy steps. He found no doorbell or knocker, only a boarded-up storm door on the screened-in front porch. William stepped inside, startled by a small boy in threadbare Spiderman pajamas, playing with plastic dinosaurs in spite of the freezing cold.

The boy frowned up at him before demanding, "What you want?"

"Is your mom home?"

The little boy jumped to his feet then whirled and threw open the front door. He disappeared into the shadowy interior, urgently yelling "Popo! Popo!"

His warning set off a commotion inside the house. Cans and bottles crashed. Loud whispers and hurried footsteps followed. A pale, disheveled man stepped into the open doorway. William inhaled the strong odor of pot.

"Can I help you, officer?"

William raised his hands palms out. "I'm not here to bust anybody. I don't want to come in. I just have a question or two."

His expression turning arrogant, the man folded his arms. "I'd like to see the warrant."

"I told you I don't want to come in. I just have a couple questions."

"Just questions, huh?" When William nodded, he relaxed. "In that case, ah . . . I'd ask you in, like outta the cold, but, ah, the house ain't ready for company."

"I'm fine right here. I'd like to talk to an Angela. Does she live here?"

"Ah, yeah. She's my sister, but she's sleeping."

William didn't believe anyone in the house had slept through the little boy's loud announcement, but he patiently played along. "Could you wake her, please? It's kind of important. Tell her I heard of her through the friend of a friend and everything is cool. I just need to talk."

Without saying another word, the man stepped back inside and into house's dark interior.

"What the hell does he want?" a female voice whispered loudly.

"How the fuck am I supposed to know? Just go talk to him. He says it's cool."

Seconds later a petite young blonde appeared wearing only panties and a tight, pink t-shirt that read "Princess Bitch." The cold air brought her nipples to attention against the t-shirt and William had trouble averting his eyes.

Carefully eyeing him, she grasped the door as if ready to slam it in his face. "You want to talk to me?"

"Just talk. I'm looking for a little insight to make sense of a situation, okay? It's about the girls that work over on 16th Street."

The moment the words were out, Angela's whole appearance turned guarded. Her hand gripped the door harder. *Damn it!* He prepared to step forward to block it open with his foot.

"I don't know what you're talking about," she countered. "Girls on the street? I don't live that life no more and I sure as hell ain't no street whore."

"No-No, I didn't mean to imply—"

"You got a warrant to be on my porch?"

"No, ma'am, but—

She slammed the door in his face before he could even move. *Queen bitch is more like it.* Part of him wanted to play hard ass, bang on the door and use the pot smell as probable cause. He immediately decided that hassle wouldn't help either his case or Angela and her family.

With tits like hers, it'll be a few years before she downgrades to working 16th Street.

As he descended through the same snowy footsteps he'd created up the yard, William pulled his notebook from a coat pocket. He reviewed the two other numbers in Gerard's handwriting. He considered how to change his approach so as not to get a door in the face again. *Late afternoon is an odd hour to be calling a hooker. I'll just say I work nights and I woke up horny.*

An aged black man, walking an even older looking poodle, strolled in William's direction. Oddly well-groomed and wearing a tiny fleece coat, the dog alternated between sniffing, sneezing and lifting its leg to pee.

The man looked him over then grunted. "You lookin' fo' a workin' girl, you wastin' time on that one." His gray head tilted toward the house. "Why's an Omaha police detective wastin' time on a little chippy like that?"

William stared at the man's familiar face, but could not place him. "Just had some questions. Stupid, really. Trying to track down a link to the girls that work 16th Street."

"The missing cop?"

"Yes."

"You don't remember me, do you?"

William examined his features again, unable to come up with the answer. "Your face rings a bell but . . . ."

"No matter. It was a long time ago. I was a security guard at that big laundromat and convenience store on Lake Street."

"The one where the kids kept busting open the coin boxes."

"Yes, sir. Remember how they was comin' through the roof vent?"

"You and I waited up half the night. Caught them all, one by one, as they dropped through the ceiling," William said, smiling at the memory. "What was your name again?"

"Smoot, John Smoot. An' your name is plumb gone from my old mind."

"William Olson. It's good to see a friendly face from the old days. I wonder what ever happened to those kids? I remember we called their parents instead of sending them to juvy. Cops could do that back then."

"One of 'em is dead." John tugged on the poodle's leash to move it away from already yellow snow. "The Fletcher kid. Got to be a real hard case after all that shit he went through with his older brother an' the cops."

"What do you mean? I don't—"

"No matter," Smoot cut him off. "Nothin' you was involved in. He got into drugs an' worse. The others are okay. Why, I think one works fo' the city parks."

William held out his hand for the man to shake. "It truly is nice to see a friendly face from the past. Glad to see you're doing well."

"I be doin' alright. Retired a few years back. Don't really know what to do with myself day in an' day out." He looked from the house to William. "You know you goin' 'bout it all wrong. The hooker thing, I mean." This time he yanked his dog back from a fast food wrapper it had dug from snow. "Chitlin'!" he chided. The dog strutted over and perched its little butt on John's shoe as if knowing it would be warmer than the sidewalk. John shrugged at William's raised eyebrows and continued, "Figure you know they's the dregs of workin' girls over there. You want to know about 'em, you gotta talk to George."

"George?"

"George Bennis. He's my nephew an' a doctor," Smoot said, beaming with obvious pride.

"He takes care of the girls?"

"Yes, sir. A lot of 'em anyway."

"Doctors don't have to talk to us, you know. But won't hurt to ask. How would I get in touch with George?"

"Big clinic on 30th Street. I got the number back at the house. You're welcome to come over. Wife's got a brisket goin' for church tonight." He winked. "We ask nice, she may let us have a taste."

"Good as that sounds, John, I need to stay on this." William said, again shaking man's hand and gently squeezing his shoulder.

"I'll call ahead an' let him know you're comin'," Smoot said. "He may not want to make time for you otherwise. You know them doctors."

"A good word always helps. Appreciate it. Nice seeing you. And it was nice to meet you, Chitlin." He bent to pet the dog who sniffed and licked in return.

* * *

Directed to the clinic break room, William found Dr. George Bennis just wrapping up his trash from a late lunch. "Sorry to disturb you. Got a minute for a question or two?"

The man smiled as he stood to shake William's hand. He waved him to a seat across the table. "Please, sit down. I assume you are the detective my uncle called about. He speaks highly of you, Detective Olson."

"As I recall, your uncle was quite the man in his day."

"Couldn't have made it through school without him." Dr. Bennis shifted, telegraphing his unease.

"I'm sorry, if I'm keeping you from something," said William.

"It's not that. It's that if you want information on my patients, I'm afraid I can't be of much help."

"Actually, I'm not interested in your patients, specifically. That would be nice, of course, especially if you had information that would lead to our missing officer."

"Ah, now this begins to make sense." The nodding young doctor relaxed. "Your best bet is to talk to a man named Bonefish. Although I'm guessing he could have high blood pressure and early onset diabetes, he hasn't sought my opinion. The office staff has speculated that he makes a very good living because he always pays in cash."

"Since he's not a patient . . . You're saying he pays the girls' doctor bills."

"Exactly. Regular check-ups, STD screenings and condoms. He's a careful man with his merchandise, if you get my meaning."

"Like any good businessman does. Where, ah, in your opinion, do you think I would find Mr. Bonefish?"

"You know those little green houses that sit right up on the sidewalk just north of Lake Street?"

"Sure."

"He owns the barbershop next door."

"He cuts hair and pimps girls?"

"I didn't say that. You did." With a practiced flick of the wrist, Dr. Bennis shot his ball of paper-wrapped leftovers into a tall wastebasket then grinned at William. "You know, diversification is key in these troubled economic times."

* * *

Memories of his uniformed days flooded back as William drove north on 30th Street from Hamilton.

The empty ground where the Pleasant View housing projects once stood triggered visions of his first murder scene, a man with a shotgun blast through his middle. Pleasant View had been home to more than a few miseries. As a kid, he'd even lived there for a few weeks with one of his mother's boyfriends. Now the once sprawling collection of welfare apartments was gone, the land vacant, covered in snow and surrounded by chain link.

At Lake Street, remnants of a shrine erected for a nine-year-old boy run over in traffic years before, poked out of the snow. He could still see the kid's crumpled body and hear the wail of the old man who'd been unable to stop in time. A bright, new, heart-shaped balloon rested among the faded and deteriorating stuffed animals and plastic flowers.

As William passed the impromptu shrine, a young black man being tugged along by a pit bull on a heavy chain shot William a hateful stare. William focused on the barbershop one block ahead. The parking lot displayed a mix of rust buckets and heavily customized luxury cars. Along the sidewalk sat a line of big-wheeled, classic Chevys that the kids referred to as donks. The centermost car, a wonder of chrome and pearlescent paint, held a license plate that read BONEFSH.

William circled the block twice to get the lay of the land then parked in a spot with easy access to the street. Reaching the shop's door, he glanced at the front window glass and the two bullet holes punctuating the painted words, Frank's Family Barbers.

Inside, laughter mixed with a radio blasting hip-hop and the buzz of razors. The front of the shop held four barber chairs backed by a mirrored wall dotted with pictures, newspaper clippings and cartoons. Opposite the barbers sat a line of old metal chairs filled with customers, each holding a number. All eyes turned to William as he stepped in. He wasn't surprised to find his was the only white face in the room. Looks of curiosity and distaste lasted the briefest of seconds, then all went back to their magazines and conversations.

"Need a trim, detective?" asked a heavyset, bald man wearing a traditional barber jacket. Moving around the first chair, he didn't bother looking up from his finishing touches on a teenage boy.

"I'm good for now, but thanks. Looking for a fellow named Bonefish."

The barber unsnapped the apron from around the teenager's neck, flicking it not unlike a matador. Freshly shorn hair drifted to the floor. "Hang on a second, son," the barber said to the teenager. He grabbed a vacuum hose from the wall, cleaned up the boy's collar then chased loose hair from his ears with a soft brush. "There you go, young man. I don't dare send you home shedding. Your mama would never let me hear the end of it."

The teenager handed him a ten-dollar bill. When the man moved to the center of the counter under the mirror and opened the cash drawer, William glimpsed a small-framed revolver by the register. The boy pulled a dollar tip from the three bills handed back.

The barber nodded. "Thank you, son, and say hello to the family." Not until then did the man actually look at William. "Haven't seen you before, but you sure as hell ain't no rookie."

"No, sir. Been around. You've never seen me because I never worked Vice." Though his eyes and expression remained blank, the barber flinched ever so slightly. In his peripheral vision, William saw two of the customers shift in their seats. "My name is William Olson."

"Bonefish is a nickname. You can call me Clarence, Clarence Jefferson. Now, Detective Olson, what would make a smart-looking man like yourself think Vice cops would have any interest in a humble barber?"

William cocked his head and waited.

A shark-like smile crept over Clarence's lips. "Alright, you got ol' Bonefish on the hook. What say we grab a cup a coffee in the back and see if you can reel me in." He snapped his fingers. In the corner seat, another jacketed barber trying hard to read a magazine jumped to his feet to take over his boss's chair.

William followed to the back of the shop to an alcove occupied by a small round table with two chairs, a pop machine and—crammed in the corner—a cardboard honor-system snack box and an odd-looking coffeemaker atop a cabinet on wheels.

"We just got this new coffee machine. Damnedest thing you ever seen," Clarence said, spinning a little chrome rack that held the coffeemaker's prepackaged coffee. "We got French roast, hazelnut, decaf. Hell, there's all kinds. I'm fond of the hazelnut myself."

William took his turn at the rack and stopped on a little plastic pod that made him smile. A grin crossed Clarence's face as William handed him his choice.

"Donut Shop Decaf," chuckled the barber. "I'd say that's just about perfect."

The two of them stood a moment as the machine groaned to life.

Clarence spread his legs and crossed his arms. "I assume you want to talk about Sgt. Gurdlich."

"Yes, sir. I understand you have, ah, dealings with the girls that work his area."

When William carefully removed his coffee, Clarence waved him to a chair at the table. "We are off the record here, just a couple a old timers talking, correct?"

William sipped his coffee and held it up in a salute. "Absolutely."

Clarence started a cup of his usual hazelnut. He looked down at William with a deceptively half-lidded glance. "You know, he was bad news. He wasn't happy just takin' money. He liked to hurt the girls."

"I've become aware of that disgusting fact. Um, are you using the past tense for a reason? Something I need to know?"

The big shoulders shrugged. "I suspect he's dead. Gone this long with no sign?" Another shrug. "But I can't say for sure and I really don't care. Heard somewheres he was retiring next month. Nobody but a fool would kick up a shit storm by killing a problem that was goin' away on its own."

The coffee machine hissed at the end of its cycle. Clarence picked up his cup and sat down with William. He sipped then arched an eyebrow. "You want to know where the nickname Bonefish comes from?"

"I'd rather hear more of what you know about Gurdlich."

"I'll get to that, but let me put things in context for you."

"Fine."

"I," Clarence said, poking a thumb to his thick chest, "am Bonefish junior. My daddy went by the same moniker. He had a barbershop over in the Bluffs and dabbled in working girls on the side. Had a reputation for treating them and his customers fair. Back then you could walk into any bar in the Bluffs, say you wanted to go fishing and they'd point you in the right direction."

William smiled and shook his head. "I get it."

"He operated for thirty years without spending a minute in jail. You know why?"

"All the cops were on the take?"

Clarence held up an acknowledging hand. "Well, the right ones was anyway. But the main reason he survived is that he had rules." He leaned forward. "Just like I have rules. No drugs, keep the split fair, take care of the girls and the customers and, above all, if the cops can't be bought, it ain't worth the trouble."

"So, you're an honorable pimp," William said slowly, feeling his way.

"Goddamn right I am." He sat back, his eyes darkening. "Some poor ugly fucker wants his joint sucked and some girl needs to feed the family? Hell, ain't nothin' wrong with takin' a cut for bringin' them together an' keepin' it safe. In case you ain't looked around lately, ain't too many jobs on this end of town."

"If it were that simple, I might be more charitable." It was William's turn to lean forward. "But we both know there's a boatload of misery that comes with that life."

"Yessir, we do. In this context, a big part of that misery was brought on by your missin' sergeant."

"Point taken," William snapped.

"You seem like a reasonable man. Unlike the bone-breakin' fucks that worked with Gurdlich." Clarence blew on his coffee, frowning as if rolling a decision over in his mind. "Just for the sake of argument, let's say I know a girl that had contact with him that evenin'." His drawl deepening betrayed his mindset. "And let's say that girl had some trouble, but had nothin' to do with his goin' missin'."

"I'd say that's a girl I'd like to talk to," said William.

"Could you guarantee she'd get a fair shake?"

William blew out a breath. "No. There was a time, but not anymore."

"I appreciate the honesty. Honor ain't what it once was around here neither." He gazed into his coffee, rolling the cup between his palms for nearly a minute. "But you'd do your level best?"

"That I can promise."

"She done a lot to fuck up her life already. I found out she's into drugs, so she ain't workin' for me no more. But that don't mean I want her tossed to the dogs for somethin' she didn't do."

William tamped down his rising excitement. "I'll keep it low-key. Bring her in quietly, put her in good hands and let her tell her side."

"Ah, the hell with it. Done all I can for the girl," Clarence said, mostly to himself. "You see that man workin' my chair?"

"Yes."

"This girl we been talkin' about is his niece. Somthin' happens to her—somethin' more than she deserves—I can't guarantee he won't shoot your ass when you be walkin' to your car some night."

"Fair enough."

Two small boys tumbled through the shop's door and raced to the small break area. Each held a plastic Iron Man action figure. The toys were locked in an aerial battle with the boys providing the sound effects. Spotting William, they froze.

"It's all right, men," Clarence said. "Say hello to Mr. Olson."

Illusion and playfulness wiped from their eyes, they stared at William suspiciously.

He held out his hand and each boy in turn solemnly shook it.

"Nice to meet you," they said in flat unison.

"Likewise." His smile was not returned.

"You boys grab a candy and get on home," said Clarence.

The boys whirled to the snack box, each grabbing a treat. Clarence playfully swatted their behinds. As one yanked open the front door, the other swung his action figure in mock attack. The door slammed shut.

"You got grandkids yet?" asked Clarence.

"Nope, not for a few years, I hope. Got one that's in his early teens."

"Ah, teenagers. They do bring on the gray hair, don't they?"

"Good god, yes, but the good usually makes up for the worry." His thoughts flickered to his oldest boy and the pride he had felt in him that morning.

"Two ten," said Clarence, like he was spitting a bitter seed.

"Excuse me?"

"Two-one-zero," Clarence enunciated. "That's the apartment she's in."

"Which is—"

"You drove the block twice before coming in. You see those apartments on the street behind my shop?"

"Yes, sir," William said, surprised that he'd been noticed.

"You park out front. She'll come down."

"Well. Ah, thank you. Appreciate—"

"She won't solve your problem," Clarence cut him off and pointed his finger. "Like I said, she didn't have nothin' to do with your crooked sergeant goin' missin'."

"I hear you."

"Good, then keep listenin'. This stays on the down low. She gets in your ride, no cuffs, no back up. Just you an' her leavin' like you're old friends. Anythin' more an' the hard cases watchin' the place will fuck you up."

Clarence stood, indicating the meeting was over. William considered shaking hands but thought better of it. The companionable truce was over. Deep behind enemy lines, he absorbed the hatred from every man in the room. Passing Clarence's chair, he caught the eye of the girl's uncle. William offered a barely perceptible nod, as if to say, "I'll take care of her."

Behind the wheel of his car, he expelled a long breath. *Well, that was interesting.* He wanted to call Dan Armour but didn't dare do anything at that moment that might incite doubt. *Why the fuck didn't I call in my position before I arrived?* After bringing the engine to life, his hand went to his Sig, then brushed his body armor for reassurance. He pulled out of the lot slowly, merging into traffic then turning quickly into the neighborhood.

In front of the apartments, he hadn't let his car idle with his foot on the brake for more than thirty nerve-racking seconds before the girl appeared in his rearview mirror. She opened his passenger door, slid into the seat and sat without saying a word. William locked the doors. Stiffly transferring his foot from brake to accelerator, he headed out of the neighborhood with his eyes scanning for threats the entire time.

"You gonna kill me?" the girl asked, clutching a shiny gold purse and biting a bloody lower lip.

"No! Hell, no! Didn't Claren...ah, Bonefish tell you who I am?"

"He say you a cop. Cops want me dead for sticking ol' Turdlick."

William flashed the memory of the barber-turned-pimp's claims. "You stuck him? With a knife?"

"You a detective?"

"Yes, my name's William. What's yours?"

"Leticia."

"Last name?"

"Alberts."

"Well, Leticia Alberts, I'm not going to hurt you. So, did you stab Sgt. Gurdlich with a knife?"

"Hell no, a rusty nail or screw or somethin'. Stuck him in his dick to get the mean-ass motherfucker off me. He was tryin' to choke me to death with his big white dick. I stuck him and he smacked my head against the wall. Look. I still got a big ol' goose egg." She turned her head and spread her black hair to expose a bloody knot. He glanced and nodded. Looking more confident, she continued, "He tried to hit me with his flick-out club but missed. He busted a big-ass chunk out of the wall instead of my head. Then I just ran."

"He didn't chase after you?" William glanced over, realizing she didn't have a coat and was shivering. Needle tracks dotted both arms. He turned up the car's heater.

"If he did, I fucked him up good enough he couldn't catch me."

"You mean the nail you stuck in his, ah his—"

"Yeah."

"Where were you exactly?"

"Sixteen Street."

"Where on 16th?"

"Glass alley. You know by the old cannery."

"You're sure you weren't further north? Closer to the grain elevators?"

"Hell, yes, I'm sure."

"I have to make a call. Let them know I'm bringing you in." William pulled out his cell phone.

The girl hunched toward the heat vents. "Whatever," she mumbled.

"William, what have you got for me?" Dan Armour said.

"A big piece of the puzzle is what. But I don't think she's the answer to why Harry Gurdlich is missing."

"What do you mean?"

"I've got the girl Gurdlich abused shortly before he disappeared."

"No shit? The hooker? How—"

"I'll tell you more when I get there," William interrupted. "The more important thing is that we've been looking too far north. Gurdlich wasn't anywhere near his last reported position."

"All right, so where are we going?"

"Send a team over to Glass Alley. I'll bring the girl to you—and only you—then meet the team there."

"On it. How far out are you?"

"Two minutes. Dan, you know Gurdlich's crew will be around for shift change. Do I need to tell you—"

"Understood," said Dan. "I'll make ready. Come to the public door rather than the garage."

"Agreed." William looked over at the girl again. Her nervously-chewed lower lip looked raw and sore. Her scrawny legs moved nervously as she shivered and rubbed her arms in spite of the blasting heater. He lowered his voice and turned toward his window. "You might get a doctor on his way, as well. The girl's jones-ing pretty bad."

William parked at a meter in front of the station. "I'm going to have to cuff you before we go in. Are you ready for that?"

Her eyes widened as she looked around in rising panic. "I never been in jail before."

"How old are you, Leticia?"

"Eighteen."

"Not a good way to start, honey," warned William. "Are you listening to me?" She nodded. "You won't get a fair shake if you lie to us."

"Si-Sixteen."

"Heroin?"

"Yeah. I-I'm needing—"

"We have medical help for that. You'll be going to an interview room first. My boss is meeting us. His name is Dan. He and I will take you upstairs together. Because of your age, your parents will be called."

Leticia groaned then bent forward. "I feel sick."

"Hold on," he called out as he opened his door.

William jumped from the car and raced to her door. She leaned out and vomited what little there was in her stomach. It splatted onto the street's packed snow. As the back of her hand swiped at her mouth, William turned from the stink but immediately back in time to catch her before she stumbled into her own mess. He held her up against the car and gently turned her to apply the cuffs in a practiced, fluid move.

"Leticia Alberts, you have the right to remain silent. Anything . . . ."

As he droned out her rights, she burst into tears that just ratcheted up her trembling. William wondered why this upset her after accepting so much abuse on the street.

19

Dan Armour reached William's side by the time he finished the Miranda speech.

On the way from curb to door, the two detectives flanked the cuffed girl, providing protection as much as physical support. The front of the police headquarters building rose in a concrete expanse leading to a bland, 1960's concrete building bristling with antennas. Beyond the front door, the desk clerks stared as they entered.

Dan waved an electronic key fob over a reader. The trio stepped from the public lobby into the more secure part of the station. When their elevator arrived, one of Gurdlich's disciples stepped off. William saw the wheels turning.

"Whadda you got there, detectives?"

"Nothing to concern you, officer," Dan snapped.

The officer continued to stare. As the elevator door slid to a close between them, he smiled and called out a snarky, "Have a nice day, sirs."

* * *

The fidgeting Leticia Alberts sat alone in a bland interview room, her forearms raw from scratching and lower lip cracked and bloodied from her nervous chewing.

"That's a brave girl in there," said William, as he and Dan Armour watched on closed-circuit television. "You know, she actually asked if I was going to kill her? I get you're pissed that I didn't check in . . . but, I gotta say, it took a lot more guts for her to get in my car than for me to walk into that shop."

"Nice try, Will." Dan crossed his arms and narrowed his eyes. "Walking into that barbershop without backup was more stupid than brave. One missing cop wasn't enough for you? Were you trying to make it two?"

"Okay, it was stupid. I just caught a break and kept rolling. I was in over my head before I realized. Besides, it had to be one old-timer talking to another. Nothing else would have worked."

"I get that, Will, but . . . goddamnit, it was reckless not to at least call in your position."

"You don't think I wasn't kicking my own ass the whole time, boss? It won't happen again." An awkward silence fell as they stared at Leticia who stood then immediately sat down again, her withdrawal obviously getting worse. William glanced out of the corner of his eye at Dan. "Ah, should I head on over to Glass Alley?"

His boss reluctantly nodded. "Yeah, I've got this end handled. A doctor is on his way for her and the crime lab should already be there waiting for you."

"Thanks, boss, and . . . " William raised his hands and let them fall to his sides. "I am sorry about not checking in. I—"

"Will," Dan interrupted him, "I've been putting this off, but tomorrow morning we need to make time for the chief."

"What? Does he need advice on covering up this Gurdlich shit storm? It's gonna come out eventually. There's no—"

"Hold it! It wouldn't hurt to tone down your attitude. He gets a whiff of contempt and that shit storm might rain crap down on all of us. Just come in first thing in the morning. We'll brief him on what we've found and get back to work."

"Sure. Nine work for you?"

"Yeah, 9 a.m. will be fine. And, by the way, I've already been told the chief will cover his ass by saying Gurdlich's planned retirement was not voluntary."

"The bastard should be in jail," snapped William.

"Sure, in a perfect world. These days it's all about intentions and spin."

"Well, excuse me, sir, but this old-timer calls bullshit on that."

Without waiting for a response, William grabbed up his coat from a nearby chair and headed for the elevator. Clearing the front door, he flipped up his collar and shoved both hands into his pockets for the short walk to his car. Heavy, fat snowflakes fell faster and faster. Moisture-heavy clouds covered the lowering sun. All around him the slow commute out of downtown had commenced.

God I hate this shit. Just as he popped the trunk to retrieve his scraper, he froze. Someone had scraped the word RAT into the snow on his rear window. Flakes had yet to fill in the letters. Without turning his head, he concentrated on what he could see in his peripheral vision. No one had stuck around to enjoy his reaction. Shrugging as if he could care less—which was true—he grabbed up his scraper, slammed the trunk lid and took several swipes to erase the slur.

Moments later, he relieved some of his anger by goosing the accelerator to rock the car over the berm pushed up by the snowplows. He had more important things to think about at Glass Alley.

Rolling slowly out of the high-rise district into the north downtown, he glimpsed the snow-shadowed baseball park's light towers rising in the distance. *Times are a changin' and not everything's for the better.*

Splitting his attention between the carefully-moving traffic and his cell phone, he noted nothing yet from Alex. His thumb dexterously entered the number to the Fitzgerald, but no one answered. The snow fell harder, driven by wind and reducing visibility. He tossed the phone into the passenger seat to concentrate on his driving.

Bundled-up for the walk to their cars, commuters streamed from the Union Pacific and the Daily Herald buildings. Trucks filled the loading docks of the newspapers distribution center.

Wonder if Manuela heard the crime lab's dispatch to Glass Alley?

The mouth of his alley destination funneled car exhaust illuminated by police cruiser headlights, an unusually pretty image in the swirling snow. A police sergeant and another officer stepped from the billowing white as William approached. A Chevy van marked CRIME LAB sat in the street facing him, essentially blocking the alley entrance.

William slowed to a stop alongside the Crime lab van. When he lowered his window the driver rolled his down.

"How fucking long?" William demanded.

"I'm sorry, sir?" The tech acted genuinely puzzled. "How long what?"

"How long have they been screwing up our crime scene?"

The tech glanced over the top of his car at the alley. "They were here when we arrived. Must have heard the call from dispatch."

William pulled ahead, parked and crawled from his car. His mounting anger compensated for the wind and cold as he made a beeline for the two officers. "So, you just had to drive into my crime scene then track the place up?" William called out. "You know better than that, sergeant."

Sgt. Ken Wilkins pounded his gloved hands together as if battling the falling temperature. "Keep your pants on, detective. We just wanted to make sure Gurdlich wasn't in there dying. We'll move the cruisers."

When the second officer turned back into the alley to move his car, Wilkins tossed him a set of keys and ordered, "Have the rookie Grant move mine and bring it around the block,"

"Officer!" William called out. "Try to stay in the same ruts you made going in."

The man waved back dismissively.

"Now, Detective Olson," said Wilkins, "what makes you so sure this is a crime scene? You really believe the crap some drugged-out hooker tells you?"

William shook his head. "I see word travels fast, Sergeant. Do I believe her without one doubt? Not hardly. What she told me was probably only half true. But, I have to check it out. If Gurdlich's dick was someplace it shouldn't have been when he ran into trouble, then that's a problem for him and the public relations department, not me."

"Just remember whose side you're on," said Wilkins.

"Not sure I like your tone, Ken. Maybe you need to take your own advice, or has Gurdlich's good ol' boy's club made you forget who we're working for?"

"Jesus fuck! You are Detective Deadbeat," said Wilkins, half under his breath.

William took half a step closer. "What was that?"

"You heard me," said Wilkins, holding his ground. "Everybody up here knows you have a soft spot for the bums. It's no surprise you'd rather trash one of us than that little doghouse runt friend of yours. Why don't you ask him where his big black friend is? We all know that guy had something to do with this."

"Everybody knows Gurdlich trashed his own reputation," snapped William. "So, what the hell are you talking about?"

"Your little friend, Alex whatever his name is. The big black guy he hangs with. He and Gurdlich tangled the night before he disappeared."

"I've talked to a lot of people in the past couple days and no one's mentioned anything about Alex. All anyone—as in everyone—has talked about is Gurdlich abusing the hookers."

"Oh yeah, you're street buddies—"

"Goddamn it, Ken!" William shouted, throwing his arms up in his agitation. "A little sixteen-year-old girl I just took into custody asked if I was going to kill her because that's what Gurdlich tried to do. She told me he tried to choke her to death with what he calls a face fuck. When she fought back, he tried to crush her skull with his baton."

Wilkins winced, then dropped his gaze to the accumulating snow. "Young, but still a drug-addicted little skank," he murmured.

"Ken, I though you were better than this. This macho, bad-ass cop bullshit's gotten way out of hand. It's the sort of thing that makes enemies and gets cops killed."

Wilkins adjusted his stocking cap and clapped his hands twice, still staring down and obviously thinking. When he raised his head and met William's eyes, he looked sincere. "Look, did Gurdlich have issues? Yeah, a lot of us thought he was way over the top. But, he was close to retirement and nobody wanted to mess up his pension. He wasn't always this bad and he saved my butt more than once."

"I appreciate the loyalty, but you can't keep his bullshit covered up and expect to find him on your own. Now, tell me about this fight between Harry and Alex's friend."

"I didn't see it, but from what I heard, Sarge was in his cruiser in front of the St. Vincent and said something to set the black guy off. He grabbed

Sarge by the neck, talking all kind of crazy. The rookie Sarge had driving, Pembroke, beaned the big guy with his baton."

"And that was it?"

"Yeah. Well all I heard, anyway. Sarge bought the kid a beer after work for a job well done."

"Why the hell didn't you tell anyone about this?"

"We told Dan Armour. He said he'd have it looked into."

William controlled his surprise. "He never said a word about it to me, but he's the boss and I'm not. Do you have a name on the big guy?"

"It's a black name, DeAnte, or something like that."

"DeAndre," said a voice from behind William. He turned to find Officer Jason Grant. "Alex told me about him at the hospital. The guy was living in a shanty next to Alex's dog house over on 20th Street before the cold snap."

"Okay, I'll check this DeAndre out. But first," William said, turning to look at the now dark and empty alley, "we have to establish that Gurdlich was here."

When the forensic tech joined them, they crunched forward through the snow.

William waved his hand at the walls of the buildings lining the alley. "Look for a fresh chunk out of the brick, three to four feet up."

The tech stopped to survey the shadowy canyon of the massive block-long buildings then looked back at William. "I might have to switch to my insulated coveralls. This could take a while."

"If it's fresh, the mark should be brighter orange than the rest of the wall. Imagine the ball on the end of a steel baton striking the brick. The girl said he knocked out a big-assed chunk."

"All right," said the tech, turning on his high-powered flashlight. "I'll shine this down the wall. You guys watch from a few feet back. Bumps and divots will show up as shadows."

Slowly, they worked their way into the alley. The long, v-shaped beam of the flashlight moved up and down first one wall then the area opposite, uncovering countless pockmarks. Each good-sized divot was examined and marked with chalk.

"I could start working from the other end if you think it would speed things up," offered Officer Grant.

"Not yet," William said. "Let's give this a few more minute—"

"Wait," Wilkins interrupted. "That's a hell of a mark, right there." He turned on his own flashlight, shining it directly into the hole. "It's fresh, too."

"This looks promising," said the tech, pulling a digital camera from his kit. He dropped a yellow flag on the ground under the divot then held an L-shaped ruler next to his target. "Watch your eyes from the flash, boys," he warned then fired off three quick frames, one straight on and two more showing the alley for reference.

While the tech made notes, William imagined the scene as Leticia had described it. Squatting, he traded insulated gloves for rubber ones and poked fingers into the snow, mindful of the shattered glass from countless broken bottles that gave the alley its nickname.

"Fucking snow," William muttered, his knees popping as he stood.

"What are you looking for?" Grant asked.

"Anything that says Gurdlich was here. Imagine his doing the hooker here," he said standing back from the wall about two feet, imitating Gurdlich. "She sticks him with a nail. He smacks her head against the wall then pulls out his baton, swings and hits the wall instead of the girl." William turned to look at the dark end of the long alley. "And she makes her escape."

"Gurdlich was fast and strong as a bull," said Wilkins. "She never would have gotten away if he had his hands on her. Something else had to happen."

"Well, he did have a hole in his dick." He glanced at the three men looking at him. "That's where she stabbed him. But he was also pissed, so I do agree."

"Maybe he splattered some blood around," Wilkins offered.

"Snow-covered now, but I can still identify it," the tech said.

"Let's form a line across the alley and sift through the snow for ten feet on either side of this mark." William pointed at the flagged divot on the wall. "If we don't find anything, I say we call in more officers to help—"

"No need," interrupted Grant. "Look." He knelt beside a hole in the snow he'd dug with the toe of his boot.

Five feet out from the alley wall lay a fully extended, metal baton.

"Bingo," said William.

They formed a circle around the evidence waiting for the tech to do his thing before William picked it up. The beam of his flashlight showed the initials H-A-G sloppily engraved on the handle. He held it for the tech to photograph the lettering.

"I'm going to call in another unit," said the tech. "This scene's gonna be a bitch to process."

William didn't pay any more attention as his mind visualized the fight. He stepped to the far side of the alley, leaning against a metal fence blocking off a recessed area once used for dumpsters but now crammed with trash. He let his eyes and mind imagine the possibilities.

"Did you guys see any openings on this building?" asked William. "I mean anything."

"Not on the alley side, but it's darker than hell out here," said Wilkins. "This place is huge. It would take a lot of time and sunshine to really look it over."

William scanned the back of the multi-story building All the way up the windows were intact. When his flashlight reached the top, he noticed ancient, half-painted-over letters.

"What's that say, guys?" William asked. "Looks like it starts with a J-E and maybe an N or M—"

"It's the old Jennings Meats building," said Wilkins. "They closed this place down decades ago. Moved out west."

William pulled out his phone and dialed Dan Armour. "Can you tell me what Sgt. Gurdlich's middle name is?"

"Hell, Will, off the top of my head, I don't know. Let me look it up. What's this about?"

"Patience, boss. Just look up the middle name."

"All right, ah, Sgt. Harry Alphonse Gurdlich. Now will you tell me what's going on?"

"We have a crime scene. Those initials are on Gurdlich's baton. We found it about fifty feet in on the east end of Glass Alley. What the girl described is mostly true, but there's something missing. I'm betting it involves her pimp. Can you press her on that? There's got to be something more than she's letting on."

"I'll get on it. The doc's in with her now, giving her something to calm her creepy crawlies."

"What's the ETA on the cadaver dogs?"

"They'll be here in the morning. Our usual handlers were working a disaster out of state."

"Dan," he took a deep breath, "there's something else."

"What?"

"Well, two things actually."

"Shoot."

"The sign on the old meatpacking plant. It says Jennings Meats. Maybe you were right about a falling out between Gurdlich and Barry Jennings. Think we can get his permission to search the plant?"

"I'll make some calls. Might be an opportunity to feel him out on his trips over the river without his thinking he needs a lawyer."

"Good thinking," said William.

"What was the other thing?"

"What?"

"The other thing. You said you had two."

"Oh, right . . . Why didn't you tell me about Alex's friend and the fight with Gurdlich?"

Dan held silent for a moment. "Because Capstain's your friend and you have a reputation for favoring the street people."

"Dan—"

"No, you'd have done the same thing in my position. This whole thing is a political cluster fuck. The Chief's on my ass to keep Gurdlich's shit from the press while the street cops are covering shit up. I thought it wise to let Davis and Gratz handle the lead on DeAndre Easton."

"Have they talked with Alex?"

"Not that I know of," said Dan. "They talked to the shelter nurse, a Miss Caldwell."

"Liz Caldwell," William added. "Was she helpful?"

"Yes. She gave us DeAndre's last name. He has no known address. He eats and sometimes sleeps at the St. Vincent . . . Hang on, I'll call up their report . . . Black, six-foot-four, well on his way to three-hundred pounds. Has a shanty over at 20th and Paul."

"That's it? No other history? I take it they haven't found him."

"No, and I told them not to spend too much time looking. I figured it was Gurdlich's boys putting up a smoke screen to keep us away from the hookers. Heck, it would be a full-time job to chase down everyone Gurdlich ever had a beef with."

"We all do what we can," William murmured, eyeing the crowd of officers, obviously both on and off duty, who had gathered at the crime tech's van. Their anxious expressions and silence spelled out their eagerness for news.

"I'll get back to you if I have anything else," he told his boss.

"Same here," Dan responded and ended the connection.

As William and his crew of three emerged from the alley the waiting cops looked at Gurdlich's baton swinging from the tips of William's gloved fingers. No one asked. They just knew.

"Print this right away," William said to the crime lab tech.

"Yes, sir. The handle's finish is pretty rough, but I'll do what I can."

"If you find any prints other than Gurdlich's, would you call me right away?" William handed the tech his card.

From back in the crowd William heard someone shout, "Rat!" followed by a mumbled, "Detective Deadbeat."

After handing off the baton, William turned to face the crowd. "Those of you who want to play schoolyard bully, go find a coffee shop waitress to hit on. Those who want to act like police officers, form up teams and start searching for access to this building."

A grumble went through the crowd as senior officers started to coordinate.

Twenty-five yards away, on the opposite side of the street, William spotted Manuela and a photographer. *She doesn't miss a beat.*

In his peripheral vision he caught a flash of Barry Jennings' face. By the time he turned his head he was gone. Seconds later, a van's dome light came on. He squinted through the snow. The dull illumination from a streetlight allowed him to identify the Angel's Wings logo. As William pushed through the crowd, Gurdlich's disciples slowed his progress.

Jumping into the street, William yelled, "Mr. Jennings! I have questions!"

Sensing he was being ignored, he positioned himself well out in front of the van and shined his flashlight through the windshield. Jennings put the van in reverse, backed enough to clear the car ahead and started to pull out. William raised his flashlight above his head and waved it so the beam moved back and forth across Jennings' face.

"Stop! Police! Mr. Jennings, I'm ordering you to stop!"

The big Ford Econoline's tires spun in place, melting quickly through the snow to the pavement.

William didn't budge from the path of the lurching van. His vision narrowed and time slowed. He saw Barry Jennings behind the wheel, the face of an angry, spoiled child. William lifted his coat, his hand reaching for his Sig Sauer pistol. Jennings flinched, tapping the brakes. The van slid slightly sideways. William moved too late. The collision spun him around, knocking him to the street.

Jumping to his feet and ignoring the pain in his hip, William limped to the driver's door, as a dozen cops descended on the van. One cop threw the van into park. Another pulled the keys. Others yanked Jennings into the street, throwing him face down in the muck.

"I'm sorry," Jennings screamed as the cuffs clicked tight. "I didn't see him . . . I couldn't stop."

Wilkins placed a hand on William's arm. "You okay, Will? Bastard looked like he clipped you pretty good."

"Yeah, hurts like hell, but I'm not gonna let the kids see," he said, glancing at a few of Gurdlich's young officers laughing at William's being knocked to the ground.

"Hey, Detective! Your pants are wet. Need a Depends?" someone taunted.

"Will," Wilkins lowered his voice, "walk away. What I'm about to do is going to embarrass you."

William did as asked but stayed within earshot.

"Pembroke!" Wilkins roared. "You and the others! Over here, now!"

In the ensuing silence, snow crunched as men moved.

"That man you just insulted was one of my training officers. He is among the best I've had the honor of working with. He's done more for the citizens of this city than all of you combined ever will."

"But—"

"But nothing, rookies. All of you will shut your goddamned mouths and start listening. I've kept quiet about this macho crap long enough. Starting now, I'm the big dawg and it's spelled D-O-G."

Wilkins' speech eased the pain as William walked to the cruiser with the very wet and indignant Barry Jennings in the back seat. He yanked open the door.

"I'm going to sue you and the city for this outrage," Jennings blurted. "When I get done, you won't have a pot to piss in."

"Good luck with that. I think one or two TV stations got your little performance on tape and, judging by the reaction of the other officers, I'd say they thought you were trying to kill me."

"I won't speak another word until I have a lawyer."

"Why did you run? All I wanted was to ask you to let us search your plant for our missing sergeant."

"Lawyer," spit Jennings.

"I'm guessing it's a 'no' on you giving us permission to search your building?"

Jennings stared straight ahead saying nothing.

"All right then, we'll get a warrant."

A smirk touched Jennings' lips.

"What was it?" William asked. "Did Gurdlich want more money? Threaten to tell everyone about your little scam to clean up north downtown? You know, transporting kidnapped men across state lines is a federal beef."

The smirk vanished.

"Yes, Barry my man, I know all about it. Your friends at city hall will drop you like a hot turd once they learn we have witnesses and financial records."

Jennings sat silent, the muscles in his jaw flexing.

20

William fingered his office phone as he asked his youngest son David, "So, did I look stupid?" He'd called home hours before to say he was okay and would be on TV, but he'd been rushed and did not give any details. Since they called him, he realized he owed them a bit more reassurance.

"No, Dad, you looked like a Husker running back." David said, his pride evident. "They played it over and over on TV. Did it hurt?"

"Well, yeah. I think I zigged when I should have zagged. I'll probably have a big bruise on my butt. I'd be happy to show you when I get home."

"Dad," David said in the singsongy tone of admonishment used when his father was acting silly.

"Do me a favor, buddy. Put your mom on the phone."

"Hope we didn't interrupt," said Susan. "The boys . . . Well, David wanted to call before bed. I told him it would be okay."

"It brightened an otherwise boring session of paperwork, Suze. Reports upon reports. I got designated to write up all this crap for a meeting with the Chief in the morning." He let silence reign a moment. "Ah, I have the feeling you had a little something to do with David calling."

"Wow!" She let sarcasm paint her words. "That's why you're the detective, dear. You see right through me. Now, about that empty promise to be careful . . . ."

"I'm sorry, hon. Something about this Jennings guy got my fur up. I certainly never thought he'd really try to run me down. He's much too concerned about his public image."

"Then you must be proud that you got him where he'll hurt the most. Are you taking notes here? For the record, how about you try to think about us the next time your fur gets ruffled."

"Not to worry. I will do my damnedest to leap aside next time. Hey, on the plus side, I heard something that made me feel a little less like an old relic tonight. But, ah, I'll tell you when I get home."

"William!" Her breath caught. "You are not old."

"Suze, I'm six years older than you. I never would have gotten clipped by that van six years ago."

"What's done is done. When you get home, I'll kiss whatever's hurting and maybe places that aren't. That should help you feel a little younger."

William could heard the boys in the background with their "gross" and "eeww."

After drawn-out goodbyes and more promises to be careful, William hung up and leaned back painfully in his chair. The hospital x-ray had showed no breaks. The doctor confirmed he just had a deep bruise that his high school football coach would have called a hip pointer.

His gaze focused on his computer. He'd written a carefully organized and detailed report and printed two copies, one for the morning's meeting with the Chief. He pulled his cell from its holster to check for missed calls then redialed the number for the Fitzgerald. After six rings, he hung up. *What the hell is Alex up to?*

The snow had slowed, but a blustery wind was doing its best to undo the work of the plows as William pulled his car from the police station garage. Instead of heading home, he turned north.

The floodlights that normally illuminated the Fitzgerald's sign were off and the interior dark as William parked his car. He had to cling to the car door to avoid the wind ripping it away. The hotel's front door had been locked and no one responded to the night bell. Fuck! He pulled up his collar against the wind, rang again then knocked, hard. Nothing. Just as he turned to leave, the door opened and an old man exited. William lunged to catch the door before it closed.

The old guy, ancient and bent, glared at him, relaxing only slightly when William showed his badge. "We're supposed to have three days," he growled. "I've paid rent here for ten years. Why do you government people want to kick me out of my home?"

"Sir, I'm not—"

"Save it. I got two words for you government types. Fuck and you," he said, punctuating each word with first his right, then left middle fingers.

Ignoring or unable to hear William's attempt to explain, the old guy carefully descended the entrance's snowy steps, checked the almost non-existent traffic then crossed the street to shuffle toward Weston's Tavern, a block to the west.

Inside the Fitzgerald, a low-watt bulb barely illuminated the first floor hallway. Beyond the office window, Gerard's domain looked like a black cave. The building itself felt like a hollow shell. The loss of tenants had drained the life from it. Soon it would be empty and rotting like so many others in the neighborhood.

William carefully climbed the creaking stairs, flashlight beam on the floor directly in front of him as he entered the cavernous second floor hall. The perfectly useless small light fixture at the far end only provided a tiny glow that didn't even reach the floor. Thinking he had reached the correct door, William flicked his light up at the metal 2 and the painted numbers beside it.

"Alex, are you home?" William called, softly tapping on his door.

A noise down the hall pulled him around. Leo, the fat man from the lobby earlier that morning, stood under the distant low-watt light. He wore only underwear and socks.

"You looking for the little fucking handyman?" asked Leo, plucking his underwear from the crack of his ass.

"Yes. Have you seen him?"

"Not my day to watch the asshole," he said, smelling his fingers. "With any luck, the noisy little bastard killed himself."

William stared in disbelief as Leo again cursed Alex then marched through a nearby doorway. A bathroom stall door slammed and flesh meeting porcelain echoed in the eerie quiet. William could almost hear his David saying "Eewww."

He faced Alex's door. The blocked thought finally emerged. *The eviction notice may have been enough to push Alex over the edge.* Glancing at the empty hall, he heard a rumble of flatulence. Flashlight squeezed under his arm, he opened his pocketknife. The thin blade easily slid behind the door's trim to leverage the old latch and release the door. As it swung open, he raised the flashlight, bracing himself for something horrific.

Much to William's relief, the room was vacant. Alex's tidy bed would have made a drill sergeant happy. His bucket of tools sat by the door. On the table a travel alarm clock sat next to a jar of peanut butter. The swing of his light caught the loaf of white bread tacked high on the wall over the table. William smiled. That was the same trick his mother had used to keep the mice from snacking.

All right Alex, where did you go?

The old mattress springs voiced their disapproval as William sat down and scrolled through the contacts in his phone before dialing.

"St. Vincent," answered a quiet voice.

"This is Detective William Olson. I'm looking for Alex Capstain, the little doghouse guy. Do you know who I'm talking about?"

"Oh, sure. Haven't seen him tonight. He's livin' at the Fitzgerald hotel now, anyway. Guess we weren't fancy enough for him no more."

"All right. Thank you. If he does show up, would you call this number? My name's Detective Olson. Does your phone have caller ID?"

"Yes, sir, Detective, sir. I'm writin' it down now on the back of my puzzle magazine. He won't be comin' in tonight, though. The doors are locked at eleven."

Back in his car, William mulled over his options. He realized he might have put Alex at risk by telling Barry Jennings he had a witness to worry about. *If the asshole killed Gurdlich . . . .*

William's fingers moved quickly on the phone's surface. Dan Armour answered.

"Dan, do you know if that Jennings fellow made any phone calls from holding?"

"He's not in holding. His lawyer appeared and got him cut loose twenty minutes ago."

"What the hell? Dan, what's going on?"

"The Chief intervened. Cut some sort of a deal. Jennings came clean and gave us the keys to his warehouse. I sent over teams and they're searching it now."

"Came clean? He confessed?"

"Only to storing flammable chemicals in that old plant. Hazmat went in first to make sure the shit was secure. I'm going over shortly. You're welcome to join in the fun, but I'm pretty sure we won't find Gurdlich in there."

"So, Jennings risked running me down over chemicals stored in his plant?"

"That's it in a nutshell," confirmed Dan. "He even has an alibi for the night Gurdlich went missing."

"It better be air tight. The guy—"

"He was playing poker with the Chief and a couple of city councilmen," Dan interrupted. "Will, we're both screwed on this one. The Chief is extremely pissed that we tossed Jennings in jail."

"Really? And what did the Chief say about his poker buddy trying to run me down?"

Dan paused. "It's not fair and I totally disagreed with him, but the Chief says you're a loose cannon who acted improperly. He said you embarrassed the city by causing us to assault a charitable organization's volunteer."

William swallowed back a tirade. "Is our little meeting with the Chief still on for the morning?"

"As far as I know," Dan responded with a shade of trepidation in his voice.

"Fucking politics, the breakfast of champions," William said through gritted teeth. He hung up the phone without saying goodbye and flung it at the passenger door of his car.

* * *

Snow had been plowed high in front of Mick's Tavern and visibility had deteriorated to only a few feet. After parking as close as drifting snow would allow, William flipped on the red and blue flashers hidden behind the grill of his car as a vicious gust shook the vehicle. He opened his door between gusts, closing it quickly to avoid its transformation into a sail.

"Cold mother out there," hollered the bartender as William closed the front door against the night's bluster. "TV weather guy says it's gonna be a blizzard."

Without the preamble of introducing himself, William demanded, "Seen Alex Capstain tonight?"

"The little guy? Yeah, he was here earlier . . . on a real bender. Drank one bottle, slept it off and took some to go."

William's gut clenched. "Any mention of his destination?"

"Hell, I don't know. The morning man knows him better than me. Last I saw, the owner ushered him out the front door . . . Can I get you a drink?"

"No, thanks. Did Alex say anything to you? Was he acting strange?"

Growing suspicious, the guy eyed him and spoke more cautiously. "His drinking that much was strange. He usually nurses the same bottle of beer for hours. The switch from beer to wine was different, too. But he was smiling when he left. Said he had a homecoming to go to. You a relative or something?"

"Or something," William quipped as he headed for the door. He had a good idea of where to look.

Shivering as he settled behind his steering wheel, he saw his phone blinking from the passenger side floorboard. The wind buffeted the car. Cursing his childish outburst with the communication device, he started the car and turned the heater on high before scooping up the phone. He had a voicemail from Liz Caldwell. He listened as he drove.

"Detective, I hope I'm not calling in the middle—"

The phone rang again, interrupting the recording. It was Liz.

William answered with, "I hope you're having a better night than I am, Liz."

"I saw the mess on television. Hope you're all right. Ah, William, I'm really worried about Alex."

"Me, too. I'm out looking for him now. You heard about the Fitzgerald closing, right?"

"Yes. Gerard called me. He's concerned that Alex never came home to collect his things."

"Best I can tell he was last seen leaving Mick's Tavern. I think I know where he was headed . . . He had a bottle."

"The doghouse?" She said as if the words hurt.

"Yeah, and in this weather . . . Well . . . I'm driving there now. I'll call when I know more."

"Please do." Her voice sounded wet, as if she had started to cry. "Bye."

Powdery snow flowed into drifts across the streets. William's car had enough weight and power to plow through for the time being, but its ground clearance and rear-wheel-drive would soon become a problem. He only had to go a mile from Mick's to the doghouse. The drive seemed endless as the near white-out conditions forced him to slow to a crawl. He had left his police flashers on and hoped that any other idiot out tonight would stay clear.

At Alex's lot, a vicious wind sucked the air from William's lungs as he jumped from his car. He pulled his coat up over his face to catch his breath then flicked on his flashlight. All he could see was driving snow. High-stepping through the knee-deep white stuff, he stiffened against wind gusts that nearly knocked him over. His foot caught on something heavy. He squatted and was relieved to see it was only a tire. Finally he reached the doghouse with its open door nearly drifted shut.

Jesus Lord, please let him be alive.

Flashlight gripped in his mouth with his lips almost sticking to the cold metal, he used both hands to sweep the snow from the doorway. The arguing wind blew it back in his face as if throwing fine needles at his exposed skin.

Finally he took the flashlight in hand and aimed it inside. At first he saw only a dirty blanket. Pursing his numb lips, he started to relax, but then the beam of light found Alex's bloody face.

"Alex!" he shouted into the confinement, his free hand shaking a flexible small shoulder. *Not stiff. Thank you, God.* Relief rolled through William.

"Detective Olson?" sounded a small, wind-shredded feminine voice behind him. "Are you back there?"

He turned to shout over his shoulder, "Liz, wait there! I'll be out in a second. He's alive but we have to get him to a hospital!"

"Should I call 9-1-1?" She sounded closer.

William almost knocked her down as he emerged, dragging Alex with him. He ducked his head against the wind and, in one motion, slung Alex over his shoulders in a fireman's carry. His legs churned through the snow, his breath puffing like a steam engine only to be ripped away by the wind. Liz stumbled along behind him.

"Rear door!" William yelled as they neared his car.

Liz yanked it open, bracing herself to keep it that way against the wind. Will literally threw Alex into the back seat. Liz crawled in after, allowing the wind to slam the door. William kept his head down as he rounded to the driver's door.

Grill light's flashing and siren wailing, William fishtailed around corners and busted through snowdrifts. He radioed ahead to the hospital. In the back seat, Liz did her best to count Alex's shallow breaths and feel for the pulse in his neck. William glanced in the rearview to see her cradling his friend, stroking his damaged face while tears streaked her own.

"Don't you die on me, Daddy," she murmured wetly. "Not now. Not when we were so close."

At 30th Street he made a wide, sliding left turn while yelling, "Hang on!" He hit the brakes and nearly missed the emergency entrance with the anti-lock system pulsing under foot. A quick gun of the engine spun the rear of the car around, pointing him back to the entrance marked in red neon.

Emergency staff met them at the door and scooped Alex from his arms. He tried to follow, but secondary staff brushed him aside as the primary medical team whisked their patient away on a gurney. Liz ran along side, crisply providing medical details.

Still on an adrenaline high, he called Dan to report what had happened. Someone shoved a Styrofoam cup of coffee into his hands and pressed him to a waiting area seat. He half-heartedly watched the muted television hanging from the ceiling in the corner. He couldn't wrap his mind around the closed captioning until Barry Jennings's face flashed on the screen. He moved closer to watch the replay of the Angel's Wings van nearly mowing him down. It all happened a lot faster than he recalled.

Maybe I should retire. I've got plenty of time in. I could putz around the wood shop, work part-time at a hardware store or something. Enjoy the kids while we've still got them at home.

Liz emerged from the treatment bay, disheveled and teary-eyed.

"What's the word?" William asked.

"He's alive. They're warming him slowly."

William noticed she wore pajamas under her coat, the flannel soaked from the top of her mid-calf boots to the edges of her long coat. The lanyard with her hospital and student ID hung over her pajama top and her fingers worried a small, heart-shaped locket at her neck.

William studied her rather distant expression. "Liz, will he be okay?"

She jerked as if startled and gave him a weak smile. "It's too early to tell. His core temperature was dangerously low. He had severe bradycardia which can be a good thing in hypothermia . . . Basically, he's in a kind of state of suspended animation. Alive but not awake." The fingers on the locket tightened. "There's no way to know if he will come back to us." As she said those words, her chin trembled and tears rose.

William opened his arms. She leaned in, sobbing as he patted and rubbed her back. The girl that William had first thought mature beyond her years just wanted to be held.

The sobs slowed and turned into ragged breaths. She pulled back, wiping her nose and eyes with her coat sleeve. "I'm so sorry."

William put a fatherly hand on the side of her face. He glanced at the IDs around her neck before his eyes came up to meet hers. "It's quite all right. So, when were you planning to tell him?"

"Tell who what?" Liz asked, confusion clouding her red, puffy face.

"That you're his daughter?"

Liz's right hand flew up to her locket. "When did you know?"

"You called him 'Daddy' on the ride in. And your hospital ID says Amanda E. Caldwell. E for Elizabeth?"

She nodded. "Caldwell's my stepfather's name. Long ago they told me my real father died when I was four. I didn't know different until a couple of years ago. My aunt told me. I'm living with her while I finish school. I was going to surprise him once he was back on his feet." The again trembling chin lifted. "Now . . . I don't know if I'll ever get the chance," she said ending on a whisper.

21

"I am Michael, one of the seven who stand before God." His powerful voice echoed off the uneven concrete floor and rough red brick streaked with lime. Gurdlich dangled, his breath shallow, his awareness drifting in and out punctuated only by guttural noises.

From a small wooden table cluttered with antique tools, Michael plucked a rusty, wood-handled ice pick. Nervous with anticipation, he searched the empty stare of Gurdlich's clouded eyes. He watched for any kind of response as he placed the pick's point in the big sergeant's left ear and pushed slowly.

None of the others had lasted this long before begging God's forgiveness.

The pop of Gurdlich's inner ear elicited a high-pitched squeal from the hateful lump's mouth. Michael needed at least a word of true repentance, just one whispered word. Without it the man would not be saved. Michael stepped back and looked around, his own gut tightening in fear of what might come to claim the man's stubborn soul.

"Repent, repent, repent . . . ." he chanted, sliding the pick beyond the inner workings of the ear into the brain. He cocked his head recalling how similar probe felt to biology class pithing of a lifeless frog. Unlike the unresponsive frog, Gurdlich's limbs jerked.

With his free hand, Michael lifted the apron to stroke his limp member. He let his mind drift, reaching and praying for the beautiful voice and warm, loving light. Those only came in a glorious gush to wash away his guilt. He needed that to survive, to banish the dirty sensation he had actually liked at the conclusion of what his mother's boyfriend did to him. Again and again he had since demonstrated his own repentance. He convinced the sinners and shared their joy.

Only this time, the sinner wouldn't break. And he could not relieve his guilt. Angry, Michael jabbed the pick in to the hilt, twirling it like the crank of a macabre jack-in-the-box. His eyes widened at the contorted smile of the face before him. It looked so like his mother's boyfriend who had crooned for him to relax and promised an ice cream cone from the Ding-Ding man.

He leaned in closer to search the lifeless, bleach-ruined eyes. Without warning, the big sergeant's eyes sparked with life. The razor-toothed mouth below snapped. A putrid breath hissed. Michael leaped back, his bloodied palms raised and trembling in terror. Screeching demons swirled up from the floor around him then swept by to grope and pull at the sergeant. Michael fell backwards onto the floor then scrambled to a dark corner. He clasped and unclasped his hands as the demons tore the shadow of the man's soul from his open mouth. They tugged the soul back and forth as if fighting for a prize. A moment later their shadows dropped back through the concrete floor, carrying Gurdlich to Hell, leaving silence and his body behind.

Michael touched his own still-intact mouth. "Thank you, God," he murmured.

* * *

The storm brewing inside William made the previous night's blizzard seem tame as he made the torturous, icy commute into downtown. Each time he convinced himself that he should march proudly into retirement by telling the Chief to go fuck himself, thoughts of his boys and college and car payments convinced him otherwise. "Whatever you need to do, I'm with you," Susan had repeatedly told him as they talked until sunup.

A call to the hospital revealed no change in Alex's condition. He could wake at any moment or never again. "We've done all we can and now it's out of our hands," the doctor had told him.

Liz had remained at her father's bedside throughout the night. William had watched her stroking his hair, telling him about her childhood, apologizing for not letting him in on her secret for fear of embarrassing him. Below the monitor screen showing his heart rhythm and blood pressure, Alex lay silent and unresponsive. William hoped the man had heard something of his daughter's words or at least sensed the love she poured out. That alone had to do what the medical doctors couldn't.

On his walk from the garage into police headquarters, William met with a few fist bumps and the occasional softly spoken "Go get 'em." He concluded news of his battle with the Chief combined with his well-publicized run-in with Barry Jennings had garnered a few fans, especially with the experienced cops grown tired of the morale's downward spiral.

Seated bolt upright with tension, Dan Armour waited outside the Chief's office.

William stopped with his back to the Chief's secretary. "Sleep much?" William asked quietly.

"Barely. You?"

William settled into the chair next to him. "Not a wink. I'm thinking it's time to retire, Dan. Tell the Chief to go fuck himself and go out in a blaze of glory."

Dan rolled his eyes. "What's the glory in that, Will? Might feel good for a moment, but it wouldn't solve any of the real problems. Did you see the paper this morning? The press is leaning our way, Will. They smell blood in the water." He flicked a thumb at the polished wood door with gold letters reading CHIEF JEFFERY P. BARNES. "The Chief's a political animal. He'll flush this Jennings guy in a heartbeat if he thinks the stink will rub off on him."

The secretary called out, "He'll see you now."

They stood in unison, but William opened the pretentious door for Dan to enter first.

Chief Barnes sat behind a large, well-organized desk. The office walls were covered in framed photographs of the Chief shaking hands with politicians and movie stars. Outside his seventh-floor window, the blanket of windblown snow made a shabby fringe of the Old Market shopping district slightly more presentable.

Without bothering to stand or greet them, Barnes barked, "Where do we stand on the search for our missing sergeant?"

"Nothing more than we had last night," said Dan. "Mr. Jennings kindly agreed to let us search his family's meatpacking plant. Hazmat took much of the night clearing the flammable chem.—"

"I didn't ask you about Jennings."

"Yes, sir." Dan didn't offer even a glance sideways at William. "Nothing new to report on Gurdlich beyond the evidence uncovered by Detective Olson."

With that opening, William began, "The baton from the alley showed only Sgt. Gurdlich's fingerprints. The lab—"

"How's the hip, Detective?" interrupted Barnes.

William let a beat of silence follow as if emphasizing he understood the game playing. "Just a hip pointer, sir, nothing broken. A little painful but manageable."

"And what the hell were you thinking, jumping in front of a moving vehicle?"

William did look at Dan this time before responding. "It wasn't moving when I stepped in front of it, sir. Mr. Jennings deliberately tried—"

"That's not what I saw on television."

"Sir, the stations showed—"

"It's come to my attention that you've been on the wrong path quite a bit lately."

"Excuse me, sir?" William did not bother to control his tone. "I don't understand."

Barnes consulted a file on his desk. "Your contact with a reporter, a Miss Manuela Garcia. Are you aware of the department policy strictly forbidding official contact with the media except through our liaison?"

"Of course, I'm aware, sir. But, Miss Garcia and I have been friends a very long time. I've never discussed an active investigation with her. Frankly, I can't stop specu—"

"I've instructed our tech people to block Miss Garcia's numbers on your cell and office phones," said the Chief.

Thrown off balance by the punch-and-move attack and keyed into his own bubbling fury, William checked his body language to hide his contempt.

The Chief pulled over a short stack of papers, rifled through them and pulled out one sheet. "What took you to 156th Street and Thomas Roads? That's the location of the West Omaha Church of Christ, is it not? I've seen no burglary reports from the church. You are a burglary detective, and . . . . " He paused to glance down then back up. "This visit was on department time, correct?"

William crossed his arms. "Have you had me followed?"

A palm slapped the paper onto the desk. Barnes arched one eyebrow. "Taxpayer dollars are too important to waste man hours on that, detective. We simply tracked the location of your cell phone. It's my job to keep an eye on those who want to do this department harm."

"Harm? I've never done anything to—"

"We have Twitter posts that say different."

"What?" Dan touched his elbow to refocus his control.

"On several occasions you publicly criticized this department on Twitter."

"Me? I don't . . . My youngest boy signed me up for that." William closed his eyes and tried to remember what he'd written before deeming it a waste of time.

Barnes turned his attention back to the papers before him. "I see references to 'keystone cops' and, ah, 'not having our act together'." He looked up and let bitterness taint his words, "Etcetera, etcetera. This is behavior unbecoming. Period."

William abruptly laughed. "Sir, those posts were at least two-years old and I was referring to a football game, not this department."

Beside him, Dan clenched his fists. William thought he heard his teeth grind just before the man said, "With all due respect, sir, our missing sergeant and his sick, not to mention, illegal, perversions will be far more damning to this department than your misinterpretation of my senior detective's online social activity."

Barnes snapped his attention to Dan. "The perversions to which you refer are unsubstantiated rumor, conjecture based on a statement from a drug addict who would say anything to harm one of our own. Frankly, I find

Detective Olson's public criticism and cavalier attitude toward this department far more disturbing than a pack of lies told by a whoring addict."

Dan took half a step forward. "Sir, you—"

"Here's what is going to happen." Chief Barnes pointed a manicured finger at William. "In the next twenty-four hours, Detective Olson, you will erase your public slander of this department. I will see a written apology on my desk and your agreement to be a team player. Plus, you will publicly apologize to Mr. Jennings for your abhorrent, disrespectful behavior. Via newspaper or TV statement, I don't care. You're damn lucky he isn't suing you and the city."

"Sir, I—"

The Chief jumped to his feet. "Detective Olson, you will shut your mouth if you know what's good for you. Now, if you chose not to cooperate, Detective, we can always use another man to watch passengers with the TSA at the airport."

"Why don't you go f—"

A ring of the desk phone interrupted William's comeback. A beat later, the simultaneous buzz of the two detective's cell phones joined in.

The Chief palmed his phone saying, "I told you no interruptions!"

Dan and William looked at their own displays then glanced at the other's to confirm the identical text message from Burt Haliday, their CSI lead investigator. *Dogs located 2 bodies in warehouse. Not Gurdlich. Still searching. Jennings in custody.*

William smirked at the Chief who listened intently on his phone. He glanced up at William then frowned. "There has to be a mistake." His free hand tousled his carefully-preened hair. "How many? In what? Any idea how long? I see. You've got to keep this under wraps. Is Gurdlich . . . Well, find the hell out!"

Dan waved his phone's screen at the Chief, who curtly waved a dismissal.

William savored the Chief's predicament all the way to elevator then looked at the thoughtful Dan, asking, "Wonder if Jennings knew the dogs were coming?"

"Hopefully we'll find out when we get to the scene. You drive." He clapped William on the shoulder. "I'll ride shotgun to save the Chief the trouble of tracking you."

"Such a funny guy," William quipped. "You have no idea how close I just came to resigning."

"Really? Bet you have no idea how close I came to beating the hell out of that political piece of shit." He shook his head. "Twitter posts? Really? He is fucking desperate. Of course, you know he was pushing your buttons hoping you'd resign."

"It was working. But, I think I'll stick around to watch the sonofabitch drown in the shit storm that's about to rain down on the whole corrupt bunch."

* * *

The Jennings' warehouse looked less ominous than it had from the dark alley the night before. As Dan and William rolled up, Manuela waved from the crowd of media gathered behind the yellow crime scene tape cordoning the street. Decked out in parkas and boots, television technicians moved around nearby satellite trucks as if settling in for the long haul.

"So much for the Chief's wanting to keep this quiet," observed Dan, smiling broadly and waving at the group.

A couple of the watchers uncertainly waved back then the wall of people surged forward. The two men ignored the shouted questions as they headed into the building's main entrance. The scent of putrefying flesh hit them as they looked over the bustle of a portable command center under construction.

An older, stocky man and CSI lead Burt Haliday emerged from the hive of activity to greet them. His eyes carried the weight of every gruesome detail he'd ever uncovered.

"We found two bodies so far and two openings where transients have been entering." He motioned them to a table covered with building plans. "What we've got here are three buildings. Over the years they were remodeled into one large complex. We're standing in the main warehouse. The second building is the largest with multiple floors. The third appears to be the newer of the three. Like this one, it is a tall, single-story structure. I've got teams searching the upper floors of the second building now, but it's going to take time. This place has more nooks and crannies than a pharaoh's tomb."

"Anything new since your text?" Dan asked.

"Let's go ask my team. They should be about ready to extricate the bodies."

22

Crossing the main warehouse floor, William noticed their footsteps echoing in the emptiness of what used to be a bustling processing plant.

"The bodies were in metal barrels, sealed tight with a clamp-on lids," Burt said, as they walked. "That prevented the usual insect activity that speeds decomp. Judging by the lack of putrefaction, they were killed sometime this fall or winter. I won't know much more than that until I get them to the lab and let the coroner have a look."

Passing into the second building through an opening protected by a massive iron and concrete fire door, they entered a darker and more deteriorated space with a low ceiling. The stench of death grew stronger. Powerful quartz lamps illuminated a corner of the floor where the two barrels had been placed on a blue tarp to be examined in detail by crime techs.

"There's a couple of good prints on this one, Burt," called out a tech, holding up a card with a graphite-laden print.

Burt opened a small jar of menthol-scented ointment and offered it to William first.

"Don't mind if I do," William said, dipping his finger in the jar then rubbing the ointment under his nose.

"We put the lids back on the barrels after the discovery. Extrication will bring the stench to full bloom. I don't need your breakfasts contaminating my crime scene."

Looking like his meal just might revisit, Dan hurried to copy William. Burt then instructed the masked techs to remove the two lids. The two detectives put on their game faces, knowing no one here would walk away unaffected.

"Holy Mother of God," Dan blurted.

The corpses were bloated and horribly misshapen, their pallid, blue-green skin cracked in some places, sloughing off in others. The smell of rotting flesh still permeated the menthol pseudo-barrier.

Burt lectured as if addressing a forensics class, "As you can see, they were placed in the barrel feet first and naked. If you look close you can identify their clothing stuffed in just under their arms there. See?"

William swallowed and cleared his throat before asking, "How long before we get a fingerprint I.D.?"

"We're done with the exterior of the barrels, so we can do it now, if you like."

"Go for it," Dan growled.

Clad in full protective gear of coveralls, rubber boots and gloves, the masked techs quickly assembled a PVC pipe frame to which they zip-tied the edges of a tarp to form a containment pool.

"We'll have to tip them, boys," Burt ordered his team. "Let gravity do the work." He turned to look at the faces of the detectives. "Ah, you may not want to watch. This isn't very tidy. It's the sort of thing that will stick with you."

William and Dan exchanged glances. Dan waved Burt to continue.

"I warned you," Burt murmured.

Slowly the techs tipped the first barrel. Three-quarters of the way over, a sucking sound announced the shifting body. Fluid trickled onto the tarp once the barrel was down. When the techs pulled at the corpse's arms, the skin sloughed off in their hands. More fluid gushed out as the body came free followed by a pile of gelatinous goo from the bottom of the barrel.

"Oh, Christ!" William groaned, turning away and pulling his coat over his face to block the cloud-like aroma surrounding them.

As the two techs headed to the second barrel, Dan waved a hand at Burt then shoved on William's shoulder. The two detectives rapidly left the scene, almost running by the time they crossed the first floor to reach the door to the outside. In the clean, crisp air, they gulped and avoided looking at one another.

William sniffed his coat sleeve then flapped his arms as if to move cleansing air through the material. He watched Dan scoop up snow and rub it over his face.

"Does that help?" he asked. At Dan's nod, he followed suit.

As they recovered, William's mind raced. "Remember my mention of Gurdlich's connection to Pastor Ahough?"

Still looking a bit green, Dan cleared his throat. "Sure." He bent and scooped another handful of snow. "God, after all these years you'd think we'd get used to almost anything. But that—"

"Judging by the stench, you've got a bad one in there," Ken Wilkins interrupted. He approached them from the makeshift command center.

"Yeah, a bad one," said Dan. "You pull an all-nighter, Ken?"

"Nah, I got a few hours sleep, but a lot of the guys are working doubles. I just came in early to give them a hand." He looked around the building with a grimace. "Is it Harry Gurdlich?"

"No," William quickly reassured him. "He's not in there, thank God."

"The way you two look, I suppose that's a blessing," said Ken. He shifted, glanced around them back at him. "Will, I'd like to apologize for what I said last—"

"Not to worry, Ken. I heard what you told the rookies after. Thanks for that."

"Meant every word. I think this whole mess will make everyone rethink their behavior."

William nodded. "Ken, you're out on the street routinely. Have you been aware of any interaction between Gurdlich and Barry Jennings?"

"No, not that I've seen or heard."

"How about Gurdlich and Pastor Ahough?"

"The TV preacher?"

William nodded.

"Nothing between them either, but Harry once told me he thinks the guy's gay. Then again, he thought anyone who didn't refer to women as bitches was gay. Why do you ask?"

"I've got two street people who say Jennings used the Angel's Wings vans to try to kidnap and dump them on the far end of Council Bluffs. If we identify the bodies in there as homeless guys, it's possible they were part of it."

"A kidnapping gone wrong and Harry was mixed up in it?"

William glanced at the thoughtful Dan then back at Ken. "Just tossing out ideas. Could be that all this is tied together."

"Harry was a bad cop, but murder?" Ken scratched under his stocking cap.

Dan asked, "Is this coming from the report the rookie took from Alex Capstain at the hospital?"

William nodded. "Got the same thing from a fellow named Terrance Sanford. On the street they call him Moon Boots."

From inside the building Burt hollered, "You boys recovered enough for the viewing?"

Seeing Ken shiver and back away, William nodded to Dan. Together they stiffened their shoulders and headed back to the door between the buildings. Burt waited holding up the jar of ointment. Both of them took bigger globs this time.

William mentally blocked the smell and focused on observation, remembering the victims were owed that much. Both bodies had been arranged on the tarps, putrid skin sagging off the bone, their humanity negligible. The clothes that had been tucked with them inside their respective barrel had been carefully laid out alongside each. Still soaked in body rot, the fabric glistened under the bright lights. One tech used long forceps to probe a victim's clothing pockets, turning them inside out. He dropped his discoveries into plastic evidence bags labeled "Victim No. 1" in black marker.

William and Dan stepped up beside Burt who waited at a plastic-covered collapsible table. The investigator rubbed his gloved hands on his protective overalls as if anxious to get on with it. He set out the bags, then selected one, opened it and used forceps to extricate a soggy wallet. He picked up another instrument with smaller points to pick at the wallet then grunted almost in triumph when he pulled out a driver's license.

"Antonio Arnold of Omaha," read Dan, writing down the name and other pertinent information in his notebook. "Thanks, Burt. Anything else of note in there?"

"A condom—still in the wrapper—, a couple of pictures and a state-issued SNAP food stamps card."

"No credit or insurance cards?"

"Nope, that's it."

Dan tossed a knowing look at William, with, "The food stamp card says he's not one of Omaha's upper class."

"Probably right," said William. "But if Jennings is our perp, why be so messy? I mean, the guy has the money, knowledge and ability to turn these guys into dog food and nobody'd be the wiser."

"Maybe he's a trophy collector," offered Dan.

An excited voice, backed by the barking of the cadaver dog, broke over the two-way radio clipped to Burt's coveralls.

"Burt, you gotta get up here. Jesus, there must be a dozen! Holy fuckin' crap!"

"Knock off the hysterics and tell me where you are!" Burt yelled back through the radio.

"T-top floor, half-way in. I'll meet you the stairwell on the west end."

* * *

Alex stood on what appeared to be an endless, rough-hewn wooden beam. Terror racked his body. The toes of his bare feet cramped in spasms as they clung to the beam's edge. He had to decide now, this moment, on moving to one side of the beam or the other. *No! Until all my options are clear, I'm staying right here, damnit.*

Beside his hospital bed, Liz watched her father's legs tremble. His feet arched, the toes stiffening under the blankets. Her throat hurt from talking nonstop, telling stories of her childhood as if bringing him up to date on all he had missed. She had drifted off to sleep, her forehead on his hand. The leg spasms had awakened her. She glanced at the monitor of the heating blanket. His core temperature had almost reached normal. The spasms were also normal as circulation returned to the deprived muscles. Studying his face, she frowned. The eye movements under his closed lids appeared almost frantic. She trailed soothing fingertips over his cheek.

"It's all right, Daddy," Liz crooned, hoping to ease whatever it was he found so terrifying. "Don't be scared. You-you can go if you have to, but I'd love you to come back. We have so much to talk about. So much."

* * *

Burt, Dan, and William automatically went for their flashlights in the dark stairwell. On the third floor landing they met Officer Grant, the lights from their flashlights shining up from below exaggerating the ghostliness of his pallid face and sunken, bloodshot eyes.

"It's not good," said Grant, turning to lead them to the fourth floor.

The cadaver dog's bark distantly echoed in the trashed, graffiti-laden mess of the fourth floor. Grant led them down a long, dark hallway, their flashlight beams swinging to quickly note the surroundings.

Something touched the side of William's head then grabbed his hair. He screeched, his arm flailing. Pistols came free of holsters and flashlights blinded him as he continued to alternate between rubbing his head and swatting at the air.

Dan demanded, "What the hell, Will?"

"Something grabbed my hair. Maybe a bat?"

"You're a lucky man," Burt said too gravely. "That was no bat."

"What the hell was it then?"

In the glow of the flashlights, William saw Burt actually smile as he pointed his beam upwards. "Dangling conduit snake." His light followed a swinging, metallic tube pulled from the ceiling by copper scavengers. "Damn things have been known to make the strongest men scream like little girls."

Even William joined in the bout of the sleep-deprived chuckles.

"I did not scream like a girl," he announced then grinned sheepishly.

"Okay, I'll agree," said Dan. "I'd classify that as more of a full-grown woman's scream."

William flipped him the finger before raising an impatient hand for Grant to continue on. The brief jovial moment faded as the recurrent putrid smell of death drifted to them. Dull light filtered through a doorway ahead. All flashlights remained on as they entered a large room, its outer wall lined by grimy or painted-over windows, some intact, some broken. Shafts of mid-morning light slanted through the few broken panes, illuminating the grizzly discovery. In the center of the room, metal drums stood in neat rows like soldiers awaiting inspection. The cadaver dog's furor kicked up dust motes and pigeon feathers that danced across the few sunbeams.

The dog handler lowered his mask. "I'll finish working this floor then head on downstairs for some fresh air. It's been a long night."

"Ah, sirs, can I go with him?" Grant asked. "After the dog hit on this room, I opened a barrel to confirm." He touched a rubber-gloved hand to his forehead. "I never want to see anything like that again."

Burt clapped him on the shoulder. "That's all right, son. I take it you re-clamped the lid?"

"Goddamn right," Grant snapped then caught himself. "Hope I didn't screw up any evidence."

"Nah," Burt reassured him, pointing at the gloves. "You did fine. No worries. Check the other rooms on this floor then head on downstairs."

"Yes, sir." William understood the kid's reluctant study of his hands as Grant added, "I-I'll just leave the gloves on then."

Burt walked to the middle of the squadron of barrels, tapping the sides as though shopping for a watermelon. All sounded dull and ripe. Picking a barrel at random, he released the clamped lid. Putrid gas hissed out. Both Dan and William covered their noses and mouths.

Burt retightened the clamp then his head drooped in disgust. "We're going to have to call the Feds. Our lab can't handle all this and," he looked up at them, "serial murder falls into their jurisdiction."

* * *

Back at Omaha Police headquarters, Barry Jennings sat in an interview room, handcuffed to the table, unshaven and unkempt. He fidgeted, huffing loudly as he sat forward then back, crossing and uncrossing his legs, all the while hating the video camera with its red light watching from its perch in the corner of the room.

After an hour of sitting alone, he jerked in his chair when the red light went out and the interview room door simultaneously opened.

"Good morning, Mr. Jennings. I'm Bill Block. I'll be acting as your attorney should you so choose." The tall, gray-haired and impeccably dressed man was known throughout the community for his outrageous but often-successful courtroom antics. "You'll notice the camera has been turned off. You may speak freely."

Jennings leaned to look around him but saw no one else. "Why are you here, Block? Where's my family's usual attorney?"

"Your family's firm is a good one. So good in fact that they wisely requested I handle your case," said Block, closing the door behind him.

"But—"

"No buts, Mr. Jennings," he interrupted opening his briefcase on the table. "This is a high-profile murder investigation—"

"Bullshit," spat Jennings. "I didn't murder anyone."

"Appearances are important, wouldn't you agree, Mr. Jennings?" Block asked, looking like a kindly grandfather.

Jennings drew his shoulders in as his chest cramped with anxiety. "Yes, of course, but—"

"Let's have a look at your predicament." Block pulled a metal chair from the opposite side of the table and sat down next to Jennings. He removed a folder from his case, opened it and read a few pages. "Attempted vehicular homicide of a police detective . . . who just happened to be searching for a missing police officer . . . with whom you have financial ties. I'd say that's very serious." He then stared into his client's eyes. "Wouldn't you agree, Mr. Jennings?"

"The Police Chief thought otherwise."

Block moved to another page then slowly, deliberately folded his hands before meeting his gaze. This time the stare hardened. "But now we have two dead bodies found inside the building from which you were trying to flee."

"What? I wasn't—"

"Do you hear that sound, Barry?" Block said, putting his hand to his ear, his face shifting from grandfather to predator. "That's the sound of your so-called connections flushing you down the shitter. Now, before the serious interrogation starts, tell me, did you or anyone you know commit murder?"

"No, of course not," Barry said, his pomposity failing in the face of Block's shark-like demeanor.

The sharp eyes returned to the folder. "What was the nature of your dealings with Sgt. Harry Gurdlich?"

This is getting fucking bad. Jennings wiped his free hand across his mouth and pressed his knees together to control their shaking. "I paid him to keep up appearances in a part of the city we are planning to redevelop."

"Bribery for turning a blind eye to something illegal?"

"No! No, he had street connections that he used to make the prostitutes and drug dealers disappear . . . I mean, hide away when our investors came around."

"So, he just cracked down on them when you wanted him to?"

"I didn't ask Gurdlich about his methods. I simply told him what we needed when and he made it happen. If that involved methods that crossed a line, it's on him."

Block nodded as if he understood the need. "Why did you attack Detective Olson?"

"Honestly, I was just trying to avoid the spotlight. I thought he would move. Honest to god, the van got away from me in the snow. It was an accident."

Block's brow furrowed. "And your reasons for avoiding the spotlight? Is there something more I need to know?" The eyes narrowed again. "Now's the time to tell me, Barry. Everything you say is privileged. It stays between us."

Jennings glanced up at the corner camera. Its light was still off. "Gurdlich told me Detective Olson had been sniffing around our redevelopment project. I was worried Olson would do something that would sour our investors."

"So, your reaction wasn't about illegally stored chemicals?"

"That was just a ruse. I had to give the Chief a reason for my actions and I didn't want him in on the redevelopment deal."

Block made some notes on the papers in the folder. "Anything else? Anything at all I need to know? I don't want any surprises once the interrogation starts."

"No, that's it. Everything." He twisted his cuffed wrist rattling the metal against the table. "Let's get this started so I can get on with my life."

* * *

Outside in the hall, William saw the lawyer peek out of the room to nod indicating they were ready.

"I'll be damned. He got ol' B. B . . . I mean, Bill Block to defend him," Dan said. "Rich boy must be scared to call in the cream of our local criminal lawyers."

"How do you want to handle this?" William asked. "Ah, given our go-round with the Chief this morning—"

"We'll be fine. I'll use the Chief angle for leverage then use this as the hammer." Dan held up the manila envelope containing their little surprise. "Before we go in, finish telling me about what this Moon Boots character and Alex said about Jennings and the church van."

William quickly related the stories. He then let Dan precede him into the interview room.

William noted Jennings staring at the upper corner's security camera. The man actually flinched when the red light flicked on.

William moved to the far side of the table, opposite the scumbag and his shark. When Jennings looked at him, he let his voice ooze animosity, "Nice to formally meet you."

The man visibly collected himself, a veil of superiority drifting over his demeanor. "Sorry about our dust-up, Detective," he crooned. "I'm afraid emotions got the better of all of us. Hopefully our little accident didn't hurt you too—"

"In spite of what you'd like to believe," Dan interrupted, "that little accident as you call it was attempted vehicular homicide. Of course, that charge is trumped by actual murder."

While William moved to the periphery, Dan took a seat directly opposite Jennings. When the manila envelope was placed on the table, both client and attorney glanced at it then each other before focusing on their lead interrogator.

"I'll have to say, you have done a bang-up job of digging yourself into a hole," Dan continued. "Wait. Forgot my manners." He flicked a steely glance at the gray-haired man. "Nice to see you too, Bill. How's it hanging?"

"Long, thick and down my right pant leg, if you must know," Block replied with a slimy smile. Jennings sneered at the crude exchange.

"All right then, now that we have the *small* talk out of the way," Dan said, leaning forward. "Let's get on with it. Mr. Jennings, for the record you agree that you have been advised of your rights, your lawyer is present and that we are recording this interview, correct?"

"Yes, of course." Jennings gaze darted to the red light of the video camera.

"Yes, of course what? Mr. Jennings, this is serious business and you need to be clear. Please speak up," Dan prompted him.

"Of course I understand my rights and my lawyer is present. I'm not a fool."

"Very well then. Let me be clear as well. Until now, your connections may have gotten you better treatment than you deserved, but connections have a way of disappearing when dead bodies start popping up. Tell me, do you think your poker buddy, the Chief, would let Detective Olson anywhere near you if he still had your back?"

"Good point. I protest Detective Olson's intimidating presence," Bill Block said.

Dan never looked away from Jennings. "If I were your client, I'd be more concerned with the two charges of murder hanging over my head." He slapped a hand on the manila envelope startling Jennings, before he rattled off, "Two counts of murder, one of attempted murder and you're a suspect in Sgt. Gurdlich's disappearance."

Jennings blinked rapidly, sweat popping on his upper lip. "My dealings with Sgt. Gurdlich were strictly business. He's retiring soon and—"

"So what happened, Barry," William interrupted, forcing Jennings to turn to look at him. "Did Gurdlich want a bigger slice of the pie for covering up your little kidnapping game? One of the guys you dumped in the Bluffs almost died."

Bill Block stiffened. He put a hand on Jennings's arm. "My client has nothing to say on that matter."

"Ah, I see this is news to you, B.B.," Dan interjected. "You'd be surprised how much your client hasn't told you. We've got two men who will testify that your client kidnapped and transported them across the state line then dumped them in Council Bluffs against their will."

"I'd like a minute with my cli—"

William cut Block off, "Oh, and those two dead bodies in your client's building? Let's make that more like a dozen, maybe more. Hell, B.B., you've got a sick fuck of a serial killer for a client."

"Gentlemen!" Dan raised his voice, bringing all eyes to him as he pulled photographs from the envelope. He melodramatically spread them before Jennings and Block. Their eyes widened on the images of the bloated, rotting, blue-green faces and the collection of barrels on the fourth floor. He pulled out the coup de grace, a fingerprint series labeled, "Jennings, Barry, C."

Block yanked his hand from Jennings's arm as though it were red hot. His horrified attention whipped from the photos to the face of the man beside him.

Jennings squirmed in his chair, eyes blinking, his confusion blatant. "I-I didn't kill anybody. That's ... I know nothing about ...." He turned pleading eyes on Block. "I was only hauling the worst of the drunks to a new shelter. They were-were everywhere, ruining the north downtown. I was doing everyone a favor, a favor I tell you," Barry stammered, sweat staining his underarms as he gesticulated with his cuffed hands for effect.

William stepped closer to his shoulder to keep up the back and forth attack. He spit out, "Keep dancing, you sick fuck. Kids will be singing songs about you. What rhymes with Jennings and meat—"

Dan slapped the table. "Tell us the truth and maybe you won't fry. Right now, I'd pay to watch the smoke curl from under the hood while your sick, twisted brain cooks."

Jennings didn't know where to look. He shrunk in his chair. "All right, I took men against their will, lots of them and dumped them in a park in Council Bluffs—"

"Shut up, Barry." Block came to his senses and returned his hand to Jennings' arm. "They don't use the electric—"

Jennings jerked away from him, shouting, "No, you shut up, you fucking shyster! I'm not paying you to make this worse!" He shivered then looked between Dan and William. "I picked up drunks in the north downtown and dumped them in park in Council Bluffs, that's all. That's all. You have to believe me." He waved his hand at the photos on the table. "I didn't kill anybody or-or even know about . . . that," he ended on a tremulous whisper.

"Were the men you picked up conscious when you left them unprotected in freezing weather?"

"I-I don't know. I never paid any attention. They were just drunken bums." Jennings wiped his shaking hand over his face. "I've told you the truth about that. It was my civic duty. I'm not some serial killer."

"We'll know more when we run these," Dan held up the finger print sheet, "against the prints on the barrels."

"Wait," Jennings jumped forward, "Those prints aren't—"

"From the barrels?" William interrupted. "No, just copies of your prints from this morning."

Bill Block huffed a breath, leering at Jennings. "I'd like to amend my client's earlier statement about not being a fool. Dan, if you plan on filing kidnapping charges, let me assure you, Mr. Jennings was only taking those poor men to a less crowded shelter. He thought he was doing them a favor."

Dan shrugged as he gathered the photos to return to the envelope. "I have no doubt you'll weasel your way to a lesser sentence in court on that one. In the meantime Barry, you will be booked into the Douglas County Corrections Center on charges of kidnapping and transport over a state line. And, you know what? That makes it a Federal offense."

William crossed his arms and smiled. "Thank you for that, Barry." When Jennings glared at him, he couldn't resist adding, "I know you could care less, but my hip is feeling a hell of a lot better with that admission of guilt."

* * *

Back in their den of offices, Dan and William met with a round of applause.

Dropping into his chair and rubbing his tired-looking eyes, Dan said, "As fun as that was, we still have a missing sergeant and a serial killer to find, preferably before the Feds take over the case. Our turf, gentlemen. Gratz, anything new on Gurdlich?"

"Nothing, sir. The hooker expanded on her story a bit. Said her pimp thumped Gurdlich on the head and that's how she got away. We're searching for a Leon Roosevelt as we speak."

The uniformed Grant came through the doors.

"Officer Grant," Dan called out, "did you just come from the scene?"

"Yes, sir," said the rookie. "The count is up to thirteen now. There were eleven bodies on the fourth floor. They just brought in a fresh dog handler to search for more."

"Had the Feds arrived yet when you left?"

"No, sir, but Burt Haliday told me to relay that the prints from the barrels downstairs matched those on the barrels upstairs."

"But no hits on those prints in the system, correct?" asked Dan.

"Nothing yet, sir."

"Thanks for your hard work, Grant," said Dan. "You look dead on your feet. Head home. Grab a shower and some shut-eye. You have five hours until your night shift begins again."

William glanced around at his fellow detectives nodding their approval and Grant's appreciative wave. *Nothing like a crisis well met and a bit of praise to improve morale.*

23

The nurse on rounds touched Liz's shoulder. She blinked awake, her head coming up off her father's hand. Her eyes went to the blanket over his legs. No trembling and no feet and toes in spasms.

"His heart rate is within normal," murmured the nurse. "Sorry for waking you. I just need to listen to his chest."

"Oh, that's all right," said Liz as she stood, moved back and stretched. "It wasn't much of a nap anyway."

The woman applied her stethoscope to several spots on Alex's chest then tucked his covers back in place. As she stepped to the in-room computer to make her notations, she smiled at Liz. "Honey, you should take a break. Go get some food. Write your cell number on the white board and I'll call if there's a change."

Liz pressed her hand to her grumbling stomach. "Guess I have been here a while. Any news on the missing policeman?"

"Just flip on the TV. It's gone from bad to worse. They've discovered something horrible. I think your detective friend is involved. At least I recognized his face on the news footage."

Liz located the television remote wrapped around the hospital bedrail and turned on the wall-mounted television. Thumbing past afternoon cable trash, she landed on a local station offering live "Breaking News." Turning the volume low, she lifted the controller to her ear to listen without disturbing the nurse.

A woman reporter, breathless yet perky, described the scene as the camera panned past somber police officers standing by the entrance to the Jennings plant. Beyond the scene's perimeter of yellow tape, a crowd had gathered, breaths puffing in the frigid air.

Liz recognized William talking with a stern-looking group of men exiting the building, some in uniforms, others wearing long wool coats. They met with another group outside, spoke briefly and broke up. Out of the huddle, a middle-aged woman in a blue Omaha police uniform emerged. Her demeanor lightened as she approached the pack of journalists. Waiting for the cameramen to get into position, she smiled tightly and swiped a tissue under her reddened and runny nose.

"Are we missing anyone?" she asked, turning to make sure all were gathered close. She faced the main bank of cameras "Okay, ready?"

"I'm sorry," said a panicked female voice. "Not yet."

"We're live," called an impatient cameraman.

The policewoman lost her smile. "What? You're live?"

Even on the small screen at the hospital, Liz saw the Police Information Officer's frustration at her nose as she wiped one more time and tucked the tissue into the cuff of her insulated jacket.

"Go ahead, officer," said one of the seasoned vets.

The PIO took the cue. "At 8 a.m. this mor—"

"Hang on!" called the same tardy female reporter.

The policewoman pursed her lips, her impatient gaze darting around the group.

The pros surrounding the ill-prepared newsgirl grumbled. She quickly announced, "Sorry, we're leading in . . . Okay, go ahead."

The PIO cleared her voice. "At about 8 a.m. this morning, while searching for Sgt. Harry Gurdlich, officers discovered human remains in a building at 16th and Webster. Mixed levels of decomposition indicate that the remains were placed here at various times. Members of the Federal Bureau of Investigation's crime lab have arrived and are just beginning to process the scene."

An uproar of questions buffeted the officer. Her impassive stare swept the crowd before she picked questioners from the chaos one at a time. "Yes, I can confirm the remains are in metal drums. No, I don't have a timeline yet. I can only say there are multiple bodies. I don't have a firm number yet. Foul play? The exact cause of death of each has not been determined. That will take time. Yes, the FBI and our local lab and investigators will be working together. No, no one has been identified."

"Is Mr. Jennings, owner of the building involved?"

The officer took a fraction of a second to identify the reporter asking and obviously hesitated long enough to mentally phrase her official answer, "Mr. Jennings is being held in an unrelated matter."

"Is he a suspect?"

"I have no information on that at this time. The investigation is just beginning. That's really all I have now. We will notify you as more information becomes available."

Previously answered questions were rephrased by the reporters in hopes of better answers. The PIO simply ignored them. Even as she turned away to return to the safety zone behind the yellow tape, the camera showed the frenzied, frustrated news pack surging forward just enough to warrant uniformed officers holding up their hands to warn them back.

A shiver coursed Liz's back. Multiple bodies. In barrels. In the building she regularly passed. A memory flickered. Alex had asked about various street people not seen recently. As the nurse left, Liz returned to his side to study his unresponsive face.

"At least you are here, Daddy," she whispered.

"Any news?" a voice asked behind her. Liz jumped at William's sudden presence so soon after seeing him on TV. "Sorry," he apologized.

"His heart rate and blood pressure are normal." Her fingers stroked Alex's hair. "He seems more relaxed. He was restless earlier. I don't know how aware of the muscle spasms he's been, but his eyes were flickering. Kinda like rapid eye movement in deep sleep."

"Interesting," William commented softly. "Wonder what he's dreaming about."

"Whatever had him agitated, he seems at peace now." As she spoke, she moved her hand to his face. "Funny," she said, one fingertip trailing down an unshaven cheek, "I've examined him dozens of times in my office, yet I've never really seen him like I do now."

"He's a good man."

"Yes. Yes, he is," said Liz, beaming over her shoulder at the detective. "Say, I just saw you on TV. The policewoman said . . . Are there really bodies in metal barrels?"

William huffed a breath, his eyes turning distant. "Unfortunately . . . yes." He focused on her with a grimace then raised his coated arm for a sniff. "Sorry if I brought some of it with me."

She shook her head and they both looked back at the man on the bed.

"Liz, what can you tell me about Alex's friend, DeAndre? How long have you known him?"

The corner of her mouth crinkled as she thought about it. "He was at the shelter when I started. I was scared of everything back then. I just about screamed when I saw him in my doorway."

"I hear he's pretty big."

"Big with scars and tattoos but he's really a gentle giant. According to Alex, he did some jail time but got his life turned around. I remember DeAndre telling me how much he once loved driving an ice cream truck and the kids calling him the Ding-Ding Man. When he laughed telling about it, that made me laugh, too." She shook her head. "Just looking at him it was hard to believe. But lots of the homeless people have contrasting life stories. Right?"

William smiled and nodded agreement.

"Alex probably wouldn't have survived the street without DeAndre," Liz continued. "He actually brought Alex and I together. We both owe him a lot." She looked up to find William frowning. "Why do you ask?"

"DeAndre's on the radar in the Gurdlich disappearance," William said, exhaling in obvious disappointment. "There was an incident between them in front of the shelter."

"I heard about it. As I told the other two detectives, I didn't witness anything, but the word was that racist jerk Gurdlich started it," Liz snapped. "He was the problem, not DeAndre."

William lifted placating hands. "Hey, I don't disagree. I'm just saying the word is out and I'd like to find DeAndre before Gurdlich's guys do. Do you know where he hangs out?"

"When he's not with Alex or the gold star guys, he's got what he calls a hidey-hole, but street people are very secretive about that sort of thing. It's a matter of survival."

"Who are the gold star guys? I haven't seen that written in the reports."

"It's a nickname for Alex's doghouse neighbors. One of them scammed a card from a casino and they spent a few days as high-rollers at Harrah's or Horseshoe, whichever one has that Gold Star thing."

William grunted. "Sounds like something my mother would have done." When she frowned, he caught himself. "Do these gold star guys stay at the shelter?"

"They're probably there now. Because of the storm, we've left the TV room open all day."

"I'll head over then. Can you think of anyone else I should talk to?"

"Paul Finnegan at Harvest House. He spent time on the street and the guys trust him."

"He's on my radar, but the Harvest House was closed when I drove by."

Liz rubbed her hand across her eyes. "It must be Friday. I lost track. Paul plays in a band at the Rose and Thistle on Friday nights."

"The Irish place in the Old Market?"

"Yeah, downstairs, off the street. I've gone there with friends from school. His group is really pretty good."

William buttoned his coat, then rested a hand on Alex's forearm. The automatic blood pressure cuff buzzed to life making him jerk back.

Liz chuckled. "You didn't do it. It's timed."

William nodded then reached to touch Alex's battered face. He whispered. "Thank god he's warm again. He looks so small without his coat and sweaters."

A lump rose in Liz's throat as she lowered herself back to her chair. Her hand flew to her mouth to stop the sob that erupted.

William awkwardly knelt to put an arm around her. "Think of all the stars that had to align to get you two back together. I'm not a terribly religious man, but I can't believe God would yank the rug out from under Alex now. He's too good a man."

"I should have told him sooner," Liz said in a tearful whisper. "But I was scared. I don't have my own place. I live with my aunt. She told me to wait. She said she understood him better than my mom ever did. And-and that he was a proud man, so I had to let him dig himself out."

William gave her a fatherly squeeze before struggling back to his feet. "I think your aunt was right. I offered him the couch in my basement and he flat refused. That's how he's wired. Now? I think it's just a matter of time before he works his way back to us."

* * *

A ringing grew then faded in Alex's ears. Fog drifted around him as he struggled for balance on the beam. Somewhere in the fog muffled voices grew louder. Something about them felt familiar, comforting. He wanted to hear more, maybe even share . . . something. Alex grabbed that thought and honed in on a decision. As temptingly restful as one side of the beam had become, stepping back into unfinished business, was the right thing to do. *I've got a job to finish. The reward will still be here when I'm done.*

He took a deep breath and let out a sigh, savoring the warmth of a cozy bed against his relaxed back muscles.

* * *

The front entrance to the Rose and Thistle sat at the bottom of a stairway yet to be cleared of snow. Lights shown through the windows but neither a knock at the door nor a second call via William's cell roused attention. He had climbed halfway back up the stairs when the door behind him opened.

"Can I help you?" asked a cautious female voice.

William turned to see a young woman frowning up him.

William flashed his warmest smile. "Hi there. I'm looking for Paul Finnegan. I heard he might be playing here tonight. I know it's early. I just want to talk to him." Showing his badge and I.D. won him a hand-wave to enter.

The various liquor signs and indirect lighting barely illuminated the shadowy bar with its low ceiling and brick walls. Through the archway to the table and chairs section, small spotlights focused on the low, cramped dais where the band was setting up. The barmaid returned to her night-crowd preparations. William leaned against the archway frame watching the barely recognizable Paul on the stage. The weary soup kitchen manager had transformed into a happy-go-lucky musician, joking with his band mates, tuning his violin, smiling.

The smile fled when he spotted William. He stepped from the lighted stage, his expression serious as he approached. "Tell me you haven't come here with bad news about Alex."

"You heard he's in the hospital?" William asked.

"Yeah, it's all over the street. He's all right isn't he?"

207

"I just left the hospital. His vital signs are good, but he hasn't come back to us yet."

Paul blew a sigh of relief then crossed his arms and spread his feet as if bracing himself. "Heard about the warehouse . . . All those cans . . . Can you tell me . . . Ah, was it street people? Some of those on the list you showed me? Is that why you're here?"

"There's nothing official yet." They locked gazes. "But, we do suspect they're from the homeless community. That's between us."

Paul swallowed. "Yes, of course."

"I'm here to ask about DeAndre Easton. What can you tell me about him?"

"A good man, has probably done more to protect the weak than the entire Omaha Police force," Paul said sarcastically. "Beyond that, I don't know much. He showed up maybe two years ago. I figured he was fresh out of jail, laying low, trying to stay out of trouble."

"Do you know where he stays when he's not at the shelter? I'm told he comes and goes."

"He picks up odd jobs from the labor pool office. There's a rendering plant south of the Interstate that pays cash. He goes there a lot and brings some of the smell back with him."

"How about sleeping arrangements?"

"He uses the shelter or his shanty. A lot of guys have hidey-holes where they go to drink or sleep during the day."

"He clue you in on his hidey-hole?"

"No. Honestly, I don't talk to him that much. He just comes and goes." Paul's eyes narrowed, his expression hardened to the point of menacing. "You know, if we lose Alex, it's on that Jennings bastard. He's killed dozens, by my count."

William shook his head. "I don't think the barrels in his warehouse are his doing. We're holding him—"

"I don't mean the warehouse," interrupted Paul. "Jennings was responsible for the Kilpatrick Center closing. Fucking, greedy bastard tossed the mentally ill onto the street in the dead of winter. That's as good as murder in my book."

William frowned. "I thought the Kilpatrick patients found new homes. It was all over the news."

"The news only reported what they were fed," Paul scoffed. "Nobody bothered to look beyond the press releases. Only the worst got new placements and even that was temporary. A lot ended up frozen on bus benches or in jail. The news painted it as a bankruptcy but if you dig a little, detective, you'll see Jennings forced their hand."

Finally ready, the drummer called for the sound check.

"I should get back," Paul said, tilting his head to the stage.

"Got a cell? I can call if there's a change in Alex's condition."

"No, I can't afford that sort of thing. What I don't spend on the basics, I put back into the kitchen pantry. Food's more important than fancy devices, don't you think?"

William nodded, feeling like shit for not being more generous himself. After shaking Paul's hand, he watched the man return to the stage to tuck his violin under his chin and mournfully stroke the bow across the strings.

"Thanks," William called out.

Paul nodded acknowledgement then let loose a wild and rousing riff that appeared to shake the weight of the world from his shoulders, if only for a while.

William hesitated in the archway as thoughts connected. *There is a pattern. Kilpatrick, Fitzgerald, dumping drunks in the snow.* Out of the disjointed cacophony of the sound check, Paul initiated a mournful Irish melody. *Was it Jennings' work at the warehouse?* The drummer added a heartbeat to Paul's haunting dirge. William's throat thickened as the sorrowful sound tugged at his heart.

"I can get you a drink if you're off duty," the waitress spoke at his elbow.

He straightened, glad for the interruption of his melancholy. "Let's say I'm on my own time. I'll have a taste of Jameson, neat."

When the waitress returned with his drink, she wrinkled her nose at the stage. "Man, I hope they play something less dreary when the crowd gets here."

William paid her and took his glass. Catching Paul's eye, he raised it, nodded his respect then downed the smooth fire in one swallow. The waitress still stood at his side, listening to the band. After handing her back his glass, he pulled out his wallet again.

"Do they have a tip jar?"

"Sure, proceeds always go to that soup kitchen, the Harvest something or other."

"Perfect." William dug out his emergency $50 bill from its special slot. "Put this in for me."

* * *

At the St. Vincent, the wind had piled snow high against the main building, burying the cars up to their roofs. William scanned the crowd as he rolled by the front of the building. He made a U-turn then parked across the street, urging the grill of his car into a drift to keep the street open.

He waited in line at the front desk as the night man doled out answers, Band-Aid's and other incidentals.

"I'm looking for members of the gold star club," William said, when it was his turn. "My name's William Olson."

"You're Liz's cop friend, right? You called looking for Alex yesterday."

"Yes, I did."

"How's he doing? Liz left word that he's in the hospital."

"Pretty rough shape but we think he'll make it."

"We're all praying for him. You come by just to tell his buddies? That's mighty kind of you."

209

"Least I could do," William said, cringing at his trading dishonesty for brevity.

"Well, DeAndre's not here and neither is Henry. Haven't seen them two for a couple-three days, but Tom and Billy are over in front of the TV, next to that big guy with the glasses. See?"

William eyed the over-crowded room. "I got it. Thanks."

Crossing to the TV, he saw the closed door to Liz's office and checked his phone to make sure he hadn't missed a call.

"Hey, guys," William greeted Tom and Billy "I've got some news on Alex. He's back in the hospital."

"You're that d-detective d-dude, ain't yah?" stammered Billy. "I seen you on the TV. Alex talks—"

"That's me," William stopped him. "My name's William." He shook each of their hands then ignored his still-painful hip and knelt so as not to talk down.

"Was it Larry that finally got him?" asked Tom. "Bastard's been after Alex for weeks now."

"No, it was the cold. He was sleeping back in his doghouse."

All fell silent contemplating Alex's intentions.

"Never thought I'd see him pushed to go back there," said Tom.

The three companionably shook their heads in understanding.

"Any of you seen DeAndre Easton?" William, asked. "I'd like to find him before Gurdlich's boys do and I'd like to tell him about Alex."

"We ain't seen him," said Billy, a little too quickly.

"Would you say the same if I wasn't a cop?" asked William.

"In your case," said Henry, "we might make an exception."

"No, you can't t-trust—"

Tom interrupted Billy, "We know you've been where we are, detective. Alex told us. We would trust you because Alex trusts you. But the fact is we don't know where DeAndre is. There's been some speculation about the old Fairbury cannery and occasional work at the rendering plant south of the freeway. Somebody else mentioned he might have a girlfriend he stays with . . . Hell, I'm not sure I even knew his last name was Easton 'til you just mentioned it."

"It's Fletcher, not Easton," blurted the big man with the thick-framed glasses. Up to that point he'd been silent, staring off into space.

Billy leaned toward William. "C-careful, man. The p-professor's l-loony tunes." One finger twirled at his temple.

"I'm all right," said the man. "My meds just make me kind of dull."

"So, you know DeAndre?" William asked.

"Yes, and his last name is Fletcher. That's what the doctors said anyway. He was a very sad case."

Billy stood to slip behind the man he called the Professor. He waved his hands and twirled his fingers to catch William's eye.

Tom smacked the kid's thigh hard with the back of his hand. "Cut it out, Billy. This is important," he growled.

"D-don't hit me," snapped Billy. "Goddamn n-nobody listens to me. It was a s-serial killer what killed old T-turdlick. N-not DeAndre. It's a serial k-killer right, detective? I saw it on the TV. Bodies in cans, right?"

"Yes, Billy," William tried to sound reasonable without being condescending. "We found bodies but I don't know who they are or even how many."

"But—"

"But right now," William interrupted, "I need to talk to the Professor. Like Tom said, it's very important."

Tom rose to put a gentle hand on Billy's shoulder. "Come on, kid. Let's you and me get in line for dinner. Leave these two fellows to talk."

As William stood his knees popped and his painful hip resisted. He winced then eased himself back to the floor next to the man now studying him with intelligent eyes.

"Professor . . . uh, I'm sorry, what's your real name?" William asked.

"Steve."

"Steve, you don't by chance know where DeAndre stays when he's not here?"

"No. He doesn't talk to me."

"The doctor you mentioned, do you remember his name?"

"Doc Moore. He helped me. Gave me the power over the demons."

William hesitated then nodded. "Thank you, Steve. Were you and DeAndre Fletcher at the Kilpatrick Center before it closed?"

"Yes, and it was much nicer than here." Steve leaned this way and that looking around. "The demons are everywhere here. I have the power over them though." He held up his odd thumb and forefinger sign.

"I want to go make a phone call, Steve. I'll be right back."

The Professor grabbed William's arm before he could stand. "Was Antonio at that warehouse? Was he in a can?"

William's eyes narrowed. "I don't know. Do you know his last name? I can check for you."

"Antonio Arnold. He was my best friend and I'm sure the demons took him."

Professor's expression remained desperate, but his body language shifted into a relaxed pose. He folded his hands and put them politely in his lap.

Seeing the war raging behind the man's eyes, William wanted to put a calming hand on his shoulder. He had been trained that sometimes invading personal space triggered irrational behavior. William went for a soothing voice instead. "Steve, when I talk to my boss I'll ask if they've identified anyone yet. Perhaps you could come help us with our investigation."

The man's body twitched, his tense expression looking like a pressure cooker about to blow. "That would be . . . Yes, that would be lovely," he enunciated carefully.

William walked to a corner and turned his back to the room to place his call.

"Whaddaya got, Will?" answered Dan.

"Another piece of the puzzle. I need a car with a cage and a couple of officers we can trust to roll over to the St. Vincent. Do it over the cell. I don't want the media picking up on a radio call."

"Hang on, I've got a couple of guys right here." William heard muffled voices as Dan talked with his phone tucked against his coat. "All right, they're on their way. What are we looking at?"

"I've got a guy who knows DeAndre Easton as DeAndre Fletcher. Turns out both he and DeAndre were residents of the Kilpatrick Center before it closed."

"So DeAndre was a mental patient. That's interesting."

"Yeah, but get this. The guy I've been talking to knows one of our victims, Antonio Arnold."

"No shit? Does he connect DeAndre to Arnold?"

"Not exactly. This guy's barely holding it together. We need to corral him and get some finger prints."

"On it," said Dan. "I'll send—"

"Wait, one more thing. There's a Doctor Moore that worked with this guy and DeAndre at the Kilpatrick. If we could track him down—"

"I'll get people on it now. Good work."

With the din of nearly eight hundred hungry, homeless men buzzing around them, William sat alone with the Professor in front of the big-screen TV. The big man's rocking to and fro diminished. William considered probing further, but instead chose the comfort of their own little pocket of silence. Minutes ticked by. The melancholy he had resisted at the bar drifted over him as he watched the line of men waiting to be fed. Images popped into his memory calling up his own turmoil and fear of homelessness.

William sighed in relief when Officer Jason Grant walked across the room toward him. They exchanged nods. Grant knelt in front of them and smiled when the man next to William met his eyes.

"Remember me, Professor?" Grant asked softly.

Damn, he's good. William's respect for the young officer climbed even higher.

"Yes, you helped me a few weeks ago." He started rocking again, looking from Grant to William and back. "Antonio is dead and stuffed in a can," he stated flatly.

Grant never even flinched. "Now, we don't know that. We need to keep looking."

The Professor stared straight ahead and the rocking stopped.

"Can you focus enough to help us find Antonio?" Grant asked.

"There's a green demon in the corner. I see him in my peripheral vision. I can shoot him for you. I have the magic," stated the Professor.

He then formed an L with his right thumb and index finger and aimed it at the empty corner. He placed the index finger of his left hand on his right thumb and made a buzzing noise through his teeth. "All right, I got that one. We can go now if we hurry."

Seeing the confident acknowledgement in Grant's eyes that he could handle the guy, William stood slowly and walked to the second officer waiting a few feet away.

Leaning closer to him to be heard over the room's chaos, the thirty-something cop asked, "What's up, Will? My rookie and I dealt with that guy a few weeks ago. Took him to the Immanuel psych ward—"

"This time we take him to the station," interrupted William. "He's got info that might help with the mess at the Jennings warehouse."

"Is he our perp?"

"I don't know, but we need to keep it low key."

"He still asking for Antonio?"

"Yup, only now we know where Antonio is," said William, shooting the officer a knowing look.

"Oh shit."

Despite Grant's soothing encouragement, the Professor's fists clenched and his breathing grew more rapid as the foursome reached the exit.

Just outside the door, Grant pointedly looked at his partner's duty belt and eased their man to a stop. "Professor, do you remember last time when we had to put cuffs on you?" The man nodded, raised his chin and put his hands behind his back. His escorts exchanged relieved glances.

As they headed to the parked squad car, a television news van careened to a stop up beside them. The next instant a cameraman emerged, his blinding light spotlighting the whole scene. The pudgy reporter at his heels rushed them with wireless mic extended, shouting at the Professor, "Are you the serial killer?"

The already stressed man jerked upright, his eyes rolling wildly. Lunging at the camera, he screamed, "Get away or I'll cut your fucking head off! Get away! Get away! Get away!"

Grant and his parter locked their arms through the Professor's, dragging him back as William stepped between them and the news hounds. His broad hand popped onto the camera lens. "Out of here now or you're going to jail! All of you!" William ground out.

The cameraman pulled backed then bobbed and weaved trying to shoot around William. At the sidewalk's edge, he tripped and fell backwards into the snow, his camera tumbling from his shoulder. The reporter, wireless mic still in hand, continued his attack, unaware that he'd lost the camera.

His voice rose over the commotion, "A dozen rotting bodies. How does that make you feel?"

Grant and his partner wrestled the Professor into the back of the squad car, leaving him face down and huddled on the floorboard, crying. At the solid thud of the closing door, they joined William's confrontation with the reporter.

Don't touch the scumbag. Don't touch the scumbag. The law enforcement mantra echoed in William's mind as he literally bared his teeth at the now wide-eyed, panting reporter. "What the hell was that? What channel are you with?"

The man's crew-cut head bobbed in his mounting excitement. "You! You're the detective that got hit by the van. How—"

Keeping his clenched fists at his sides, William shoved his face closer and enunciated dangerously, "What. Station."

The reporter swallowed but stood his ground. "Action Five News. We're just doing our job. Like you. It's a public sidewalk."

"How did—"

"We got a tip." He stiffened his spine and shoved his face back at William. "That's all I'll say. Action News protects its sources."

William sucked in a deep breath aware of the uniforms flanking him. He glanced around at the after-dinner-smoking crowd eagerly watching the entertainment.

Unaware of his cameraman's preoccupation with getting his camera back up and running, the reporter misinterpreted William's crowd awareness as backing down. He abruptly poked the mic in William's face. Reflexively, William jerked it from his hand and violently flung it across the street.

Amidst the applause of watchers, he bent down to speak through his teeth, "You're a slimy, piece of shit."

"Hey, that—"

"You'd fuck your own mother for tens seconds of fame."

"I'm a journal—"

"The fuck you are! I'd have my uniforms here toss your ass in jail if I had time." His pointing finger didn't contact the scumbag's chest. "Don't think for a second this is over. I'm gonna shove that mic so far—"

The cameraman was back up, his light on. William's expression blinked from rage to concern. "That's all I can say at this time. Have a good evening," he said calmly.

The reporter's face screwed in confusion as William pivoted away. Behind him the man recited, "Well, there you have it, ladies and gentlemen. Police brutality plain and simple—"

"We don't have shit," yelled the cameraman. "Check your mic."

"I don't have a fucking mic," screamed the reporter. "Go wild. Switch to on-camera. Still have the cop car in frame?"

"Go!" yelled the cameraman.

William stopped at the squad car to confer with the two uniforms. The three of them looked back to smile at the camera.

"There you have it, ladies and gentlemen. Police—"

"That's a nice camera," said a toothless man, stepping into the shot. "What's one a them things cost?"

The reporter shoved him back. "We're trying to work here."

Shouting their own questions, the shelter crowd enveloped the Action Five news team.

"Think they'll make it back to their van in one piece?" Grant asked. "Should we call a car to help?"

"Nah," his partner said, winking at William. "They're about to become stars in their own reality TV show. Wouldn't want to stand in the way."

As William jogged to his vehicle, the cruiser headed down the street on its way to headquarters.

24

A tear trickled down Alex's cheek. Alone in his room, unable to make his body respond, he listened to televised reports from the Jennings plant.

Quiet footsteps and the opening whoosh of the curtain to his room raised Alex's spirits, then the smell of Old Spice aftershave sent a spike of fear through his helpless body. He heard the slick brush of winter coat fabric and the creak of a leather duty belt as Old Spice came close.

Inside Alex screamed for help. Outside he showed only an elevated heart rate.

On the television, new excitement gripped an anchorman's voice as he announced a breaking development. "This just in, raw video of an arrest . . . Just forty-five minutes ago, police took a man into custody."

"Get away or I'll cut your B-E-E-E-P head off! Get Away! Get away! . . . "

The sound of the Professor's panic and Alex's own terror sent a violent tremor through his body. His eyes flashed open.

Old Spice stood over him, surprised then smiling malevolently. "Well, look at you! You're back," the uniformed officer crooned. He glanced around then pulled the cap from a syringe in his hand. "As long as you're awake, you should know the big nigger was seen entering the old cannery over by Glass Alley. He's next on my hit parade."

Alex strained to coax out a hoarse, unintelligible whisper as his fingers clawed at the end of useless arms. *Nurse's call button. Find it, find it, find it.*

The cop leaned onto the bed, crushing Alex's lips with an index finger. "Shut the fuck up, you piece of shit. You go quiet and I'll let that little dyke nurse friend of yours live."

Alex stared at the syringe of clear, colorless liquid. The cop slid its needle into the injection port on the IV line. Alex glared at the thumb of the wide hand settling on the syringe plunger. The machines watching over him ticked and pulsed as that thumb slowly, fractionally pressed down.

He silently focused his entire being on the arm with the IV. God, make it move. Move!

The arm violently jerked, pulling the IV line away and dislodging the syringe. The counter tension of the officer's hand sent the syringe flying. Alex tracked it through the air until it hit the wall and bounced out of sight.

"Cocksucker!" spat the cop in a coarse whisper. He dropped from sight to search for his miniature weapon.

"Well, Mr. Capstain, nice to see you're back with us," said a nurse flicking back the curtain. "Oh, you have a visitor." Her surprised expression changed with a professional smile as the officer straightened.

Old Spice smiled convincingly. "I was just talking to him and his eyes popped open," he said, with feigned excitement. "A little late for a Christmas miracle, but, by golly, I'll take it."

Alex looked from the nurse to the cop then down to the hand resting on the grip of his holstered pistol.

The nurse stepped to the bedside and turned her attention on her patient. "Alex, can you move your fingers for me? Good, now how about your toes? Very good. You gave us quite a scare."

Alex tried to speak, but couldn't. The words just wouldn't leave his throat.

"That's okay," she reassured him "Don't try to talk just yet. We had to intubate you for a while there. Your throat's going to be sore for a bit."

Above and behind the woman, all niceness left Old Spice's narrowed eyes. The back of a broad hand swiped at a bead of sweat trickling from the hairline below the stocking cap.

The blood pressure cuff on Alex's arm hummed to life, gripping his bicep then hissing in release. He could hear the tap of nearby computer keys as the nurse added notes to his chart. The woman glanced over her shoulder at the white board as she palmed her cell phone.

"Is that Liz Caldwell's number?" the officer asked.

"Yes. She slipped down to the cafeteria. I promised—"

"Hey, she's a good friend," Old Spice interrupted her. "I'd love to deliver the good news myself."

"The poor kid's been here since last night. She needed a break." The cell phone disappeared back into the pocket of her scrub jacket. "Tell you what, you go retrieve her and I'll alert the doctor."

"You gotta deal, ma'am." When her attention returned to Alex, Old Spice cocked a warning eyebrow that made him stiffen.

"You just relax, Mr. Capstain. Your numbers are normal, so no worries. The lab tech is rounding. She'll be in momentarily to draw some blood then we'll see about a quick bath and careful shave." After looking over his IV site, the nurse stepped out of the room as silently as she had entered.

Old Spice took her place at the bedside. "You've got more lives than a fuckin' cat," he whispered before glancing at the half-drawn curtain then bending to look around the floor. "Fuck me," he growled in frustration, bolting upright as a cart with squeaky wheels passed by. When the curtain didn't move he pointed a warning finger. "Keep your mouth shut or I will add that little dyke shelter nurse to my list. You got it? It's your word against mine."

Alex jerked an awkward nod then the cop disappeared beyond the curtain.

He blinked back tears as he tried to move. The low beep of the heart monitor increased as he grew frustrated with the maddening slowness of his uncooperative limbs. Toes then fingers flexed. He groaned in triumph when one leg then the other shifted. A violently trembling hand gripped the half-rail at his side. He stared at the symbols on the railing until he recognized the one that would raise his head. Finally upright he fought a brief dizziness.

Breathe in, breathe out.

With supreme determination, he turned onto his side and slid his legs until they dropped over the edge of the mattress. He flexed his toes, circled his feet then straightened his lower legs, sheer will driving blood and muscles. As he pushed off from the head of the bed, his butt slipped. The next instant his feet settled on the floor but his knees buckled. He crashed to the floor, the IV line, blood pressure cuff and monitor cables pulling taut.

Fuck this shit!

He clawed to free himself from everything. Above him alarms sounded. Right in front of his eyes his clothes and parka filled an under-the-bed storage basket. As he pulled his clothes to him, he spied the uncapped syringe on the floor. Blood trickled down his arm from the dislodged IV site as he meticulously picked up the syringe. His shaking hand dropped it onto the seat of the chair next to the bed.

Oh, God, please. Please ....

He continued to mentally beg as he moved. Despite the bone-sawing pain, his joints and limbs worked better and better. The urgency of the continued alarms spurred him to a super human effort to pull on his clothes. Any moment staff would crash into his room and discover him.

With easier movement and increased circulation, his mind cleared. He knew Old Spice would not search out Liz. DeAndre was another matter. Knowing DeAndre was in the cannery basement was not the same as finding him there. If the rumors were true, the predators and junkies that called that cavernous underworld home would not welcome the cop's intrusion.

With super-human effort, he levered himself to his feet and leaned against the bed.

Running feet sounded in the hall accompanied by someone shouting "Crash Cart!" The activity moved away then over the hospital intercom came "Code 99. ICU 8. Code 99. ICU 8."

He looked up at the white board and saw his room was ICU 2. The Lord had delivered him a chance. His energy returned by miraculous leaps and bounds. He pulled the hospital gown off. Ignoring underclothes and socks, he struggled into his pants, shirt and tennis shoes. Bending to pick up the syringe by its barrel almost toppled him back to the floor. He took deep breaths and, hand over hand, steadied himself along the bed. One foot dragged the parka with him. After settling the syringe onto the narrow metal tray at the bottom of the white board, he splayed one hand for balance and used his teeth to pull the cap from the wet marker. The block letters looked childish, but he nodded at the accomplishment.

DeA AT C. COP TRIED KILL ME.

He drew an arrow from the word "kill" to the syringe in the tray.

Holding onto the wall, he bent to retrieve his coat. One foot in front of the other, he cautiously moved by the curtain. Down the hall, staff milled and voices shouted. No one looked in his direction. He turned in the opposite direction. By the time he reached the elevator, his confidence was high that he would make good his escape.

The elevator dinged and the doors opened. A teenager gripped the handles of a wheelchair occupied by a disheveled, wrinkled old woman. The girl looked him up and down then curled her lip in distaste. He gripped the railing and glanced from the lit-up "Lobby" button to the girl.

"Do I look that scary?" his voice croaked. "I was in a car wreck last night."

The old woman blinked at him, her expression concerned. "It's a blessing you weren't hurt worse, young man."

He pointed up. "Angels and the grace of God, ma'am."

She nodded, saying, "I'll pray for you."

"Gram!" the teen admonished, her disgruntled attention on the elevator numbers above the door.

On the first floor he stepped into the lobby with them. When the old lady wiggled her fingers in parting, he waved back. People hurried about on their way to their business as he was headed to his. The weakness in his legs had become merely an afterthought. The sensation reminded him of the first time he'd caught a second wind while running high school track.

When he exited the revolving front doors, the cold hit him hard enough to flutter his heart. He sucked in a frigid, life-giving breath before flipping up and tightening his fur-edged hood and beginning his march to the cannery.

Surviving two close calls—the hypothermia and Old Spice's needle—in as many days buoyed his spirit. Despite the pending danger and present bitter cold, he focused on savoring the beautiful evening. Birds flitted and chirped, the setting sun shown yellow-to-red reflecting off snowy rooftops and sparkling in the windows of the university buildings. At street level the clean blanket of snow had its usual rough, brown hem but that was just a small, inevitable and ever changing part of a much grander scene.

How could I have been so blind as to want to throw this all away? He thought back to his response to the old woman in the wheelchair. *Angels and the grace of God. Where the heck had that come from?*

A memory of his time between worlds struck him hard, freezing him in mid-step. His eyes widened and chest heaved. He'd seen it all while standing on the beam. *Angels do exist. They are all around, DeAndre, Liz and William. Good is battling evil through all of us.*

The epiphany sent a renewed and miraculous rush of strength and purpose through his damaged body. He stood straight, shoulders back, his limbs strong, his mind confident. Nothing could stop him from fulfilling his purpose. Good would win out over evil.

* * *

At police headquarters, William frowned at the video monitor showing the Professor in animated conversation with an empty room.

"He was semi-coherent until those TV assholes lit him up. Now we won't get anything," William growled at Dan. "How the fuck did they know?"

"They were probably tailing you, Will. This is a big story and they're desperate to scoop each other."

"If they'd done their fucking job when the Kilpatrick closed . . . ." William mumbled to himself.

"The Kilpatrick? What about the Kilpatrick?"

"Nothing, boss. Another issue."

"So, what do we know about this big fellow beyond his being batso and knowing one of our victims?" Dan asked.

"At the shelter he told me his name is Steve. Alex apparently gave him the 'Professor' moniker because he once worked at the university." William flicked his hand at the screen. "I'm guessing schizophrenia. The rookie, Grant, said this guy sees demons that he shoots with some illusionary power he believes he can fire from his fingers. We'll know more when the doctor gets here, I guess."

"Growing up, there was a kid on my block that was like that." Dan stared at the monitor. "My mom told me not to play with him, but I did anyway. He was weird . . . and scared all the time. Said he saw pirates and monsters everywhere. We all played along, our imaginations battling whatever monsters the kid said he saw in his head."

William grunted. "You'd be amazed what I saw growing up in the shelters. My own mom was bipolar. Seemed like we were always on a roller coaster of super highs and lows. People don't realize the percentage of mentally ill among the homeless. They think they're all lazy or drunks."

"It's about twenty-five percent," offered a visitor, stepping into the video room in the company of the front desk clerk.

The detectives turned.

"About twenty-five percent of those in the shelter system are severely mentally ill," the man continued with an authoritative tone. "If you consider some less-debilitating conditions, it's closer to forty percent."

"Detectives Armour and Olson, this is Eric Moore," said the clerk. "He says you asked him to come in."

"Doctor Moore?" Dan asked.

"Technically yes, but I'm not practicing at the moment. The train wreck at the Kilpatrick Center soured me on the system and I decided to take a break for a while."

His open coat revealed a red polo shirt tucked into is khaki pants. Noting the thoughtful expressions of the two detectives assessing him, he waved a hand at his clothes. "I manage a Target store these days. After this last Christmas, I can tell you with one-hundred percent certainty that retail is a form of madness all to its own."

That got the chuckles he had obviously aimed for. He joined the two men turning back to the video screen where the Professor was aiming his fingers at an imaginary foe.

"I taught Steven to do that," Moore murmured.

"That thing with his fingers?" asked William.

"Yes, it's a coping mechanism. He sees demons and sea monsters. To him, they are as real as I am to you. I convinced him he has the power to disarm them." Moore leaned a little closer to study their man more intently. "I assume he's had some medical attention. Otherwise, with this much stress, that room would be trashed by now."

"Yes," said William. "Before he flipped out at the shelter, he said something about his meds made him dull. I don't know what kind." He shook a definitive finger at the screen. "I do know—or rather see—that he's working his butt off trying to hold onto to some sense of reality."

Dr. Moore gave William a surprised look of respect. "Very perceptive, detective. Right now he's maintaining, but it is an obvious struggle. So, did he hurt someone? Is that why I'm here? If he did, it was probably an accident. He yells and threatens, maybe throws the furniture, but I've never seen him actually act out to hurt another person."

"He's only part of the reason we asked you to come down," said William. "We're also looking for DeAndre Fletcher."

Dr. Moore's face fell.

"You know the name," Dan observed.

"Saddest case I ever dealt with." The doctor pulled out a chair to sit down. "I was sure he'd be dead or in jail by now." He looked from William to Dan. "Tell me, is DeAndre a suspect in the serial killings on the news?"

"Yes, I'm afraid so." Dan sat at the narrow table across from him. "What can you tell us about him?"

William remained standing, too nervous to settle.

"God, I don't know if I should even be talking . . . HIPAA privacy laws and all." He paused for a long moment, his eyes on his fingers drumming on the table. Abruptly, he slapped both palms down and snapped his head up. "Hell with it! All the fucking rules couldn't save my patients from a goddamn condo developer. This will take a while. Do you have someplace totally private?"

As William escorted the psychologist from the video monitoring room to a small conference room, Dan grabbed coffee for all of them. By the time he arrived with three small Styrofoam cups balanced in his hands, William already had a few notes on a yellow legal pad.

"The DeAndre Fletcher I dealt with was a chameleon of sorts," said Doctor Moore. "He had a knack for becoming who you needed him to be. Not surprising considering all he's been through."

"Could you expand on that?" asked William.

"As a child, DeAndre suffered more torture and humiliation than you can imagine. He described his mother as extremely religious. She may have had mental health issues of her own, but that's speculation. She apparently had a live-in boyfriend who was a sadistic pedophile."

Both detectives shifted uncomfortably.

"The physical and sexual abuse went on for I don't know how many years. When DeAndre came to us, he had burns, bruises and old fractures that had healed badly. He wouldn't talk. His hair was falling out. And . . . he had to be treated for anal and oral syphilis."

"When did the abuse happen? I mean, do you recall any specific dates?" asked William.

"Hard to pinpoint a year. DeAndre was probably twelve to fourteen when I first saw him. He was old enough that the boyfriend had lost interest and began using his little brother."

"Jesus," said William.

"Yeah, it's sick. Not in the least uncommon, but sick nonetheless," said the doctor. "Bearing witness to the evils of the world is something I don't miss." He grasped his cup of coffee and slurped the too-hot liquid without blowing on it. He winced as the liquid hit his mouth, but didn't look up. "It takes a toll. Of course, as police officers you deal with—"

"Yes, sir," William interrupted him, "And simply documenting instead of acting on it has its own price. Many a good cop has grown immune and cynical or been pulled to the dark side because of it," William said, remembering a younger and more principled Gurdlich.

Dr. Moore took a second wincingly-hot sip before he continued, "When DeAndre learned the boyfriend was hurting his brother, he told his mom. She gave DeAndre a black eye for talking dirty."

"Nice," Dan said, his hand unconsciously brushing the grip of his pistol.

"Out of desperation, our young DeAndre told a policeman. But rather than immediately calling child welfare and having the boys removed, the officer and his partner stopped by the apartment to beat the living hell out of the boyfriend. Goddamned Neanderthals thought they could knock the pedophilia out of him."

William sat forward, his pen at the ready. "Was he able to tell you the officers' names?"

"No," the doctor said then frowned at the two men. "I would think there would be a record in the system . . . unless they didn't file a report."

Both detectives shrugged.

The doctor shook his head. "No, they had to have filed one. Shots were fired. At some point during the beating, the boyfriend broke free, grabbed DeAndre's mother and a handgun and shot at the officers. One of them returned fire just as young DeAndre jumped in between. The bullet tore through his bicep and lodged his mother's throat. I remember him sobbing as he told me his mother bled out in his arms."

The heavy silence in the room made William's heart ache.

"Any possibility this was imaginary? Something conjured by DeAndre's condition?" Dan asked. "We've combed our system for a DeAndre Fletcher and came up empty."

"I'm certain there should be a record. The intake paperwork at the Kilpatrick referenced it in detail. Of course, what happened to those records after we were shut down, I have no idea."

"So what's DeAndre's coping mechanism?" William asked.

"Schizophrenia is a coping mechanism for DeAndre," said Doctor Moore. "Yes, it is a mental disorder. But the mental misinterpretations of reality simply allow some schizophrenics like DeAndre to cope. They compartmentalize, trying to ignore what can't be changed and confront or force what they think can be changed. They are simply not able to move beyond ugliness because it taunts them. I was never able to help him like I could Steven. It's one thing to see monsters. It's another to become one."

In boss mode, Dan asked, "You're saying DeAndre becomes a monster?"

"Well, no, monster isn't really the right term," said Dr. Moore. "In his mind, he becomes Michael, an archangel. It's from the Bible. Remember, I said his mother was extremely religious. She skewed his ability to see abstract principles in her version of religion. His reality hurt too much."

"Um, if we're talking Saint Michael, he was the biggest bad-ass archangel of all of them," Dan offered.

William and the doctor merely looked at him without taking his point.

Dan pulled a chain with a Saint Michael medal from under his shirt collar. "I take it neither of you is Catholic." He tapped a finger on the medal. "Saint Michael's the patron saint of cops. He kicked Satan's ass into Hell."

That clicked for William. "So, our defenseless little boy copes by becoming a biblical super hero?"

"Yes, that makes sense," Dr. Moore said, equally enlightened. "But the little boy is now a six-foot-four, two-hundred-and-sixty-pound man. He can do incredible damage when he breaks with reality."

William was almost afraid to ask, "What causes—"

"The trigger?" Moore interrupted.

William nodded.

"It's logical in DeAndre's case. Sex," stated Moore. "Look at his history. The last time I saw him flip at the Kilpatrick, it was because of something sexual on television. He was twenty-years old. Something on a daytime soap opera set him off. I swear, he grew six inches taller right before my eyes. He announced that he was Michael, one of seven archangels and that he was sent to cure the sickness."

Dr. Moore stood up to act out the rest. "Then he strutted over to the heavy, old, thirty-two-inch, wall-mounted CRT television, ripped it right off the wall and hurled it across the room like it was nothing."

"Jesus," William whispered.

"Exactly," agreed the doctor. "And get this, the TV hit the wall so hard, it broke the 2x4 studs."

"How'd you get him under control?" asked Dan.

"Didn't have to. Once the sickness—as he called it—was destroyed, Michael reverted back to DeAndre. He sat back down in his chair like nothing had happened. Surprised the hell out of the entire staff."

"So, do you think he could be responsible for the bodies in the warehouse?" asked Dan.

The doctor deflated and sat back down. "He's certainly capable. But I'd lay the responsibility at the feet of whoever set him free on the streets. DeAndre should never have been put where he couldn't be watched and controlled."

The vibrating of William's cell broke him out of his campfire-horror-story daze.

"William, it's Liz," she said, before he could say hello.

"Hey, Liz, I've got news on—"

"He's run off. He's just . . . gone. I- I went to the cafeteria—"

"Hold on," William cut her off, jumping to his feet. "Slow down. What do you mean he's gone? Are we talking about Alex?"

"Who else?" she said through obvious tears. "He took his clothes and vanished. He-He left a note on the board but it doesn't make any sense. I texted a picture of it to your phone. Did you get it?"

"Settle down, now. I'll look and call you right back." Ending the call, William frantically thumbed the cell's screen then looked at his boss. "Dan, how the hell do I get this thing to show me a picture in a text?"

After a few seconds of pressing buttons and scrolling menus, Dan brought up Liz's photo. "What are we looking at, Will?" he asked.

223

"A note left by Alex at the hospital." William took back his phone and squinted at the image. "Apparently he's out of his coma and on the move." He pulled a pair of reading glasses from his shirt pocket and looked closer. "Shit! Goddamn motherfucker!" he yelled, dialing Liz's number. "Liz, try not to react to this question. Is there an officer there with you now?"

"No, though the nurse said one was here earlier. He was supposed to look for me—"

"Good. Right now, go find some company, but make sure it's not a cop."

"Will, what's—"

"Just go now. Please, go! Is that still ICU 2?"

"Yes," she said, his commanding tone obviously ending her tears. He discerned voices in the background. "Okay, I'm in a crowd now, at the nurse's station. Will, what the hell is going on? What did that message mean?"

"Tell the nurse to put on rubber gloves and return to that room to bag what she finds at the end of that arrow. You do not leave that station. Got it?"

"Just a minute." He heard her give the instructions to the nurse before she returned to the line. "So, where did Alex go?"

"Somebody is after him and DeAndre and I think Alex went to warn his friend."

"It was the cop?" Liz asked.

"Apparently. What the nurse is collecting is evidence."

"This is a nightmare."

"Keep it together, kid. The officer that comes for you will say Chief of Detectives Daniel Armour sent him. If he doesn't say exactly that, make a stink, a loud one."

"Okay. What did the nurse need to collect?"

"Tell the nurse to close and lock Alex's room. It's now a crime scene."

"Oh, my gawd," Liz murmured.

"What?"

"She's showing me the bag. It has an uncapped syringe in it. She said she closed the door and put tape over the entry with her initials. What do I—"

"Your job is to wait for the officer with the right words. He'll bring you here. I'm going after Alex. I know where he went."

25

God's thunderous voice woke Michael from a terrifying dream.

"Take this and eat. This is my body broken for thee."

He had been mired in a pool of deathly blackness, his powerful angel's wings beating until they ached. No amount of effort could pull him free. Heart hammering, he looked around at the cellar. The demons that had come for Gurdlich's soul were gone, leaving the lifeless gray husk now mottled in true death.

Gurdlich was his first failure. The others he'd lovingly packed away to await the rapture. He did not know what to do with the remains of the unrepentant sergeant.

The powerful voice of God returned. *"Take this and eat. This is my body broken for thee."*

* * *

As Alex approached the cannery, the day's end sucked away the light. Above ground, the multi-story concrete skeleton stood as an empty, crumbling ruin. Jagged, cinder block fingers rose ominously into the darkening sky. He had heard plenty about its underground labyrinth of shelter for addicts and predators.

"I gots to crawl through the steam tunnels," DeAndre had said.

Alex prayed for access to those tunnels somewhere in the cannery basement. He had no time for caution. Looking around for any sign of the predatory cops, he quick-stepped the last half block to the small gap in the cannery's sagging front gate. He first peeled off his coat. In an awkward, sideways limbo, his arm and coat went through first followed by his head, boney shoulders and chest. Something caught at his waist. Cursing, he dropped the coat to grab the rusty chain link to support himself while the other hand worked to free his belt buckle.

A monstrously large pick-up truck roared up, jumped the curb and slid to a stop inches away. Two tall, hefty men jumped out.

Alex fell free of the gate as the hand of one of the muscled men shot through. Fingers clawed at his threadbare canvas shoe but Alex jerked away. He scrambled the first ten feet on all fours then caught his balance, rose and ran as fast as his bad leg would allow. The shout "I'll take the shot!" drove him harder toward the cannery entrance.

"Jimmy! Not out here," a voice echoed. "He's headed to the nigger."

Just as he reached the door, the truck engine roared and metal crashed behind him as the vehicle took out the fence. Alex burst into the deepening shadows of the building, frantically peering about for a way below ground. Tripping over a pile of debris, he switched to a rapid shuffle to maintain his footing. Pounding footsteps echoed behind him just before a flashlight's beam swept the wall in front of him. His bobbing shadow briefly danced on the wall beside a doorway. Through the opening he saw the downward-slanted railing of a stairwell.

"I'm on him! You wait for Sarge!"

Heart pounding, breath ragged, Alex descended the blackness of the stairs. The hand sliding down the wall kept his sense of space oriented. Stumbling slightly at the first landing, he turned to take on the second flight. Above him the faint beam of the flashlight flickered and his pursuer's feet thundered.

The stairs ended. Alex used both trembling hands to feel for the basement access door. Discovering the edge of the doorframe and sensing the emptiness beyond, he hobbled into the darkness, one hand in front of him, the other sliding along the wall. He glanced over his shoulder just at the doorway was dimly outlined by the moving flashlight.

Out of the darkness a dainty hand flew past Alex's face then an arm fell on his shoulder. He collapsed against the wall, grappling with his assailant. His leg gave way. Twisting and screaming he hit the floor with a stiff, unforgiving foe covering him. The distant flashlight beam swept past then back, locking on target as the circle of light revealed the feminine face of a clothing store mannequin. The expressionless painted face exploded, showering plaster and fiberglass as a gunshot boomed off the basement walls.

In a surge of adrenaline, Alex rolled free and was up. One step, two. Flat cold metal smacked him in the face. *Dead end.* He dropped to his knees just as the second shot tore into the metal inches above his head. Alex frantically slid his hands upward, found the knob then yanked on the metal door. He fell through the opening as the third deafening gunshot vibrated his eardrums. *Like a depth charge in a WWII submariner movie.*

Again surrounded by blackness, he edged forward with one hand on the wall. His shoe encountered another set of stairs leading down. He tried to catch himself on the wall but still tumbled. On his back at the bottom he took quick inventory of his surprisingly still intact body. Glass crunched under foot as he rose. Beyond the ringing in his ears, nearby rodents squeaked and scurried.

"Nice shot, dickhead! You shot her face off," a sarcastic voice echoed from above.

"Shut the fuck up, Carl. I can't hear!"

Door's still open. They know where you are. Of course, idiot . . . .

"Both of you shut the fuck up and hold your fire!" roared a third voice.

"Hell, Sarge, I was shootin' over his head."

"Then quit fucking around. The little doghouse runt may not be much but the big nigger'l eat you alive if he gets the jump!"

Staring up at the faint light coming through the doorway above, Alex backed into another doorknob. Through that door he found a cavernous space illuminated by barrel-contained fires. The wavering flames reflected off their rising smoke giving the area an eerie orange cast. His chest still heaving for air, Alex gently shut the door. He squinted into the shadows searching for DeAndre.

"You don't be bringing trouble in here or you be dead," rasped a deep voice from the depths of the space.

Alex coughed and fought for air. "No choice . . . cops want . . . to kill me . . . and DeAndre."

"Alex? That you?" said the disembodied voice.

Marginally reassured that he was recognized, he moved forward slowly. "Yes."

"Motherfuckers hit you with them shots?"

"No, they shot . . . the mannequin." Behind him heavy feet descended the final flight of stairs.

"They shot my Jasmine?"

"If that was her name . . . Ah, yes." He looked over his shoulder at the still closed door.

"Let'em fuckin' come," said the voice. "We'll show'em who runs things down here."

A flashlight beam flickered under the door.

"They're here," Alex whispered loudly.

"Go on and find a hole over there behind you. No, to the right. You watch the show," said the voice.

A shrill whistle brought the dark, earthy cavern to life. Shadowy forms moved. Thumps and scrapes sounded.

Hand on the damp wall, Alex scurried to his right to a jagged break in the concrete blocks and crawled in.

The cops burst through the door into the sub-basement, their flashlight beams arcing like light sabers in the thin smoke. All three took the same stance, knees bent, guns raised with flashlights pointing down the barrels of their weapons.

"Omaha Police!" shouted the sergeant.

In the cavern, footsteps scurried. Someone coughed and someone in another location laughed maniacally. The rapid guttural slurs coming at them turned the flashlight beams into a laser light show of confusion.

"What the hell is this, Sarge?" called out one of the cops.

A chunk of concrete crashed at their feet. All three jumped, their guns and lights swiveling.

"Fucking crack den or something. You see where that came from?"

A larger, softball-sized chunk of concrete caught the sergeant on the shoulder, knocking him back. "Fuck!" he screamed, firing his shotgun at a flash of movement.

Alex pressed his hands over his ringing ears.

"We're not fucking around," the agitated Jimmy yelled. "We will kill—" A thrown brick tore into his forehead.

Alex glimpsed a dark form moving from the floor to jab something into the sergeant's back sending him stumbling forward. Turning his ankle, he fell. The shotgun clattered away from his out-stretched hands. At the same time, a small, bat-faced man ran forward in a crouch, the length of pipe in his hands whizzing toward the legs of the third cop, Carl. He shrieked in pain and went down.

Projectiles rained in from all directions.

Scrambling to his feet, his arms protecting his head, the sergeant screeched, "Get out of here!"

Jimmy swiped at the blood coating his face, his voice rising in panic, "I can't see shit. Sarge! Sarge!"

Dodging and ducking, the sergeant grabbed the shotgun then Jimmy's collar, pulling as he retreated toward the stairwell. Alex gave the man credit when he returned for Carl. Obviously the army of assailants didn't. A hefty block of jagged cement caught the sergeant between the shoulder blades. He arched his back, but kept his footing and retrieved his last man. Only a few projectiles followed him as he dragged the man to the doorway.

As he clawed for the doorknob the sergeant yelled, "Get up!"

Jimmy threw his arm up over his head, only to flinch and cower when a brick hit his hand. "Should we call for back-up?"

"No! I'm not here!" the sergeant roared as he finally got the door open. A broad hand shoved Jimmy through as Carl came to his knees and crawled after him.

Projectiles peppered the closing door then a roar of victory rose up from the underworld.

Alex strained to see the occupants of what had once been the cannery's physical plant. He dug in his pants pocket for a Mick's tavern match. As it flared he saw that she had crawled into an earthen hollow carved out by a failing storm sewer system. When the tiny flame guttered, burning his fingers, Alex dropped it. Cautiously, he moved back into the smoky haze of the cavern. He cleared his throat then called out, "Hey, out there! You, ah, know me?"

Close to the door, a man slipped out of the shadows like an eel emerging from its underwater nest. "I seen you at the St. Vincent. You the doghouse man. What brings you to down here?"

"Yeah, and why'd that fucking trouble follow you?" called out another, less friendly voice.

Alex held his hands up as if to calm the tense atmosphere. "Those cops want to kill my friend DeAndre. I have to warn him."

The doorman waved a hand at the shadowy cavern. "I got this." He put his hands on his hips. All Alex could make out were ragged clothes, thinness and an unshaven face with sunken eyes almost hidden in a veil of long, straggly hair. "DeAndre come through every now and then, but he don't stay. Sometimes he brings food. I ain't seen him today."

Disappointment deflated Alex. "So, this isn't . . . Do you know the steam tunnels?"

"'Course. They run all over under downtown. Most on this end ain't used no more."

Hope surged. "DeAndre told me he uses the tunnels to get to his hidey-hole. Do you know where that is?"

"Can't be far. He don't have a light. But where he go, ain't none a my business." The man crossed his arms and bent to peer harder at Alex. "You goin' in the tunnels to look for him?"

Alex nodded. "Got to. Where do they open? Is it down here?"

"You ain't much to look at, but you got balls. See them big-ass tanks over there?"

Alex could see little more than a big mass of something in the darkness. "I think so."

"Behind them big tanks, that's where the steam lines come out."

* * *

William rolled to a stop in front of the broken cannery gate as Jimmy and Carl hobbled to their truck. Both pretended not to see him.

He hurried from his car cataloguing their appearance. "Looks like you were on the losing end of an ass kicking, gentlemen."

The bloodied Jimmy glared over Carl's shoulder as he strong-armed him into the truck's passenger seat.

"What the hell were you doing in there? You two have knowledge you need to share?"

Jimmy waved a hand between himself and his passenger. "See these clothes, Olson? We're on our own time. We—"

He moved in closer, enough to let them know he wasn't fooled or intimidated. "What happened to the leg, Carl? Might need an X-ray."

Carl jutted his chin out then snarled, "We fell down the stairs in that old building. Just looking around."

"Is that right? Curiosity killed the cat, you know."

Jimmy sneered, "And how's your hip?"

"Hurts. I don't heal as fast as I used to, being an old guy and all." He leaned back to look at the cannery. "So, you find anything interesting in there?"

Carl glanced at Jimmy. "Nope, we just got a tip that Gurdlich might be in there."

William nodded then backed up to get a broader view. He glanced down at the fur from Alex's coat poking out of the muddy rut carved by the truck's tires.

He turned an icy stare on the two men. "A tip from who?"

"None of your mother fucking business," said Jimmy, taking one big step to be within inches of William's face. "It's not like you give a shit anyway. You'd rather play kiss-ass with the winos than help a fellow cop."

Loosening his stance to move quickly and tightening his back and stomach for action, William met belligerence with soul-deep cold confidence. "Try kicking my ass if you want, kid. I've been a cop longer than you've been alive. There was a time when us real cops would have buried an animal like Gurdlich."

"So much for the honor of the good old days. Go fuck yourself, old timer," Jimmy said through tight lips.

"So I guess that's a negatory on you kicking my ass." William smiled at the kid.

Jimmy laughed and looked at Carl, "I think the old guy really wants to play. All right show me—"

William's hand whipped from his coat pocket, the sections of his metal baton extending in flight. It thumped hard into Jimmy's carotid artery, dropping the muscled jock like a sack of shit.

"Hey, asshole!" shouted Carl, scooting to the edge of the truck seat just as William slammed the door on his mangled leg.

"Motherfucker!" he screamed, clawing at his waistband.

"It's a bitch, drawing from that holster in the sitting position isn't it?" Carl froze with William's Sig Sauer pistol leveled on him.

"Cheating son of a bitch," Carl muttered through clenched teeth.

"Cheating? This ain't high school, ass wipe."

"Fuck off, old man!"

William leaned against the door, pressing it harder into Carl's leg. The younger man trembled to control his reaction but a groan still escaped.

"Was it Alex or DeAndre that kicked your asses in there?"

"Don't know . . . what you're talking about," Carl panted.

William pulled back the door then slammed it hard.

"Fucker! We were . . . chasing the little guy but . . . lost him."

"Was anyone with you?" When Carl showed his teeth in a belligerent snarl, William raised an eyebrow and pulled the door back for another assault.

"Stop! Larry Jenkins told us the black guy was down there. He's in some steam tunnels or something. We saw the little guy going in. Tried to follow but he lost us. That's it."

William's laugh did not sound humorous. He slammed the door again. Carl jerked and gagged.

"And who is us?" William enunciated.

"Just me . . . and Jimmy. Honest, detective."

"Who kicked your asses?"

"Crack heads. In the dark. A fucking army of 'em . . . came at us with rocks and pipes."

At William's feet a quiet, childlike sob came from Jimmy's drooling mouth as he rolled to his side.

"You boys take care," William said, giving the door one last shove and stepping over the kid. He backed to his car, pistol in hand.

* * *

Alex went through most of a book of matches before locating a small hatch below a pair of insulated, fourteen-inch pipes. It opened on darkness. Leaning in, he struck another match. The tunnel was actually tall enough for him to stand up. He ducked through the doorway into the tunnel then patted his shirt pocket to make sure he still had the stack of matchbooks.

Striking the last match from the first pack, he walked forward. He cupped the flame and made it ten yards before touching the dying flame to its empty cardboard jacket. That got him another twenty yards. He held onto it until the last second, checking the tunnel as far ahead as possible. Deciding to save his light, he proceeded in darkness, one hand on the wall, the other outstretched before him.

The wall's concrete surface slid by rough, cold, and in places, slimy. Then the wall disappeared altogether. Confused, he struck a match from a new pack and discovered he was at a T-intersection. *Jesus, it's a damn city beneath the city.*

The steam pipes suspended on hangers overhead connected with a manifold that appeared to be fed by a much larger pipe running perpendicular to the smaller ones.

When another short-lived match became history, he rubbed his eyes to recheck what he thought he saw. A distant, dim light to his right beckoned. To his left he only found blackness. One foot in front of the other, he cautiously headed toward the light.

Just got a handle on the goodness of life, God. Don't let me die down here where no one would even hear me scream.

After what felt like a hundred or so yards, he stopped to tune into his surroundings. Something didn't feel right. He reversed direction, returning to the T-intersection. It took several matches to examine the walls. Twenty yards to the left of the T he found an orange extension cord coming from a caged light fixture without a bulb. He followed the wire to a four-foot high, metal door with a broken deadbolt, the wire pinched in the doorframe.

Well, DeAndre, looks like you have all the comforts of home.

Lined with old brick and bulging mortar instead of concrete, the new tunnel proved to be too cramped for him to stand. Crawling while holding a match proved problematic and time-consuming. When the tiny flame went out, he crawled on in the dark, the former match hand following the electrical cord. His gut told him it led to DeAndre's hidey-hole. He remembered the man's words of "I gots to crawl through the steam tunnels."

The darkness in the cramped space grew suffocating. Alex's imagination ran wild. A cave in, buried alive, his mouth and lungs filling with dirt. His chest tightened as his heart raced. He fought the urge to scream. Finally, when he could take it no more, he stopped and struck a match. *What if I'm stuck and can't turn around?* He held his breath. Raising the match, he stared at the end of the tunnel and a metal ladder leading up to an ancient, wooden door.

26

"Dan, I just tangled with a couple of Gurdlich's boys," William said into his cell phone. "They chased Alex into the old Fairbury cannery and lost him. Apparently they ran into a bunch of crack heads and barely made it out. They looked pretty banged up."

"Fuck," cursed Dan. "Now everybody'll know Alex is on the street. How'd you get the story from 'em?"

"It took a little persuading, but I'm confident I got the truth. They said DeAndre is in some sort of steam tunnel under the cannery. They were hoping Alex would lead them to him."

"You persuaded? Wait, I don't want to know. So, the kids are trying to clean up after their sergeant. What a cluster fuck. Goddamn it, we don't need this crap right now."

"Is Liz there yet?" asked William.

"No, but my guys have her and say they're on the way in."

"Thanks, boss. Keep me posted. I'm heading in after Alex—"

"No-no-no!" Dan stopped him. "That's a negative, my friend. You've taken more than your share of chances lately."

William huffed a breath and counted to ten.

"I can hear your brain working, Will," Dan cut into his thoughts. "I'm ordering you not to enter that cannery. Alex is safer in there than out in the open and you know it."

He worked not to grind his teeth. "Okay, I hear you and you're probably right."

"I'll send in SWAT to deal with the cannery," Dan continued. "Have to wake up public works and try to get some maps. Those damn tunnels run all over the downtown."

William looked around his location and almost slapped his hand to his forehead. "Dan, something just occurred to me. Jennings' building is right behind the cannery. Is he still in custody or did the Chief cut him loose for poker night?"

"Real cute, Will. No, he's still here. Probably won't be moved to the Douglas County jail until morning. The political types have abandoned him. Are you expecting me to ask him if those tunnels connect to his buildings?"

"See? That's why you're my boss. You can read minds."

"Smart ass. I'll go chat with him then talk to Burt. He's still on scene. Oh, and you know that female member of the FBI forensics team?"

"Someone mentioned her. Marshall, isn't it?"

"That's the one. I hear old Burt has the hots for her."

"Good for him. It's about time he found a fellow geek and settled down."

"I shared that bit of gossip so you wouldn't step on toes."

"Me? I'd never—"

"I'll call or text with what ever I get out of Jennings and send the maps to Burt. You get with him and proceed however you see fit . . . without offending anybody important."

"Thanks, boss. I'm on my wa—"

"Will, you did some good work today. Now, don't screw it up by doing something stupid. I mean it. I know you're worried about Alex but—"

"Not to worry, Dan," Will cut him off. "I'm walking around the block to the Jennings plant now. Keep me posted on the cannery. Shoot me a text when you have Liz. And tell SWAT to go easy on Alex, if he's still in there. I'd hate to lose him now."

"All duly noted," said Dan.

* * *

Dan watched Barry Jennings shuffle into the interview room looking tired and disheveled. His escort, a heavy-set female corrections officer, held up her keys waiting for Dan's instruction.

"Leave them on. We won't be long," said Dan. "Take a seat, Barry" He took a closer look at the man. "Say, that's quite a lump on your lip. Making new friends are we?"

Jennings glared up at the closed-circuit camera. "Not a word without my lawyer," he growled.

"What is it about that camera that bugs you so much?"

"You Tube."

"Really? You really think you have a reputation left to protect?"

"Lawyer." Jennings clamped his lips, though the belligerent effort was lost when he grimaced.

"You ever hear the one about the little rich guy in jail?" Dan paced a moment. "I'll take your silence as a no. Well, it seems that on his first night in lockup, his new cellmate—a man almost twice his size—asked him whether he wanted to be his husband or his wife. When the new guy said he'd prefer to be the husband, his cellmate smiled and told him to come right on over and suck his new wife's dick."

"Lawyer," the man in the orange jumpsuit repeated through clenched teeth.

"Now, Barry," said Dan, "I'll be happy to help your expensive lawyer log a few billable hours, but what would you say if I told you we were looking at somebody else for these murders?"

"I'd say you've finally pulled your head out of your ass, because I certainly had nothing to do with it."

"What can you tell me about the old steam tunnels under your meatpacking plant?"

"Well, I was . . . Wait, is this some sort of trick? I want my lawyer."

* * *

Sgt. Ken Wilkins had entered the closed circuit camera viewing room to join Detective Emma Gratz just in time to hear the Chief of Detective's predictable intimidation joke. They had shared a companionable laugh but were now listening intently.

Wilkins fidgeted and loosened an aching shoulder. "Wonder what he's after."

"Will Olson called in some intel about old tunnels under his buildings," Gratz offered. "Armour sent my partner to pick up the public works director and hunt down some maps." She turned at his awkward movement then looked him over more carefully. "What the hell happened to you, Sergeant? You look like you got rolled in an alley or something."

"Searching for Gurdlich, on my own time, I might add. Stumbled into a nest of crack heads. This whole thing . . . It's a helluva mess."

Her expression turned sad and she patted his shoulder. "I know you're pushing it because he was a close friend. It's hard, but you gotta be careful, too."

He let tears shine in his eyes. "We'd have probably found him by now if he was alive."

"I'm sorry, Ken," she spoke with sincerity. "Tough way to spend your down time. You hang in there. Armour and Olson have shaken some things loose."

He nodded. "No point in sticking around for this interview shit. I'm heading back out to look some more."

"You might hit the locker room and clean up a little. On the other hand you could blend in with those street people."

"Naw, just as well be in uniform and on the clock," His shrug sent a stab of pain between his shoulder blades. *More than a deep bruise? What do I care? Bigger worries to deal with.*

* * *

The stench drifted in the air near the meatpacking plant and only worsened when William entered the building doorway. Despite the cold, he understood the need for ventilation fans beyond the command center tables. The FBI's big budget, high tech presence made Burt's original makeshift lab look like a kid's playhouse kitchen. A huge LCD screen sat at the end of a row of tables filled with computers and complex scientific gear.

William approached a white-coated tech clicking away at a keyboard. "Seen Burt Haliday?"

The tech looked carefully at his displayed badge before answering, "I believe he's up on four with our agents. Do you know how to get there?"

"Oh, yeah. Unfortunately I was up there this morning."

At the stairwell, William paused, looked up, then opted to head to the basement instead. He flipped on his flashlight and descended, his footfalls echoing and flashlight sweeping. A quick survey found the area empty but for a few pieces of ancient machinery too large for scavengers to carry. He aimed his light beam on the far walls. *Hell, I don't even know what a steam pipe looks like. I'm wasting time.*

Back upstairs, Burt and two members of the FBI team met him on the main floor landing.

"I hear we're taking this investigation underground," Burt joked, eyes twinkling over the top of his glasses. "Nice catch on the utility tunnels by the way. Will, I'd like to introduce Special Agents Elizabeth Marshall and Mark Bennett. They're heading up the FBI lab."

"Nice to meet both of you." He shook hands. "I'm William Olson, Omaha Police Detective." Both agents were around Burt's age, well dressed and keen-eyed.

As Burt moved to the female's side and the two exchanged looks, William caught the first whiff of geek lust. Special Agent Marshall wore square, black-framed glasses that complimented her nerd essence. He smiled when Burt put a hand to the small of her back as they turned to exit the stairwell. She didn't object.

"So, Burt tells us that one of our suspects frequents utility tunnels in the area," said Bennett as they walked.

"Yes, DeAndre Fletcher, also known as DeAndre Easton. He was a patient at the Kilpatrick Center before it closed."

"Kilpatrick was a long-term mental health facility," Burt added.

"Detective Olson, do you know if this DeAndre is a big man?" asked Marshall.

"Reportedly six-foot-four, well over two-hundred pounds and suffering from schizophrenia."

The female agent looked over her shoulder at her partner. "That would fit."

"Fit what?" William asked, confused.

"Sorry, Will. Let me bring you up to speed," said Burt. "We've determined that most of our victims' throats were cut. They died of exsanguination. Trouble is, there's a definite lack of blood."

"So, they were killed elsewhere and brought here," William stated.

Burt nodded. "That's where the evidence is pointing."

Marshall continued, "And it would take great strength to transport that much dead weight to the fourth floor without the help of an elevator."

"Or whoever it was who helped," threw out her partner.

William scowled at him. "That's an ugly thought."

"And unlikely considering the length of time it took for the collection up there to accumulate," Burt stated confidently as he slid into the chair in front of the closed laptop labeled "Forensics – B. Haliday" He opened it and tapped keys as soon as the screen lit up. "We hadn't even thought of looking under the building until Dan called with your discovery. Let's see if they've sent us the maps."

From the tiny speakers, a sensuous female voice purred, "You've got mail, stud muffin."

The tips of Burt's ears turned cherry red. "I'm sorry." He cleared his throat. "One of my guys is a comedian—"

Standing at his right shoulder, Special Agent Marshall didn't miss a beat. "And who's to say your email alert is wholly inaccurate?"

A snicker sounded nearby. The usually unflappable Burt stiffened, his neck flushing deep red, almost purple.

"Ah, yes," he blurted in relief, pointing to the screen. "Here we go. These look like PDFs of what is under this block." He turned his head to catch the eye of a white-coated FBI crime scene tech manning one of the laptops on their table of hardware. "I'm sending some files to your server. Can you put them up on the big screen?"

Seconds later, the foursome stood in front of the huge LCD monitor, parsing decades and in some cases, centuries-old cartography.

"The steam tunnels didn't go in until the '60's," said Burt, "Maybe we should separate these by date." He looked over his shoulder at the FBI tech. "Can you separate these on the screen for us?"

With a patient smile, Special Agent Marshall tapped Burt's arm then stepped up to the LCD. Just by sliding her fingertips across the touch screen, she quickly rearranged the pictures by date. Burt's face glowed with fascination and admiration. When she reoriented the images to the north-south orientation, his enamored expression was downright embarrassing to William and the observant Mark Bennett. They looked at one another, grinned and shrugged then focused on the job at hand instead of their co-workers.

It didn't take long to discern that there were no steam lines running directly to the Jennings plant.

"I recall the data indicating this building had been constructed in the 1920's," Bennett pointed out. "Let's start at the beginning of the map records and work forward."

Meticulously arranging and scaling of the early maps revealed a rat's nest of utility lines. The plant had actually been a composite of three old buildings built at different times and cobbled together. Endless map discrepancies arose. Finally, the attentive FBI tech used Photoshop to drop the background out of the newest map and laid it over the older maps. A distance discrepancy of twenty feet appeared.

"So, the main line that feeds steam and water to the cannery could be much closer to this building than these old maps indicate," said Burt.

"Close enough that a thermal imager might show the heat signature of the steam pipes," pointed out Bennett. "We've got one in the truck." He motioned to the tech with his hand. "Alejandro, do you mind?"

The man deserted his computer and headed for the door. The uniformed Ken Wilkins entered as Alejandro exited.

"Jesus, it's a damn media circus out there," commented Wilkins. "I think I just saw Lester Holt from the Today Show."

After making introductions, William asked, "Where's your rookie, the Grant kid?"

"Learning to work traffic over at the sports arena. Miserable damn night for that. I was just at the station and heard you might need a tunnel rat."

"First we need a tunnel," said Burt.

"Well, this should give us a little help," said Special Agent Bennett, removing a FLIR infrared camera from the case brought in by the tech.

"Are the basements separate or joined by doors like up here?" asked Marshall as her partner readied the camera.

"Separate spaces," said Burt. "Only this building and the next have basements. The building furthest west was built in the '70's, according to the plans."

Together they clanked down the metal stairs into the first basement. Flashlights swept the walls as they walked to the far end. Bennett powered up the infrared camera, its screen coming to life with brilliant blues and purples on its LCD screen.

"Blue, not so good. We're looking for a yellow . . . like that," the agent explained, pointing to the yellow silhouette of Sgt. Wilkins walking in front of the camera.

"Hey, Ken," William called out, "The camera says you're hot."

"You know it, baby!" The sergeant's laugh echoed. "The ladies say it's my after-shave."

William rolled his eyes. "Yeah, that Old Spice never goes out of style for us older guys."

The walls of the first basement gave up nothing. Discouraged, they plodded back up the stairs, across the big empty floor and into the second warehouse where the stench of the first two bodies still lingered. Below ground, the dissipating odor of death mixed with a root-cellar smell that reminded William of his grandparents' farm.

Finally, the infrared screen showed a faint yellow ribbon just above floor level, running the length of the north basement wall.

"Bingo," Bennett called out. "Now, if there's a hole or a doorway, even a crack, this should show it as yellow or orange."

After twenty minutes of careful moving examination, they still had nothing more.

"I can't believe the tunnel would be so close without some form of access," said Burt. "I mean, it isn't just steam lines in those tunnels. There's electric and water too in some cases."

"Maybe there's a hatch in the floor," suggested William.

All five formed a line, flashlights in hand, walking the floor until its entirety was covered, both with the naked eye and the infrared camera.

"So much for that theory," said William. He pulled out his cell phone to check for a text about Liz and progress in the cannery. The lack of a signal made him curse and shove his phone back in its holster.

"We're all over-tired," Burt said, actually assessing the only female in their group. She gave him a disgusted look.

Circled up with their flashlights reflecting off their faces, William thought they looked like campers about to tell ghost stories. The eeriness of the scene and their situation kept him from voicing his thought.

Marshall waved her hand toward the stairwell. "Let's head back up and have another look at the building plans. We may have missed something obvious."

* * *

In the narrow brick tunnel, Alex planted a hand and a foot on the ladder then dropped the spent match. In darkness, he crawled upward, trading the fear of being buried alive for thoughts of surprising DeAndre.

At the top of the ladder, he wrapped an arm around the uppermost rung and struck a match. The old wooden door's black paint was cracked, peeling and streaked with lime. Its latch looked to be an ancient bar and lever arrangement.

Better go slow. Scaring the big man would be a good way to get my skull cracked.

He blew out the match and slowly pushed open the door. Its corroded brass hinges squeaked with each incremental movement.

A putrid smell accompanied the glaring electrical light greeting him. Squinting from being so long in the dark, Alex hoisted himself up through the doorway onto his knees on the floor of what appeared to be an ancient cellar.

DeAndre's hulking form stood silhouetted and motionless against the light of a single bulb dangling from the thick wooden joists above. In front of DeAndre, the light fell on a small wooden table. Next to him, in the shadows, something hung heavy, connected to the overhead joists by large hooks.

Suddenly apprehensive and unsure, Alex kept silent. DeAndre retrieved something from the table. A black apron draped his front. The glow from the overhead bulb streaked down his back, highlighting the crisscross of paler scars and pockmarks down his bare back and broad buttocks. The sight made Alex wince, his insides tightening with sadness. *Wow, there's a lot you haven't told me, my friend.*

DeAndre lifted a long, thin-bladed knife as if to study it under the light bulb. He turned to face whatever it was that hung next to him in the dark and began to cut.

Awareness slammed into Alex. The putrid smell, the apron and knife, the carcass hanging from hooks . . . DeAndre was so hungry that he'd pulled rotten meat from a dumpster.

Alex struggled to his feet, about to speak, when a blood curdling bellow shook the room.

"Take this and eat! It is my body!"

Alex shrank back, confused and disoriented. *That wasn't DeAndre's voice!*

The shadowy hulk held a slice of meat in his hand, tilted his head back and dropped the morsel in his mouth. Alex listened to the smacking lips as the man chewed. The hulk swayed, metal creaked.

Alex fought the urge to vomit as hard as he fought to comprehend. *Is DeAndre dancing or convulsing?* A singsong of gibberish like a mix of ancient language with a hillbilly twist poured from DeAndre's mouth. His arms flailed and his body spun. As the big man turned, the light clearly showed DeAndre's face and the black apron, both caked with blood.

Now totally terrified, Alex backed slowly toward the floor hatch. Images flashed across his mind of a frantic race through the tunnels with a knife-wielding DeAndre at his heels.

In his dance of madness, DeAndre's arm caught the hanging lightbulb. It swung in a wild semicircular arc, casting pulses of light on the dangling carcass. Alex froze. The carcass had a face. A human face. Alex's vision narrowed. In the diminishing pulses of light he saw the big square head and high, tight crew-cut. Gurdlich's face looked gray, his eyes milky white. His tongue lolled from his gaping mouth.

A high-pitched, ear-piercing, primal scream filled the cellar. DeAndre froze, arms outstretched, knife in hand. Slowly he turned, his confused eyes locking on Alex. It wasn't until Alex gasped for breath that he realized the scream came from his own mouth.

"Hey, Little Man," DeAndre spoke in his own voice again, his gold-toothed smile framed in that gore-covered face. "I took care of the sickness like God told me."

Alex stiffened to control the violent tremors that coursed over him. He sputtered, "You need help . . . you're s-sick . . . That's G-Gurd—"

"No, Little Man," DeAndre interrupted him in a perfectly reasonable voice. "He the sick one. He hurt that little girl. His sickness won't hurt nobody no more. God told me. Look," he said sawing a hunk of flesh from Gurdlich's chest, "It be good and holy now. The sickness is gone." DeAndre popped the morsel into his mouth and smiled innocently.

Maybe I died in the doghouse and this is Hell.

Unable to take a breath, Alex wretched like a dog and fell forward on his knees. As the contents of his stomach came up, DeAndre dropped the knife and ran to his aid. Panicked, Alex shoved him back with all his might.

"Don't . . . touch me . . . freak!" he croaked, choking on his own vomit.

DeAndre's smile faded, his face changing before Alex's horrified stare. He stood tall, seemingly gaining six inches in height. In one stride he loomed, his huge frame casting a menacing shadow. Alex didn't recognize this being or his voice.

"I am Michael, one of the seven who stand before God."

27

Dan hadn't called with news of Alex, but had sent the text saying Liz arrived safe and sound.

A second review of the building plans had been fruitless. William rubbed his temples in frustration. The solicitous Burt watched Marshall attempt to roll the fatigue from her shoulders, then looked around the room at the various people who had been at their work for such long hours. He knew what was coming.

Burt announced loudly, "I say we reconvene in the morning for a fresh look at the basements. We're done for the night, Alejandro," said Burt, to the last, remaining FBI lab tech who proceeded to walk along the table punching off the various laptops and closing their lids. "Ah, shall we gather again at eight-thirty or nine?" Burt asked, looking from Marshall to Bennett then back at Marshall. Their gazes locked.

"How about a 7:30 breakfast meet?" murmured the female agent. Burt's head nodded.

Bennett glanced at William. They shrugged simultaneously then followed along behind the zoned out couple. After she collected her shoulder bag from a table, Burt's hand comfortably settled at the small of her back. The two spoke low enough that only they could hear.

"Think they're discussing the case?" muttered Bennett to William.

"More like techy stuff."

Bennett barked a laugh. "Yeah, that would turn her on. Did you notice that the two of us were not included in that mention of a breakfast meet?"

It was William's turn to laugh. Alejandro beat them out the door and headed to the truck-mounted generator. At the temporary power box near the doorway, Marshall waited for Burt to flip the breakers. The cavern of the building went dark, quickly followed by the perimeter lights as the generator powered down. In the suddenly quiet night, the only sound was the idling cruiser of two officers left to assure the security of their crime scene.

Now ahead of the lagging couple, William walked alongside Bennett listening to the crunch of their shoes in the snowmelt recently cast on the sidewalk.

"Hey, Mark," called Marshall from behind. "Burt's giving me a ride home. You go ahead."

Without turning, the agent waved an acknowledging hand then grinned at William, catching him mid-yawn.

William caught himself. "Sorry. God, this has been a long day. I'm parked on the west side, around the corner."

Bennett consulted his watch. "And a short night. See you at nine."

Dialing Dan Armour as he walked, the puzzle of the steam tunnels still played in William's tired mind.

"Hello, Will," his boss answered.

"Hey, Dan, it's Will."

"I know, it's you. That's why I said 'Hello, Will'." Dan's yawn triggered another jaw-cracking one of his own. He barely heard Dan commenting, "You need some sleep, my man."

"My body says the same but my mind isn't letting go. What's the status of the steam tunnel search?"

"Nothing yet," said Dan. "Took forever to clear out the rat's nest in the cannery basement. Units are still working the tunnels but it's slow going. They have orders to call if they have any luck. What's new from your end?"

"Nothing." William paused to rub his sleep-deprived eyes and crack another yawn. "We can't find any connection from the meatpacking plant to the cannery. The tunnel is close enough to show on thermal imaging but we can't find access from the Jennings plant." He paused to scoop up a handful of snow and rub it on his face. "I can hardly keep my eyes open. Anyway, the plan is to come back with fresh eyes in the morning. At nine."

"Okay. By the way, that Jennings prick wasn't much help. He doesn't recall any steam coming from anything but their own boilers."

William looked at his wristwatch. "Jesus, Dan, you still have him in interrogation?"

"Hey, we're not the Gestapo. He went to lock-up hours ago, probably asleep by now, just like we should be. He'll go in front of a judge in the morning. If he's still got the juice, he'll be released. That means, my friend, if you've got questions now would be the time to demand answers."

The snow had cleared his muddy thoughts somewhat. "Hm, there is something bugging me about his plant."

"Rousting Jennings this time of night might upset the other prisoners," said Dan, his tone betraying a smile. "I'd be happy to make a personal appearance. You know, make sure his cellmates know who's responsible for disturbing their beauty sleep. So, what is it you want to know?"

William stopped and turned to study the looming building beside him. "Ask him about the furthest building to the west. It looks different, cheaper, like it was an afterthought. Ask him why. Something about it won't let go."

"That's it? Okay, I'll call back when I know more."

William reached the west end of the building and rounded the corner onto 17th Street, his car in sight. The shell of the cannery rose over a frigid landscape lit by a nearly full moon.

Damn it Alex, what are you up to? Where did you go?

242

As he tugged at the keys in his pants pocket, the sound of a quarter hitting the wind-swept sidewalk made him pause. For a moment he considered walking on, but a quarter was a quarter. His eyes swept the moonlit walk abutting the building. Something caught his eye where the foundation met the walk. At first he thought it was a reflection, either the moon or the dim corner streetlight on his coin in the slope of the snow. He stepped closer. A sliver of light shone through the crumbling mortar surrounding a gas pipe protruding from the building's foundation.

Light? What the hell?

Palming his flashlight, he toed away the snow then ignored his protesting hip and dropped to his knees. Nothing. He turned off his flashlight. The light returned. He wasn't imagining things.

There's no power to the building, so what the hell is this?

The sliver of light escaped through a crack in the foundation. A light was on in the building's *basement*? Like a sprinter, he bolted from his kneeling position, into a full-out run back to the plant's main entrance.

As he neared, the door of the cruiser on guard popped open. The officer's flashlight beam hit his face. "You! Stop!" the man shouted.

William slowed, throwing up his hands. "Detective Olson here. I just left but, something caught my eye."

"Sorry, sir," said the patrolman. "I—"

"Get on your radio. Have dispatch contact Burt Haliday. He's in his car. I need him back here now. Warehouse three. Got it?"

* * *

Back at the station, the very tired Dan Armour placed his gun and cellphone in a small locker before being buzzed into the holding area.

"Hey! Jennings, wake up!" Dan Armour yelled, flipping on the lights to roust the sleeping men. Moans and curses arose. Some of the men covered their eyes, rolling away from the disturbance.

"Jennings!" Dan bellowed.

The man on the bunk next to Jennings, kicked him awake.

"What now?" whined the sleepy-voiced Jennings as he sat up.

Feeling more invigorated, Dan cheerily announced, "One more question."

Jennings squinted then growled, "Lawyer."

"All right, but I'll stand right out here and keep talking until he gets here." He raised his voice a notch, "You fellas don't mind my chatting with Jennings, do you? I can talk all night. In fact—"

"Answer his fucking question, rich meat," hissed an angry voice.

"Oh, for Christ's sake," Jennings said falling onto his back in his bunk, his arm over his eyes. "What is so goddamn important?"

243

"Have it your way. I can ask here. At the old plant, why is the western-most building different?"

Jennings groaned. "A fire. In the seventies, I think. It was the oldest building." The arm fell away from his face and he continued in a bored voice, "My grandfather started the business there. He used the building's storm cellar to dry-age sides of beef, but after it burned, my dad threw up something quick for storage. He—"

The hallway door clanged shut behind Dan and the lights went out.

He scooped his cell phone from the locker and punched in William's number. The call went straight to voicemail. As he rapidly strode back to his office, he scrolled his list of contacts and dialed a second number.

Burt Haliday answered. "I'm on my way back to the site now. Got William's message a minute ago."

Dan stopped. "What message?"

"That he found something in one of the buildings as he was leaving."

"Did he say what? He's not answering," said Dan. "I need to tell him that the western most building at the plant was rebuilt after a fire. Jennings said it has a storm cellar. Can you tell him when you see him?"

"Storm cellar? Hang on, I'm with Special Agent Marshall. Let me tell her about it."

After a moment of Burt's mumbling, he heard Marshall say "There wasn't anything like that in the plans."

"Burt, I've got a bad feeling about this. I'm putting out an officer needs help call. Don't you go in that plant without backup."

"Does the FBI count as backup?"

* * *

With no access to turn on the command center's generator, William flipped on his flashlight. Gun drawn and flashlight sweeping the dark, he quickly crossed the echoing expanse of the first two warehouses into the third. In his stark, relatively narrow beam everything looked older, more ominous. Each of the doorways between warehouses was protected by massive concrete and metal fire doors held back by ancient pulleys and weights. The sounds they made opening made William think of something from the Middle Ages and dragon-like monsters coming for him in the dark.

The western-most warehouse had seemed empty with the exception of a towering collection of dusty wood pallets stacked in the corner near where the gas pipe emerged on the outer wall. Turning off his flashlight, he stood in the dark, letting his eyes and ears adjust. Beyond his own breathing and the overhead creak of ancient rafters, he thought he heard faint voices. Straining, he turned his head slowly. A dim light glowed beneath the pallets.

He re-powered his flashlight. Walking carefully he discovered a winding path through the mountain of wood. In the middle of the pile with the pallets well over his head, he went dark again. The glow returned as his eyes adjusted. Fifteen feet in front of him, a thin line of light shown up through the floor.

I'll be damned.

Moving across the concrete floor, he found a wooden hatch, gray with dust except for a heavy metal ring. He stored his flashlight then, tightening his hold on his gun, tugged at the ring. The hatch rose slowly, creaking on a spring-assisted hinge. A narrow wooden stairway slanted down.

"Who's there?" called a familiar but shaky voice.

"Alex, is that you?" asked William.

"Don't come down, William. It's not safe," warned Alex.

"Sorry, buddy, but that's my job." The weight of his footfalls creaked on the stairs. "Anyone armed down there?"

"Not at the moment. Please, just—" Alex stopped speaking as William came into view, gun extended.

William's brow furrowed as he scanned the scene. A huge, nearly naked black man sat on the floor, hugging his knees and rocking violently. At the edge of the dim light, a large and naked male corpse hung gray and slack from thick meat hooks embedded in the overhead joists. The lower half of the body had mottled to purplish black, so it had hung there long enough for gravity to collect the bodily fluids. Blood, both old black and new burgundy painted much of the room. He glanced over arterial sprays on the walls and pooled stains on the concrete floor beneath the corpse. His attention ended on the dried blood caking the big black man's hair, face, arms and what appeared to be his only garment, a black apron.

Alex sat on his knees beside the man, one hand gently rubbing a broad knee, his eyes round in a sad, beseeching expression.

When William cautiously stepped from the stairs onto the floor, DeAndre stopped rocking. The sudden cessation of the big man's movement chilled his law enforcement soul. He did not lower is weapon. If the time-bomb of insanity before him exploded, he would only have seconds.

"It's all right, DeAndre," Alex said in a singsong, soothing voice, as if speaking to a small child. "This man's a friend. He's here to help us."

"Alex," William spoke just as softly, "you should introduce us."

Alex barely nodded his head. "Call me Little Man," he said. "Like my big brother DeAndre does. Michael was here but I asked him to leave for the time being."

Without moving his head, William flicked his gaze into the cellar's shadows. "And where did Michael go—"

"Why he got a gun, Little Man?" DeAndre interrupted, his rocking resuming with slightly less fervor.

"I'm sorry for the gun, Little Man," crooned William. "I didn't know it was you down here." The gun's barrel drifted down but his grip remained ready. "It's really cold down here. Upstairs there's warm blankets and something hot to drink."

"That's a good idea, William. I am freezing," Alex said, holding out his hand to DeAndre.

DeAndre's rocking intensified.

William recalled Dr. Moore's stories and saw them playing out in this tormented man's staring eyes.

"DeAndre, it's okay for us to leave, really." Alex gently tugged on DeAndre's arm.

"Little Man, God told me to kill the sickness. You heard Michael. He knowed what to do." Tears streamed from DeAndre's eyes as his chin trembled like a child in fear of punishment.

"You aren't in trouble, DeAndre," crooned William. "Just come on upstairs. Lets get warmed up and talk this—"

"You stay right where you are, you fucking sicko!" shouted Ken Wilkins from the stairs at William's back. William didn't have to look to know the man had his .40 caliber Glock aimed and ready.

"Ken," William continued his crooning with an undertone of authority and warning, "back off. It's handled. Go get us some blankets."

The steps creaked as Wilkins stepped down further. As William turned, the man's free hand pulled the hatch closed over his head. The Glock's aim swung toward him. He dove for the cover of the corpse a fraction too late. The bullet's massive punch caught him low in his vest, spinning him sideways. He hit the floor hard, but came up firing.

The first round from William's Sig creased the side of Wilkins's face, tearing off a piece of his left ear before punching through the wooden hatch.

DeAndre rose up between them. William jerked his aim just in time, his second shot striking the cellar wall.

"I am Michael, one of the seven who stand before God!" DeAndre roared in a stentorian voice. His arms lifted as if they were magnificent wings as he strode toward Wilkins, his demeanor powerful and invincible.

William blinked at Alex's cat-like spring from the floor, a long-bladed knife slicing forward and up into Wilkins' groin. His body weight behind the thrust carried the svelte blade all the way to the officer's pelvic bone. Mouth open in a scream, Wilkins slammed the barrel of his pistol down on Alex's head. The weapon discharged, burning hair and flesh as the bullet cut a deep furrow and blood flowed.

Clutching at the wet corner of his vest and desperately digging for air, William failed to bring his gun up as Alex crumpled.

The rage of the delusional angel beat him to it. With one huge hand, DeAndre grabbed Wilkins by the neck. Like a frenzied dervish, he whirled, slamming the gaping man against the blood and lime-streaked cellar walls. Two quick blasts from the Glock echoed with craters of flesh and bone exploding from DeAndre's back. The embattled figures tumbled to the floor. The Glock fell free. DeAndre's hulking form went slack as they landed at William's feet, Wilkins sprawled atop DeAndre, the broad black hand still clutching his throat. Two feet away, Alex squirmed and moaned, his eyes blinking, the top of his head still smoking.

William leveled his pistol in Wilkins's face.

"Shit," Wilkins spat, one eye lolling oddly, blood leaking from his ears and nose.

DeAndre's hand fell away as he looked up at Wilkins, his face wrinkled in confusion. "Why you want to hurt us?"

"Jesus," Wilkins gasped. "You don't remember me do you, kid?" Blood and spittle flecked as Wilkins coughed and looked at William. "Why the fuck did you jump in front of that pervert?"

"What pervert?" wheezed William. "What . . . the hell . . . you talking about, Ken?"

"Gurdlich. Gurdlich and I . . . we go to this kid's house," Wilkins said, nodding to DeAndre. "This guy's little brother was getting ass raped . . . " Wilkins coughed and drew a ragged breath.

"That was . . . you and Gurdlich?"

"You heard?" Wilkins raised a shaking hand to wipe at his face, but the hand dropped onto DeAndre's chest. "Chief covered up . . . that shit."

"Who shot . . . his mother?"

"Harry. Kid jumped in. She wasn't supposed to . . . die."

Wilkins's eyes grew distant.

"Ken!" William croaked.

Wilkins gasped. "Gurdlich figured out . . . this was the kid," he said, blinking down at the attentive DeAndre. "When Harry disappeared . . . I figured . . . revenge." His tongue flicked out. "Thirsty."

DeAndre frowned then turned his head to look at Alex.

"You okay, Little Man?" he asked in a clear voice.

Alex raised a weak hand to swipe at a trickle of blood near his temple. His blackened scalp smoldered as he gave a loving blink and a slight nod.

"You find your girl," DeAndre whispered. "She needs her daddy." His gold tooth caught the dim light as he smiled. His breath sighed as his eyes fluttered then stilled in nothingness.

Alex glanced at William. When they looked back at DeAndre's face in a crystalline moment of time, they beheld the face of an angel at peace.

William closed his eyes in reverence as Alex released a mournful wail.

* * *

An eternity later William thought he might be hallucinating as he watched the Chief of Detectives descended the creaking stairs, his weapon drawn. A uniform with a shotgun followed on his heels.

"Holy Mother of God," Dan whispered, his eyes rounding at the horror show.

Smoke from the shootout still hung heavy, acrid. William lay covered in blood spatter and bone fragments. He blinked rapidly, but couldn't form words. He held onto every second, forcing a shallow, sucking breath that didn't seem worth the effort. Dan edged forward looking at the tangled bodies of Ken Wilkins and DeAndre Fletcher. He only glanced at the unconscious Alex.

"Will, you hit?" asked Dan, gently pulling the weapon from William's lax hand. The words sounded as if down a hallway.

"Can't breath," mouthed William.

Dan ripped open William's shirt exposing the copper-jacketed bullet lodged in his chest wall partially stopped by the edge of the Kevlar vest. William's fingers fluttered over the crimson blood bubbling from around the puncture wound.

Burt pushed Dan aside and knelt to touch the wound. "Pneumothorax," he pronounced then yanked an ever-handy rubber glove from his pocket and slapped it over the site. William groaned at the eruption of pain and fought to stay conscious. Burt yelled out, "Somebody get me some duct tape. Now! Get the paramedics down here ASAP!"

"They're crossing the building," came a distant voice at the stairs.

"Holy fuck, Will. Even rookies wait for back-up," Dan chastised as he fumbled with the roll of wide silver tape shoved into his hands. He tore off strips that Burt pressed around the edges of the glove. William's next shallow breath came easier, but the pain sparkled and raced throughout his chest.

His hearing blossomed with acuteness then faded. He captured the urge to laugh when feet stumbled nearby and a young voice sputtered "It's a hell house in here."

"Found Gurdlich," William murmured as his awareness faded.

Somewhere in the shadows hands manipulated his body. Needles pricked his arm. Voices drifted in and out. A sharp pain rammed his side and he took deeper, easier breaths. The world came back into focus with Dan tapping his face.

"Hey, William. You back with us, guy? Come on. Give me some lip!"

"Go . . . fuck yourself."

"There you go . . . With a mouth like that, you'll never have my job."

"Never," he repeated adamantly. His head had been secured on a back board. Towering above him, people seemed shoulder to shoulder in the cellar. He jerked, his eyes straining in panic to look around. "Where's Alex?"

Dan patted his shoulder. "Already in the squad and stable. You're next."

William fought nausea as he was lifted. His view of the cellar bobbed and weaved as paramedics hauled him up the stairs. He caught a glimpse of the sheets covering Wilkins and DeAndre. He knew good ol' Burt had already photographed the scene, even as the living were cared for.

Cold air and flashing lights smacked William as they carried him from the Jennings plant. A crowd of cops and media craned to see. He allowed himself to float in the clean smells and warmth of the squad, the murmurs of the paramedics and even the siren became a background of white noise.

From the corner of his eye he could see Alex on his gurney, a bandage on his head, IV hooked up to his arm and a smile on his face.

They must have given you some good stuff. Sweet dreams, buddy. You earned it.

The ride to the hospital was a short one. Paramedics worked efficiently, radioing ahead so all would be ready. At the hospital, cold air rushed in through the open squad doors. William saw Liz greet paramedics and follow Alex inside.

Dan appeared at his side. "What the hell happened down there?"

He grunted in pain as his gurney's legs locked into place and touched the ground.

"Let us get him stabilized," a doctor ordered. "I'll let you know when you can question your man."

Susan and the boys arrived as the gurney neared the hospital doors.

"Stop!" William shouted out. That effort and the abrupt halt sent out a stab of pain he tried to hide as his family reached him. His wife sobbed as she clutched at his hand. "No need for tears, Suze," he soothed, his thumb sweeping her knuckles. "I'm okay. The vest caught the worst of it. A little puncture hole is all. X-rays and a couple of days in bed, I'll be good as new."

He looked to the foot of his gurney where the boys stood big eyed and struggling to be stoic. "Boys, take your mom to the waiting room. They'll let you know when I'm free, right, Doc?"

The doctor nodded and waved the boys aside so they could get to work.

*   *   *

"It looks a lot worse than it is," one of the nurses told Liz as clutched her hands to her chest and watched them clean the mess from her father's hair. She knew they had expected to see brain tissue. As they washed away the gore, it became clear the bullet had carved a furrow in Alex's scalp but had not fractured his skull.

"I think that look on his face might qualify as a smile," said the doctor who'd treated him just days before. He humphed and shook his head. "With what he's been through, I'm surprised he's with us at all."

"God knows we're not done," Liz murmured.

His head wound treated and battered body cared for, Alex was again moved to intensive care. Consciousness had not yet returned, but his smile never left.

What are you dreaming about? Liz squeezed his hand then leaned in to kiss his whiskered cheek.

In Alex's heaven-sent dream, four-year-old Amanda Elizabeth Capstain stood on a kitchen chair, playfully coaxing cheesy powder from a foil envelope into a pot of steaming macaroni. He stood next to his daughter who had put him in charge of measuring and pouring in the milk. Payment for his service came in the form of a kiss on his cheek.

"Mac, mac, macaroni," Amanda sang, tapping the envelope's backside. "Come on Daddy. You're not singing."

Alex joined in their musical tradition, singing the macaroni song while stirring the milk, powdered cheese and butter to make his daughter's favorite meal. When all was ready, a dance added the finishing touch.

"Mac, mac, macaroni," they sang, Amanda dancing atop her father's work boots as they swayed and twirled. "Mac, mac, macaroni, mac, mac, mac." As the final three macs were sung, Alex dipped her backward like dance partner positioning a fancy ballerina.

In the hospital, the dream danced across Alex's expressive face. Liz watched, wishing the tangle of wires and sensors connected to her father's body could offer a glimpse of what was playing out in his mind.

* * *

Cops filled the hospital lobby, spilling onto the entrance sidewalk. At their fringes, Manuela stood, ears attuned to comments, observing and making notes for her follow-up to this morning's blockbuster story. She shivered as much from the cold as anticipation of the shockwave her story would carry.

A white panel van sporting a picture of a rolled up newspaper pulled into the half-circle drive in front of the hospital. A harried-looking man hopped out, sliding open a side door to reveal bundles of papers fresh off the press. Manuela watched eagerly as the man hauled a bundle to the news rack, unlocked, dropped and propped the rack's door against his leg.

Bored officers sauntered over in search of a diversion. One of them held the news rack's door open to assist the circulation man as he cut a bundle's plastic binding.

"You mind?" asked a burly cop, offering the required number of quarters.

"Sure go for it," said the circulation man, handing over the paper. "It's all about you guys today anyway."

As he read the six-column headline, the cop's jaw dropped. *MISSING COP AT CENTER OF CITY HALL CORRUPTION*. Manuela couldn't control the grin that split her face as the man's eyes flicked over the thumbnail pictures of a uniformed Harry Gurdlich sitting alongside the Mayor, Police Chief, Pastor Ahough and Barry Jennings. A much larger photograph showed a head-on view of a maniacal-looking Jennings behind the wheel of an Angel's Wings van as Detective Olson ha leaped for his life.

The captions of the photographs tied financial connections between the Mayor, the Chief and Jennings to Jennings' release after the incident.

Manuela controlled her urge to dance as the significance of her story played out on the officer's face. She noted anger then acceptance followed by relief. His reaction attracted attention. Other officers crowded in. The papers sold-out quickly as the shockwave spread and reactions became more vocal. Those who expressed outrage at the story were quickly shouted down by those re-emboldened by the corruption finally being exposed.

Seeing the good guys winning for a change created a glow of warmth in Manuela's chest. *We'll be all right . . . .*

* * *

William had accepted a mild pain medication in order to be alert for the inevitable barrage of questions. Dan milked every detail from him, periodically inserting appropriate chastisements. After giving that official statement and signing it, his family was allowed in.

Susan yelled for David to slow down as he rushed in. William's oldest, Mike, entered at a more dignified pace than his little brother, but could not contain his smile. There was handholding, an awkward, wincing group hug and an embarrassingly, long kiss between husband and wife, after which William showed them his chest tube and his sutured puncture wound.

"So, dear husband," said Susan, "about that promise to be careful."

William sobered and stared deep into her eyes. "Not to worry. I'm done with it. Putting in for retirement as soon as they let me out of here."

After a sigh of relief, she cocked her head as if doubting him then shrugged. "Any word on when that will be?"

"A couple of days to make sure the insides have sealed up okay."

She cocked an eyebrow. "You sure you won't be tempted to move to the Chief's office?"

William's expression soured, his eyes rounding in horror. "Why the hell would I want anything to do with than son of a—"

Susan held up the front page of the newspaper. William stared at the headline for a long, silent moment then took the newspaper from her hand and read further. "I'll be goddamned," he said. "Manuela's kicking ass and taking names . . . This didn't come from me . . . Son of a bitch but this is great—"

"It was some rookie named Grant," said Susan, "and a whole lot of other people. She's got records and statements from everywhere, including somebody named Bonefish."

William laughed out loud, then winced at the pain. Turning the paper to look below the fold, his celebratory mood darkened. A small story below the fold, headlined, Homeless American dreamer key to breaking case.

"Have you heard anything on Alex? Is he doing okay?" he asked.

"Last I heard he was in intensive care, but that's been a few hours," said Susan.

* * *

In Alex's room the monitors beeped and ticked. Liz still stood at his bedside focused on the smile on her father's face. Her Aunt Deb entered quietly, letting a muffled whimper escape in seeing Alex's tiny body and damaged head. Liz cuddled her in a comforting hug.

"My god, that's just like him," said Aunt Deb.

"What?"

"That smile," said Aunt Deb. "Maybe it has something to do with this." She pulled a morning paper from her large canvas tote, handing it to Liz. The paper was folded so that the story on Alex was most prominent.

Liz read it, eagerly. "My god, Daddy, you did good," she said aloud, her eyes welling as she touched his face. Alex's smile seemed to intensify. Liz unfolded the page to see the package of stories in its entirety and gasped, realizing the impact the news would have.

Unaware of his wounds or the goings on around him, Alex dreamed that he was back in his wood shop sweeping up the sawdust and shavings from a completed project. He savored feeling younger with strong arms and sure hands. He wore a canvas and leather shop apron over a blue chambray shirt and crisp blue jeans.

After sweeping up and disposing of the trash, he stepped to his workbench and removed a fine, wood-and-brass square and a mortising chisel from his apron pockets. Carefully, he placed each in its appropriate spot on the bench's well-organized tool board.

Satisfied that all was in order, Alex untied the waistband and pulled the neck strap of his shop apron up over his head to hang it on a wooden peg near the shop's front door. Light streaming through the door's glass panes retained the soft glow of a warm summer evening. *Time to go home.*

Hand on the light switch, he turned to look back at his shop and his life's work. All was square. All was finished. He flipped off the lights and opened the door to a glorious sunset. He blinked then remembered. Before him lay the wooden beam on which he'd stood on just days before. It led from the door but came to an end a few feet away. Once rough-hewn and unfinished, the beam was now smooth and rich and oiled to gleaming perfection.

With eyes wide open, thinking of his little girl's cherubic face, he confidently stepped off the beam and into his peaceful, heavenly reward.

* * *

It seemed like they had been talking for hours when she realized she couldn't actually be talking to him. The dream had taken Liz back to her old office at the St. Vincent. Her father sat on the battered metal stool by her desk. He looked good. Happy, healthy, he had some meat on his bones for a change and he was clean-shaven. He smiled and laughed as they talked. It was the same laugh she remembered from childhood and it warmed her soul to hear it. Her consciousness had risen to the point that she could wake if she wanted, but she chose to sink back in and enjoy this dream a little longer.

"You know you've got a good one in Officer Grant," Alex said. "He's a listener and he's kind-hearted, just the sort I'd always hoped you'd marry."

"He is special . . . Wait, how did . . . " Liz couldn't find the words, then reminded herself this was a dream. "Yes, he is special," she said, settling back in. "He reminds me of you in some ways, maybe not so many fun little jokes . . . ." Liz stared into space for a moment then took the plunge. "You know I'm sorry I never told you . . . I almost did when you gave me that Christmas letter . . . I really wish I had before I lost you."

"I figured it out before I left," said Alex. "Remember that smile on my face?"

"Yes," said Liz. "We all talked about your smile during the move-in party last night. What was that smile all about?"

Alex beamed. "Lots of things." His eyes twinkled, an infinite, all-knowing expanse. "I saw macaroni dances and Christmases. I saw my little girl all grown up and getting married. I couldn't dance with you at your wedding, but I was there. Most of all, I could see that everyone would be okay and my work was done."

Liz gasped awake. She felt the tickle of tears that had run down her cheeks, pooling in her ears.

"You okay?" Jason asked, rolling over to gaze at her with sleepy eyes.

"I just had the most wonderful dream."

"Alex?"

"Yes." Liz smiled at him.

"I had a fairly interesting night myself," said Jason. "Must have been the move and that bottle of wine William brought over as a housewarming gift."

Liz rolled to him, wanting to talk as he sat up on the edge of the bed, his back to her. She rolled closer, rubbing a hand on his lean, lower back, "Don't you want to tell me about it?" she asked.

"Maybe at breakfast," he said, pulling on the blue jeans he'd worn the day before, his back still to her. His hair stuck out in all directions as his head popped through the neck of a police academy t-shirt. "We've got a lot of work to do today. Lots of unpacking. You want pancakes?" he asked, stepping into his sandals. "I think I saw a pancake mix in one of the boxes."

"Sounds good," She let concern edge her voice. "I can make them though, you did a lot of heavy lifting yesterday."

"Nah, I'll get it," he said, nearly sprinting out the door.

Liz's mind churned with worry.

Maybe buying this house was a mistake. This was my childhood, not his. Maybe it's too much. God, and I just told him I was dreaming about my dad . . . .

Liz crawled from bed, pulling on clothes continuing to worry she'd really screwed things up. They'd gotten the house for a song. It had been empty since Alex's eviction, bouncing from one failing bank to another. But for a young couple just starting out, it had been a bit of a stretch.

During the move-in party, the talk was all about Alex. William had fawned over the home's woodwork while Aunt Deb told stories of childhood. The guys from the shelter and the Harvest House told funny stories about street life and people. Liz had added stories of macaroni dances, ruby red heart-shaped Christmas ornaments and Play-Doh cupcakes. Almost two years had passed since that awful night.

It's time to get on with life. Stop living in the past. She hustled down the stairs to the kitchen, an apology perched on her lips.

The kitchen was empty. Jason hadn't even hit the on switch on the coffee maker they'd set up the night before. Liz pawed through the boxes, locating the pancake mix and half a bottle of syrup. They had plenty of paper plates and plastic utensils but the largest item, a mixing bowl eluded her. She heard a commotion in the basement as she flipped the switch on the Mr. Coffee.

She stood at the top of the stairs. "You all right down there?"

"Yeah, I'm fine. I'll be up," Jason called out. "Can you start the coffee? I forgot."

"Already did, sweetie." Discovering the bowl, she eyed the mix instructions and continued with a raised voice so he would hear her, "I'm sorry for talking so much about my dad. This should be about us, our new beginning."

"What?" hollered Jason, "Give me a minute, I can't hear you." His voice sounded a little cross.

Embarrassed, Liz searched for an elusive measuring cup.

What the hell is Jason doing? We need to talk this through.

She slammed down the pancake mix and poured herself a cup of coffee, staring out the window and angry with herself. The stairs creaked. The coffee burned her lips as she took a bracing sip.

"I'm sorry this move has been more about the past than our future," she blurted, as Jason appeared, looking like a little kid with his hair all a mess. In his hand he held a small, cloth-covered box.

"What? Are you okay? You look all tense."

"I'm fine, but we need to talk. This move, it's just—"

Jason held out the box, smiling too broadly. Liz thought the box looked familiar, but hung on to her determination to talk. Jason waved the box up and down, insistent and looking a bit silly.

"Okay, what's this?" she asked.

"Don't you remember it?"

"It's . . . familiar, but—"

"Alex told me about it."

Her breath caught. "When . . . Where . . . What are you talking about?"

"At the gas station." Jason beamed and moved the box at her again.

"What?" She set down her cup and finally took it from him.

Jason scratched his head then shrugged. "It was the weirdest thing. Last night I dreamt I was getting gas at the BP station up on Harrison. And there was Alex sitting in a pick-up truck, motioning for me to come over. It seemed like we talked for hours. I'd never seen him so happy."

Liz stared from him to the little box in her trembling hand.

"Some of it's a little spotty, now that I've woken up . . . but I remember he said something about elves . . . and a magic cookie slot?"

Tears welled and Liz could hardly get out the halting words. "Yes, the mail slot by the front door. He-He used to say . . . elves left cookies in there for me . . . ."

Jason laughed and said, "Alex told me you're old enough now to know they were the leftover cookies from his lunch. He also told me where to find that . . . box you're holding," he stumbled over the last words as his own tears trickled down his cheeks He managed to whisper, "It was in a little space up under the basement stairs."

Her vision a bit blurry, Liz lifted the frayed and dog-eared lid. Her finger pushed aside brittle tissue paper to reveal the ruby-red, heart-shaped Christmas ornament.

—THE END—

255

ABOUT THE AUTHOR

During the first thirty-four years of his story telling career, Kent Sievers' tool of choice was a camera. Working as a newspaper staff photographer with the occasional assignments for national media outlets, Kent has collected a wealth of real-life experience that he now puts to good use as a writer of fiction.